ENTER THE LION

"This is a fine spy thriller complete with all the appropriate elements—ladies in distress, confusion as to who is on whose side, and all the other trappings of a good cloak-and-dagger work. As a Sherlockian book, this is certainly among the best....Thoroughly satisfying."
—*St. Louis Post-Dispatch*

"A rollicking good mystery."
—Minnesota *Post* Publications

"The authors have whipped up a lively, complex plot involving a rare diamond necklace, a dashing former American slave named Captain Jericho, and the intricacies of British politics. Holmes fans will especially enjoy the banter and deduction rivalry between young Sherlock and his equally brilliant brother as they go about solving the case."
—*Publishers Weekly*

"An engaging bit of lunacy, action, ratiocination, and humor."
—*Library Journal*

"*Enter the Lion* deserves its own rather special spot in the Holmesian literature."
—The Houston *Post*

ENTER THE LION

MICHAEL P. HODEL AND SEAN M. WRIGHT

PLAYBOY PRESS
PAPERBACKS

FOR *THE* WOMEN:

Terry, who believed; and
Mary, who was there
                    —MH

AND

Nancy: All my love
(Who'd appreciate it more?)
                    —SMW

CONTENTS

Mycroft Holmes of the Foreign Office, as depicted by Sidney Paget in the pages of The Strand Magazine, *September 1893, to illustrate the case of "The Greek Interpreter."*

FOREWORD

Mycroft Holmes. The name is unfamiliar to all but the most dedicated *literateur,* mystery buff, or Baker Street enthusiast. Even so, it certainly is not so well known to them as that of his famous brother, Sherlock. There are even some who, though they are fairly conversant in the Holmes Canon, have somehow glossed over the two glimpses of Mycroft Holmes that are vouchsafed to us: "The Greek Interpreter" and "The Adventure of the Bruce-Partington Plans," which first appeared in the pages of *The Strand Magazine.*

Within the pages of *The Baker Street Journal, The Sherlock Holmes Journal* and other periodicals of Canonical "higher criticism," speculation about Mycroft Holmes has ranged from a theory that, in his youth, Mycroft Holmes was himself a detective called Martin Hewitt;* to a suggestion he is really Albert Edward, Prince of Wales, later King Edward VII.**

But, even with all this guessing and speculating, Mycroft Holmes has remained the most enigmatic figure in the Watsonian chronicles, and would have continued as such had I not been prowling through an antique shop on Ventura Boulevard in Los Angeles during the spring of 1977.

As is my wont, I was searching for some possibly Holmesian relic. At other times I have found a bust of Napoleon, a Persian slipper, a dark lantern, and other potential "Canon-fodder." On this day, I was admiring

---

* J. Randolph Cox, "Mycroft Holmes: Private Detective," theorized in an article in *The Baker Street Journal.* The Martin Hewitt stories by Arthur Morrison appeared in 1894 and continued until 1903 in the pages of *The Strand Magazine.*
** Wilber K. McKee, "The Son of a Certain Gracious Lady." Both of these monographs are noted in *The Annotated Sherlock Holmes* 1:591, and will also be found in *The Baker Street Journal* 8, No. 3 (1958).

a handsome tantalus that would have looked very nice on my sideboard. I discovered that I was a few dollars short of completing the transaction when it occurred to me that a friend worked at a radio station just a few doors down the street. That is how Michael P. Hodel became involved in this book.

Mike and I have collaborated on several adaptations of the Holmes cases for radio plays and he does a weekly science-fiction program, called "Hour 25," among other duties at the radio station. In this hour of decision, I decided to put the arm on my friendly poker foe for the extra cash. The proprietor returned to his crossword puzzle and I went off in search of Mike.

My deerstalker cap elicited a few comments from the receptionist (she was new), but I forged ahead and, amid an avalanche of tape, found Mike, who welcomed me heartily. That is, until I told him of the reason for my visit. When I told him that the object of this loan was to purchase a tantalus, he declared himself surprised that they yet existed, that he had never seen one and that he would be happy to " 'turn aside and see this wonder.' "

Back in the antique shop, Mike announced that he liked the spirit-tray and that he wouldn't mind loaning me a few dollars toward its purchase. He confided to me that he could also bring down the price a few dollars if he had just a few minutes alone with the proprietor. So, because such sordid bargaining is foreign to my nature, I continued my browsing.

In the rear of the shop, half-hidden under a boatload of knick-knacks, stood an old-fashioned rolltop desk. Hand-crafted of mahogany, it was one of those triumphs of the cabinetmaker's art in the last century. It was honeycombed with pigeonholes and drawers, one of which—the large double-drawer on the right—was ajar. I bent over to close it. It was stuck. I exerted a little more force; still no success. So I tried the opposite tack: I pulled on the drawer and, after a short period of resistance, it gave way.

Within the drawer was a fairly large, dusty old ledger, bound in cord, with gray end-boards and leathern corners. Opening it, I turned the pages, entranced to see that it was a manuscript, written in a beautiful, neat copperplate style of handwriting. Absently thumbing through the pages, I glimpsed the name "Mycroft." How unusual, I thought. Then it came to me: this was a find of the first order! I replaced the book and closed the drawer.

I caught Mike's attention as the phone rang and the proprietor excused himself. Leisurely, Mike walked over and asked what it was that I wanted. "Open the lower right-hand drawer," I said. He opened the drawer and drew out the ledger. He too thumbed through it. His eyes also popped out. "I think we'll have to buy the desk to get it, don't you?" he said. He looked at the book again. "I've always wanted a rolltop desk, anyway." The tantalus forgotten now, he produced his check-book and headed for the proprietor. I've never seen a transaction completed so quickly.

The desk was delivered two days later. We waited with apprehension as the delivery man set it against a wall in Mike's living room and left with a rather generous tip. The door shut and we raced for the drawer. I won, by dint of a stride and a bruised set of knuckles.

As I retrieved the book, a note fell out. It was written on heavy, engraved stationery; the legend at the top read: THE DIOGENES CLUB, PALL MALL, LONDON. The note was written in the same hand as that used in the ledger and dated 22 June 1934, addressed to one Calvin Trent.

> *Dear Trent:* [it read]
> I am dying. No more Ascot; no more Albermarle. They have me on a diet of milk and porridge—it is not going to help. As I told you when last you dined at the Diogenes Club—was it really a decade ago?— I have a favour to ask, though not one that I would have anticipated.
> Enclosed, you will find a manuscript, wormed out of me by a publisher during a weak moment. With Sherlock now ensconced in Sussex, and the continual shifting of governments at Number Ten, it may be a last remembrance of an age long since vanished.
> Although I am distressed to learn that I am in my anecdotage, the publisher assures me that the sales of my story will handsomely augment my pension— though for what need at this point in my life is quite

beyond my reckoning. Reading it over, I find that I have changed, incredibly so, from the youth who originally wrote of these events. I have since had the chance to refine my notes and, in some ways, improve upon my prose of that time. Hopefully, it may not now seem to be too ridiculous.

You will find mention of yourself within these pages, Trent, but do not worry. Your role, then as now, is exemplary. I send you this manuscript hoping that you might read it and possibly set aright any faults of memory. I hope that you may also obtain the necessary permissions to publish what might yet be secrets of state in your own country. I know that your closeness to the President puts you in a position to help.

Of course, if diplomatic reputations require, I shall obscure or even delete any incidents that you may specify. Discretion is still my watchword!

I hope that this account of our first meeting brings you and Mrs. Trent as much joy to read as its writing brought to

> *Yr. Ob'dt S'v'nt,*
> [signed] MYCROFT HOLMES

There was a postscript: "Please refrain from getting any whisky stains on this; it is my only copy. -M-"

Clipped to the letter was a handwritten reply from Calvin Trent. For the sake of space, I will not repeat it in full. It was on official-looking letter paper, and its gist was that the President, whom Trent referred to as "The Chief," felt there was still too much political dynamite in the narrative to reveal it to a world and a nation as yet in the grip of universal economic depression, while petty dictators were saber-rattling up and down the length of Europe, Asia, and the Far East.

Trent went on to say that FDR "read the manuscript and liked it," characterizing the story as "a real ripsnorter." Even so, the story remained, to him, one for which the world was not yet prepared. As if in answer to Mycroft's postscript, he included a lighthearted note about the President's setting a whisky decanter on the manuscript, without doing it any apparent harm.

Although I am somewhat conversant with the history of the Roosevelt administration (alphabet-soup commissions, court-packing, Yalta, etc.), I knew of no one named Calvin Trent associated with it, nor could I find any mention of him in any histories. I finally asked a member of "The Red Circle," the Washington, D.C., scion society of The Baker Street Irregulars, to do a little digging for me. She discovered the following.

Calvin Trent was a member of the United States Secret Service from 1872 to 1909. With the ascendancy of Taft's administration, he was named to the rank of deputy director, a position he maintained for eighteen years. He acted as a special advisor to three presidents before removing himself from the District of Columbia in the mid-1930s. He made a secret visit to Berlin for President Roosevelt and died shortly after his return.

His widow, Elizabeth Trent, retired to the Los Angeles area after his death; she lived there with her daughter's family until her own death in 1949. Having learned where the daughter resided, we now understood how the desk of a D.C. bureaucraft found its way into a San Fernando Valley antique shop.

What is not explained is why the ledger was not removed before the desk was given up by the family; why Calvin Trent did not return the ledger to Mycroft or why Trent's answer remained with the ledger, rather than being sent to Mycroft Holmes.

In a large manila envelope, there are several notes alluding to other adventures that Mycroft apparently wished to write about. Mike and I found them within the ledger too. My theory is this: When Calvin Trent learned that President Roosevelt wished not to have the book published, he returned it to Mycroft. But, since Mycroft decided not to publish, he sent the manuscript back to Calvin Trent as a memento and, either intentionally or inadvertently, included the notes of some other exploits. These may be revealed at a future time.

For those unfamiliar with Mr. Mycroft Holmes, it is appropriate that we briefly introduce him.

The first indication of Mycroft's existence is made in the case entitled "The Greek Interpreter," published in

The Strand Magazine for August 1893. It is revealed by Sherlock that his brother is seven years older than he and insists that Mycroft has even greater powers of observation, deduction, and inference. No one has heard of him because Mycroft, extremely Falstaffian in appearance, is incredibly lazy and would rather be considered wrong than go to any trouble to prove his deductions.

When first introduced, Sherlock tells his friend Dr. Watson that his older brother holds a minor office as an auditor of various governmental departments. It is not until "The Adventure of the Bruce-Partington Plans" that Sherlock takes Watson (and the reader) into his confidence:

> "I did not know you quite so well in those days [says Sherlock]. One has to be discreet when one talks of high matters of state."

When Holmes asks Watson if he knows what brother Mycroft does for a living, Watson recalls that he had some small office under the British government:

> Holmes chuckled. . . . "You are right in thinking that he is under the British Government. You would also be right in a sense if you said that occasionally he *is* the British Government."

Sherlock goes on to explain:

> "His position is unique. He has made it for himself. There has never been anything like it before. Nor will be again. He has the tidiest and most orderly brain, with the greatest capacity for storing facts, of any man living. . . . All other men are specialists, but his specialty is omniscience. We will suppose a Minister needs information. . . . He could get his separate advices from various departments on each [point], but only Mycroft can focus them all, and say offhand how each factor would affect the others. They [the government] began by using him as a short-cut, a convenience; now he has made himself an essential. In that great brain of his, everything is pigeon-holed, and can be handed out in an instant. Again and again,

his word has decided the national policy. He lives it. He thinks of nothing else."

Mycroft Holmes, then, fulfilled the function that government and industry now reserve for their most sophisticated computers.*

On the whole, Mycroft Holmes shunned any deviation from his normal circuit:

> His Pall Mall lodgings, The Diogenes Club, Whitehall [the location of the government buildings in London]—that is his cycle,**

says Sherlock. In fact, Mycroft's visit to Baker Street in "The Bruce-Partington Plans" is so extraordinary that Sherlock is moved to remark, "Jupiter is descending today."

Sherlock's metaphoric use of the largest planet in the solar system is not entirely a literary reference. It is also very descriptive. Dr. Watson delineates Mycroft's appearance:

> . . . heavily built and massive, there is a suggestion of uncouth physical inertia in the figure, but above this unwieldly frame, there was perched a head as masterful in its brow, and so subtle in its play of expression, that after the first glance one forgot the gross body, and remembered only the dominant mind.†

In our present manuscript, Mycroft Holmes has not yet gained all the weight we associate with him in the Canon. In his late twenties and tending toward obesity, we discover a more attractive man than the great rotundity described in Dr. Watson's writings.

Nor is he without a sense of humor. In "The Greek Interpreter," Sherlock and Watson leave Mycroft at the Diogenes Club and walk back to Baker Street, only to be

---

* There have been several "Mycroft-as-computer" monographs published in *The Baker Street Journal*, and it is no accident that, in at least one science-fiction novel, *The Moon Is a Harsh Mistress* by Robert Heinlein, there is a computer by the name of "Mycroft."

** "The Greek Interpreter."

† Ibid.

astounded to find Mycroft calmly smoking a cigar, firmly ensconced in an armchair at 221B. Mycroft takes great delight in explaining that he took a hansom directly after Sherlock and Watson left the Diogenes Club and passed them as they walked. As Sherlock says, "Art in the blood is liable to take the strangest forms." Thus does Mycroft display the same "flair for the dramatic" exhibited by his brother at the drop of a deerstalker.

The present manuscript is dated 1934, and concerns events that occur in 1875. Mycroft is therefore twenty-eight years of age (b. 1847). He lacks, as his own words will indicate, a certain maturity and intellectual depth, retaining a measure of adolescent naïvete, an unusual characteristic to be found in a government employee, even for Victorian England. This naïvete seems to stem from his intense shyness—also implied from the manuscript—which was a lifelong curse. Never comfortable among the masses, Mycroft sought refuge in a private sanctum sanctorum, the Diogenes Club, which he co-founded. Sherlock provides us with this description found in "The Greek Interpreter":

> There are many men in London, you know, who, from shyness, some from misanthropy, have no wish for the company of their fellows. Yet they are not averse to comfortable chairs and the latest periodicals. It is for the convenience of these that the Diogenes Club was started, and it now contains the most unsociable and unclubbable men in town. No member is permitted to take the least notice of any other one. Save in the Stranger's Room, no talking is, under any circumstances, permitted, and three offenses, if brought to the notice of the committee, render the talker liable to expulsion. My brother was one of the founders and I myself have found it a very soothing atmosphere.

And from that rather offhand comment, we discover that Sherlock himself may have been a member of the Diogenes Club, too.

Aside from the two cases I have so extensively quoted, there are two others in which Mycroft is mentioned: "The Final Problem" and "The Adventure of the Empty House."

In the former, Mycroft is so distressed at Sherlock's danger from the evil ex–Professor Moriarty, that he is finally shaken from his ease at the Diogenes Club to assume a disguise as the "very massive driver" of a small brougham, "wrapped in a dark cloak . . . tipped at the collar with red." As such, he drives Dr. Watson to Victoria Station so that he and Sherlock might leave England.

In the latter case, after Sherlock returns from a three-year disappearance, he tells Watson that brother Mycroft had kept paying the rent to Mrs. Hudson for 221B and arranged that everything should be kept as Sherlock left it. Mycroft also has kept Sherlock solvent throughout his travels and kept him informed as to events in England.

Interestingly, the late Monsignor Ronald Knox, the founding father of Sherlockian "higher criticism," has found evidence from these two cases to say of Mycroft that he "was, at this period of his life, in the service and in the pay of the ex-Professor [James Moriarty]."* Such a suggestion is refuted by this manuscript, in Mycroft Holmes's own words.

This is not to say that Mycroft was not above indulging in some big-brotherly teasing with Sherlock. There is the otherwise unrecorded Manor House case, for example. After buttering up Watson with "I hear of Sherlock everywhere since you became his chronicler," Mycroft proceeds to twit his brother by utilizing the old one-two punch:

> "By the way, Sherlock, I expected to see you round last week to consult me over that Manor House case. [Here comes the first poke in the ribs.] I thought you might be a little out of your depth."
> "No, I solved it," said my friend, smiling.
> "It was Adams, of course?"
> "Yes, it was Adams." [Ready, round two.]
> "I was sure of it from the first."

Such baiting—by both brothers—appears in this narrative also.

It should be mentioned that Mycroft Holmes has been hypothesized as the uncle of the famous American detec-

* To be found in Msgr. Ronald Knox, "The Mystery of Mycroft," *The Annotated Sherlock Holmes* 2:591.

tive, Nero Wolfe, of West Thirty-fifth Street, in New York City. Certainly Wolfe's portly figure, and the deductions made from his armchair, are reminiscent of Mycroft, as his association with Archie Goodwin is reminiscent of Watson. However, Goodwin's literary agent, the famous mystery writer, the late Rex Stout, said little about such a relationship, and may not be above pulling his readers' collective leg. "If I'm not having fun writing a book no one's going to have any fun reading it," he is reported to have said.*

As for this manuscript, there are certain incidents that will be of interest to Baker Street Irregulars and other Holmes buffs: where Mycroft lived before moving to his lodgings in Pall Mall in the fashionable St. James area of London; some revelations about Sherlock's and Mycroft's youth; and the truth concerning the beginnings of the Holmes-Moriarty feud.

As to the events of this book, the reader may be assured that they are true. We have Mr. Mycroft Holmes's own word on it. It is only because the government of the United States, in an opinion expressed by a member of the present administration, still considers the events detailed within as being too delicate for its citizens, that this book is being published as fiction.

Come now to the London of 1875. Victoria has reigned for some thirty-eight years. Benjamin Disraeli and William Gladstone are taking turns at being prime minister and an American mercantile delegation is in a carriage, approaching the British Foreign Office in Whitehall. A mysterious black man is now moving in social circles quite unused to a man of color in their midst. And a young man by the name of Sherlock Holmes is about to become involved in the second case of his budding career. Deep within the bowels of the British Foreign Office a man is toiling at his desk. What follows are the words of Mycroft Holmes.

SEAN M. WRIGHT, BSI
Locksley Hall
Los Angeles, California

---

* The reader may make his own judgment by reading the various Nero Wolfe mysteries as well as the biographies, *Nero Wolfe of West Thirty-Fifth Street* and *Sherlock Holmes of Baker Street*, both by the late William S. Baring-Gould.

"It is always a joy to me to meet an American. . . ."
—My brother, Sherlock,
as quoted by Dr. Watson in
The Adventure of the Noble Bachelor

TO THE READER

Having been a civil servant to Their Majesties, privy to the confidentialities of state for more than a half-century, I am unaccustomed to having my deeds bruited about in the public prints. Even so, certain personages in Fleet Street assure me that the time is come to recount some of my exploits so as to satisfy the public curiosity. I am personally unaware of any pandemic inquisitiveness, but the publisher insists otherwise. The following is, therefore, an attempt to satisfy this purported demotic phenomenon.

My brother, Sherlock, takes up a considerable amount of space in the pages following. I hope that what you will read does not diminish his escutcheon, so carefully burnished by Doctor Watson. It may be possible that some minor points will appear at odds with the doctor's portrait. I beg you to excuse them. They are seen through a lens considerably older, yet lacking the continual perceptions afforded the good doctor. It is also true that this particular episode took place some five years before Doctor Watson met Sherlock. My brother's methods had not as yet crystallised, nor had his powers attained the maturity which later won the recognition of the masses, as well as the admiration so ably provided by his friend and biographer.

The events recounted are true. I have deleted certain related but unimportant details in an effort to spare the reader's attention. Rest assured that they make no difference to the present narrative, but would only clutter up what is, in some ways, an already congested account.

I add one more note of caution. It is always difficult to reconstruct thoughts and conversations, especially those which took place nearly six decades ago. Sherlock's allegations of my omniscience notwithstanding, I do not pretend to have perfect recall, at least not in *every* regard. What you are about to read is a re-creation of the events and conversations appertaining to this memoir.

MYCROFT HOLMES
Pall Mall, London
1 May, 1934

1

"THE LION LOOKS
IN ALL DIRECTIONS"

An early snow had lately visited itself upon the city of London on that day in late November, in the year of Our Lord 1875. I was seated at my desk in the Foreign Office, in a private chamber that was mine by virtue of my position as assistant to the Right Honourable Jerrold Moriarty, the Foreign Office liaison with the military. Among other duties, I audited certain government books: military expenditures and such. In this way, I became aware of many departments of the government, and occasionally was asked to contribute my thoughts to other agencies.

At this time, I was fondly hoping to proceed with my forecast of economic trends in Ireland, then as now a thorny problem. But Mr. Moriarty was graciously allowing me to devote my early afternoon to a justification of his theories concerning military usages of the island. After reading through his memorandum, I was once again determined that he was—once again—out of his depths. The man's lack of historical perspective appalled me. Moriarty was a career diplomat but he had no real knowledge of the differences between the wildly sentimental Irish and the practical orderliness of the Britannic peoples. Political inclinations, international affairs, and the like were really not his *forte*. To be truthful, he owed his present situation to political influence, not political acumen.

Although I consider bodily exertions an absolute waste of effort, I was seriously considering a minor perambulation around the block when my secretary, Sylvanus Griffin, entered my spacious but drafty chamber to announce the arrival of my brother, Sherlock.

Even as an undergraduate, my brother bore some of the physical characteristics that would distinguish him in later life: Though not quite so tall as I, he is still well above the average height. Seven years my junior, he was, at the age of twenty-one, beginning to lose his hair above the temples of his high forehead. His large nose—hawk-like is the description that comes to mind—is, like my own, a family attribute. One need only view the likeness of Horace Vernet, the French artist, on the Albert Memorial to discover whence it was inherited.

Sherlock was always lean, wiry, and quick, always enjoying the out-of-doors with the same devotion he gave reading. He was especially drawn to the more arcane studies of crime and criminals. He could recite the names of axe-murderers, garrotters, highwaymen, arsonists, and cutthroats, together with their respective deeds, mind you, in a litany of almost religious intensity. He pored over newspaper accounts of crime with the same interest I gave the practical arts and sciences. I could accept the wisdom of my teachers and books and be content with formulae and methodology. But Sherlock was not satisfied until he had directly observed the matter himself. For this reason, he excelled at chemistry and anatomy, dissection and the like. While we are both paragons of cause-and-effect deduction and induction too, once I was sure of my logic, I was content to leave it as stated. Sherlock would check and re-check his conditions, ready to obtain the knowledge first-hand if need be. And it served as one measure of the difference between us. As his older brother, I sometimes felt compelled to explain things to Sherlock, but it was always his own driving curiosity that would compel him to substantiate my testimony. This attitude seldom vexed me and sometimes was quite amusing. Oddly enough, we got on quite well together.

He strode into my office, the picture of the dilettante student: a bowler on his head, his overcoat slung over one arm, swinging a walking stick in a cavalier manner, the elbows of his off-the-peg cutaway shiny and the knees of his pants almost out. His bemused expression was almost redundant.

"Good day, Mycroft," he said in greeting, laying his *accoutrements* aside. "What keeps you indoors on Her Majesty's business this afternoon: Ireland, I presume?"

Since a map of that stormy island lay on the side-table

with several pieces of foolscap nearby, it was not so splendid an inference and I told him so.

"Have you any other daring feats of ratiocination with which to amaze me?" I asked rather heavily.

"Merely that you are overworked and lacking a proper amount of exercise," he replied. "Also that you had kidneys for lunch."

"You're getting better," I admitted with a smile. "Kidneys have a distinctive odour all their own. As for being overworked, you are again correct. But let me see what you would conclude from the following." I stepped over to the map and picked up a sheet of figures. "It is stimulating to see how often people are unable to take isolated pieces of information and connect them into meaningful patterns. Look here." I handed him the paper, a page from a recent report. "The Ulster potato crop has declined by twenty-six percent in the past six years. Military enlistment has increased by forty-six percent over the past three years and the civil authorities in Londonderry report that the number of illegitimate births has risen by twelve percent. Conclusion?"

"No you don't," my brother smiled. "I confine my knowledge of economics to a strictly personal application. And it is for precisely that reason that I have come 'round to see you, Mycroft."

"You need to borrow some money," I said. He nodded ruefully.

"Victor Trevor has invited me to Donnithorpe and I am without a farthing."*

"My Government stipend is hardly the Cheapside Hoard, Sherlock, but I suppose I can spare you a small amount."

As I made out the cheque, something else occurred to me. "Sherlock, it's after hours; you won't be able to change the cheque until tomorrow. Why don't you and young Trevor meet me for dinner at Goldini's Restaurant tonight? I'll be happy to play host and it may impress your young aristocrat."

* The reader will be referred to "The Gloria Scott," a case found in *The Memoirs of Sherlock Holmes,* in which Holmes discusses the circumstances under which he met Victor Trevor and, indeed, undertook his first investigation. That case occurred approximately one year before the present narrative. MH/SMW

Sherlock nodded absently as he deposited the draft in his wallet. He found it uncomfortable to talk about money. As his wants were simple, he lived well enough on the small paternal allotment he received each month, although it was sometimes necessary for me to augment it. The sordid part of his visit over, he now allowed his eyes to stray over my bookcase. As I returned to my desk, I noticed that his gaze lingered on the mathematical journals I kept.

"Yes, Dodgson is still there," I said in anticipation of his unasked question, while I read another page of Moriarty's memorandum. "But I must say that I've kept his works only for the sake of inclusivity." I put down the report. "I fail to understand why you continue to sit at the feet of that mathematician of ill repute. I mean, he insists upon writing those silly fables. 'Lewis Carrol' indeed! I understand that the Dean's wife has forbidden him entrance to her parlour."

Sherlock's face flushed. "Yes, she has," he replied, heatedly. "And I must say that it is a foolish *contretemps* at best. Charles Lutwidge Dodgson is a first-rate professor and his less serious avocation should play no part in his colleagues' judgement of his work."

"Balderdash," was my response to his objections. "Few enough of those academicians read anything more recent than 1789 anyway, let alone know about his career as a nonsensical *literateur*. It's his infatuation with prepubescent girls that is ruining his reputation," I added, warming to the discussion. "If he is to teach impressionable young undergraduates, he must set an example of sterling character."

My brother's response died on his lips as Griffin knocked, then entered, to tell me that a trade delegation from America awaited my attention. I bade Sherlock goodbye as my secretary handed me a note from Ames, Mr. Moriarty's secretary, which he said would explain the situation.

The situation needed some explanation, for it was highly unusual for me to receive outsiders on official business, nor did I interview those who wished to speak to Mr. Moriarty: that was properly handled by Ames. I felt it a trifle beneath my official dignity to be placed in such a position. But then, orders are orders.

Ames' note did little to clarify this break in my routine. He advised me that the Americans were representing the business interests of Alabama, one of the states of the American Union. I was being asked to conduct a preliminary interview so as to ascertain whether they warranted Mr. Moriarty's time or no. Once more I was struck by this anomaly: my superior held a vital position in the Foreign Office hierarchy, though of a second rank. I mentioned that he was the civilian liaison between the FO and the military. Never before had "business interests" intruded themselves into his office. This department worked closely with the Admiralty, being an admixture of civilians and officers. That I worked closely with some economic developments seemed to be the only link—and a tenuous one at that. I wondered if these Americans had been directed to the wrong office to begin with or if Mr. Moriarty actually had an idea of their stated intentions.

Griffin patiently awaited my final digestion of the contents of the message, and, at my request, ushered the visitors into my office. I would have to gather more data before I made any further inferences.

The members of the Alabaman delegation were all former military men, entering as though by order of rank. The leader was an elderly, white-haired gentleman who strode in with a marked military cadence. Though he wore a malacca walking stick, it saw little usage. He carried himself with ease and stood as straight as a ramrod. He even had a handkerchief tucked up his sleeve, a custom universal among soldiers whose tunics have no pockets. He also affected the goatee that had become an obligatory style for the French, Italians, and all former military officers since the accession of Louis Napoleon.

He was followed by a burly man, just as tall, but some twenty years younger and five stone heavier, four of which he could have shed with no ill effect. He too sported a long imperial, though of a deep russet colour. He was slightly winded and must have been out of condition for the four flights between Mr. Moriarty's office and my own to affect him so. His smooth palms told of a well-cared-for existence, while the man's choleric face and the scars on his right cheek and neck told of his short temper and experiences as a sabre fencer and duellist. The hard flints that stared at me confirmed that he was uncompromising and direct. Interestingly, the thickened lateral surfaces of his forefingers were indicative of an early training and continued skill as a horseman. He must have been in charge of a cavalry unit at one time.

As for the two others, they were both barely thirty and shared some common traits: brown, longish hair and well-bred youth; both were tall and aristocratic (in an American sense, of course). One was clean shaven, while the other asserted his individuality by being dramatically moustached, each mustachio carefully waxed into a long graceful sweep against his smooth cheeks. These two were obviously of little importance to this meeting; I would be speaking to the older gentlemen.

"Mr. Holmes," said the white-haired man in a soft Southern drawl, "I am Colonel Mordecai Leland of Alabama. My associates: Captain Ravenswood." The fleshy duellist brought his heels together and nodded curtly. "Tyler Carteret." The young man with the spectacular moustache did the same. "My nephew, William Bankhead," who followed the lead of his companions.

Being used to military decorum, I gravely nodded in response to each of my visitors, then gestured to the worn leather-covered sidechair for Colonel Leland, and the others to the nearly swaybacked divan facing the office fireplace. I took my place next to the heavy oak swivel chair behind my desk. But, before sitting, Colonel Leland reached into the breast pocket of his morning coat, brought out an envelope, and handed it to me.

"We have a letter of introduction, sir," he said.

The heavy-grade white bond and blue coat of arms announced a message from a member of the diplomatic corps, the Right Honourable Cyril Harvey, British consul general stationed in New Orleans:

> *My dear Moriarty* [it read]:
> This will serve to introduce Colonel Mordecai Leland and his party, a trade delegation to London from the state of Alabama. I am sure that they will receive every courtesy and all co-operation from yourself and

your office. In turn, you will find their ideas highly beneficial and of great import.

Best Regards,
[signed] *Cyril P. Harvey*
Consul General

The last sentence, underlined as it was, caused me to raise an eyebrow. Harvey's words, innocuous though they were, indicated much more than a mercantile deputation being sent off with the blessing of the consul general. While pretending to study the note, I inspected the Americans closely. The younger men were perhaps more tense than the circumstances warranted. Colonel Leland sat in dignified silence, calmly looking at the wall behind me; had he been standing he would have been at parade rest. Only Captain Ravenswood was discernibly examining me. So intent was he that his face, already choleric, was becoming redder by the moment. Although Ravenswood was the only member of the delegation unable to conceal his agitation, his fellows also seemed to expect some immediate recognition after my reading of the Consul General's message. I resorted to some discreet dissimulation.

"Commercial delegation, eh?" I said, rising to return the note to the dignified Colonel. "I am afraid that you gentlemen have been misdirected. You should have been referred to the Ministry of Trade."

This was a blind, of course. Cyril Harvey had been most specific that these men should see my superior. I wanted to know if the Americans knew as much. I received my answer with the Colonel's next words.

"We were told that the lion looks in all directions."

These portentous words caught me off guard. That phrase dropped all pretense of a commercial delegation from the Americans. Known only to a few members of the FO, the phrase in effect said: "I have important military information of great significance." I had been entrusted with the knowledge, but I was powerless to take charge of the matter. No one less than Jerrold Moriarty could act on this matter. Although I knew the response, and could answer, because it concerned the military liaison's office, I could do nothing but report it to Moriarty. The Americans had made a mistake. Officially, I could not take the slightest recognition, for the message was for Mr. Moriarty's ears alone, and they would have to wait for him to see them.

Blandly, I began: "The Ministry of Trade is located. . . ."

"We'd best speak to your superior, young man," interrupted the duellist, "or things may go hard with you."

The solemn Colonel raised a peremptory hand.

"Don't be foolish, Ravenswood." To me he said, "Please forgive Captain Ravenswood's outburst; we had a choppy crossing and I fear that my friend has not yet recovered."

"I quite understand."

"Now then, you were saying?"

"That the Ministry of Trade is . . ."

"Look here, Colonel," said the Captain, his face growing redder as he refused to be restrained. "We didn't come this far to be put off by some bureaucratic wet nurse."

Jumping up from the sofa, he loomed over my desk, his crimson face glaring down like a vengeful sun. "You will give that letter to Mr. Moriarty, or you will live to regret it!"

A look of actual pain crossed the face of Colonel Leland, as the Captain continued his hysterical tirade: "I assure you, Mr. Holmes, we are not here on some idle whim! Neither shall we be shunted back and forth between departmental mollycoddles!" His voice now dropped dramatically. "If you are not aware of the import of our visit, you had best direct us to those people who are!" He was staring directly at me with those two hard pieces of flint burning in his face. "I promise you we shall brook no delay," he snarled.

The Colonel stiffened. "Captain Ravenswood!" he barked. "That will be quite enough. You may be seated!" The Captain turned, staring at him resentfully.

"Now, sir!"

Ravenswood tried to stare down the old man, but finally he stalked back to his seat, still in a rage. In any other circumstances, I should have had no further dealings with such people and shown them my door. Only the portent of the message and the Colonel's calmly authoritative demeanor kept me from following my instinct.

"I am truly sorry for the Captain's ill temper, sir," said the Colonel, relieving the tension in the room several degrees. "At the same time, I must agree with Captain Ravenswood in one regard. I am sure that Mr. Moriarty will be most eager to receive our message. The more quickly he receives word of our arrival and Mr. Harvey's note, the better it will be for all concerned."

"I shall see what can be done."

"I appreciate your help, Mr. Holmes," said the Colonel, rising. "And again I apologize for my friend's rambunctiousness." He turned back to Captain Ravenswood, "I'm sure that he does also. Come, gentlemen."

He gave me a stately nod and led his companions to the door. Captain Ravenswood hung back, ostensibly to pull on his gloves. Seeing that the others of his party were in the outer office, he completed his task and stepped over to my desk, grasping the sleeve of my coat.

"You should be aware that we are keeping cases on our friends, Mr. Holmes." He stared at me grimly. "And our enemies."

I regarded his hand coldly and pulled my arm away. He turned to leave, pulling the door shut behind him with just a bit too much force.

Hastily, I drafted a note to Mr. Moriarty, informing him of the visit and of the diplomatic *gaffe,* deleting any reference to the animosity displayed by Captain Ravenswood. No purpose would be served, I thought. I rang for Griffin and asked him to deliver the message immediately.

When my secretary departed, I reached into the humidor on my desk and took out a cigar. Cigars are to me what pipes are to my brother. Aside from becoming an extension of one's personality in conversation, a good cigar can be a friend and comfort *par excellence.* The cheerfulness they inspire is a boon to contemplative thought: a remedy for depression, a balance for excitement.

I cut off the end and struck a match, drawing the vesta along the length of the panatela to awaken the bouquet of the fine Havana wrapper. I lit the cigar and leaned back in my chair, watching the smoke rise to the ceiling, and considered the implications of the visit. An American delegation—Southerners—ostensibly on a trade mission, come to Whitehall armed with a note and a phrase, a string of words which they should not have known and surely not used as they did. They demanded audience with the civilian liaison with the military. And that underlined sentence in Harvey's message. . . .

Those were the facts. The Captain's emotional tirade and the Colonel's quiet insistence indicated some personal feelings over and above normal foreign affairs. They were involved to a great extent in whatever plans or information they sought to communicate to Mr. Moriarty.

For a brief moment I considered sending a friendly note to the American embassy in Grosvenor Square to acquaint them with the matter. But I stayed my hand. Whatever the business, it was not yet far enough advanced to breach the diplomatic integrity of the Foreign Office.

Griffin returned. He informed me that Mr. Moriarty had left for the day, but that Ames had left the note on his desk. Such information came as no surprise; Mr. Moriarty often left the office immediately following luncheon.

Griffin moved to go, then turned back saying, "Oh, and Ames sent down the invitations to the Admiralty Ball for you and your brother." I thanked him and he left.

The Admiralty Ball. I usually had little time to bother with such occasions, as Griffin knew. These *soirées* are little more than functions at which to show off or make connexions. And that would be my purpose: to make a connexion for Sherlock. I was determined to introduce Sherlock to some department heads. I felt that it was time for him to consider a career, a steady profession for which to prepare after he left his studies, desultory as they were. It would give him a head start and a goal for which to prepare himself, despite his talk of preparing himself for an uncertain future as the "first consulting detective"—whatever he meant by that.

The clock now read 6.10. Griffin was gathering up his belongings and my cigar had gone out a while before. My office door opened and Griffin asked if there was anything else to be done. Upon learning that I had no further need of his services for the day, he nodded and left. I shrugged into my greatcoat and left the office, taking a final leave of Griffin on the steps of the Foreign Office. I had earlier mentioned my plans to eat at Goldini's and he wished me a hearty appetite before he departed.

The snow, though light, had slowed the traffic. An over-turned hansom cab halfway up the block was making its contribution to the evening confusion. I saw that I would make better time if I walked. So, with great misgivings, I launched myself from the steps of the FO and propelled myself into the endlessly eddying stream of humanity on the sidewalk.

I was less than four blocks from the restaurant when a man bumped into me from the rear. In trying to keep his balance on the icy sidewalk he wrapped his arms about me. I felt a slight tug at the front of my coat, but was so engrossed in keeping my balance on the slick pavement that I paid it little mind in the confusion. Righting ourselves, he made a quick apology over his shoulder and hastened into the crowd. I never saw his face, although I had the impression that he wore a bowler and white knit comforter around his throat. I paid him little mind as I brushed the wrinkles out of my coat. I gave a reassuring pat to the inner pocket containing my pocketbook and found the comforting lump was missing. The man was a cutpurse! I looked in the direction in which he fled, but no one in the immediate crowd could be identified as a fleeing criminal. I quickened my pace as a heavy-set man peering nearsightedly over an armload of packages nearly bowled me over. When I again regained my equilibrium, there was even less hope that a trace of the culprit could be detected.

I pushed ahead, staring into each face I passed, staring at their habiliments, hoping to see some familiar piece of clothing. Nearly a block away from my mishap, I paused at the entrance to a pub. I was slightly winded, but the major reason for stopping was because I noticed that the door was slightly ajar. The probability that the thief had taken refuge within the establishment's precincts was enough to be an interesting speculation. Through the etched glass in the door I perceived perhaps a dozen men lined up before the bar, drinking, talking, and awaiting service from the comely barmaid. A knot of four men at the farthest end of the bar caught my attention; one of whom seemed to eye me with a trifle more curiosity than my presence demanded when I entered. There was something familiar in the billy-cock and comforter he wore. And another thing caught my eye which made him a likely suspect.

As I finished my inspections, a constable, about to return to duty after finishing his evening meal, wiped his mouth on his sleeve and stood up, calling out a good-night to the proprietor. I stopped him as he approached.

"Just a moment, Constable, if you please."

He look at me with the dull annoyance one feels when being pressed back into service after enjoying a satisfying meal.

"What can I do for you, sir?"

"I have reason to believe that one of the men in here is now in possession of my wallet."

"Well," he said, unimpressed, "that's an awful peculiar way o' stating a complaint."

The man needed convincing. "I'll wager your mother in Nottinghamshire wouldn't think so."

"Here now, you leave my mother out . . ." His voice trailed off as he was hit by the full import of my little parlour trick. ". . . How'd you come to know about my mother?"

"Never mind that now. Just tell me," I turned back to the four men. "You've been here for some time?"

"A good half-hour."

"As I thought. Now, who was the last man to enter?"

His eyes narrowed in concentration as he scanned the noise and smoke of the room. "Well now, I'm not altogether sure," he said, "but I would say that it was one o' those men over there." He indicated the quartet.

A tall, rough-featured man sidled up to us. " 'At's right, guv," he observed. "But they all come in together—'bout a minute or two 'fore this toff." He jerked his thumb to indicate me.

"They must all be in on it," said the policeman. "Well, now, sir, you just point out the one who lifted your money. You just do it quick an' John Lawr'll take 'im off to the pile." But while the policeman blustered, the four stood firm, drinking their dark ale as though they had not a concern in the world.

"We h'ain't got this blighter's bloody pocketbook," said one of the four unconcernedly over his shoulder. Another of the men gave a snort. "A man can't even stop for a pint o' bitter wivout some smart Johnny an' a bobby tryin' to pinch 'im anymore. H'it's a bleedin' shyme, I say."

"Here now," the bobby commanded, "no more o' your lip, you."

"You tell 'im, Alfie," a voice cackled as the room grew silent at the prospect of an impending arrest.

The policeman held firm, his thick moustache bristling. "Go on; point out the man and your property and John Lawr'll hand it right back to you." A round of laughter resulted. This was an obviously unsympathetic crowd. Undeterred, I watched the quartet for any sign of guilt, but they merely continued to sneer at me with an unspoken enmity. But two of them had turned around, their backs now to the bar, their elbows resting lightly on its surface. Getting ready for trouble, I thought.

"You," I said. "You on the end," I pointed. "That's him, Constable."

The policeman darted forward and took hold of the man by the scruff of his neck as he blanched with guilty discovery.

"And you." I whirled around on my heel to take hold of the man behind us who had volunteered the information. He lunged for the door, but a number of now-willing hands prevented his bolting and brought him back, struggling.

Two short blasts of the constable's whistle brought some more uniformed police into the pub, enough to subdue the two prisoners until the police van was finally brought.

"You'll find my wallet in this man's coat pocket. It's black morocco leather. There is a card inside of it identifying me as a member of the staff of the Foreign Office."

"Here it is," said one of the bobbies, reaching into the man's pocket and bringing out the wallet. He opened it and removed a card. "It's just as you said," he told me as he handed the *portemonnaie* back to me. The banknotes and other papers were untouched. The police van pulled up outside the pub and the prisoners were escorted outside by the police.

"A neat trick, and that's for sure," said the constable named Alfie. "But tell me, how did you guess that it was the short bloke?"

"I didn't guess, officer. I knew it was that man." I smiled as the policeman took off his helmet and scratched his head.

"Beggin' your pardon, but how could you know?"

My smile broadened. "Very simply. Note the ale-mugs of the other three men. They are now very nearly empty, and were so at the time I entered. The fourth has hardly been touched, indeed, is less than a third empty now. There is no other glass, so that was his first drink. Now look closely at that glass."

The officer did so.

"The publican has kept his kegs in a cold storeroom and you note that the fourth glass still has condensation on its sides from the recent entry of a very cold liquid. Not another ale-mug in this room has any condensation on it. So, then, despite what was said, the men almost certainly did not enter together, although they seem to be acquainted. Had the man not come in later, he would have consumed as much as the others and the ale-mug warmed to room temperature. Equally obvious, the man who lied, saying that all of them had come in together must have had some reason for trying to put us off."

" 'Cause he was the one holding the loot." The policeman laughed as he concluded my deduction. "Well, that's a pretty good trick, I must say."

I left my card with him so that I might be notified by the court, should they need my testimony. I then took my leave of the place, resuming my walk to Goldini's.

My brother and Victor Trevor were already seated when I arrived. Watching their hands, I could see that they were involved in spirited conversation. Making my way to their table, I saw that the intensity of their discussion caused them to take little notice of the pointed stares coming from other tables.

"Ah, Mycroft. Perhaps you can make this low, country-bred patrician understand," was Sherlock's greeting. Trevor sat, grinning at me from atop his athlete's body: "Mr. Holmes, your brother is as single-minded as a stick. And almost as intelligent."

"Now, now," I said soothingly. "What's all this about?" Despite—or perhaps because of—my being seven years older than my brother, I invariably sound avuncular in his presence. Not that I mean to, he just keeps putting me in that position.

"I was merely saying that there's absolutely no sense in your brother's obsession with this 'consulting detective' business. No money, no social standing—it's a ridiculously flamboyant gesture."

"Akin to slaying dragons, searching for the Holy Grail," answered my brother with quiet irony. "Or perhaps stealing from the rich and giving to the poor."

"Now, Holmes," Trevor ran his stubby fingers through his buttery-yellow hair. "You know what I mean." He absently began to chew an end of his almost invisible blond moustache.

"My dear Trevor," answered Sherlock. "Merely because I choose not to go through the pointless rigmarole in becoming a solicitor, nor waste my time in government—meaning no offense, Mycroft—nor to bore myself to distraction working my way up in business, you say there's no sense to it? I mean to make my own way in the world. And did you know," he went back to the topic at hand, "that there were four hundred eighty-six murders committed in metropolitan London last year? That Scotland Yard solved but two hundred four of them? That means, Trevor, that there are—barring multiple murders—some two hundred eighty-two murderers walking the streets tonight, free to kill again if they so desire."

I knew my brother during these periods; he refused to be mollified.

"And those figures don't even begin to speak of a legion of other crimes: larceny, robbery, arson, forgery, rapine, and the rest. They go unpunished, indeed in many cases they are unknown, because the police have not a sufficient number of men or the time to detect them. And even if they did have the brains to solve such cases, their methods . . ." He shook his head scornfully. "Trevor, you have no idea! These people are using techniques that the Romans would have found barbaric!"

Trevor raised his hands in mock surrender, laughing. "Enough, Holmes, enough. No further need to preach at me again tonight. I believe you; I really do. But being a detective is so terribly"—he searched for a word—"so terribly . . . common."

"I'm sure my brother is letting his rhetoric overcome him."

"Not in the least," said Sherlock. "Mycroft, do you recall the murder of the young fishmonger in Deptford last month?"

I shook my head. Such doings are meat and drink to my brother; however, they concern me but slightly.

"Someone smashed in his head with a stone. And do you know how the police solved the case?" He looked back and forth to Trevor and me. When we made no response, he continued. "The man belonged to a gang of some sort. The police merely had the members rounded up and beat them senseless until one or the other of them confessed. Romans! I daresay that even the Babylonians might have found such methods a trifle archaic." Sherlock now sat back in the leather chair, his long arms folded in front of him.

"But Holmes," said Trevor, "it worked. On such low life you use the tactics they understand best. "An eye for an eye," he ended virtuously.

"My dear Trevor," Sherlock replied with feigned patience. "The idea is not to meet force with force, but to overcome such barbarism with the most important weapon possessed by man: the human brain.

"Science," he continued, swinging into his favorite subject, "that's the key to criminal investigation. Not a cosh on the head or a knife in the ribs. It's the chemistry, the analysis; the knowledge of a criminal's habits, patterns of behavior. These are the things that the police should be studying, and what they should know."

Trevor shook his head. "I recall how you put all this to good use with the Governor's affairs and straightened me out last year, so I don't understand why you don't want to become a member of the police force.* And I don't mean the uniformed force," he added, when Sherlock made another move to protest. "I mean the Detective Department of Scotland Yard.** You were saying just last week that the Yard has less than twenty detectives for the

* For the history of this incident, which Sherlock considered his first investigation, see "The Gloria Scott" mentioned previously. Trevor is referring to his father as "The Governor." MH/SMW

** The Detective Department of the London Metropolitan Police (Scotland Yard) began in 1842 with two detectives. It was reorganized in 1878—three years after this conversation—thereafter renamed the Criminal Investigation Department, the CID. MH/SMW

entire area. Why, with your brain and attention to detail . . ."

"The police," said Sherlock, folding his arms about him even more tightly, "are too slow, too clumsy and too inefficient for my liking. And too regimented," he said as an afterthought. "Why, any decently intelligent criminal could think rings around them. The problem is that no real intellect has taken up the profession."

"Which one?" Trevor asked with a chuckle.

"Either," Sherlock admitted with a wry smile. "If there were any talented criminals who studied their craft with an equivalent amount of time and study such as I hope to devote . . ."

"I'm glad there aren't," said Trevor.

"Ah, but there will be, some day," said Sherlock. "Mark my words, the thing is inevitable. And when that day comes, they'll need someone with my skills and talent."

For an instant, I glimpsed an aspect of my brother that I had rarely seen before. Beneath the adolescent bravado, there was a core of iron resolve, a singleness of purpose akin to my own feelings about my chosen profession. Indeed, such devotion is a characteristic trait of our family.

"Speaking of skills," I interposed, to change the subject, "the chef here is a friend of mine and is reputed to possess such culinary art that he can turn a relatively minor *truite amandine* into ambrosia." I beckoned the waiter to give him our orders.

The ritual of dining is one that I truly enjoy. I have no patience with those like my brother, who treat a good meal as if it were merely fuel for stoking a furnace. There is as much taste, imagination, and artistry utilised in the preparation of a fine meal as in, say, a concerto or an oratorio. I must confess however, that I am perhaps overly appreciative of what I find to be the zenith of English cuisine, a hearty shepherd's pie.

We had finished our repast, and Sherlock was lighting the briar-root pipe I had given him the Christmas before, when a voice boomed above the quiet murmuring of Goldini's patrons. Though I had not heard it before, it was instantly recognisable.

"I know he's here, an' I insist upon seein' him," proclaimed a voice directly from Dixie's land. Looking up, I saw young William Bankhead gesturing heatedly at an anxious waiter. The attention of the diners was immediately focused upon the man who stood at the top of the stairs leading into the main dining room. As the headwaiter hurried to intercept this barbarian in his temple, the beefy youth caught sight of me and waved. He galloped into the room toward our table while warding off functionaries with one arm.

"I've had the devil's own time finding you, Mr. Holmes. You've got to come quick. Right now! Something terrible's happened."

I rose to my feet and, placating the attendants, attempted to soothe the young American stallion.

"Calm yourself, Mr. Bankhead; here, sit down and give me your tidings."

Trevor hooked a vacant seat from an adjoining table and our intruder fell into it. His red face and trembling hands told me of recent exertions. He pulled a large red handkerchief from his pocket and mopped his brow. He looked questioningly from me to my companions. I hurriedly introduced them and assured him of their discretion.

"Now, sir, what is your problem?"

"It's Colonel Leland," said Bankhead in an urgent stage whisper. "He's been shot!"

"Have you gone to the police?" asked Trevor.

"No," said Bankhead. "We daren't. Word might leak out to the newspapers. It's a very delicate matter, you understand."

"Yes," I nodded. To Sherlock and Trevor I said, "I'm sorry, I must leave." I pushed back my chair.

"Wait, Mycroft." My brother shot out a restraining hand. He turned to the visitor.

"Mr. Bankhead, this delicate matter of which you speak —do I understand that the attack may be related?"

Bankhead glanced back at me. When I nodded, he said, "It seems possible."

"Then," my brother continued, "since you cannot go to the authorities, perhaps I may be of assistance to you. As you have sought out my brother for advice, I infer that there is some connexion between this occurrence and the Foreign Office. Unfortunately that branch of the government is not provided with investigators. I have had some experience with such enquiries, so if I may offer my services . . . ?"

His tone was cool, but I recognised the eagerness behind Sherlock's calm *façade*. His eyes had lost their customary hoodedness and were sparkling with anticipation as he watched the young American intently. Bankhead weighed the alternatives. I was prompted to speak, but hesitated. In my silence, Bankhead spoke: "I'm not empowered to accept your offer, Mr. Holmes. I would have to speak to the others . . ."

"I might remind you, sir," said Sherlock with the casual air of a peddler in Portobello Road, "that time is certainly of the essence. The trail grows colder each moment you delay."

Trevor watched in fascination. But before he could say anything, Bankhead suddenly smashed his fist into the damask tablecloth. The plates and glassware jumped and, I must admit, so did Trevor and I.

"By th' Eternal, you're right! Very well, I accept your offer. Come, I have a cab waiting to take us back to the hotel."

I had just enough time to pay the bill and follow them out into the early snow skirting Gloucester Road. As we entered the landau, Sherlock whispered fiercely. "Can you acquaint me with the details privately?"

I nodded, making a mental note to warn Sherlock about interfering in what could too easily become a diplomatic incident. I was sure that my presence would mitigate any feelings of surprise that might be felt by the Americans at our appearance.

Victor Trevor began his farewells, but Sherlock brushed these aside and pushed him into the carriage. "No, Trevor," he said, "you may be of service." He smiled. "Besides, you can be a first-hand witness to what I was talking about before dinner."

"But Holmes," protested Trevor, "What are you getting me into?"

2

MY BROTHER
BECOMES INVOLVED

As our landau rattled off toward Regent Street, we tried to achieve some degree of comfort within. But four large men in so small a conveyance made this virtually impossible. Sherlock and Trevor were hunched together on one side, while Bankhead and I faced them uncomfortably. The young man sat beside me, stiffly distraught. A soldier he might have been, but inside, he was still not ready to accept the possibility of death, especially at such close quarters.

Raising my voice over the squeaking of the springs, I attempted to divert him from his melancholia by enquiring about the incidents leading up to this evening's adventure. The young man seemed grateful for the question.

"We were on our way back to the hotel after dinner," said he. "Carteret and I were escorting the ladies . . ."

Sherlock raised his eyebrows in a questioning look. Bankhead saw it and explained. "Miss Rachel Leland, Colonel Leland's daughter, and her friend from school, Miss Millicent Deane; they came with us to begin a continental tour."

"Or at least, that's why you say they're here," said Sherlock.

"Yes," Bankhead agreed enthusiastically. "It was the Captain's idea. What a strategist!"

Sherlock smiled while Trevor turned his laugh into a cough. Bankhead stared at them for a moment. "Does my admiration for my commander amuse you, sirs?" he asked, his eyes narrowing.

"Oh no, not at all," said Sherlock smoothly. "Merely gratified to see my small deduction about your friends has proven to be correct."

That seemed to mollify the young man for he continued,

"As I say, Carteret and I were escorting the ladies about five, maybe ten feet behind Colonel Leland and Captain Ravenswood. Miss Rachel stopped us to point out a gown in the window of a shop, but within a short time, we continued on our way. A few seconds later, and without warning, two men jumped out of a doorway. One of them pulled out a pistol and pointed it at the Captain and Colonel. Before we could move to prevent him, he shot and hit Colonel Leland, while the other man swung out, striking Captain Ravenswood a glancing blow. He used some sort of sap—a cosh, I think you call it here. Anyway, seeing us, they turned and ran. Carteret ran after them, but lost them in all these twisting streets. I helped the Captain to his feet and flagged down a carriage. We put the Colonel in and the ladies and picked up Carteret on the way. When we got back to the hotel, the man at the desk sent a messenger for a doctor.

"In all the confusion, I thought of you and ran off to your offices. I would never have found you, if the porter hadn't recalled hearing you say to your clerk that you had to go to Goldini's to meet your brother to pay . . ."

Now it was Sherlock's turn to cough.

"I'm extremely sorry to hear of this turn of events," I interjected. "Yet perhaps this is an opportunity to learn more details about your, ah, mission."

Bankhead nodded grimly at my companions. "I think not, sir," he said. "It's not that I don't trust your friends, you understand . . ."

"My dear Mr. Bankhead," my brother said, reaching to relight his pipe. "I can assure you of our discretion. If you are truly serious about wanting our assistance, then we must know every pertinent fact."

The sulphurous flare of his vesta illumined all our faces as he struck it in the silence. While Bankhead thought this over, the resultant glow from the incinerating tobacco in his pipe revealed my brother's attentive stare.

At last Bankhead smiled. "I suppose you're right, Mr. Holmes. It's just that we've been so concerned with secrecy and such . . ."

"A perfectly valid concern, sir," I said. "I have always placed a high premium on confidentiality. But," I added, "in this instance, I find myself agreeing with my brother."

This had the effect that I wanted. Bankhead acquiesced completely.

"Very well. What would you like to know?"

"Let us begin with a more detailed account of your activities," said Sherlock, trying to settle back into the upholstery, his hands resting atop his walking stick. "You might start with what you did after your arrival in port today."

I laughed to myself and said, looking into Bankhead's amazed face. "I can assure you, sir, I mentioned your visit to no one. This is what my brother means by a little deduction."

"But how could you know?"

"There are any number of indications," Sherlock smiled. This was not quite true. There were two indications, one of which was rather a long shot, considering that Bankhead had changed his clothes to dine, Sherlock explained.

"The most outstanding feature is the remnant of shine left on your boots. Not even the snow has been able to efface the finish completely. It is indicative of that gloss given by bootblacks of the Cunard line."

"Also," I said looking back at him significantly, "the right lace was broken and replaced while he was onboard ship." The wonderment on Bankhead's face was not so meaningful to me as was the puzzlement on Sherlock's. He leaned forward and looked at the lace again, smiling appreciatively. "Mycroft, how can you say that it was replaced on board the ship and not, say, in the hotel?"

"I've had occasion to make a small and as yet incomplete study of aglets," I said casually for my brother's benefit. "But enough to know that the metal aglets used on ships are different to the celluloid kind used on bootlaces sold by cobblers and bootblacks on land. You would do well, Sherlock, to study footwear a little more closely. You might even find your researches of use to your classroom studies in logic."

Bankhead's admiration was apparent as he said, "Your industry is to be complimented, sirs." I half expected him to rise and bow from the waist. Then he continued his narrative. "We arrived this morning on the *Britannia*, took the train to Victoria Station and then a hansom to the hotel . . ."

"The Langham," said Trevor.

"You too?" exclaimed Bankhead. "How did you know?"

Trevor said, "I heard you tell the driver."

Bankhead, slightly disconcerted with Trevor's humorous interjection, went on with his story. "Well, we registered, had our luggage taken up and went straightaway to Whitehall and Mr. Moriarty's office in the Foreign Office. We then returned and dressed for dinner. And excepting that, we've all been together.

"Of course the ladies stayed behind, when you visited Whitehall," I said.

"Well yes," said Bankhead. "But we've been together until the accident."

"It was no accident," my brother broke in, impatiently. "Can you recall any specific details about your attackers; their faces, their clothes?"

"Uh, let's see," Bankhead strained to recall. "One had on a plaid overcoat and the other . . . No, no. I just can't remember; it all happened so quickly. It was dark and they were some distance away from us when they struck."

"You can't recall any distinguishing characteristics, or something they might have said?"

"No, they seemed kind of ordinary. One was short, I remember. Oh, wait a minute; one of them said something about a duke. 'Get the duke,' I think I heard him say."

Further enquiry was forestalled as the landau pulled up before the hotel. Grateful to leave our cramped quarters, we clambered out and stood in the snow while Bankhead paid the driver. We then followed him into the welcome warmth of the hotel lobby and up the stairs to the fourth floor. A few yards down the hallway, Bankhead rapped at a door. It opened and we followed him into the suite.

Captain Ravenswood was seated on a couch, a discreet bandage on his forehead. He was comforting a young lady, evidently Miss Rachel Leland, if her resemblance to the Colonel was any indication. The young lady seated opposite them in a sombre wing-chair had a friendly face, filled with concern. This was Miss Millicent Deane, the young school companion. The remaining member of the party, Tyler Carteret, interrupted his distracted pacing as we entered.

"Bankhead, where did you dash off to?" snapped Ravenswood. Then seeing me, he harshly demanded, "What are you doing here, Holmes?"

"I brought him, Captain," Bankhead replied, a bit puzzled at the uncivil tone used by his superior. "I thought that since he's the only man we know in London, I'd . . ."

"Bankhead, you're a fool," barked the Captain.

"Now, see here, Captain Ravenswood," Bankhead retorted. "You can't . . ."

I decided to head off this angry exchange. "Captain Ravenswood, your associate brought us from dinner to see if we could be of any help."

Ravenswood's temper subsided a minor degree. "I am sorry that he inconvenienced you gentlemen."

I held up a conciliatory hand. "Please say nothing further about it. How is Colonel Leland?"

"The surgeon is with him now," Ravenswood gestured reluctantly toward the bedroom door with a wax vesta he had fished from his coat. "The hotel management rounded one up for us.

"We've had precious little time to make any other arrangements, damn your London thugs!"

"Captain Ravenswood," my brother began mildly.

"Who the hell are you?"

Sherlock stiffened, his eyes becoming cold and dark beneath hooded lids. I introduced him and Victor Trevor with as much diplomatic aplomb as I could muster. I too was put off by the offensive manner being displayed by the American. There was an awkward silence as we awaited to be introduced to the ladies. Finally, Bankhead did the honours.

"As I was about to say," Sherlock said, the faintest note of disdain in his voice, "we have come to help you. Mr. Bankhead has agreed to . . ."

Ravenswood jumped to his feet, "Bankhead, you have no authority to commission any arrangements for this mission." To Sherlock he continued, "I repudiate any such verbal contract that has been made. Now if you gentlemen will leave us, we'll . . ."

"You'll what, Captain?" My brother's voice was icy. "You may insult us or you may threaten us as you will. But such threats are empty and you know it. If Mr. Bankhead spoke truly in the cab, you dare not call the police."

His eyes swept the length of Ravenswood's bulk contemptuously. "And I don't believe that you could remove us bodily yourself."

"Now, Sherlock . . ."

"Mycroft, we offer our assistance to this man and receive naught but abuse. Now," he turned back to Ravenswood, speaking in measured tones. "I understand your anxiety. You were hit over the head and your friend may be near death. But you are still bound by the rules of civility. I am sorry for the hurt you have sustained. I should like to help you bring the felons to justice."

Ravenswood assessed my brother with a steady gaze. Then his shoulders slumped. The tension in the room eased slightly; Carteret and Bankhead moved from where they had frozen. Out of the corner of my eye, I saw that Trevor had relaxed. He had been wound tight as a spring, ready for any action that might have been needed.

"You are quite right, of course, Mr. Holmes," said Ravenswood in a milder voice. "I do apologise. I've been overwrought, you see . . ." His voice trailed off as he nodded toward the bedroom door.

As if on command, it opened, allowing me—with the aid of the large mirror atop the bureau opposite his bed— to catch a glimpse of the white-haired figure bundled under the blankets. The man who emerged was younger than I would have thought, but his bulky medical bag and the fairly pungent aroma of carbolic acid proclaimed his profession to be that of physician. He quietly closed the door and Miss Rachel Leland stood up, going across the room to him. She held a crumpled, twisted lace handkerchief. Her concern drew the doctor from his weariness.

"He's asleep," said the doctor, in a faint Scots burr. "I think he's over the worst of it. There'll be no need to take him to hospital. But he'll need four days' bed rest at least and plenty o' quiet."

"Four days!" exploded Ravenswood.

The doctor turned to him. "Your friend was very near death," he said curtly. "An inch higher, or if he'd lost any more blood, and you'd a' been ordering a coffin for him. I canna' understand your objection to a few days' bed rest." The doctor, in his soft-spoken way, was a match for the volcanic Ravenswood. The American just stared until Miss Leland moved to interpose herself between the two men.

"Oh doctor, we're so grateful," she said, in a charmingly light Southern accent. She reached out for his hand impulsively. "I can promise you, sir, that he'll get the very best of care." She smiled at him and the room seemed to grow the brighter for it.

Even Ravenswood seemed to be affected by her charm: "I'm sorry," he said, "I didn't mean to imply anything, doctor. We've all been so worried."

"I understand, sir," said the physician. "I dinna mean to take off your head. I've had a beastly day myself." He turned to Miss Leland. "I would suggest that, should he seem feverish later, you apply cold compresses. There's a chance that he might be a trifle delirious when he awakens."

Miss Leland started, her hand darting to her lips.

The doctor quickly added, "But I think this unlikely. Oh, he may babble a bit, but I hardly think he'll become violent. And this will pass."

Miss Leland became visibly relieved.

"Have you any laudanum here?"

"I have some," Miss Deane said, speaking for the first time since we entered.

"Then you should give him three teaspoonsful mixed in a small tumbler of water, no oftener than thrice daily, should he awaken and be in pain."

"I will be happy to do so," said Millicent Deane. "Will you be calling on him tomorrow?"

"Certainly, unless Lady Finsdale's confinement should prevent me."

"I've had some training as a nurse, Doctor. If I can help . . ."

"Excellent," the physician beamed. "Probably, it will not be necessary for you to re-dress the wound between my visits. However, if there is considerable drainage, you should dress it after bathing the area in boracic acid. I have left a small bottle in the night-table for that purpose. If there is any change in his condition, I can be reached at this address," he said, handing her his card. "Agar is the

name. Dr. Moore Agar. Good evening, ladies, gentlemen."
The front door closed behind him.*

With the physician gone, Captain Ravenswood resumed
a less friendly manner. He removed a cigar from a silver
case taken from his coat pocket. "Well, gentlemen," he
said, striking the vesta and turning to the members of his
entourage, "it appears that we face a delay. Mr. Holmes, it
seems as though we must see your Mr. Moriarty without
the company of Colonel Leland. Can you arrange for us
to see him, as you told the Colonel this afternoon?" he
asked through the pungent smoke.

"I don't know, Captain," I said. "I've already notified
Mr. Moriarty of your message. I will be seeing him tomorrow, and I have no idea as to how he will wish to proceed."

"Oh, I expect he'll see us," said Carteret smugly.

"I expect he will," I agreed, considering the note from
the Consul General, "though I suspect that his schedule is
already filled."

Actually my superior did not work that hard, but I felt
impelled to break that serene confidence the Southerners
carried about wtih them so arrogantly.

"Speaking of busy schedules," my brother interjected,
"I'd like to clear up a few minor points, so that we may
leave you to your rest, Captain Ravenswood." The Captain
turned to him. "Mr. Bankhead has told us that you haven't
been out of each other's sight since you arrived this morning." Ravenswood shot a sharp glance at his youthful
companion, then returned his gaze to Sherlock.

"That is correct, young man. We got off our train, hailed
a cab, and came directly to this hotel. We then visited Mr.
Moriarty's office and were referred to your brother, though
I am still not sure that it is any of your business." The
cigar smoke wreathed his heavy face with acrid grey
clouds.

"That is . . . very interesting, sir," Sherlock responded
slowly.

Ravenswood's tone changed, and he became almost

---

* This must be the same Dr. Moore Agar of Harley Street mentioned in the beginning of "The Adventure of the Devil's Foot," in
the collection *His Last Bow*. But is this Agar's "dramatic introduction to Holmes" about which Watson says he "may someday recount"? MH/SMW

friendly in his sudden concern. "Well, you must all be quite wearied by this evening's tumult. Mr. Holmes, I hope that we will be seeing your superior soon and that I may bid you a good evening."

"Yes, of course," said Sherlock slowly. Then his manner changed abruptly. "Well, you too must be wearied by your experiences this evening. And if you have no more business to conduct, Mycroft," he turned to me; I shook my head. "Then we will take our leave and bid you a good night."

And so we left, Sherlock virtually pushing us out of the room. On the way downstairs, I asked why he made us make so precipitous a departure.

"I for one am glad we did," Trevor put in before Sherlock answered. "I don't believe that I could have endured that horrible aroma an instant longer. Those American cigars are no better than hemp."

"They aren't American," Sherlock and I chorused together.

Trevor stopped in his tracks. "The devil you say!"

"They're East Indian," I replied. "A dark leaf binder, shade grown, with an undistinguished burley filler. Their only redeeming feature is their Sumatran-leaf wrapper. They're sold ten for a shilling practically within twenty-four hours after harvesting, obviously his habitual smoke, seeing how well they fit his cigar-case."

"And there are only three shops in London with the cheek to carry them," my brother went on for me. "And not one of those tobacconists is anywhere near where our American cousins told us that they'd been today.

"Which means that they are lying," Sherlock declared flatly.

3

A DISCUSSION IN
MONTAGUE STREET

"Holmes! Are you certain?" asked Trevor.

"Of course," came my brother's impatient reply. "I tell you, that cigar cannot be purchased within two miles of Regent Street."

I could not dispute my brother's conclusion, but I was more concerned with its implications. Why would the Americans lie over so small a thing? To what end? And what other portions of their story would prove false? Trevor echoed my own thoughts when he added, "You don't suppose then that the attack on Colonel Leland was also a ruse?"

Sherlock shook his head. "No, that was real enough. One doesn't get a Harley Street physician involved in such a plot on such short notice. No, the attack and the injuries are real enough. Without additional data, I would have to agree that it was a simple matter of encountering foot-pads. After all, Regent Street is as likely a spot to be robbed as any other in London, and considering the wealthy residents of the Langham, perhaps even more so. Still, there is something wrong with the Americans' story."

We were, by this time, outside the hotel. The doorman beckoned a carriage and we directed the driver to Montague Street, where my brother had rooms near the British Museum. During the drive, I gave Sherlock and Trevor a brief account of my first meeting with the Americans. By the time I had delivered this history, my brother's frequent questions notwithstanding, we had reached his lodgings. I accepted his invitation to join them in a glass of sherry.

Although I was feeling the exertions of the day—eight flights of stairs are not within my normal regimen—I nevertheless laboured up the several steps to my brother's second-storey flat. I would have preferred to return to my own modest rooms near King's Cross, but I sensed that we had not finished our discussion.

Sherlock pushed some books off his shabby settee of faded purple plush and tossed some newspapers into a corner which was apparently reserved for them, judging by the growing stacks already in residence. Room thus made for me, he lifted his violin from a disreputable red velvet and rosewood armchair, into which Trevor then threw himself. Remembering his stated purpose, Sherlock searched out three clean though unmatched glasses from among the various utensils littering his cupboard.

I must remark here upon my brother's habit of locating items among seemingly unrelated objects. In this instance, an undistinguished bottle of wine was found amid the clutter adorning a deal-topped chemistry table. The habit had been developed in childhood. I can still recall our father's vehement objections when Sherlock insisted that his cricket bat should be located among the beautiful walking sticks in my father's rack. No amount of parental displeasure could break him of the habit, however. I believe he thinks it to be a superior form of camouflage and I have no doubt but that he continues to practice this peculiar vice to this very day.

"I can understand Holmes living in this rather Bohemian colony of Bloomsbury," said Trevor, looking about the room with familiar disdain, "but it seems a bit out of character for you, Mr. Holmes."

"Not at all," I said, awaiting my sherry. "If you were a minor official in the government, you'd find the convenience of Bloomsbury, or more properly, St. Pancras, eminently preferable to the slums of Lambeth, for instance."

"Oh well, yes, Lambeth. But Mr. Holmes, it's so, so . . ."

"If you weren't such a prig, Trevor," said Sherlock, handing him a glass, "I'm sure you'd find the informal atmosphere quite congenial. I prefer my rooms here if for no other reason, because of the handiness and proximity of the British Museum, a short walk 'round the corner."

While Trevor and I sat and sipped, Sherlock doffed his coat and donned a plain navy-blue dressing gown. Then he paced the room, glass in hand, pipe in mouth. Without warning, he stopped abruptly in his perambulations and asked, apparently to no one in particular, "What do you think of Miss Leland?"

Trevor and I exchanged a glance.

"Charming lady," I said. "Obviously well bred, schooled in the social graces, handled Captain Ravenswood's distemper very well. Quite intelligent though a poor cook. I should say. Make some man a good wife and hostess. She had every man in that hotel room captivated."

As Sherlock regarded me narrowly, I hastily amended my statement: "Well, almost every man, then."

Sherlock stopped his pacing and loomed over me. "Did you notice her eyes, Mycroft?"

I tried not to look at him stupidly. "Of course. Blue."

"That's not what I meant. She was watching us most intently. You in particular, dear brother."

"My dear Sherlock, you are imagining things," I said. "She's merely a beautiful young woman, that's all."

"For that matter, so is Millicent Deane," said Trevor.

"No, Mycroft, I'll wager she's more than that," said Sherlock, ignoring Trevor. "You yourself said that she is quite intelligent. But time will tell."

With that, he put down his glass and retrieved his violin, setting his darkening clay pipe in the Persian slipper hanging from the mantelpiece in which he kept his stinking shag tobacco. I knew from long experience that it was time to depart. I like to think of myself as a music fancier and I knew that the sounds Sherlock would shortly draw from the instrument would bear little relationship to anything approaching music. This is not to say that he is a poor musician, but his introspective moods produce a questionable taste in composition. Trevor too understood the sign and bestirred himself from his chair, into which Sherlock poured his languid form. As we gathered our hats and coats, the violin was transferred to his knees, tuneless noises beginning to emanate from it, as Sherlock scraped the bow across its strings. I drained my wine glass.

"Time for me to be abed," I shouted over the shrieks of the violin. "Mr. Moriarty will demand a full accounting first thing tomorrow."

Sherlock made no response. I raised my voice a little more.

"I'll have to phrase it simply for him; he's not at his best in the mornings, I'm afraid." Still no answer.

Trevor and I looked at each other. He shrugged. I nodded. We left. Nothing less than a cannon shot fired across the room could have or would have interrupted my brother's cerebrations.

It was a quarter past eight next morning when I arrived, a full fifteen minutes past my usual time. Griffin, knowing my habits, had the fire lit and a pot of tea ready. "He's here already," was his greeting. No need to tell me who the "he" was. I nodded ruefully, and opened the door to my sanctum. Jerrold Moriarty was pacing in what could only be called a swaggering waddle, awaiting my arrival. In appearance, he was above normal height, a high forehead doming out, a thin bridge of hair separating it from the bald spot behind. He had cavernous sockets, in which gleamed dark, beady eyes. His complexion was sallow, and spindly limbs protruded from a fullblown pot belly. He habitually wore high-waisted trousers and short waistcoats which emphasised that ungainly appendage as though it were a sign of prosperity. Doubtless, he had had a difficult childhood. And although he lost no opportunity to impress his subordinates with the virtue of hard labour in Her Majesty's service, I myself was of the opinion that his career owed less to diligence than to well-placed friends.

"Keeping bankers' hours, eh, Holmes?" he snapped. "What's this business all about? And why should I want to talk to these colonials?"

"An apt choice of words," I responded gravely. "But first, would you care for some tea or toast?" I gestured toward the rack, noticing that two pieces were already missing.

"Never mind the blasted tea," he retorted gruffly. "I'm meeting with the Lords of the Admiralty at nine and I want to know if they should be made aware of this."

"I'm not quite sure, sir. As I said in my note yesterday, the Americans put forth a note written by Cyril Harvey, our man in New Orleans. But something occurred last night that makes this meeting less imperative and, conversely perhaps, even more so, than it was yesterday." I paused to sip my tea.

"Well, which is it? Stop shilly-shallying, man! Tell me what happened."

"The leader of the party, Colonel Leland, was assaulted and shot last night."

"Is he dead?" Moriarty asked anxiously.

"No sir, but gravely wounded. It seems to have been a small-calibre weapon; the bullet must have been deflected by a rib." I then advised him of the story told us by Bankhead. He listened thoughtfully, cocking his head to one side in a characteristic way, the small, red-rimmed eyes fixing themselves on me throughout. When I finished, he nodded.

"You might want to see them, sir, this coming Thursday."

"Why?"

"Because Colonel Leland mentioned that 'the lion looks in all directions.'"

He looked up sharply, but said nothing for a few moments. When he spoke, his tone was nonchalant. "So you suggest that I see this Captain Rookbait . . ."

"Ravenswood, sir."

". . . have a preliminary meeting and hear him out. That seems a sound enough idea, but I want to receive some *précis* information about them . . . from up the line. Is that all?"

"Yes, sir. Would Thursday fit into your schedule?"

He seemed distracted for a moment. "Humm? Oh yes, very well. Thursday."

He made for the door and turned back, hesitating a moment before he spoke again. "Tell me, Holmes . . ."

"Sir?"

"What are your own feelings in this matter?"

I considered my answer for a moment before I spoke. "I really have no feelings about them, sir. They were most anxious to see you. And as they have important military information, you should see them directly."

He shrugged in reply. "You're right, I expect," he said, turning to open the door. Then he stopped to face me again. "Actually, as one who is slated for rapid advancement, I can tell you that I am cognizant of several other developments as yet unknown to you. There are certain elements of policy being discussed in confidential quarters and some highly secret plans drawn up at this moment by our military. In close consultation with myself, I might add," he puffed.

His hand was now on the knob.

"It seems entirely possible that your friends, an unofficial delegation to be sure, might fit into a larger picture already being considered. I cannot say more, but I may have cause to trust you with more information."

He opened the door, then shut it without leaving.

"Oh, and Holmes, that reminds me; after you finish that Ireland business, I want you to make a few lists for me."

"Yes, sir."

"I want to know about the state of readiness of the Aldershot regiments, also. I recollect there were some speeches made by the MP from Manchester last year. Ramsey, I believe is his name."

"Yes, sir."

"They were about navy allocations, if I recall aright."

"I believe that is true, sir."

"Just so."

From this point, the conversation became quite technical, delving into the politics concerning military funding for the succeeding six months and opposition views in Commons.

Shortly after Mr. Moriarty left, I'd sunk myself into the Irish morass once more. It was still forenoon when my clerk entered.

I will digress a moment here to describe and praise my clerk. Sylvanus Griffin had been with me since I entered the foreign service, and he was in some measure responsible for more than can be told. He was three years older than I and physically unprepossessing; I'd be surprised if he came to my shoulder standing in his boots. His predominant feature was a shock of unruly brown hair, which he was forever pushing out of his eyes. Although he took pains to dress correctly, he had the unfortunate habit of wiping his pen nib across his sleeve, no matter what he was wearing at the time. It was commonplace to see a thin line of ink across his wrist that instantly defined his occupation. But he was tireless, efficient, and on the few occasions on which I sought his advice in official matters, I found his judgment both perceptive and accurate.

His one anomaly was that his usual quiet demeanor was ofttimes broken by stray fits of laughter, as though he were recalling the ending of an untold humorous anecdote. I was able to keep him with me as I assumed greater responsibilities in the government and I daresay that not one man in ten thousand was so well served by his clerk as was I. Though his forebears were Cockney, his immediate family was of more gentle birth, and he was one of the first in the city to gain his post through the civil service. I am proud to have worked with him.

"Yes, Griffin? I'd asked not to be disturbed."

"So you did, sir, but this seemed to be important."

"Why is that?"

"There's a young foreign lady here to see you, sir."

"Indeed?"

"Yes, sir; a Miss Rachel Leland. A Yankee," he added, with some faint derision.

I considered this momentarily before I bade him show her in.

"Oh, and Griffin . . ."

"Yes, sir."

"There is more than one kind of American," I said, fighting a smile.

"Is there, sir?" he said, cocking a brow.

"Most definitely—Miss Leland is one of the *other* kind."

"I see, sir."

"And for heaven's sake, don't ever let her hear you describe her as a Yankee."

A small smile played across his lips. "As you say, sir."

With that he ushered Miss Leland into my office. We exchanged greetings.

"It's so good of you to take time out of your busy day to see me."

"Oh, please," I deprecated. "It's nothing at all. How is your father?"

"A bit better," she said. "He seems to be resting as well as he can, under the circumstances. Millicent—Miss Deane —is watching over him, so I know he's in good hands."

"Of course. Please sit down. Make yourself comfortable."

She took her place on the swayback couch, bequeathed

to me by generations of bureaucratic forebears. I sat down on the almost-matching chair, of equal antiquity and wear.

"I hadn't time last night to thank you for your kindness. You all left so hastily," she said. "It was very kind of you and your brother to come, and Mr. Trevor as well." She hesitated. "And I want to apologise for Captain Ravenswood's behaviour. But he's been under such terrible strain." She gave me a wan smile. "We all have. And then his getting hit over the head—well, I just wanted to . . ."

"Please say no more about it," I murmured. "I quite understand."

Seeking to change the subject, I asked, "Would you care for some tea?"

"Why yes, sir. That would be pleasant." She rose and inspected the view from my window. Unfortunately, all that can be seen from my window is the western portico of the Foreign Office under a wedge of the leaden sky which boded more snow.

Griffin brought in the refilled teapot and vanished. Miss Leland returned to the couch to take charge of the tea things, displaying an easy mastery of the ritual despite her youth. I watched her, marvelling not only at her easy manner but at the similarity of costume she exhibited to the clothing worn by women in England: The jacket and full, ground-sweeping skirt were both made from merino wool, dyed a rich umber. Her hair, upswept in front, tight ringlets of honey-blonde falling behind down her neck, supported one of the silly feathered hats then in the height of fashion. She removed her kid gloves to pour the tea and pass a cup to me.

"You'll please to pardon my lack of grace, Miss Leland," said I. "I am quite unused to entertaining such charming company in my chambers."

"I never thought I'd be having tea with a British diplomat, myself," was her demure response. "Miss Storke's Academy for Genteel Young Ladies did not really prepare me to entertain such distinguished company."

The bright smile she gave me with the tea was not shared by her eyes. In fact, a lurking fear reposed therein. It led me to an untypical frankness.

"Tell me, Miss Leland; why did Captain Ravenswood feel it necessary to lie to us last night?"

She averted her gaze. "Lie? Why, whatever do you mean, Mr. Holmes?" Her voice was steady, but her manner betrayed her. Nevertheless, I continued.

"What I mean, Miss Leland, is that the Captain told us that no member of your party left the hotel save for the purpose of their visit to these offices yesterday and then for dinner. Young Bankhead told us the same."

She continued to stare at the carpet. "And what makes you think they're lying, Mr. Holmes?" She took a handkerchief from her sable muff and proceeded to twist it compulsively.

"The cigar he was smoking last night was purchased in this city, in a place nowhere near the hotel or Whitehall."

"But how could you know that?" she said, staring at me incredulously.

"Cigars are a hobby with me, Miss Leland. Now, that particular type of cigar which the Captain smokes is impossible to obtain along the itinerary mapped out for us by the Captain and Bankhead. Someone in your party must have ventured out much further into London than they would have us believe.

"So then, Miss Leland: what is the truth of the matter?"

The fear in her eyes became more uncontrolled.

"Surely you can be mistaken, Mr. Holmes," she said falteringly.

"I!" I cocked my brow. "Am I mistaken, Miss Leland?"

She looked like a cornered deer. Then, with a sudden movement, she balled up her handkerchief and threw it on the carpet. I rose, bending forward to pick it up.

"Let it lay," she exclaimed. "It's a gift from *him*."

I resumed my seat. "Captain Ravenswood, you mean."

"Yes . . . that beast!"

Her words were spoken with such loathing, that, I confess, I lost some of my professional aplomb.

"Oh, Mr. Holmes," she continued, "he deceived me too. I don't know what I can do; I'm just a poor helpless girl." Her words rushed out now.

"I'd hardly call you helpless," said I, hoping not to sound too dry.

"I must tell someone," she said fervently. "Father won't listen and Tyler and Billy—why the're little more than boys. They can't do anything to help. I need someone else to talk to." Tears were forming in her eyes.

Awkwardly, I moved from my chair, sitting next to her on the couch. Slowly, I placed my hand on one of her own. There was no stopping the tears now. She wept openly, sobbing, her cheek resting on my shoulder, her soft blonde curls brushing my face, her bonnet now fallen onto the rug. With difficulty, I extracted my own handkerchief from the breast pocket of my frock coat, proffering it to her.

Accepting it, she dabbed her eyes delicately, the scent of her perfume filling my nostrils. Her eyes were dry now, yet she remained close.

"Oh, you must think me an awful child," she sniffed prettily, still dabbing at her cheeks.

"Not at all," I attempted gallantly. "Merely—merely a beautiful woman who finds herself in need of help." I hoped I was not sounding like one of Thackeray's swains. I despise insincere sentiment.

"And you'll help me?" she asked, her eyes now lighting with hope.

"I'll do—what I can." I was not about to be won over completely. I found her open manner too forthright, too lacking in reserve. I had found this to be true of many Americans and such lack of discretion usually puts me off. But Miss Leland was very nearly ecstatic at my answer.

"Oh, Mr. Holmes, I don't know what to say." She took my hand in both of hers. "Thank you, Mr. Holmes."

"Now then," I asked while extracting my hand as gently as possible, "what can you tell me about the Captain's cigars?"

She hesitated. "I really don't know if I should, Mr. Holmes." She looked away. "I'm wondering if maybe I've said too much already. If Samuel found out . . ."

"My dear Miss Leland," I interjected. "If you want your mission to succeed and the Captain is working against the very government to which he has come for help, then it is he who is doing your cause a disservice. That I have already discovered him in a lie is one reason for my recommendation against associating ourselves with you." I looked at my hands. "But he is not the head of your delegation and I am sure that your father knows nothing about his

other involvements. If you do, it is your duty to tell me."
I returned my gaze to her. "It really is, you know." If she
was going to be indiscreet, I might as well take advantage
of it.

"You're right, Mr. Holmes. We arrived in London yesterday morning and registered in the hotel. My father went
into his room and took a nap. Tyler and Billy were sitting
in the parlour, reading. Millicent and I were putting our
clothes away when the Captain came to our door to say
that he was going out for a while and would be back soon.
He said it was confidential and that we needn't worry ourselves about it." Her eyes fell. "He hinted at something . . ."

"Something?"

She looked up again and sighed. "He mentioned that it
had something to do with The Cause."

" 'The Cause?' I must say, Miss Leland, that I have no
idea what that may be."

"The Cause," she said again, softly. "Mr. Holmes, I've
lived with The Cause all my life. It's what we in the South
call the War Between the States." Her face grew hard as
she continued: "I have become so tired of hearing about
our 'glorious heritage' and the 'blot on our honour.' . . .
Mr. Holmes, please understand, I love my father and I
know of his devotion to the Southland, but we lost the war.
We lost and we should rebuild what was destroyed, not
just go on about the past. We should look to the future . . ." She looked at my handkerchief in her lap. "You
know, Mr. Holmes, such talk would be considered traitor-
ous at home. But everyone is so backward . . ." She choked
back a sob and stopped.

I considered what she'd said. I had paid scant attention
to the southern half of the United States since the war. I
am afraid that we in England took it for granted that the
Union was sound and that the dissidents who may have
remained in the late Confederacy were effectively muzzled.
But Miss Leland's words bespoke a deeper resentment than
I had thought existed among the citizens of the South.

"Miss Leland, you mentioned that Captain Ravenswood
deceived you too. In what manner?"

"I did a foolish thing yesterday," she said. "I told Millicent that I wanted to go out for a walk, but what I really
did was to follow Captain Ravenswood."

"But you said that you trusted him."

"Oh, Mr. Holmes, these games of intrigue and deception, they're not for me. I went out because, well, I'm to be betrothed to Captain Ravenswood. Daddy was to have announced it last week, but then we had to go on this mission. We were going to be married in the spring."

"This is very interesting, Miss Leland, but . . ."

"Mr. Holmes, I'm not really in love with him," she said, her eyes becoming hard and unfeeling.

"Then why are you consenting to . . ."

"I must, Mr. Holmes; it's my duty."

"Of course, Miss Leland, I understand." The age of prearranged marriages of convenience had not yet passed. Miss Leland explained.

"You see, before the war, Daddy was part of what we call the Southern aristocracy. Of course," she added coyly, "it doesn't begin to compare with yours."

I smiled back tolerantly.

"He owned the second-largest cotton mill in the South and we had three thriving plantations. But during the war, he lost them and after, them damnyankees and Scalawags took over the mill."

"You lost everything, then?"

"Well, not quite everything. We still had one plantation left to us and it was our largest. We call it 'Ilium,' but so much of the surrounding acreage was stolen by freedmen and the Yankees that we hadn't very much left for our own crops, only about twenty-five thousand acres. I suppose that sounds like an awful lot to you here on this tiny little island, but back home, why that's barely nothing at all."

I nodded.

"Well, anyway, Captain Ravenswood had been more fortunate. He was able to preserve much more of his holdings. He and Daddy had been business associates before the war and he thought to help Daddy after. Poor Daddy. He didn't have much of a chance to do anything else but what Captain Ravenswood proposed, so they struck a bargain." Her voice became very low as she continued. "He said that he would help Daddy financially, for what he said he considered a very small and reasonable price." Her lips trembled. "Myself. I was to be the price, when I came of age. Against my will I was promised to him."

She raised the back of her hand to her brow. "And now I am a pawn in all this."

I was captivated by her story. "I see. Bankhead mentioned that your coming to England at the start of a continental tour was a ruse."

"Well, yes and no," she said. "We were going on a tour, but the Captain found a way to use it to fit into his own plans for Alabama."

I wondered more about the Captain's plans and said, "Can you tell me any more about Captain Ravenswood?"

"To be honest, Mr. Holmes, I don't really know as much as I should about him. He came to New Orleans, shortly before the war, I know. He's in shipping and has investments in some other businesses all through the South. He has a terrible temper and he's an excellent marksman. He's fought in several duels back home. That's about all I know."

I leaned forward in my chair to study my visitor. Her face was flushed and her careful *coiffure* was in danger of falling. In general, she gave the impression of innocent helplessness, only slightly belied by the strong, yet delicate white hands, so carefully kept and manicured. I searched her face for any sign indicating a lack of truthfulness. She dropped her eyes, continuing the story of her previous day's adventure.

"The Captain took a cab, I saw him get in, but I wasn't able to overhear the destination."

"Then you did not follow him?"

"I didn't say that," she said flashing a brief smile.

"All right. I assume that you too hailed a hansom, instructing the driver to follow Captain Ravenswood's cab."

"Exactly. We drove around the city for nearly an hour. Then we crossed a bridge . . ."

"Do you know which one?"

She smiled helplessly. "I'm afraid not. But he had his driver stop at a saloon near the river and went inside. I didn't dare follow him in; besides, it was obviously not a place in which a lady should be seen."

"Certainly not," I agreed half-heartedly. Then I brightened. "I take it that you asked the driver to what part of London he had driven you."

"Oh yes," she smiled again. "I surely would never have

known where I was otherwise. Ever'thing's so twisty here. It was in Southwark, he said, near the river."

"Very good, Miss Leland. And the name of the sal . . . the pub?"

"Oh!" She looked startled. "I never thought to look, or even ask the driver. I felt so daring just going out alone! He went out again today, so I thought it best to come right over to see you before he returned."

This disquisition was not ending on the same bright note of promise on which it was begun.

She obviously did not know who the Captain was to see, nor how long he would take. This annoyed me also, but there was nothing to do about it, save to end the interview. "I appreciate your coming, Miss Leland, and trusting me with your story. As yet, I am not at all certain how I can help you, if indeed I can. But your advice about Captain Ravenswood's movements have been to some extent enlightening."

"Well, you were so nice last night, Mr. Holmes. I thought that, well, maybe I could confide in you. And," she paused, looking up at me with large eyes, "I just had to tell someone."

Tears were beginning to form; I decided to steer her to the door. "So you said," I told her gently. "Now I suggest that you return to your father before the Captain discovers you missing. That would be most unfortunate."

"You're right, Mr. Holmes. Thank you again for being so kind to a stranger."

We rose together and, as we came to the door, she leaned forward and, like a small child, lightly kissed my cheek.

"That wasn't necessary." I said brusquely.

"I know," she smiled brightly. "That's why I did it." She picked up her bonnet. At the same time, I retrieved her handkerchief from the floor, proffering it to her.

"I'd rather keep yours," she said, coquettishly.

I gave her a gracious little bow and smiled in return.

"Oh, but that will leave you without a handkerchief," she said, giving her hat a final adjustment.

"That's true."

"Well," she said, looking directly into my eyes, "you'll just have to keep mine, I guess."

I must have looked a trifle confused; I retained enough presence of mind, however, to give her another little bow and then lead her to the door. For a while after she left, the scent of her sachet lingered in my otherwise stuffy office.

With the distraction of Miss Leland's visit over, I returned to my duties. It was nearly six o'clock before I finished the work Mr. Moriarty had laid out for me. Griffin had been sent to secure copies of the speeches made by Ramsey, the MP from Manchester; there was no one else in the anteroom. I was just finishing part of my report when the door opened to admit my second unexpected visitor of the day. By the time I did look up, I saw a man standing about midway between my desk and the door. He was an American Negro, dressed as a gentleman. He wore a high silk hat, long frock coat, grey-striped trousers and highly polished boots. The only oddment in his attire was a bright plum-coloured, silk brocade waistcoat, dominated by a heavy, tastelessly constructed Albert chain. The long blue fob hanging from his watch pocket contributed to the distressing picture he presented.

"I don't have much time, Mr. Holmes," he said, approaching my desk. He was at my side before I could rise. In a voice like quicksilver he spoke again. "I must talk to you about the American situation."

The American situation! This man must have some connexion with Colonel Leland and his companions. I had to learn more. My reply, however, was so much bluster. "Now see here, I don't know who you are, but . . ."

Without seeming to move a muscle, he suddenly had a gleaming Derringer in his hand.

"I'm not here to bandy words with you, sir. I will have that discussion and I will have it with you now."

Just then, there was a knock at the door and a familiar voice called out my name: "Mycroft? Are you in?"

"You'd best put your gun away," I said softly. "He'll be in here in an instant."

The dusky intruder faltered, looking back to the door, then back to me.

"Do it now," I snapped, "or you've come for naught."

He pocketed the pistol.

"Come in, Sherlock."

The coloured man stepped clear of my desk as the door opened.

"We shall speak more of this later, sir."

On cat's feet, he walked swiftly out. He paused at the door for a second as he passed my brother and the two silently measured each other. They were within an inch of the same height, although the Negro was somewhat bulkier. Sherlock flashed me a glance, sensing danger, mutely asking if he should attempt to hold the stranger. I gave no signal and, in the next instant, the man was gone, the door closing softly behind him.

"Who was that?"

"I don't know, Sherlock. He didn't have time to introduce himself. What do you make of him?"

"American; not long in England; horseman, judging by his gait. Abominable taste in waistcoats."

"Yes," I continued. "Well educated too. Rather expert in the use of firearms. He told me that he wanted to discuss the American situation, whatever that was supposed to mean."

Sherlock sank into my visitor's chair and steepled his fingers together in front of his face. "Ravenswood and his crowd, do you think?"

"I wonder. He drew a Derringer on me. It must be a very important thing for him."

"A Derringer! Well, why didn't you have me stop him?"

"No purpose. If he wants to talk to me he doesn't wish to kill me."

"I must say you're very cool about this, Mycroft."

"Oh I shouldn't worry about it, Sherlock. The only reason he was able to come in today is because I sent Griffin off to the archives. He'd never have been able to get in otherwise. If he comes by tomorrow, I'll be sure to have him searched first."

"I should be careful all the same, Mycroft," he said gravely. In a moment, though, his tone lightened.

"I see that he wasn't your first visitor of the day."

"Oh?"

"Miss Leland's scent. I noticed it last night before Ravenswood lit that abominable cigar."

"Very astute, Sherlock."

He laughed at some private thought. "Come, Mycroft,"

he said. "It's time for dinner. My treat tonight. Will Simpson's-in-the-Strand serve your appetite?"

I confess I stared at him. "Simpson's? You'll treat me?"

"Your cheque, remember; I stopped at the bank to change it."

I laughed. "Very well, Sherlock. Now tell me, what have you learned?"

"No, dear brother, my story will wait. I want to hear about Miss Leland."

In the hansom, I told Sherlock what I had learned from Miss Leland. There really was little to tell him. Merely that Miss Leland was betrothed to Ravenswood; that she had been deceived by him; and that she had followed him to Southwark and left him there. Sherlock listened attentively but said nothing until I finished.

"We have another thread to our bow," he said. "I sent Trevor off to keep an eye on them. He'll be reporting back to us tonight, and we'll see if there is something new to be learned after all."

The hansom pulled up to the restaurant. I paid our fare and the cab disappeared in the traffic of the Strand.

Simpson's was crowded, but a gratuity to the headwaiter procured a table for us on the ground floor. We sat in the window, allowing us to observe the Strand with its scurrying throng of humanity. While awaiting dinner, Sherlock and I used the time for our favourite exercise.

"The little man there, Mycroft, in front of the baker's, just paying the driver of the hansom . . ."

"Draughtsman, married. Rather, about to be married."

"A senior clerk, from the look of him. First marriage, I surmise."

"No, Sherlock, his second. Note the condition of his hat brim."

"Oh yes. Nearsighted, too."

"And given to heavy exercise."

"Spends much of his time in his club."

"Possibly the reason for the ending of his first marriage. I hope his second wife is more understanding."

"Or more muscular." We laughed and the scene changed.

"The woman calling for her child under the street lamp."

"Housewife, has two children, the other somewhat older

than the one she has with her," I said. "Lives in Camden Town. Bringing home her dinner now."

"Oh?"

"Note the package under her arm. It has been wrapped by a poulterer."

"Ah, yes, so it was: the pinkish paper and cord. I hope her husband's not home yet if she's only getting tonight's dinner now."

"Ah," said I, "The policeman talking to the lamplighter. Isn't that your friend, Sergeant Lestrade?"

"Friend?" said my brother with a smile. "Well, after a fashion, I suppose."

The policeman left the lamplighter and plodded across the street, crossing in front of our window. Sherlock rapped on the glass and waved. Lestrade looked up, startled, saw Sherlock's smiling face, snarled something and continued away. Sherlock laughed.

"What was all that about?"

"You may have read in the papers a few days ago," my brother laughed merrily, "that Lestrade was put in charge of the investigation of those housebreakings in Locksley Street, near Limehouse. I sent a note 'round to him at the Yard, suggesting that he investigate the whereabouts of a certain housemaid who had been dismissed by no less than three households within the vicinity. The answer he sent by return post took the form of a suggestion that I kindly stay out of his affairs."

"Yet I see that he took your advice after all."

"Thus it would appear, Mycroft. He only becomes that nasty after he's proven to himself the correctness of my advice. And speaking of appearances . . ."

"Hullo, Holmes; good evening, sir," said Victor Trevor in greeting. He was disheartened as he sat down in the vacant chair at our table.

"Lose him?" asked Sherlock.

"Yes, damn it. The Captain is as devious as you had predicted, Holmes," said the discouraged giant. "I followed him only as far as Saint Paul's before my cabbie's horse threw a shoe. By the time I was able to catch another empty hansom, the fellow was gone without a trace."

"What wretched luck," said Sherlock with disgust. "Ah well, there's nothing for it. You tried your best, Trevor. I suppose there's nothing left but to invite you to join us. We may as well enjoy the meal if not your results."

We spent the remainder of the dinner speaking inconsequentially. Or rather, Trevor and I did so. My brother kept silent, scowling, obviously deep in thought. Suddenly, he threw down his fork and pushed Trevor away from the table.

"Mycroft—Trevor! There's not a moment to lose!"

I had only enough time to pay for the unfinished dinner—at which I was supposed to be my brother's guest—while Sherlock gathered up our hats and coats for us and propelled us out of the restaurant. We stood in the snow while Sherlock explained his behaviour:

"Mycroft! The black man who was your visitor this afternoon—if he is who I believe him to be—I only just remembered that I read about him last week in the penny press. He's a former American slave. Back in 1860 he led a number of his fellow slaves in a series of mutinies against their masters. Rumour has it that he's a brilliant tactician, though where he learned his art I have no idea. Anyway, he escaped to the continent in '70, made a deal of money at the tables in Monte Carlo. Now he's a highly paid soldier of fortune. Styles himself 'Captain Jericho.' "

"Somewhat melodramatic," said Trevor with a sniff. "But what's all this about?"

Briefly, I told him of the encounter I'd had with the Negro.

"You mean he just put the pistol back in his waistcoat and walked out as cool as that? What brass!" exclaimed Trevor when I finished.

"That's his manner," said my brother. "Damn! There's never a cab when you need one!"

"You should have called the police," said Trevor to me.

"The man's broken no law," said Sherlock.

"You're forgetting about the pistol," I said, drily.

"Well, none that can be proven," rejoined Sherlock. "He moves anywhere he wishes and no one knows anything about him, save what he chooses to tell."

"But what could he want to talk to you about, Mr. Holmes," asked Trevor.

"It must concern the Southerners' mission in Whitehall," said Sherlock impatiently. "Now, let us consider what reasons he might have for discussing the American delegation with you, Mycroft. As a former slave he would have a natural curiosity about an American delegation from a Southern state, composed of former officers, active during the late Confederate campaign. Under any other circumstances, his interest would most likely end there. However, this delegation presents itself to the military liaison in Whitehall. For what possible reason?"

"Sherlock, these are now matters of state, I think . . ."

"A man points a pistol at you and all you can think about is protecting a possible state secret?" cried Sherlock. "What is the heart of this matter, Mycroft? That is what must be discovered." I subsided.

"Do you think this Negro might want to stop the American delegation?" asked Trevor.

"The signs would point to that probability," said Sherlock, retreating once more to his introspective pose. "As a former slave, he might want to somehow discredit these Southerners, most likely themselves former slaveholders. Which would then make one suppose that this Captain Jericho has a personal reason for intruding himself into this business."

"Maybe he was a slave to one of these delegates!" cried Trevor, joyous at his own perception.

"That would make the situation an urgent one, eh, Mycroft?"

"Obviously," I said. So much I had deduced for myself. I was happy to see Sherlock wanting to aid me in this episode, but I was more concerned that this remain within the precincts of the FO. I had my own ideas, but as yet, even I did not know all the facts myself.

"Well, for whatever reason," said Sherlock, mulling it over in his mind, "he's up to no good. And it bodes ill for the Southerners. He'll not cavil at murder, you may be sure."

"Good Lord, Holmes!" Trevor belatedly exclaimed, "We have to warn them!"

"Precisely!" Sherlock called back while he stood in the street in an effort to flag down the hansom with his stick. The driver finally saw him and turned into the kerb.

"Quick, Mycroft, get in," he said, tugging me to the door of the cab. "Take this man to the Langham," called Sherlock up to the driver. To me he continued, "There's no time to spare."

"But Sherlock . . ." I protested.

"You're the only one. You're much better acquainted with them than either of us." I saw the wisdom in this and stepped into the hansom.

"But Sherlock," I said, turning on the step. "What about you?"

"Trevor and I are going in search of Captain Jericho," was my brother's gleeful answer, as he pushed me into the cab and closed the dash.

"We, old boy?" said Trevor, eyeing Sherlock quizzically. "What can I contribute to this quest?"

"Your calming presence," I yelled out from the window in the dash, the cabby whipping up his horse. "There's nothing like a sixteen-stone, six-foot-four university rugby man to make people think twice about violence."

Trevor's reply was lost in the wind as my cab sped away into the falling snow.

4

ANOTHER
UNFINISHED MEAL

Arriving at the Langham, I distractedly handed a florin to the driver. It was a trifle more than the ride was worth, I admit; in my hurry, it was the first coin I reached out of my pocket. Doubtless, had I fished out a sovereign I would have left it without hesitation. I dashed past the manager's desk and climbed the stairs two at a time, reaching the door to the Americans' suite puffing mightily. (I have since welcomed the advent of the lift.) Millicent Deane answered my insistent knocking and I wheezed out an apology for my unannounced arrival with a request to speak to Captain Ravenswood.

"I'm afraid he's not in, Mr. Holmes. Everyone is out to dinner."

This intelligence raised the question in my mind as to the safety of the Americans outside of the hotel. But I asked, "The Colonel—is he resting?"

"Yes," Miss Deane answered, now alerted to some possible danger. "Is there anything wrong, Mr. Holmes?"

"I trust not. May I come in?"

"By all means, young man," came a vigorous bellow from the open door of the Colonel's bedroom. "Rescue me from this motherin' female."

"I just gave him his medicine," said Miss Deane, her face going red. "He's been very restive today."

"Perhaps I can ease his agitation," I answered, hoping to calm my own disquietude.

She smiled, but it did not belie the shadows under her eyes. She was under a strain, caused no doubt by her "restive" patient. "The worse the patient, the better the nurse," I told her, dropping my gloves into my high black-silk hat which she then took from me, with a thankful smile. I then presented myself at the door of the Colonel's room.

"Hand me that damn quilt, young man and if you'd be so kind as to adjust that paraffin lamp beside me, I'd be most grateful. And shut the door; I think the draft is the cause of my chill."

I shut the door and retrieved the quilt from the seat of a chair, arranging it on the bed for the Colonel.

"Thank you, young man. You know, Millicent's a charming girl, but I've not been able to convince her that I'm not standing on the banks of the Styx. Not quite yet, anyway."

"I hope you're resting easily."

"Hah!" he responded. "It would take more than some puny English popgun to do me in for good and all." He arranged himself on the pillows: "The last time I took a bullet, I could secure no better than a narrow cot for my convalescence. And that was in a drafty tent in a chill field at Chickamauga. This," he indicated the broad expanse of coverlet, "is sheer paradise by comparison." He laughed. "You know we had a good chance to win the war, back in '62 or thereabouts."

"You mean The War between the States," I said.

"What other war was there?" he snapped. I smiled inwardly. I could have mentioned several other wars, but thought better of it. The Colonel continued to talk, telling me of his career during the late campaign. His experiences took him to Pennsylvania, "deep in the heart of Yankeedom," as he put it, thence to Virginia and North Carolina. "I was a fighting officer, not one of those damned bullet-dodgers in Richmond," he explained.

I was surprised at his garrulousness and even more surprised to find myself enjoying his narrative, spiced as it was with his forthright opinions. In spite of my usual disdain for immediate *bonhomie*, ˉ ˉˉˉ ˉ ˉˉˉ vself warming to this multifarious American gentlem⌐⌐

"At any rate, I'm glad you stopped in," Colonel Leland said, pausing in his account, "to listen to my meanderings. It's pleasant to relive the past now that I'm a general without an army. Sought refuge in Cæsar's *Commentaries*, but I wasn't able to concentrate on him, what with Millicent and the doctor running in and out all the while. Everyone else is out and even when he's here, Ravenswood keeps dashing about like Quantrill's Raiders. Never around when I want him."

"I too had hoped to see Captain Ravenswood this evening."

"Came to tell him that Mr. Moriarty'd see us, eh?"

"Something on that order. But I find him at dinner."

"Good military dictum," the Colonel nodded. " 'Eat whenever you have the chance.' You never know when you'll have to miss a meal or two. Missed several in my time." He reached a corncob pipe from his night stand as he glanced at me shrewdly. "Doesn't appear that you've felt the pangs of hunger recently, Mr. Holmes." I found myself surreptitiously drawing in my stomach as the Colonel chuckled.

"You know, that Dr. Agar's got the right attitude," said Colonel Leland. "While he was here last night he told me about an alcoholic concoction that sounded very tasty. You do imbibe, I hope?"

I averred that I did.

"Excellent!" He waved to the tantalus across the room on the bureau. "You'll find what we need in that contraption over there. The newest form of medicinal torture: they put the spirit-tray out of reach and then lock it on you besides."*

Fortunately, the key hung from the handle of the receptacle so there was no problem in liberating the decanter which the Colonel had requested. His eyes glistened and his tone became conspiratorial as I brought the decanter to him.

"Bring those two glasses over there," he commanded. "You know, the others don't know it, but that bullet didn't do very much damage."

* A tantalus is a spirit-case constructed in many designs, the most common of which is a fenced-in tray, with an arm that swings down between the uprights of the handle to embrace the stoppers of the decanters which fit snugly within. The arm can be locked to prevent pilfering. Its name derives from the mythic king, Tantalus, who was condemned to stand in a pool of water, a branch of fruit hanging over his head. When thirsty and bending to drink, the pool dried up; when hungry and reaching for the fruit, the wind blew the branch out of his reach. The irony of the Colonel's remark becomes understandable. MH/SMW

"I deduced as much, sir," I said. "Dr. Agar mentioned that the bullet had been deflected. He recommended a light dosage of laudanum, a soporific anodyne. Such a prescription told me that he had little fear for your well-being."

"Very good, young man," said the Colonel. "He patched me up and spent the rest of the time talking about what fools my would-be assassins must be by botching a relatively simple murder at close range." He laughed softly. "Well, he mixed up a little of this nectar last night and we enjoyed ourselves. Yes, sir," he chuckled, "that man's a better doctor than he let on to you last night. 'He might be a trifle delirious when he awakens,' I heard him say." Colonel Leland laughed out loud. "That was just in case I woke up in an inebriated state."

During his tale, I had poured a measure of Dr. Agar's prescription for each of us and we drank heartily. Colonel Leland then smacked his lips and wiped them on the sleeve of his nightshirt. "Good liquor!" he exclaimed. "Dr. Agar called it 'Scotch Mist,' and damned if I don't feel as comfortable as dew on the grass."

We sat for a moment, silent while he regarded his tumbler's golden contents.

"Now then, Mr. Holmes. I appreciate your visit, but I'm sure that a busy diplomat like you didn't come here merely to visit a sick old man. So tell me, just why did you come, sir?"

Whether because of the drink or because of his perspicacity, I told him. "My brother and I were speaking about your ordeal of last evening and we thought there was cause to believe that there might be another attack on your party tonight."

"And what led you to this conclusion, sir?"

"I had a visitor, who is, my brother believes, an adventurer, a soldier of fortune who uses the *nom de guerre* 'Captain Jericho.'" I paused, looking the old gentleman in the face, "Are you acquainted with such a man, sir? He didn't mention you by name."

Colonel Leland lit his pipe and pulled hard at it. After a moment he said, "If I didn't like you so well, Mr. Holmes, I would detail for you all of my thoughts regarding that insolent scoundrel who betrayed my trust and affection. He is a mad dog, sir. He deserves to be shot on sight." He studied me through a blue-grey cloud of smoke. "How do you come to know of him, sir?"

"I exchanged words with him this afternoon, in my office at Whitehall." I paused. "I believe he wanted some information as to your appearance at Whitehall."

The Colonel looked at me levelly. "And what did you say to him, Mr. Holmes?"

I returned his gaze. "As a matter of fact, I told him nothing. The interview was interrupted by my brother. However, I've been a civil servant long enough to know when not to betray a confidence. I have no idea what you wish to see Mr. Moriarty about, in any case."

My answer satisfied him. He relaxed against the pillows again. His thin frame was almost lost beneath all the bedding.

"I thought I was rid of him when he fled to the North," the Colonel said at last. "It appears that I was wrong." His eyes rested for an instant on the portrait of a woman on the table beside his bed. The resemblance to Rachel Leland was unmistakable. "Maybe Lily was right," he said. I noticed that he was tiring; his speech was slowing and becoming disjointed. "The Yankees are ruinin' us . . . the nigras aren't ready . . . we've got to do something else . . . Hell no . . . Ravenswood can't do it alone. He's too busy just looking out for himself . . . we must send someone else, gentlemen. . . ."

Suddenly the Colonel's eyes opened wide and he looked directly into mine. "You think this boss of yours will be ready to see us soon?"

"I'm sure that Mr. Moriarty will be at your service on Thursday."

He grunted and studied the wall behind me. He spoke again, as if to himself. "I suppose Lily was right . . . I could have stayed home and let Ravenswood . . . someone else come instead . . ." Then his eyes brightened and a fiery determination took hold of him. "No! No, by God! I've got to do this myself!" This resolve exhausted him. He fell back into the pillows in a faint. He was breathing regularly as I picked up his pipe and laid it on the night stand and quietly made for the door. But I was stopped in my tracks by strange, low male voices talking, followed by a muffled scream. I dashed into the parlour only to see a short, swarthy man swing around and train a small pistol on me. Millicent Deane struggled vainly in the hairy grip of his large, burly accomplice.

"Step in here, mister," he invited. "We'll have the both of you in the same room, if you please."

Moving slowly, I complied. By now, the hulking Manchester brute, a bare-knuckle prize fighter, if his flattened nose and calloused ears were any indication, had pressed a dirty rag against Miss Deane's face. He held it there for a few seconds until she slumped forward, unconscious, to the floor. The rag was saturated with chloroform.

"And who might you be?" asked the man wielding the gun.

I said not a word as I assessed my situation, looking from one man to another. Incorrectly believing me to be a somewhat befuddled gentleman, the brute dropped his guard and laughed, "He's just a simpleton, that's all." Even so, the gunman approached me warily. He had been a sergeant in the Royal Marines, I saw, recently cashiered, who preferred his new acquaintances to those in his former life. All of this seemed highly irrelevant as I faced his pistol.

He stopped about a yard away from me and as he did so, I brought up my foot in what my brother had taught me was a *savate* manœuvre."* Even then I was no athlete, so it would only be accurate to say that it was the sheer effrontery of the motion that caused the gunman to cringe momentarily at my assault. When he recovered, it was too late for him to fire. My foot connected with his knee and he awkwardly dropped to the floor, his pistol flying beneath a chair. The goliath with the chloroform lunged for it, but I threw him back. He tried for it again. I still carried my walking stick and I put it to good use. I waited until he was almost on me, then brought the large knobbed head up hard—and into his stomach. He doubled over in pain. Dropping the stick, I locked my hands above him and

* *Savate* is an old form of boxing which enjoyed a long vogue in France. Blows are delivered by employing either feet or hands. No doubt, Sherlock learned this ancient form of self-defense at about the same time that he learned *baritsu,* the system he used so effectively in "The Adventure of the Empty House," the first case recounted in *The Return of Sherlock Holmes.* MH/SMW

brought them down with as much force as I could muster. He fell to the floor with a groan.

This episode caused me to ignore momentarily the man's partner. As his accomplice fell, he jumped on my back and we crashed down on his nefarious colleague.

"Hit 'im, Tom, hit 'im," cried the little man in a thick, strangled gurgle.

The last I remember was hearing the whistling of the blackguard's cosh before the darkness came.

My eyes watered as pungent smelling salts assaulted my nostrils. I became aware of my head, throbbing with a sharp, mind-pervading ache. I became conscious of a dampness, and it was only after several moments of concentration that I realised it to be caused by a cloth being held to the pulsing lump. Groaning, I attempted to rise.

"No, no, Mr. Holmes: please don't try to get up just yet. You're going to see double for a while. Just keep your eyes shut tight," came Miss Deane's Southern lilt. But I squirmed a little and opened my eyes, finding that indeed, I was double-visioned and dizzy. I shut my eyes as tightly as Millicent Deane had told me, before I became nauseated.

"Just a few minutes more. When you can focus your eyes, you can get up. Not before."

I grunted something meant to be an acquiescence and turned my head slowly to its recent resting place. Some moments passed before I spoke again, my eyes still shut. "The Colonel?" I croaked.

"I saw him through the door, Mr. Holmes. He's snoring soundly. He slept through the whole thing. I would have gone in, but your groans were too urgent to ignore."

"And you, Miss Deane?"

"Well enough, Mr. Holmes. A little unsteady, but nothing serious."

I now ventured to open my eyes again. The room had ceased to spin and I could see the windows clearly now. I tentatively sat up, moving slowly and with no little distress. But not enough to prevent me from attaining a more dignified position on the settee.

"You have a terrible knot," said my young companion, now sitting next to me and examining my head in a professional manner. I touched the swelling gingerly, finding a lump the size of a goose egg. We rose to inspect the damage.

I saw that the parlour was virtually untouched. My hat still sat on the table by the door where Miss Deane had left it; my stick was in the middle of the room where I dropped it. A few pillows had been thrown about . . . the furniture barely out of place that was all. We then went into the Colonel's bedroom.

He still slept, as Miss Deane said. She counted his pulse and found it to be normal. We replaced the pillows that had been searched. That done, I noticed that the night-stand drawer was open, making mention of the fact to Miss Deane. She turned to close it, but instead cried out "It's gone!"

"What is that?"

"The Colonel's pistol, his beautiful pistol!" she exclaimed. More calmly, she explained, "It was a gift from his regiment after the first battle of Manassas."

I looked into the drawer. "Is there anything else that you know to be missing?"

She looked in at the contents. "I believe not, Mr. Holmes."

I took a small bottle from the drawer of the night table. There was no label on it. "What is this, Miss Deane? the boracic acid?"

"No, sir. That's the bottle of laudanum I used for Colonel Leland. I had just given him a dose before you arrived."

I looked at its contents. "I recall Dr. Agar mentioning three teaspoons dissolved in water to be given the Colonel. His language implied a powder, yet I see that the contents of this bottle are in liquid form."

"Yes, the doctor brought it this afternoon. He said that he suspected my supply might be running low. I thought at the time that it was fortunate he did so: I had almost used all of what I had."

"I see," I commented, replacing the bottle. "Dr. Agar was on his rounds."

"Oh no, Mr. Holmes," said Millicent Deane, "it was Dr. Fordyce who . . ."

"Dr. Fordyce?" I asked, "I thought Dr. Agar was treating the Colonel."

"That's right, but Dr. Fordyce came to the door this afternoon and told me that the hotel management had asked him to look in on the Colonel. He found him resting and suggested that I use this bottle of laudanum in place of the other."

I quickly unscrewed the cap, asking, "When did you administer the latest dosage?"

"Just before you arrived. About five minutes or so." She watched me as I tasted the liquid. This was no laudanum, but a powerful tincture of pure opium.

"How much did you give him?"

"Dr. Fordyce prescribed two tablespoons." She noticed my concern. "There's nothing wrong, I hope . . ."

"No," I said, looking back at Colonel Leland. "Two dessert-spoons will cause him to sleep deeply and for a long time, but there's no danger."

"What was it?" she asked. Her eyes opened wide with terror when I told her.

"But not to worry, Miss Deane," I continued comfortingly. "It will actually do more good than harm. He will only sleep deeply."

"Of course," she said, composing herself once more. "There'll be no trouble. Thank you, Mr. Holmes."

I next turned my attention to the suite. As we tottered from room to room, we saw that they had been thoroughly ransacked. The suitcases, valises, and the portmanteau shared by Miss Deane and Rachel Leland had been entirely emptied, the contents strewn about the floor. The closets were a shambles, the clothes thrown pell-mell all about the rooms. Coming back to the parlour, I again referred to the man who had left the opium.

"I am curious about this 'doctor' who came around this afternoon. Did you notice anything out of the ordinary about the man?"

"Not especially, Mr. Holmes," she said. "I remember that the Colonel told me after he left that he had a grip like a mule skinner, though. Oh, wait—I did notice something."

"Yes? What was that?"

"He had thick calluses on the sides of his forefingers.

I noticed them when he took my hand in greeting, but thought nothing of it then. But I've never known any doctors to have such thick calluses."

"Nor have I, Miss Deane. That was most perceptive of you. I fear that the man was an imposter. I must take my leave now, Miss Deane. Promise me that you'll open the door to no one other than your friends or to Dr. Agar."

"You have my word on that, Mr. Holmes," she said earnestly.

"I daresay you have seen the last of this Dr. Fordyce, but it will not hurt to be on your guard."

"Yes, Mr. Holmes. And once more, thank you for your help."

I decided to not mention Captain Jericho to the young lady. I had no doubts that these intruders were his own men. They had done their work here, so there was no need to burden Miss Deane with fears for her friends.

I took a cab home. The incident in the bar notwithstanding, this was my first real brush with elements of London's underworld. I would not have been averse to being spared the introduction altogether. There was something of consequence in the air. The Americans, the Negro, the two assailants of tonight's adventure: They all fit together, I knew. But there was much data missing. Most definitely, I wished to be close to Mr. Moriarty on Thursday afternoon to find out more about this mysterious affair.

Perhaps it was the blow I had suffered that caused me to be slightly dizzy as I climbed the mercifully short flight of stairs to my flat. As I unlocked the door, however, any vestige of confusion was instantly driven from my mind by the voice that called out to me from the darkness of my room:

"Come in, Mr. Holmes, but please avoid making any sudden moves."

5

CAPTAIN JERICHO
COMES TO CALL

"I told you we'd speak again."

"Captain Jericho, I presume," I said, with as much equanimity as I could muster.

"At your service, sir." Although it was utterly black in my parlour, I could sense the sardonic bow implied by the man's tone of voice.

"I prefer that the lamps be left unlit. Darkness suits me."

"As you wish," I said, closing the door. By instinct I found the desk and placed my hat and gloves upon it. My coloured visitor sat in the Morris chair in a corner of the room by the draped windows. I took a seat on the end of the couch opposite.

"I trust that you'll put your cane aside also," said he as I sat down. "I'd hate to muss up that handsome vest of yours with a bullet hole."

I winced at having my waistcoat referred to as underwear, yet I complied by placing my stick on the floor. I had fleetingly thought of using it as a weapon; Captain Jericho's words decided me otherwise.

"You will recall, Mr. Holmes, that at our previous meeting, I had an important matter to discuss."

"Yes, I do. The American situation," I replied, "whatever that may mean."

"Oh, Mr. Holmes, Mr. Holmes," Captain Jericho sighed mockingly. "You must surely know—or at least have an inkling—of what I mean. Anyone who has already discovered the name of an anonymous visitor in this short span of time . . ."

"Very well," I said. "I do have the ghost of an idea that you are somehow connected with an American business delegation that appeared at my offices on Tuesday. But I tell you now: I shall answer no questions concerning the confidential business of Her Majesty's Government. I trust that I make myself clear."

Captain Jericho again sighed. "I must say, it's as I expected. Would it do any good to remind you that my weapon of this afternoon is now aimed directly at your top left-hand vest pocket?"

"Threats are useless," I said, a little more bravely than I felt.

"We're not likely to be interrupted," said Jericho, "yet perhaps I can negotiate an exchange of information that will benefit both of us. Would that help you to change your mind?"

"It is, at least, a trifle more reasonable a demand," I responded. "With what do you have to bargain?"

"Something you must be dying to have, if my information about you is correct: background, history and a sense of perspective."

"And in return, you want . . . ?"

"Mere details. What is it that Leland and the others are after? I believe that I have some information about their plan already. But I would appreciate having that knowledge confirmed."

I frowned. "I am not sure that I have much information, Captain. But if you are as resourceful as I believe you to be, you must have all the details I have and much more besides."

"You may be right," he conceded. "But how can I be sure until I hear from you myself?"

I thought about what plans of resistance I had at hand. In a drawer in the table beside me was a .22-calibre pistol pressed upon me by Sherlock which I might try to use to my benefit. But I discarded the idea immediately. My eyes had adjusted to the darkness of the room and I could dimly make out the form of my visitor. Jericho had been able to make out the stick I carried close to my body, so I knew I would be foolish to make any sudden movement now. I had no doubt but that he did in fact have the Derringer I saw earlier levelled at my heart. There had been a few moments of silence while I pondered my situation. Now his rich baritone chuckle drifted across the room as though he read my thoughts.

"I see that I must have you between a rock and a hard place, if I can cause you so much deliberation."

"I've been weighing the better course of action," I replied candidly.

"I see. And what plan of action have you chosen?"

"Before I decide whether I should divulge anything at all to you, I want to know something."

"Anything at all," was Jericho's good-natured response.

"Who the devil are you? You roam London at the head of some secret organisation, you may have infiltrated the Foreign Office already, and you could precipitate a diplomatic crisis."

"Whoa, whoa now. That's an awful lot to tell even you," he answered with a sardonic laugh. "As to my identity, you've learned my name already. Or, at least, the name I'm currently using.

"Regarding my organisation and the means by which I come to know things—" I could sense the shrug of his shoulders—". . . well, let us say that I have a thousand eyes and ears aiding me."

"As well as an overly developed sense of the melodramatic," I added drily. "Thank you for your detailed report."

"Not at all, I'm sure," he said lightly. "And now, it's your turn; what do you know about me?"

In the darkness, I recalled the man as I had perceived him for that brief moment in my office that afternoon. "You are an American Negro, a former slave born in the South, on a plantation in Alabama, if I am correct about the origin of your accent. You became proficient in the use of both sword and pistol, are more or less self-educated, and fond of horse-riding. In your youth, you worked in the fields . . ."

"Choppin' cotton fo' de ole massa," he mockingly interjected.

". . . but graduated to the kitchen where you became a passable cook."

"Cook?" he exclaimed. "I was a *chef de cuisine!* Veal tetrazzini, lobster thermidor, and Bordelaise; why my creole sauce was famous throughout the bayou districts. Besides that, I make a pretty good mess of hamhocks and grits."

"You were then sold to another family in Alabama. You worked mostly in the stables breaking horses, you planned a daring escape and are, without doubt, the most vainglorious man I shall ever meet."

He laughed, delighted with my observations. "You are as perceptive as I've been told, Mr. Holmes," he said. "Perhaps even more so," he added softly. "Needless to say that you are correct on all counts." A hard note entered his voice. "I was a slave. I was sold as a chattel to Colonel Mordecai Leland before the war. I escaped in the early part of 1857 via the seven circles of hell called the 'underground railroad.'" He paused. "But I returned to the South with a band of former slaves who are still unequalled in courage, determination, and daring. I led them in a series of uprisings throughout the South. When the War began, we bedevilled the Confederacy in a thousand ways, before finally heading west in '63. The killing was sickening to me. And when some Yankee buck found the Southerners' battle plans for Antietam rolled up and hidden in a cigar, the South never knew what hit them. The fight went out of them. They were beaten and they knew it. It was only sheer cussedness that made them keep up the fighting until '65." He paused for a moment, lost in thought.

"Out west we became cattle drovers. We were thus engaged when the news reached us of Lee's surrender at Appomattox Courthouse. My men cheered for half an hour. We were free, they said. The old plantations would be chopped up for us. We'd go back to get forty acres and a mule. But I knew better. I knew that the old hatred and prejudice would die hard, if at all. But I was hopeful because I also knew of Mr. Lincoln's plan to get the country back together as quickly as possible." Again he paused and his voice, which had lightened, took on the same hardness with which he'd begun his story.

"But then Mr. Lincoln was shot. We were still on the trail when word came to us, only a week after we heard about the war's end. That's when I knew for certain that there'd be no end to the bitterness. Old Andy Johnson tried his best to keep Lincoln's plan, but the Northern politicians finagled their way around him. The carpetbaggers came south and the army ran the elections so all the black folks could vote, while keeping the whites away. Hell, even I knew that was stupid. A whole lot of nigger politicans were voted into legislatures who didn't even know how to read, let alone run a state.

"Then the Klan started up, and the other terror groups. And that's when I returned to the 'fair' South. We shot up the countryside for a while, but I could see that we were causing more harm than good. The Negroes were beaten, no matter what. Right then and there, I decided to quit helping everyone else. I vowed to get all I could, devil take the hindmost. So we quit the night-riding and the shooting. We dispersed among the white folks down South and looted the homes of carpetbaggers, politicians, and generals alike.

"We made so much by despoiling the homes of the rich and powerful that there was soon a general alarm spread and we found things getting too hot. So we came to Europe to fleece the white folks of the old world. . . . The pickings were easier than I had imagined, and I soon had white folks working in my setup here. Well, I bettered my financial circumstances in many ways . . . it's unimportant how . . . and now I come face to face with Mr. Mycroft Holmes"—his voice once more became mocking—"concerning Colonel Leland and his flock." I heard him shifting in the chair.

"I have certain knowledge, Mr. Holmes, that my former master and his friend, Ravenswood, represent a party of— well, let's say some 'concerned' Southern folks, who plan to offer your government a deal which will resubjugate my people." He took a breath. "No need telling you that I plan to stop them. And I will."

I knew that he wasn't boasting.

"But I want your help. I'd rather that you aided me without coercion, but I'm not averse to using force if necessary. Now . . . will you help me?"

I played for time, "But surely, with all your informants in the Foreign Office, you don't need me."

"None of my informants is quite so well placed as are you. What I know of the Southern plans I knew before the Colonel left Charleston."

"But I'm not really at liberty to help you. I must have time . . ."

I heard the hammer of Jericho's pistol cock and, though he sat silent and unmoving, I sensed the pistol swing around in his hand to point its evil little barrel directly at my heart.

". . . But then again, I appear to have little to say in the matter."

"Ah, but Mycroft, you above all should know how deceptive appearances can be."

The draperies parted. It was Sherlock!

"What the devil!"

"Come now, Captain Jericho, you can do better than that. Before you do, however, you may forestall any untoward accidents by handing me your pistol."

I saw my brother's distinctive silhouette against the window as Jericho surrendered his firearm to him.

"It seems as though I've underestimated you . . . both of you," said the black man.

"Very good. All right, Trevor, turn up the light."

Trevor stepped through the window from the small balcony outside and turned up the gas jet. The flickering flames illuminated a vivid tableau: Jericho in my chair, Sherlock standing beside him, a pistol pressed to the American's brow. It was an ironic reversal of our first encounter.

"How long have you been standing there?" I asked.

"Since a few seconds before you entered the room," my brother answered, smiling. "I told you I'd locate him, Mycroft. Are you so surprised I kept my word?"

Exhaustion and my throbbing head prompted my outburst. "Do you mean to stand there and tell me that you've been listening in from the first? You jackass! You took bloody well long enough to announce yourself! I almost had heart failure!" Sherlock said nothing until I ran down.

"If you've finished your ranting, Mycroft, you will perhaps realise that I waited to find out the motives of your gentleman friend here. No point in acting until the facts are made clear."

"You're awfully cool about all this, I must say." I turned to my cupboard and poured out a glass of brandy. My head was still throbbing from the attack. "This man threatens to murder me and you just stand there!"

"You were never in any real danger, Mycroft. Trevor and I were on either side of Captain Jericho and within easy reach of him."

"Pardon me for interrupting, but I'm curious to know

how this young man got here after me?" Jericho quietly interposed.

Sherlock fixed him with a confident gaze. "Actually, we arrived before you. I made some enquiries concerning a coloured man in the area. There aren't many in the vicinity, you know." He smiled as he said, "Especially those wearing gaudy waistcoats. We found you eating in a pub— several Scotch eggs were on your plate. We followed after you left. We situated ourselves where we could hear you give your instructions to the driver and then Trevor and I took a hansom along another, more direct route. We spent some few moments awaiting your appearance at my brother's front door, then climbed up to the balcony and bided our time until my brother arrived."

"But I never saw a trace of you!" said Jericho, amazed.

My brother coughed modestly. "Of course not. I didn't intend that you should."*

Jericho laughed heartily. "Well, I must say, sir. I enjoy a man who can best me so coolly and with such finesse. I could have used you in my raiding parties during the war!"

"And speaking of the war, Captain Jericho, perhaps you'd be so kind as to resume our conversation," I prompted.

Jericho turned back to me eagerly. "Then you'll join us?"

"I didn't say that. You must understand that my first allegiance is to the Crown. Whatever my ultimate decision may be, it will be, first and foremost, in the best interests of Her Majesty's Government."

Jericho nodded. "I expected you to say just that, sir, and I think I can assure you that your Queen and council will be happier without getting tangled up in these people's plans."

I nodded to Sherlock, who removed his pistol from Jericho's temple, after the coloured man gave us an assurance that he had no wish to threaten us further. Sherlock pocketed his pistol; he and Trevor then took seats and brandy was poured all 'round.

* This sounds suspiciously similar to the exchange Sherlock has with Dr. Leon Sterndale in "The Devil's Foot"—what the late Monsignor Ronald Knox has dubbed "the Sherlockismus"—a verbal riposte found throughout the Holmes Canon. Has Mycroft lifted an instance from Dr. Watson's later account, or was the latter occurrence a stylistic refinement on Sherlock's part? MH/SMW

"I believe that the man is right, Mr. Holmes," said Trevor, taking the straightbacked wooden chair near the front door.

"I beg your pardon?"

"I mean about Great Britain keeping out of any American intrigues," Trevor continued, after taking a sip of his brandy. "Her Majesty's Government remained neutral during the last American unpleasantness, as I recall. I'd say that there'd be little sympathy for any involvement in an internal matter concerning the United States at the Court of St. James."

"That's very soundly put, Trevor," said I. "But it's not quite that simple." I sat, staring into my glass. "I suppose you were too young to understand the diplomatic ramifications of the event, but in 1861, a hostile action by the Washington government almost brought this nation into their conflict."

"That must have been what our newspapers called the *Trent* Affair," said Jericho.

"What was it?" asked Trevor.

"The United States ship *San Jacinto* stopped the British mail packet *Trent* on the high seas, boarded her, searched her and removed two Confederate ambassadors, Mason and Slidell, who were later detained in Boston," I said.

"But why were the Confederates on board?" Trevor continued, perplexed.

"The Union forces had the Southern coastal ports blockaded," Jericho responded. "The only way for the ambassadors to break out was by booking passage on board a neutral ship."

"According to maritime law," I added, "passengers on board a neutral ship cannot be molested if outside the territorial waters of any hostile nation. We felt that the North would respect the freedom of the high seas, and so did the Confederates."

"But they didn't, eh?"

"Well, officially, the Washington government was not aware of what had happened. The captain of the American ship was acting without orders. Although Secretary Seward and President Lincoln had been informed that Mason and Slidell were leaving, they made no move to stop them. The captain of the *San Jacinto* acted on his own authority," I continued, "even though the North wanted to prevent any official recognition of the Confederate administration by the United Kingdom, the most effective way being to prevent any diplomatic manœuvering by the South.

"Of course the incident created an uproar in Parliament. The PM demanded the immediate release of Mason and Slidell, and insisted that they be allowed to resume their mission. Parliament also demanded an apology from Seward as secretary of state."

"I recall that a whole bunch of troops appeared on the Canadian border, prepared to back up your demands, too," interjected Jericho.

"That is correct. Eight thousand of Her Majesty's troops were deployed along the border, with a promise of more should the need arise, before Mr. Lincoln and Mr. Seward saw the wisdom in respecting the rights of ships on the high seas. They ordered the release of Mason and Slidell and made an apology, a rather nice one at that."

"But what about the diplomatic legation from the Confederates?" asked Trevor. "The mission obviously failed."

"True." I replied. "But they generated a great deal of good will and sympathy for the Southern cause. It was ended only by the singleness of action taken by Prince Albert. He convinced the Queen, who in turn persuaded the PM, who then prevailed upon the Cabinet that such an intrusion would face too much European opposition from the League of the Three Emperors. Alexander, the Czar of all the Russias, was doing a great deal of sabre-rattling at the time. Aside from that, other nations on the Continent were quick to show us their displeasure.

"Aside from these considerations, our whole colonial system would have been jeopardised by the removal of troops from our many territories to bolster our offense within North America. Such an action would, no doubt, have fomented insurrections among the natives. Most damagingly, our whole course of action could and most likely would have united both North and South against us, engendering the possibility of an American invasion of the United Kingdom. It became imaginable, for the first time in history, that every nation of the civilised world would be compelled to align themselves into two opposing forces.

Think of it, gentlemen, the entire race of man would be engaged in a conflict encompassing the globe!

"But aside from these considerations, gigantic as they are, the most telling point of the Prince's communication to the Queen was his concept of the moral aspect of such an action. He said that we had lost the North American colonies after much bloodletting during the last century, and that any further bloodshed between the English-speaking nations would be the reprehensible act of a morally ruined government."

"You seem well versed on this subject," said Sherlock.

"I have seen the memorandum," I said softly. "Prince Albert was most eloquent and most emphatic in his warnings." I reflected upon my words for a moment before saying, "I don't believe that the situation has changed sufficiently to consider another course."

I saw the look in Jericho's eyes as I spoke; it was a look to a long-vanished time. As we sat in silence, I was able to give a few seconds' thought to the late Prince Consort for, like many another Englishman, I had been genuinely fond of him.

Although a German, he came to our country for the love of our Queen, a country well known for its contempt of foreigners. He studied our ways, mastered our language, and gave of himself freely for the benefit of the poor, the disenfranchised, the forgotten. His philanthropies became publicly acknowledged, but not so evident was his good counsel, ofttimes found in smoothing over governmental vicissitudes. When he died, our nation lost a spark of decency and goodness within Her Majesty's Government.

It is common knowledge that Queen Victoria continued, after his death and until her dying day, to mourn for him, becoming known as "The Widow of Windsor." Yet I believe that our nation lost even more than she. An able statesman, a philanthropist in the most Christian sense, a man possessed of a first-rate mind, imbued with a strong will to do good: that was Albert of Saxe-Coburg-Gotha.

I paused in my ruminations and looked up at my audience. Jericho, Trevor, and Sherlock were all watching me intently. "The economics of the situation certainly are not in our favour either," I continued. "It may well be worth it to the Prime Minister and the Cabinet to lend aid, or to declare war or whatever else, for if we won, we would once again have the virgin wealth of the entire North American continent at our fingertips." I considered my next words carefully before I spoke: "The British Empire would circumscribe the earth, we would be masters of the greatest regnancy ever attained by a single people and sovereign. And, barring any internal insurrections . . ." I looked up at Jericho who gave me a friendly nod ". . . we might just be able to hold sway over that empire for a thousand years."

"So we aren't just playing at marbles," said Trevor, with a low whistle.

"Not at all," I replied firmly. "Not at all."

No one spoke for a few moments. Then Trevor, with knitted brow, put forth an interesting question. "But look here, Mr. Holmes, how could such an event help Leland and Ravenswood? Surely they would be happier with an independent America, no matter which side won their civil war."

"Allow me to answer that point, Mr. Holmes," said Jericho. "Mr. Trevor, there are quite a few people in both North and South who would only be too happy to sell our country down the river, so long as they could make a profit for themselves on the deal. I daresay that we'd hear about a lot more of them, but they have neither the money, nor the imagination, nor the number of followers to make the role of Judas enviable. Unfortunately for us, Ravenswood has all three of those commodities, and a whole lot of well-wishers down South who'd stand by, neither helping nor hindering him.

"He and a great many other die-hard rebels want a return of the tired old plantation life, slavery, and the prosperity they think they had in the antebellum days. These people want this so much that they'll sink to any depth, wallow in any filth, so long as they can assure themselves that the old days will return."

"It would further appeal to a certain number of people who presently sit at desks within the Foreign Office and in the Admiralty, who would be driven by fantasies of Clive and hope to vie for the title, The Man Who Won Back North America. Oh, yes," I said, "there are many desks in Whitehall whose occupants could entertain such thoughts, Megalomania is rife within the confines of government, and the number of those stricken with it increases the higher one rises in civil service."

"But surely," said Trevor, "The Queen, Parliament—this country is at peace with the United States. We are friends of the Americans, are we not?"

"Officially," I answered. "But maybe only because no one else has given them any other alternative. There was a lot of feeling back in '61 that our troops in Canada should invade the North while the Confederates kept the major forces busy in the South and near Washington City. General Burke could have brought all 8,000 of Her Majesty's troops already stationed in Canada and more—many more—if Prince Albert hadn't advised the Queen against it." Once again, I thought of the memorandum he wrote to Her Majesty. "His advice to the Queen concerning the handling of that situation was the last thing he did before he died."

"But that was nearly fifteen years ago," said Trevor. "Surely the old feelings have changed?"

"Not so much as one might hope. Very few of our ministers now have the same sense of history as Prince Albert had."

Sherlock, who had kept silent during this whole conversation, now proffered an opinion. "I believe that statement might take in your own superior, Mr. Moriarty."

"Oh yes," said Jericho, "I've heard of the ambitious Mr. Moriarty."

His remark caught me unawares, but I had to agree.

"Quite so, Captain. He lacks the capacity to see things in perspective. He disregards events which don't fit his preconceptions."

"And you think Ravenswood can persuade him of the validity of his plans?" asked Jericho.

"Easily. Regaining something such as the American continent? Why, such is the stuff of which dreams—and careers—are made," I answered.

"Then how can we stop Ravenswood?" asked Trevor.

"That will be difficult," I said.

"You're right again, Mr. Holmes," said Jericho. "He's a fanatic. But the terrible thing is that there are many more just like him, all through the South. I must tell you some other things, Mr. Holmes. But I must have the word of your brother and his friend that the story will not leave this room."

They readily assented.

"Then you must know that there are nearly a hundred thousand soldiers, clandestinely recruited throughout the South, who take part in secret manœuvres in strongholds located in Texas and in the territories to the west."

I nodded to myself.

"I expected something, but not that—certainly not on such a scale!"

"And Colonel Leland—what's his place in all this?" asked Sherlock.

"He's basically a decent man. In fact, he's not all that interested in a return of slavery. His quarrel is with the federal government. Actually, he is one of the more rational within their councils," said Jericho.

"From what he said tonight, I don't believe that he'd share that compliment with you." I said. "In so many words, he let me know what he thinks about you."

"That's just his way," Jericho smiled. "He never forgave me for escaping. Thought I should appreciate all his efforts to 'civilise' me more. And I know that the others —Carteret and Bankhead—aren't really sure of the extent of the plan at this time, either. They, like Rachel Leland and Millicent Deane, are window dressing."

"Ah, yes," said Sherlock, " 'the continental tour.' "

"That's not important right now," I said. "Let's get back to the matter at hand. Now that Leland's incapacitated, the government will most certainly have to deal with Ravenswood, and I fear our having to deal with him. Captain, can you tell me anything more about him?"

"Ravenswood is brave, seems impetuous, but underneath there's more cunning and conniving in his mind than anyone I've ever met. Once set on course, he will not deviate a hair's breadth until he's attained his goal. He is a pretty good strategist, but he's not adaptable. He lacks the resourcefulness to meet unexpected challenges to his plans."

"Sounds as though he should get along wonderfully with Mr. Moriarty," I commented archly.

Jericho smiled. "They do sound similar, don't they?"

I was about to ask how he knew, but Trevor spoke before I could.

"But just a minute," he said, and we all turned to him. "Look here, aren't we forgetting that Ravenswood isn't heading the delegation—Leland is."

"What makes you so sure that he will continue?" asked Sherlock, quietly drawing at his pipe, leaning back in his chair with his fingertips together once again. We all turned to him. Jericho found his tongue first.

"Of course! It was Ravenswood who planned that attack on Leland, I'd swear it!"

"And if Leland dies, Ravenswood becomes the spokesman for the would-be Confederacy," I added. As I spoke, though, another thought struck me. "But wait, that might be too transparent."

"My thought exactly, Mycroft. It might be one of the others," said Sherlock.

"What, Bankhead—Carteret? They're striplings," said Jericho.

"Striplings perhaps, but surely capable of sabotage. There are also the women," said Sherlock.

"I should think we could safely dismiss them as suspects," I answered. "I find it difficult to think of Rachel Leland, his own daughter, in such a role. And certainly not Millicent Deane, whom I have seen struggling for her very life." I then briefly detailed the attack we had suffered in the Americans' suite, admitting that I had no idea as to why my assailants rendered us unconscious only to steal the Colonel's pistol, except to theorise that the bogus doctor was obviously a member of their gang.

"Callousities on the outer edges of the forefinger, eh? Humm." A horseman, then," said Sherlock, his fingertips remaining steepled.

"More precisely, a coachman," I countered.

"The purported doctor's strong grip, 'like a mule skinner,' I believe you quoted the American as saying. That indicates the training of horses—if not of mules."

"Yes, but extend the inference, Sherlock. Don't be so timid. A coachman's or a cabbie's horse may very well be changed daily; a firm hand is therefore indicated in those professions also."

"A firm hand, certainly, Mycroft, as the scars readily attest."

"My dear Sherlock, the testimony of the scars is indicative of the brutality of this handler, which met with determined resistance. I would therefore suggest that this 'doctor' is more likely to be a discharged coachman—or cabbie—with a penchant for cruelty toward the animals in his charge."

At this point Trevor turned to Jericho, "They do this all the time, you know," he said, rocking his chair back against the wall, his head narrowly missing the gas jet.

Jericho stood up and stretched. "What makes you so sure that you can dismiss the girls so easily?" He began to pace slowly, his hands in his pockets. "It's possible that one or the other of them may have staged the whole of tonight's encounter for your benefit, Mr. Holmes."

"Nonsense," I answered.

"Besides," scoffed Trevor, "would a lady associate with such low life? And what man would take orders from a woman?"

"English gentlemen ruled by a king in petticoats come to mind," Jericho said deridingly. "You certainly have a lot to learn about women, Mr. Trevor."

"Trevor's dealings with the fair sex are not the point at issue here," said Sherlock shortly. "We are speaking of foiling Captain Ravenswood and this fantastic scheme—not the plot of some lurid penny-dreadful."

"I was wondering if Ravenswood is all we have to worry about." said Jericho, ending his pacing.

"I wonder, as well," I said, eyeing him closely.

Trevor chuckled. Sherlock glared at him.

"I cannot believe that anyone in the party could know that they would be attacked tonight," said the blonde young man.

"I remember the person whom we originally thought responsible for such an attack tonight," I remarked.

Sherlock now stared at Jericho as well. The Negro was leaning insouciantly in the doorjamb, directly behind Trevor. His elbow rested on the handle of the gas jet, as he yawned elaborately.

"I wish you all had a little more practical experience with women in general, not simply knowing that they might be 'reasonable horsewomen.'" Again he yawned and stretched.

"It's getting past my bedtime, gentlemen, and I have pressing business elsewhere. You know," he laughed, "I find myself in jeopardy of losing my reputation as a rogue. But I shall do my best to get it back!"

As he spoke, the room was simultaneously plunged into darkness and we heard Trevor and his chair fall to the floor with a resounding crash. The black devil had turned off the gas jet, throwing the young giant over so quickly that it seemed as though long minutes had elapsed before Sherlock and I could dart to the door, stumbling over Trevor's flailing form. Captain Jericho's mocking laughter greeted our fumbling as a sliver of light marked his departure through the doorway of my flat.

Too late, we scrambled to our feet and into the hallway beyond, but there was no trace of him. We ran down the stairs and opened the front door, but the street was empty. Back in my parlour, the gas turned up once more, we all looked at each other sheepishly for having let down our guard.

"I'm sorry, Trevor," said I as the young man rubbed his shoulder. "I did not mean to kick you."

"Think nothing of it, Mr. Holmes. I'm only sorry he disappeared so fast. I should like to teach the brute some manners."

"It's fortunate that he is on our side," said Sherlock.

"I *hope* he's on our side!" Trevor returned, breathing heavily. "What possible reason could he have for such an uncalled-for departure?"

"I should say that our coloured friend has a wide theatrical streak in his character. I only hope that this is the worst example of it we must witness," said my brother. He turned to me. "We would do well to give careful consideration to those we trust in future."

"I quite agree," said I. "I did not say so before, but I've half a notion that that coloured fiend is responsible for my shattered head."

"And I have another half a notion that you are quite correct in that assumption," Sherlock concurred with a smile.

I poured another stiff brandy all around to restore our

shattered pride. Within the quarter-hour, we had agreed to meet again the next evening for dinner. I showed Trevor and Sherlock out, musing upon the fact that they'd needed no help to get in earlier.

The brandy proved most therapeutic in its application to the pain of my throbbing head, so, after taking another small libation, I was able to go to bed and sleep soundly.

6

MORE AMERICANS

It was snowing as I made my way to the office the next morning. I had a comparably light day of work ahead of me, for which I was thankful. My cranium had not yet fully recovered from last evening's onslaught. Griffin suppressed a smile at the unaccustomed rakish angle of my top hat which concealed a still tender lump, the prize of last evening's escapade. Pointedly ignoring him, I proceeded directly into my office. I had now to tackle the task laid on me by Mr. Moriarty, that of the Manchester MP. With any luck at all, I should be clear of my desk by the middle of the afternoon.

Early on, it became evident that my schedule would go awry, when Mr. Moriarty abruptly flung open the door to my office. He was livid and I seemed to be the cause of his ill temper.

"Holmes, you idiot!" He waved a paper wildly in the air. "Do you know what this is? My ruin, sir, my ruin! And yours also! I shall see to it. I shall see to it, so help me!"

With that he tossed the missive onto my desk. The words *United States of America* leapt up at me. I had no idea as to its content, but I knew I could rely upon Mr. Moriarty to provide a vociferous, if somewhat garbled, account.

"Those blasted Yankees want to know what we're up to with that mercantile delegation from the States. The phrasing in this note is just short of a severance of diplomatic relations." The choler in his voice rose with each word. "We are requested, nay, *ordered*, to appear this afternoon in Grosvenor Square with a complete report of our meeting with these people." His voice cracked and he drew in a deep breath. "What *are* we doing with these people?"

"So far as I know, sir, you are still awaiting *précis* in-

99

formation, as we discussed yesterday. Until you receive it, I was prepared to do nothing more. You'll recall I told you that the Americans will say nothing to me."

"I recall that you insisted on sending them to the Ministry of Trade, if I remember our discussion yesterday," he said sarcastically. "And that even after you had that note of Harvey's and they had given the sign. You had best explain that action, Mr. Holmes." He sat down petulantly. "I suppose you gave them the countersign, too."

I strove to keep my equanimity. "No, sir. I know that only you can do that, or someone of the same or higher level. My hands were tied. I had to direct them to the Ministry of Trade and prepare a report on the meeting which I had my clerk send up to you yesterday."

He stood up impatiently. "I suppose you are right, but I should have been consulted immediately, Holmes. You should have brought up that *précis* yourself." He took a breath. "Well, that clears me of any responsibility. But an answer must be given to the Americans in Grosvenor Square. It must be found quickly or we—you," he quickly amended his speech—"shall be disgraced and dismissed. You have my assurance of that." He sat. "Have some tea brought in," he said glumly. "I should like to have some just now."

I rang for Griffin. When he returned with the tea, Mr. Moriarty found time to compose himself and I had my first chance to read the communication.

Without doubt, the Ambassador was stirred. His handwritten note was couched in a tone best described as fury. He demanded to know the extent of any conversations between ourselves and the American delegation and he insisted that Mr. Moriarty appear at the embassy at two this very afternoon, accompanied by all relevant documentation and information.

I glanced over at my superior after finishing the note. His earlier pronouncement notwithstanding, Moriarty stood an excellent chance of being sacked and, as he said, I along with him. The mission we undertook to the American embassy would be a delicate one. Our only defense would be that Moriarty knew absolutely nothing about the intended goal of the former rebels. And neither did I—at any rate not in an official capacity.

Moriarty w-s pouring his second cup of tea with a hand that grew unsteadier by the minute. Yet, as I concluded my reading of the note, his voice was exceedingly calm.

"Well, Holmes?"

"It seems that the situation is an obvious mistake and that it can be cleared with little difficulty."

"Oh? And what do you propose to do?"

"We have two, possibly three choices: firstly, we go to the embassy and tell 'he Ambassador what he wishes to know; secondly we go, but refuse to tell him anything resting on the grounds of privileged information."

"And the third alternative, Holmes?"

"A most unpleasant one, sir. Should we not explain ourselves adequately enough for the Americans and they proceed to make things a bit nasty with the ministry or with the PM we might have to resign."

"Resign? Throw away thirty-five years of service to the Crown? You must be mad!"

"Merely being complete, sir. I didn't expect that we should choose that alternative."

"Well, that's better, then. So let us consider the two real choices. Comp'y or defy, I'd say." He chuckled slightly. "Humm. Rather c.--- +o an epigram, that. Comply or defy. Yes. I rather like it."

"Yes, sir," I .greed gravely. "But to return to the matter at hand . . ."

"Yes, yes. Should we choose to go to the embassy, what do you propose we tell them?"

"Only what you know about them, sir. That is, that the Americans attempted to see you, were referred to me, I sent you a memorandum of the conversation I held with them, and that is all."

"Ah, yes. But are they not on my schedule for this very afternoon?"

"Yes, sir. But that is not the business of the American Ambassador."

"Of course, of course." He paused, lost in thought. "A bit ironic, actually."

"I beg pardon, sir?"

"Nothing, Holmes," he said brusquely. "We must be sure not to stay at the embassy for any length of time. There is no reason for the colonials to know about this meeting when I greet them this afternoon. It might be a sword to hang over their heads, for one reason or another."

"Yes, sir."

"Should we find it necessary to remain, I shall leave you in my stead. I know that you can ably represent the Crown in my absence."

"I appreciate your confidence, sir."

"I don't believe we will mention the communication from Cyril Harvey, shall we, Holmes?"

"I cannot see any advantage that that will give us, sir."

"Yes. No use tipping our hand before we know exactly what cards we're holding. And, should you be detained, I shall be learning more about their worth." He chuckled softly again.

"I appreciate your confidence, sir," said I. "And yet I feel impelled to remind you of the other course of action open to you."

"Eh? Being what?"

"It would not be inconsistent with our past policy for you to draft a note, politely requesting the Ambassador to refrain from intruding himself in the affairs handled by this office. After all, he has no right to interfere with the conduct of the business of Her Majesty's Government. We might then inform him that we will apprise the embassy of any business conducted which we believe to concern the government of the United States."

"A definite possibility, Holmes," said Moriarty, as he picked out a cigar from the humidor on my desk, sniffing at the leaf wrapper. "But hardly one calculated to assuage the rancor of the American eagle, my dear boy." He took another cigar and, with its mate, deposited it in the breast pocket of his morning coat.

"No, my boy, conciliation is called for at this juncture. The long and usually cordial relations between our two great nations must be maintained and should be paramount in our thoughts; it would not be meet to disturb them—at this time, in any case."

"And have you spoken of this to Sir Robert Hyde yet, sir?" Sir Robert was Mr. Moriarty's immediate superior. This was an unfair thrust, but Moriarty's tendency to express himself in rhetorical generalities sometimes called for puncturing. As I expected, he blanched to the roots of this thin and wispy hair.

"Tell Sir Robert? Are you insane, Holmes? This is no more than a mere misunderstanding. Even so, Sir Robert would have me dangling from a gibbet at Tyburn within the hour. Why, should he learn of this rift, I'd be fortunate not to have my head fixed atop a pike on London Bridge!"

"He does have a responsibility for such matters, sir."

"Well, I don't believe that we have to bother him with this trifling matter, this—ah—unfortunate quarrel. The man's a killer, you know that, Holmes. I'm sure you recall how he gave poor Rogers the boot last year, simply because he took an opposite side during the debate over Russian expansion into the Balkans."

"Yes, I recall the circumstance."

"Well then, you understand." He looked down at the open humidor and shut the lid with a snap. He looked up at me inquisitively. "Come to think of it, you spoke to me about the Russian expansion of influence before the conference. I told you that the Czar was no one to worry about. . . ." He ruminated over this, then sighed. "Ah, but you young hotheads simply won't listen, will you?"

I refrained from pointing out to him that I had been correct in my conclusions about the Balkan situation. This was not the time to burnish my laurels. Mr. Moriarty once more lifted the lid on the humidor, staring at the coronas within.

"No, we'll not inform Sir Robert of this particular thorn just yet, my boy. The matter falls wholly within the discretion of my office and I'll treat it accordingly."

"As you say, sir." I waited a moment to see if he'd take another cigar. He did. "I might remind you that Ambassador Schenck has requested your presence in Grosvenor Square at two o'clock. You have some five hours to reflect on your course of action."

"I'm well aware of the time, Holmes," he snapped, shutting the lid hard. "There's no need to remind me."

"Yes, sir."

"Very well, then." His annoyance subsided. "I appreciate your thoughts, Holmes. I'll let you know what I decide." He left. As I knew from long experience, I would not have long to wait for a note to be sent from his office to mine.

The best way to handle Jerrold Moriarty was to allow him his own circuitous route to arrive at your conclusions. Thirty minutes after he had departed my office, Griffin handed me a communication from upstairs.

"We leave for the embassy at 1.30." It was signed "Moriarty."

I smiled briefly at the laconic message. There had never been any doubt in my mind. The memorandum brought another question to bedevil me, however. By what manner had the Ambassador learned of the appearance of Colonel Leland and the others in Whitehall? This business had all the confidentiality of a story on the front page of the *Daily News*.*

Upon our arrival, we were kept waiting some few minutes before the lanky, rawboned secretary ushered us into the embassy's *sanctum sanctorum* and withdrew. Although I had visited the American Embassy previously, during the incumbency of the present Ambassador's predecessor, this was my first meeting with Robert Cumming Schenck, former congressman, career diplomat, now envoy extraordinary and minister plenipotentiary to the Court of St. James. I was relieved to see that the large brass cuspidor—his predecessor's constant companion—had been removed.

The Ambassador did not rise as we were shown into his office. We stood for an awkward moment by the door at one end of the long room, while he continued to sit behind a massive oaken desk, rather ostentatiously looking over some papers resting in a neat pile before him. We advanced down the room in silence. In the general stillness, I was able to take an inventory of the man's character. The scrupulous neatness of his desk top, immaculate hands, well-manicured fingernails, and a softly pervasive scent of bay rum, bespoke a fastidiousness seldom associated with Americans in this country. The cunningly embroidered carpet and stencilled tracery on the walls around the windows, combined with the rich, almost garish, use of red

* The *Daily News* was founded in London in 1846, a champion of Liberal viewpoints. Mycroft's simile here is especially noteworthy, for he is quoted by Dr. Watson in "The Greek Interpreter" as having advertized for Paul and Sophy Kratides within its pages. Mycroft was obviously a long-time reader. MH/SMW

and gold-fringed wall hangings denoted a conflicting sense of taste, while the man's beautifully appointed suit told of a more personal sense of quiet opulence.

On this day, Mr Schenck's appearance was marred by a slight, although perceptible, growth of beard. I also noticed that the points of his wing collar were less than pristine, although a recent attempt had been made at smoothing them. Such a condition was at odds with his other character traits so it must be a severe crisis to require Mr. Schenck to wear yesterday's collar with today's cravat. The business must be serious, for I saw that the man had been working throughout the night, only just resuming his collar, cuffs, cravat, coat, and waistcoat before we arrived. This fact was even more evident when I saw that the buttons in the deep folds of his ample waistcoat were misaligned, a manifest sign of a haste to make oneself presentable. Finally taking note of our presence, Ambassador Schenck rose.

"I appreciate your promptness, gentlemen," he said. "I apologise for the delay, but another matter required my attention."

"Completely understandable," responded Mr. Moriarty with unaccustomed expansiveness. "It's good to see you again, Mr. Ambassador."

"I wish the circumstances were more pleasant, Mr. Moriarty," he returned coldly. "I do not believe I know your colleague," he continued, turning to me.

"This is Mr. Mycroft Holmes of my office."

"Honoured to meet you, sir," said Mr. Schenck, extending his large hand. As I grasped it, surprised at its lack of vigor, I noted the weariness in his eyes. Some grave event had sapped the strength from this big, bluff man, possibly to be found in the pages until recently occupying his attention. As he walked from behind the desk, I found his darting, black eyes, beaked nose, and fringe of grey-white hair reminiscent of the American bald eagle displayed behind him, in the brilliantly coloured reproduction of the Great Seal of the United States on the wall. He waved us to a long couch of wool plush in front of the office fireplace while reaching for the bell-pull beside him.

"It's a bit early for tea, I know, but please join me; I've not had a bite of food all day."

The long-limbed secretary now reappeared.

"Hank, ask Trent to join us and be sure to load up the tea-waggon with those biscuits and scones I had yesterday." The Ambassador looked at us. "I've developed a taste for oatcakes and scones during my term here. Best-tasting things in the world. That'll be all, Hank." The young man, whose red hair and freckles seemed so at odds with the formal cutaway he wore, disappeared whence he had come.

The small-talk continued. Mr. Schenck allowed as to how he thought the custom of having tea in the afternoon was most civilised. We agreed, although I knew Mr. Moriarty would not have turned down a somewhat stronger libation. We spoke of the price of cotton being up in Syria, while that of rubber was down in the Malaysian archipelago. Mr. Moriarty was almost to the edge of his seat awaiting the real reason for our visit. when the tea and scones were brought in on a tea-waggon by a young man who was at once the most obsequious, yet most intelligent-looking man I could ever recall meeting.

He was of slight build, with thinning brown hair and an almost invisible moustache. He had a very softspoken manner to him, as we learned when he was introduced by Ambassador Schenck.

"Gentlemen, this is Mr. Calvin Trent, my personal secretary. Trent, this is Mr. Jerrold Moriarty and Mr. Mycroft Holmes of the FO."

"Pleased to meet you," Trent responded with the grip of a boiled cod as we shook hands. Once more I noted the subservience of his manner, so at variance with the perceptive depths in his expression. He wheeled the tea-waggon between the Ambassador's overstuffed leather arm-chair and the sofa upon which we sat.

"I'd like you in on this, Trent," said the Ambassador, pointing to the beautiful but uncomfortable straightbacked Sheraton side-chair next to his own chair. The young man nodded and obediently took the seat at his master's left hand.

"Now then, Mr. Moriarty, I feel that we have much to discuss."

"I too feel that there is much to say, but I must tell you right off that I cannot enjoy your company for very long, Mr. Ambassador," said my superior. "My agenda is extremely crowded and I had to postpone no fewer than four previously scheduled appointments, many having to do with the gravest matters of state."

"I appreciate that you have no particular desire to be here, sir," the Ambassador said coldly. "Unfortunately such matters do not accommodate themselves to individual schedules."

I sighed inwardly. Mr. Moriarty was beginning to crumble. We were not to have an easy time of it. Removing a small memorandum book from the pocket of his coat, the Ambassador began his remonstration: "On Tuesday last, you were visited by a group of four men who presented themselves as members of a mercantile delegation representing business interests for the state of Alabama. Oddly enough, they have not seen fit to present themselves to this office under the established and accepted forms of protocol, even though I represent their country. Or do I?" He referred to his book, as though making sure of what he had just said, then closed it with a snap. He continued in an overly kind, sarcastic voice. "Is it possible that these men are not what they represent themselves to be?"

Mr. Moriarty squirmed in his seat.

"I have learned," Mr. Schenck went on, "that each of these men is a trained military professional, and that all are former officers in the late Confederacy. One of them is even being sought in connexion with a murder inquiry in ... ah ..."

"Mississippi, sir," Trent prompted quietly.

"Thank you. Mississippi. He is said to have killed a man who contested his assertions that the late President Lincoln was a Jew."

"An African Jew," Trent amended.

"Six of one, half-dozen of another," Mr. Schenck remarked with a shrug. "In any case, he should be extradited here and now, back to Mississippi to stand trial. But this," he fumed, "this is of slight import, for he is now apparently protected by diplomatic immunity, if my information is correct. Still, I have not been informed of their presence in London directly from them and I am forced to return to the original question: Why have they not presented themselves to me? I can only suppose that they have come to this country for a purpose which I would find inimical to the best interests of the United States."

"I—I don't know what to say," began Mr. Moriarty, falteringly. "You see, Mr. Ambassador, ah—I—uh, never set eyes on them, myself. When they asked to see me, I was engaged elsewhere. My secretary directed them to Mr. Holmes, here, when I proved unavailable."

The Ambassador swung his gaze toward me.

"Well, young man, what have you to say?"

"Very little, sir. As you say, they represented themselves as a trade delegation, asking to see Mr. Moriarty. In fact, they insisted on seeing him and, as a consequence, they told me very little, directly."

Ambassador Schenck stared at the floor, as though regarding the weave of the carpet intently as he spoke. "Gentlemen," he said softly. "We seem to be at an impasse." He continued his inspection of the floor. "And I get the feeling that I am being played the fool." With that, he threw his head back and his dark eyes locked upon our own as he roared, "And I won't have it!"

The outburst took us both aback.

"At this moment," shouted the Ambassador, "those men may be conspiring to overthrow the government of the people of the United States of America, a country I have served with devotion and fidelity all my life," he continued passionately, "and I will not allow *you* to countenance treason against her!"

There were a few moments of an awful silence before a shaken Moriarty ventured, "Surely—surely you don't look upon us as abetting traitors against your country, Mr. Ambassador?"

"That you must answer for yourselves, sir," thundered the American. "I'm sure you must know the answer better than I."

These words had an almost electric effect upon Mr. Moriarty. Although remaining seated, he drew himself erect and he lapsed into the formal tongue of diplomacy. "Your Excellency, I must remind you that you are speaking to the representatives of Her Royal Majesty, Victoria, Queen of England . . ."

"I know who *she* is, sir, I assure you! What I want to know is what you're doing with this so-called trade delegation! Why does a *trade* delegation seek out the offices of the military liaison within the Foreign Office?"

The Ambassador's words were like a body blow; Mr. Moriarty looked as though someone had just stepped on his stomach.

"Why I never . . . I never thought . . . it never occurred to me . . . ," he stammered.

"I give you my word, sir," I jumped in, "neither Her Majesty's Government nor Mr. Moriarty are guilty in any way of conspiring against the United States nor have they any knowledge of such a conspiracy."

"And what about you?"

Discretion is the better part of diplomacy, I told myself. "Well, sir, I did have the one encounter with them. After which I offered to direct them to the Ministry of Trade."

Trent coughed circumspectly as the Ambassador returned to his desk.

"If I may ask a question, sir . . . ?"

Schenck waved his hand absently.

"I'd like to know, Mr. Holmes," asked Trent, adjusting his collar, "if the members of the delegation actually went to the Ministry of Trade?"

"Don't answer that, Holmes!" barked Moriarty. He rose majestically and, with a dignity I had never seen before, he gravely marched to the Ambassador's desk. "I've had just enough bullyragging from you, sir. Now just you listen to this." He turned to me.

"Holmes," he said, with all the power of the Royal Navy, "Holmes, you are being given a direct order: this entire affair is hereby made a matter of state. You shall answer no questions that may be put to you by these men without specific instructions to do so." He turned again to the Ambassador, whose mouth had fallen open in surprise and amazement.

"And you, sir! How dare you act in this manner before the representative of Her Majesty's Government? Just who do you and your upstart nation think you are? I promise you that Your Excellency has not heard the last about this feeble attempt at intimidation. Further discussion about this matter will come from the office of Sir Robert Hyde, if not from Mr. Disraeli himself!" He strode back to the sofa, picked up his hat, and said, "Come Holmes; we are leaving this nest of vipers." Without another word, he collected his hat and stick and swept out of the American office with me in his wake. I can remember—or am I only thinking that I remember—the Ambassador bemusedly murmur, "I didn't think the old stuffed shirt had it in him!"

In the carriage returning to Whitehall, Mr. Moriarty chuckled.

"Not a very diplomatic ending, I'll admit, Holmes, but that political popinjay always affects me adversely with his boorishness. Imagine shouting at me as though I were his valet. Humph. He actually expected Her Majesty's representative to cower at his feet as though he and those Washington ruffians owned the world. Well, we'll just see about that! Sir Robert will be told about this meeting directly." He laughed again, a little more nervously this time. "That American will think twice before he attempts to tweak the tail of the British lion again!"

"I would say that you carried it off quite well, sir. But the repercussions . . ."

"Bah, what repercussions? Schenck acted like a clumsy lout. Why, if I chose to make this incident known, he would become the laughing-stock of the entire diplomatic community. I daresay he'll cool down soon enough. I may even send an apology over to him and that will be the end of it."

"I hope that you are correct," I added grimly.

We travelled in silence for a few blocks before Mr. Moriarty spoke again.

"See here, Holmes, I do believe that you've earned the day off." He consulted his watch. "It's only just two-thirty; plenty of things for you to do by way of preparing for the Admiralty Ball, I'll wager, eh?"

"That is true, sir."

"Well then, I'll tell you what: why don't you take the remainder of the day off to finish those preparations?"

I accepted with alacrity. His unaccustomed heartiness made me no less cognisant of the fact that he was meeting with the Leland delegation, Captain Ravenswood now in command—at least until the Colonel was given ambulatory permission by Dr. Agar. I had the feeling that my superior was attempting to be sure that I would not be about when the Americans told him their plans. I was also sure that if, at a later date, I wished to learn of the business conducted,

I need only phrase my request to Mr. Moriarty in a way that would not alarm him.

I would also have been foolish not to take advantage of a few more hours of leisure time to do just what Mr. Moriarty suggested. My tailcoat was then at the tailor shop being let out, and my tailor had hoped for another fitting before final adjustments were made.

I expected Sherlock and Victor Trevor to be early for dinner that night. Not that my brother cared one whit for food, of course, but I knew that his friend's appetite would not allow Sherlock to dally.

After leaving off Mr. Moriarty at Whitehall, I bethought myself to book a table for us at the Café Royal, and so informed the driver. While the cab was stopped in traffic, however, I recalled my dwindling supply of banknotes. I removed my pocketbook and counted my money. There was enough, but the prices at the Café Royal were dear and it was still nearly a week until my salary came due. I then happily recalled that my landlady had returned from a visit to her relatives in the west country. Sherlock and Trevor were to meet at my rooms in any case. . . . Fortunately Mrs. Crosse loved to cook and did it well. End of difficulty.

I instructed the driver to forego stopping at the restaurant but to take me directly to my home in St. Chad's Street. We drove up Regent Street past the Café Royal and toward the Langham Hotel. The Langham—where the thugs had hit me for six the night before. Where Colonel Leland lay smoking his corncob pipe. Where Rachel Leland might now be sitting perhaps, doing needlework or maybe reading. The hansom moved on and I caught sight of the Langham, now stark against the hastening gloom. We drew near and I stared at the building from out the small side window of the cab. And then it was gone.

We continued up Portland Place to the Park Crescent, passing Regent's Park, turning thence into Euston Road. We proceeded along, passing Tottenham Court Road, Gower Street, Woburn, and Eversholt; we came to St. Pancras Station. I recalled how, when I was house-searching, I had hoped to find something near St. Pancras, for it was built from the prospective plans for Whitehall, designed by Sir George Gilbert Scott. He wanted to make it a companion to the Houses of Parliament, but his plan was rejected. He therefore, transferred the design to St. Pancras Station. I took it as a good omen—so to speak—when I found Mrs. Crosse's vacancy shingle so near.

The driver followed the curve of Euston Road, past King's Cross Station, then turned right, into St. Chad's Street, where my flat came into sight.

I am always at a loss to explain to myself as to why it was that my landlady took such a lively interest in me. Mrs. Bridget Crosse was a pleasantly attractive young widow whose husband, a second lieutenant, had lost his life in India a very few years before. She was in the latter half of her third decade at this time, but as efficient and conscientious as a woman with twice her experience and age. She was what is popularly termed "black Irish." Not at all the Irish lass of the music hall, complete with red hair and freckles, she possessed the translucent complexion, raven hair, and dark, sparkling eyes of the true Celt.

Her husband, a man of apparent foresight, had inherited a small sum, sufficient to purchase the house at Number 42. He then instructed his wife to take in a lodger to supplement the not-too-munificent pay of a second lieutenant and went off in service of Queen and country.

As I mentioned, the young man died overseas—of some tropical disease. His young widow was left with the merest pittance of a pension, this circumstance forcing her to take in a second lodger, myself.

I spoke of her merits as a cook. This is not an idle compliment. The woman set the best table between here and Charnwood. Her *pâté de fois gras* pie, scalloped oysters, chicken curry, and Lancashire hot-pot were unexcelled. As long as she remained my landlady I ate the best-prepared food in London, if not in the whole of the British Isles. The lady took it as a personal rebuke if I was not at home to enjoy one of her meals. Although she kept a small staff of servants, they were unobtrusive. To me, this was more than a convenience, for even at this time, I was prone to keep myself to myself.

But as wonderfully run a household as she kept, this paragon among landladies had her own peculiarity. She was religious—excessively so. It is actually part and parcel of the soil in Ireland, but I believe that the death of her beloved husband intensified her natural tendency. Every new tract concerning the most recent "apparition," every new pronouncement made by His Holiness, the Pope, found its way onto my breakfast tray. At other times, I found medallions and "holy cards" imprinted with the features of one saint after another. But the lady was sensitive in this way and her sensitivity prevented her from leaving anything but pre-Reformation saints who would be therefore acceptable to my C. of E. background.

I received likenesses of Saints Agatha, Lucy, Christopher, Jude Thaddeus, Peter, Paul, Patrick (of course), the Archangel Michael, and St. George—both spearing their respective dragons—and many others who took up space in my chest of drawers. My favourite of this celestial company was the picture of St. Dymphna which I found one morning beneath my napkin, next to a reprint of some piously written account of the vision of the Virgin Mary at La Sallette.

I found a frame for St. Dymphna—also spearing a dragon—and for many decades, it sat on my desk in Whitehall, to the amusement or consternation of my colleagues. I had the private enjoyment of knowing, alone among all those who labour within the Foreign Office, that St. Dymphna is the patroness of those afflicted with nervous disorders. In my profession, I will accept all available assistance.

I feared that I might have to listen to the latest declaration made by Cardinal Manning concerning home rule for Ireland from Mrs. Crosse. The pronouncement had been reported by the newspapers that morning. I had already perused His Eminence's remarks some days ago in a copy he had graciously supplied to the Home Office; the cardinal issued these bulletins in advance of publication, he said, in a spirit of fair play. I suppose he meant for the Government to issue some kind of rebuttal on the same day. So far as I know, however, the Government never rose to the bait. It is also true that one could traverse a certain storey in the Home Office and listen to several pairs of teeth gnashing in impotent rage.

The policy of the Crown in regard to the isle of her birth was always a sensitive issue with Mrs. Crosse, and the cardinal's remarks were sure to inflame her tender feelings.

I entered the house with a feeling of unnecessary dread, however, for the lady was absent. Congratulating myself for having escaped her political opinions, I left a hastily scrawled note informing her that I would have company for dinner. Such a note was actually gratuitous, for Mrs. Crosse invariably prepared more food than was needed. What was not eaten during the meal was sent 'round to the poor in various soup-kitchens in Whitechapel.

Opening the door to my rooms, I found an unexpected visitor.

"You have a delightful collection of ancient coins, Mr. Holmes."

Of all the people that I would ever hope to meet in my rooms, commending me on my antique acquisitions, I should never have anticipated Calvin Trent, the self-effacing American attaché.

"I never thought I would have the pleasure of exhibiting them to you, Mr. Trent."

"I see you've not met your landlady. She let me in before she left."

"You must have impressed her with the urgency of your mission," I responded coolly.

"I told her that I had to see you on most important governmental business."

"Your government or mine?" I asked shortly.

My latest American visitor held up his hands placatingly.

"Ease up, please, Mr. Holmes, you're off duty now."

My eyebrow arched.

"Meaning that you are not, sir?"

"In a manner of speaking, let us say. My visit here is not known to Ambassador Schenck. I've come to ask you about a Negro. Calls himself Captain Jericho."

"Indeed? And who might this biblical buccaneer be?"

He gave a slight smile.

"I was hoping that you might tell me. He was in these rooms not twenty-four hours ago."

I smiled ruefully and gave a short bow. "That well-advertised Yankee shrewdness," I said. "I must learn to guard myself against it." I waved him into the very seat Captain Jericho had occupied the previous evening, while I took a place opposite him.

"Well, sir," said I finally. "Why am I sought out by the American Secret Service?"

Trent's face became a blank. "What makes you think that you are being sought out by that organisation?"

I allowed the man to squirm while I removed my snuff-box, tapped it and opened it. "My dear Mr. Trent, you arrive in my domicile in this melodramatic manner after making my acquaintance scant hours ago. Really, sir, what do you take me for?"

"I might be here for other purposes; why do you say the Secret Service?"

After proffering some to the American, which he refused with a wave of his hand, I took out a pinch of snuff and placed it on the back of my hand, saying, "Within the American embassy, you replaced one George Atkinson, another member of your American Secret Service, although he was listed within your embassy as cultural attaché." I inhaled the snuff and removed my handkerchief from my pocket. "I need not reveal to you my methods for discovering that fact, but I can tell you that a junior clerk would do well to learn the names and faces of the diplomatic community within his capital city." I sneezed and replaced my handkerchief.

"Needless to say, I do know the name and face of every clerk, junior clerk, secretary, attaché, confidential secretary, and the exact number of foreign nationals employed within each legation."

"But that's impossible," Trent protested.

"Not at all, it merely takes some concentration and memorisation. The trick is to keep the information current. But to return to your own case, you replaced George Atkinson, whom I discovered to be a Secret Service man, masquerading as an attaché. It is not too long a shot to infer that there is no one better to replace a Secret Service agent than another Secret Service agent." I paused, as much for effect as to light a cigar. I was enjoying the American's consternation. "Both you and Atkinson are cut from the same bolt of cloth: quiet, retiring, and much more knowledgeable than is warranted by your so-called position as 'personal secretary.' "

"But those are such very inconsequential reasons for your conclusions."

"Those very inconsequentialities are what commanded my attention."

"I may have to bring you to the attention of my superiors," said Trent, with a rueful smile, "but as of now, Mr. Holmes, I propose a bargain, a truce if you like. I believe we are working toward the same end and I would appreciate your co-operation. Besides," he said, shrugging his almost nonexistent shoulders, "two minds are better than one, even one as keen as your own."

I lifted my hand in warning, "I am prepared to listen to such a proposal, Mr. Trent, yet I am compelled to remind you of Mr. Moriarty's orders, spoken in front of you this afternoon, to which I am bound by oath."

"I am aware of your responsibility, Mr. Holmes, as clearly as I am aware of my own. However," and his eyes took on a sly look, "if I already know what it is pertaining to this matter that you know also, and if I can perhaps give you a few more particulars, in exchange for your aid, would that be breaking your oath?"

"We shall see. I can promise nothing."

Trent shrugged again. "I suppose I'll have to gamble," he said. "You know then that the Americans are not a trade commission sent by the state government of Alabama. I surmise that you might even know something of their true purpose in coming to London in the first place. And that you received such information during one of the two visits made by Captain Jericho."

I allowed no reaction to cross my face.

"I don't know all the particulars, myself," Trent went on, "but I've heard rumours of men in the South, former rebels, who've been training under arms." He gave a slight shrug. "I must admit that I have no independent verification of such tales, but you must be aware that such a circumstance is contrary to the martial law that has been imposed on the South since the end of the war. God knows that we've few enough soldiers to patrol that vast region. There are some places so remote I suspect that they may be still fighting George the Third!"

I politely returned his smile.

"Actually, we know damn little for certain. I'll wager that Jericho knows more about what's happening than we do."

I nodded noncommittally. Trent sat silently, awaiting my reply to his gambit. I was spared the necessity of replying by a knocking at my door. My brother and his friend had arrived for dinner. I excused myself and Trent rose as Sherlock and Victor Trevor entered my sitting room. I made the introductions, omitting any reference to Mr. Trent's occupation. It made little difference, for Sherlock's first words to the American were, "How do you do. I'm sorry that your new duties do not allow you the opportunity for target-practice that you enjoyed in the army."

Trent was taken aback for a moment, but was equal to my brother's sally.

"What makes you believe that I enjoy shooting?" He smiled and added, "I see that the talent for quick identification runs in your family."

"Thank you," said Sherlock. "I mentioned your ability because of the slight, smooth depression worn into your right cheek, where you habitually rest it on the rifle stock. It would follow that a man who had done as much shooting as you should enjoy it."

"You confuse pleasure with necessity," Trent replied with the same smile.

I interrupted before Sherlock could answer. "You've arrived at a most propitious time, Sherlock." I turned to Trent. "My brother and his friend have become involuntarily involved in this matter, Mr. Trent. They were able to interpose themselves at an opportune time last night, checking a possible threat to my life, and remained to hear Captain Jericho's singular narrative concerning the very events of which you speak. It is only proper that they hear what you have to say also. I can assure that their discretion is complete and absolute."

"Besides that, we have an invitation to dine," Sherlock observed.

Calvin Trent eyed the two arrivals closely as they took their places about the room. When Trent next spoke, he weighed his words carefully.

"Captain Jericho spoke to you last night. I believe he told you about the plans to capture the country with the help of the British government. But did he mention a jewelled necklace valued at more than one and a quarter million dollars—that would be worth some two hundred fifty thousand pounds here?"*

Trevor gasped, "No, not a word."

Trent shook his head, "Well, I don't suppose he would. But your supposed patriot had his eyes firmly fixed on those people from Alabama for some less idealistic reasons than he may want you to think.

"You see, back in 1863, there were a number of prominent Confederates who had thrown away their rose-coloured glasses and were prepared for a Federal victory. But they weren't preparing to live with that outcome. They were determined to be quit of the Federal government; the Confederacy might fall but these Confederates weren't going to fall with it. It was decided to petition a foreign country where they would be welcomed, treated with respect and allowed to retain their slaves.

"They had a country in mind, too: Brazil, ruled by Dom Pedro II. These men would form some kind of 'government in exile' by offering 'colonisers skilled in agriculture, industrial methods, and railroad construction.' In return, the Confederates would receive land grants to be apportioned among them.

"Well, the idea was enthusiastically greeted by many, including some of those involved with the government in Richmond. Six men were chosen to represent the Southern interests and these men—one of whom was Colonel Mordecai Leland—decided to ensure the success of the mission by sending a lavish gift to the Countess Isabella D'Eu, the daughter of the Emperor Dom Pedro."

"That woman," I muttered. "Our relations with Brazil have always been stormy and uncertain because of her influence over the Emperor."

"Exactly. That's the reason the committee thought to send a gift to her. And knowing her tastes, they knew that they could not be penurious."

"Very astute of them."

"Indeed. Colonel Leland had the idea, and a sharply reasoned one it was," Trent agreed. "Leland had resigned

* At the time of this adventure, the pound sterling was worth approximately $5.00, the dollar being worth exactly 100 cents. Today's (1980) dollar fluctuates between 2 and 5 cents in equivalent purchasing power and continues to fluctuate daily. MH/SMW

from the army, but was continually asked for advice by congressional committees from Richmond about popular reaction to proposed legislation.

"Well, after the decision, contributions were solicited throughout the Confederate states, among five hundred thousand 'superior people,' as they termed themselves. In all, the committee raised a fund of more than one million, two hundred fifty thousand in gold. This money was entrusted to two young Southern officers whom you've met."

"Not Tyler Carteret and William Bankhead?" gasped Trevor.

"The same," Trent smiled grimly. "Upon the recommendation of Mordecai Leland."

"The pieces begin to fall into place," muttered Sherlock. "Pray continue with your story, Mr. Trent."

"They boarded a blockade runner which rendezvoused at sea with the *Laurel*, a small Confederate vessel, which had on board the most influential secret agent representing the Confederacy in Europe . . ."

". . . James D. Bulloch," I broke in. "I have heard of his exploits before. But I have never heard of this one."

"That's how well kept a secret this was and still is," Trent acknowledged. "It's taken many years to learn what I know about it. After Tyler and Bankhead met with Bulloch they returned to Alabama. The *Laurel* sailed to the Madeiras and encountered the *Shenandoah,* purchased by Bulloch . . ."

". . . for forty-five thousand pounds from Her Majesty's Government," I interjected. "It was formerly known as H.M.S. *Sea King.* That I knew about, but no one knew the reason for the purchase, aside from the fact that it was to be added to the Confederate fleet."

"She was to be the successor to the *Alabama,*" Trent replied. "The *Shenandoah* was to raid the islands frequented by the North's whaling fleets, a source of abundant wealth to the North and a training ground for able-bodied seamen.

"But first," Trent continued, "Bulloch met with its captain, James I. Waddell, concerning a personal mission to precede duty in the North Pacific. Bulloch explained to Captain Waddell what the young men had brought with them in the chests now in his possession.

"'I am to use all of this money to purchase the most beautiful and expensive diamond necklace in history,' he told the Captain. Waddell then transported Bulloch to India, to the diamond mines there.* He was aided by experts, spending weeks selecting, bargaining, and buying the gemstones to be assembled for the necklace.

"Then he went to France, to Boehmer and Bassenge, the same company whose founders had created the fabulous half-million-dollar necklace ordered by Louis XV for Madame du Barry. They spent almost a year in bringing into existence the most exquisite piece of jewellery in the world today. Then Bulloch met again with Captain Waddell on October eighth, 1864, in Liverpool.

"Bulloch charged the Captain with the journey to Brazil, giving the diamond necklace into his possession. The Countess D'Eu had been informed of the gift and was expecting a 'presentation from the people of the Confederate States of America suitably expressing their admiration for her.'

"Waddell was told to continue to seek out and destroy Federal ships, but that while he did so, he was to find or make an opportunity to visit Rio de Janeiro without arousing suspicion as to his true purpose. While in port, Captain Waddell was to present the necklace to the Countess.

"Waddell had taken leave from his command, and again the ship *Laurel* was appointed to meet with the *Shenandoah* in the Madeiras. The Captain boarded ship. Two days after his arrival, he departed Maderia.

"Ten days after putting out to sea, the *Shenandoah* captured the Federal barque, *Alina,* en route to Buenos Aires from Newport, England, with a one-hundred-thousand-dollar cargo. After several other successful raids, Waddell and his crew arrived in Melbourne harbour in Australia on January twenty-fifth, 1865.

"While in port, eighteen members of the crew deserted, apparently taking the necklace with them. Captain Waddell attempted to replace them with Australians and came under fire when the Melbourne police accused him of violating British neutrality laws. But by the end of the month, the police had rounded up fourteen of the missing deserters

---

* At this time, India was the world's leading diamond-producing country. MH/SMW

and brought them back to the ship, where they were put in irons.

"The authorities now insisted that Waddell leave or face internment. But the Captain continued to remain in port, urging every effort be made to apprehend the four men still missing, yet not deeming it wise to mention the disappearance of the necklace.

"On February third, with internment imminent, the police informed Captain Waddell that the four men had disappeared from Melbourne and that his ship would be seized unless he cleared out of port immediately.

"Waddell obeyed, ordering the sailing master to set a direct course around the horn for Rio de Janeiro. But the ship had hardly cleared port when the Captain issued new orders. They were to sail north instead of to Brazil.

"The *Shenandoah* captured seven ships in the following weeks in the northern Pacific. When Waddell captured the U.S. ship *William Thompson,* her skipper indignantly informed the Captain of Lee's surrender at Appomattox and that the Civil War was ended. Nevertheless, on that day, June twenty-sixth, 1865, Waddell defiantly told his officers and men that so long as his ship remained afloat, he would continue to fight until the South became free. He was, no doubt, also fearful of returning his mission a failure, the necklace lost."

"I recall the incident that followed," I said. "It was in the newspapers here that while the *Shenandoah* anchored off Vancouver, one of our captains, ah, James Lonsdale of the frigate *Metabel,* came aboard and gave Waddell a friendly warning: If he continued to raid and sink Yankee ships he would no longer be considered a Confederate patriot but a pirate."

"That's right," said Trent. "The *Shenandoah* ceased preying on shipping in the Pacific, sailed through the Strait of Magellan and landed in Liverpool, dropping anchor on November sixth. The sailing master charted a remarkable course: for seventeen thousand miles the ship was not sighted until they reached the mouth of the Mersey River.

"Not until then did Waddell haul down the flag of the Confederacy and formally surrender the ship to the British Navy."

"Yes," I nodded, "but we didn't want her. The ship was

an embarrassment to us and we were also fearful that the United States would seek reparations for the toll she had taken in Yankee shipping."

"So what happened to the ship?" asked Trent.

"The Admiralty put a new crew and stores aboard and before the American Ambassador could do anything about it, they had the *Shenandoah* sailed off to the most remote spot upon which the admirals could agree: Zanzibar. There she was refitted, repainted, her cannons were removed, and she was then presented to the Sultan of Zanzibar for use as a pleasure yacht.

"But the Sultan didn't like the ship and, after a single cruise, sold her to a wealthy Greek named Eppinus, who went down with all hands in a typhoon in the Indian Ocean shortly thereafter."

"And that is all that history knows about the *Shenandoah*, eh?" asked Sherlock. "But what of the necklace? I can only suppose from your narrative that the four seamen who deserted must have taken it with them."

"One would think that," Trent continued. "Waddell thoroughly searched the fourteen deserters who were returned to the ship. None of them had it, indeed they all stoutly denied having taken anything off the ship, except nineteen hundred pounds in English gold. After he surrendered the ship, Waddell undertook a journey to Melbourne in a forlorn hope of finding the fourteen deserters and the missing necklace."

"And nothing was found," said Trevor gloomily.

"Oh, something was found. Melbourne police found four skeletons in the wastes near Oodnadatta, some nine hundred miles northwest of Melbourne. Half hidden in the sand were found a brass belt buckle and a wooden seaman's knife. Both were stamped 'Naval Arsenal, Charleston, S.C.' and the initials of one of the missing deserters, Paul Terhune, were found carved in the knife handle. But this was all circumstantial evidence, though it convinced the police that they had found the four deserters.

"But no conclusive proof was found linking the men to the lost necklace, nor that they ever had it. Captain Waddell died two years ago, convinced to the end that the necklace is lost somewhere amid the sun-scorched scrub of the Australian bush country," the American said, ending his tale.

"But if Jericho is after it, the necklace must have been found," said Sherlock.

"It was never lost," said Trent quietly.

"What!" we chorused.

"That's right," said Trent. "A man's body was found in Jasper, Alabama, eight years ago. He'd been dead for two days before it was discovered. He had been living under the name of Phineas Tourney. I would stake my reputation within the Secret Service that that man was aboard the *Shenandoah*. Unfortunately the ship's log is lost."

"So the man had never deserted at all, but had rifled the Captain's safe, found the necklace and hidden it aboard ship," I said.

"That's correct, Mr. Holmes," Trent replied. "At least, that's my theory as well. He brought it off the ship, kept it out of sight for more than year and hoped to sell it to the highest bidder. But that opportunity never came. He had been murdered but nothing of value was to be found. I daresay an inescapable fact emerged when I began researching the background of Captain Samuel Ravenswood. In 1867, Captain Ravenswood visited Jasper, Alabama, on business, a few days before Tourney was found dead.

"My theory is this: Tourney sent word to Ravenswood, telling him about the necklace, most likely in veiled terms. The Captain discovered what it was that Tourney was offering to sell him, killed him, and brought the necklace back to his home in Montgomery.

"I now believe that Ravenswood is somehow involved in these rumoured movements back in the Southern states. I believe that he has dangled the necklace in front of whatever ruling body is making these secret arrangements and has therefore gained considerable prestige and influence within the group. I also believe that Colonel Leland and Captain Ravenswood have been sent to England to put the necklace to its original use."

"So what was originally meant for a countess, they now intend to give a Queen," said Sherlock, reflecting on the story.

"But no one can bribe the Queen!" Trevor declared stoutly.

"Of course not," I agreed, "but some of Her Majesty's

ministers may not be so ethical. A gift of two hundred fifty thousand pounds is one not likely to be ignored, and can have heavy implications. In some quarters, it may do what months of negotiation fail to do."

"So if Jericho's story is to be believed," Trevor burst in, "then . . ."

"It will be used to arm, supply, and supplement the army raised by Ravenswood and his people," Sherlock concluded.

"Then these rumours are true," said Trent, triumphantly smiling at me. He had gained the information I could not reveal. I could do nothing but to give him a sporting nod.

"But," Sherlock added, "that's only if they still have it."

"What do you mean?" asked Trent.

For the second time in twenty-four hours, I recounted my adventure with the thugs in the Langham Hotel. At the conclusion of my tale, Trent asked. "Do you think Captain Jericho was behind the attack, and do you think he has the necklace now?"

I looked at my hands, ignoring the first part of his question. "I think not," I said at last. "The Confederates surely hid it too well for them to find in the short span of time that Miss Deane and I were unconscious."

"Tell him about the callouses," said Trevor.

Sherlock and I exchanged smiles. Trevor was always a good audience.

"We believe one of the thieves, or a henchman, rather, to have masqueraded as a doctor, though he was formerly employed"—Sherlock paused, glancing my way—"at a livery stable."

There was a knock at my door. It was Mrs. Crosse.

"Would you like your dinner served now, Mr. Holmes?"

"By all means, Mrs. Crosse. Oh, and we'll have one more guest to dine." I turned to Calvin Trent. "Mr. Trent, I insist that you sup with us tonight."

"Oh yes, Mr. Trent," Mrs. Crosse said quickly. "There's plenty for everyone."

"Well, I'd really like to . . ."

"Good. Then I'll set another place," said Mrs. Crosse, brightly. "You look as though you could use a good home-cooked meal," she added, appraising his thin frame closely.

"Yes, ma'am. Thank you," was all the hapless American could say before she bustled out the door.

7

A BRIEF ENCOUNTER
AT THE ADMIRALTY BALL

"Wake up, Mr. Holmes. It's just six o'clock. Hurry yourself and I'll be back up with your breakfast in half an hour. Your bath is drawn and ready. Hurry before it gets cold."

And so my Friday began with Mrs. Crosse's dulcet Irish tones. I proceeded to the daily ritual of preparing myself to meet the world, a prospect with which I am never too comfortable.

After a not too leisurely bath, I dressed with my usual punctiliousness. I do not mind sharing a part of my toilette with the reader, for I am certain that most of the male population shares this inconvenience with me. And that is the arrangement of the necktie.

Sherlock and I have always detested this inconsequential and totally useless part of a gentleman's apparel. It serves no purpose, nor is it put to any use. Quite independently, we arrived at the same conclusion while I was away at college and Sherlock still in the early forms. Our answer was to wear the easiest kind of necktie we could find. I might add that neither one of us cares for the wing collar; we use the *revers* collar exclusively.

After attaching the collar, we tie a simple bow knot, then tuck the whole thing under the collar. Therefore, the ends need not be straight nor even. One merely centers the knot and that is the end of it. I am sorry to say that, although this style used to be commonly worn during the last century, it has all but disappeared in the early part of the twentieth century, save its relegation to evening wear.

My morning ablutions over, I sat down to enjoy my breakfast in accustomed ease. Aromas from the silver-covered platters appetisingly assailed my nostrils. I would be partaking of another culinary masterpiece, courtesy of Mrs. Crosse. Not only did the woman cook exceedingly well, but she made the meal attractive to the eye. The poached eggs were always placed just so, cooked to the exact setting. The toast was in the rack, properly cooled; the kippers and bacon piquantly arranged around the eggs. But I digress. . . .

The public prints contained no account of the mysterious assault in the Americans' suite, just as there had been no word of the shooting of Colonel Leland. There was no other news of interest to me in the *Telegraph,* nor yet in the *Daily News,* though I took exception to the editorial. As I put the papers aside, I was minded of Sherlock's fanciful habit of studying the agony columns in the various daily periodicals. I occasionally glanced at the weird and oddly worded notices. They often took the shape of vulgar expressions of infatuation or pleas from deserted wives, husbands, parents, and sweethearts. Such twaddle repulsed me even more than the advertisements.

I now considered paying a morning visit to Colonel Leland. After last evening's revelations I wanted to keep a particularly close watch on him.

Mrs. Crosse took away the dishes, reproving me for not having eaten more while she was away.

"Very perceptive, Mrs. Crosse. In my own defence, I can only say that after having tasted your ambrosia, I find most other victuals more like cannon fodder than food."

She laughed merrily, "Ah you're just like my late Kevin." Then she added a wistful "God rest his soul."

"He must have been a very good man to be gifted with your cooking."

"Oh, aye," she said with a faraway look. "He was always out of sorts when he had to eat in the officers' mess."

"I can well understand his feelings in the matter."

"Yes, yes," she went on, while collecting the last of the dishes. "He used to tell me that he would have to let out all his uniforms after our wedding." She grew briefly pensive. "Ah, but he was a lovely man."

"And his brother in Surrey? I would suppose that he is in better health now, what with your ministrations and your cooking."

"Listen to the man go on," she said with a giggle. "Sure and you've a touch of the blarney in you this morning, Mr. Holmes. But he is much better, saints be praised. Mr.

Crosse always said that Kerry was born to be hanged, so's I knew that no throw from a horse would keep him long abed. Just between us, a few prayers for him wouldn't be too many."

"Another soul to add to your prayers, Mrs. Crosse. Why with all the people for whom you pray, you will be close to the Throne yourself, when the time comes."

"What a lovely thing to say, Mr. Holmes. But, you know, I don't do it to be rewarded. Still, it's an awfully comforting thought." She smiled as she refilled my tea cup. "Will you be late tonight, sir?"

"You might say yes and you might say no," I told her in an affected Irish brogue. She laughed. "Seriously, I will be home at five, but you'll recall that tonight is the Admiralty Ball, so I expect that I shall be coming in at about two. I'll be sure not to disturb you."

"Disturb me, the way I sleep?" she laughed. "Not likely. But before I go to bed, I'll leave some tea and biscuits for you."

"Thank you, Mrs. Crosse, but the Army-Navy Club sets a table that is almost as delectable as your own. I'm sure that my brother and I will be quite bursting at the seams by the time we return. Still . . ."

"Ah, that one," she said with a disapproving frown. "There's no meat on him at all. Skin and bones he is and that's all. I'd like to have him live here for a month. I'd get him to look healthy quick enough."

I chuckled at the thought of Sherlock being forced to eat. Mrs. Crosse would have to tie him to his chair. But it was now time that I leave. The morning was brisk and clear. The snows of the past few days had turned to slush. The bracing atmosphere cheered me so much that even Griffin's unusually dolourous countenance was unable to lessen my enthusiasm.

"What's the matter, Griffin? You look as though . . . ah, but I have it. Your wife went against you and took in the boarder after all."

"A good wife is hard to find and that's a fact, sir. But how . . ."

"Simple enough. Your boots aren't blacked up to their usual sheen and you've cut your face in no less than four places while shaving. Your suit isn't brushed and you've neglected to pomade your hair. Obviously your wife is not speaking to you, let alone making, your clothing presentable this morning. You must have left the house in great haste. The row was a frightful one last night, eh?"

"Indeed, sir. But how did you know . . ."

"You mentioned the possibility of a dispute last week. I merely applied that knowledge to the present state of your untidiness."

"You're a blooming wonder, sir."

"Thank you, Griffin. I suggest that peace of mind will come only after you put your foot down and explain the matter to your wife. Having a boarder sharing your home will take away the privacy you value so highly."

"That's it precisely, Mr. Holmes."

"Well, surely a man of your skills can make the situation clear to your good wife?"

Griffin's face grew longer. "You've not met the missus, Mr. Holmes. It will take more strategy than that to make her see the light." He turned to go.

"Oh," he said as he was almost out the door. "I forgot. His Nibs himself left you a note; it's on the desk."

"Mr. Moriarty's here this early? Why he's only been in once before nine that I can recall."

"He's still only been in once before nine. He left it last evening before he went home."

"Humm. Working late. Most unusual."

With that, Griffin resumed his official impassivity and left my office. My habit of being familiar with subordinates had more than once earned me a disapproving lecture on the subject from Mr. Moriarty, but I found it satisfying to have those in the lower echelons friendly. Griffin and I were both careful to respect the proprieties, never overstepping the boundaries of station. But early on, we agreed that we might just as well be cordial than not, and it had turned into a stimulating friendship.

Moriarty's note had evidently been written after some drinking. The penmanship was less disciplined than was his usual style.

Holmes [the note read]:
Be sure to have Ames send invitations to the Admiralty Ball to the Langham. Captain Ravenswood and

his party are to be in attendance. I may be late tomorrow morning.

J.M.

I had Griffin summon the messenger to Moriarty's secretary with instructions to take the invitations to the Langham.
I then busied myself with the remainder of the day's work
and spent time in the various tasks of my office, none of
which concern this narrative.

It wasn't until after luncheon that Griffin entered my
office with the mail from the first post of the afternoon*
to break my routine. There were two messages. Mr. Moriarty sent me word that he would not be coming in that day,
which was hardly surprising, and Sherlock sent a curious
wire:

MYCROFT:
THERE IS SOMETHING DEFINITELY AFOOT. CANNOT AC-
COMPANY YOU TO ADMIRALTY BALL. WILL BE IN TOUCH
LATER. ENJOY YOURSELF TONIGHT ANYWAY.

SHERLOCK

After I had moved heaven and earth to get him an invitation! After all the trouble I had taken to be sure that
there would be some well-placed acquaintances disposed to
see him! I was livid. Such cavalier ingratitude! I attempted
to continue working but the incident clouded my thoughts,
as the clarity of the morning gave way to a midday overcast. Finally, I gave up all pretense of work and left the
office, with nothing but the most curt nod to the mystified
Griffin.

A yellow fog swirled past the window pane, as the cab
approached St. Chad's Street. The leaden air matched
my mood. It was not until long after dressing that my usual
equanimity returned as I anticipated the Admiralty Ball.

The line of carriages approaching the Army-Navy Club
inched along. I had taken a hansom and I could hear my

---

* Those of us now burdened with the incredibly inefficient postal
system of the modern era might look in wonder at the mail deliveries of a more attentive age, when the postman came around eight
times daily. There was a hue and cry from London's populace when
the service was cut to only six daily deliveries. MH/SMW

driver hurling curses through the roof at me. I was no doubt stealing time from him which he could have put to better use finding other fares. I caught sight of Lord and Lady Tarleton, who had apparently decided to send their coach home, braving the heavy, wet fog while they walked the last four blocks. I was in no hurry to rush out to greet them; Lord Tarleton was one of those whom I had asked to meet my brother tonight, with the idea that a position might be found within his lordship's large banking concern.*

After some minutes, we had proceeded no more than thirty feet, so I clambered out of the hansom, paid my fare (to the driver's great relief), and walked the rest of the way alone.

The Army-Navy Club, an imposing architecture, was resplendent this evening. High above the dining room, lit by the spectacularly cut crystal chandeliers, the walls fairly bristled with the arms and armour of mediæval England Interspersed among the regimental colours and drums were pictorial representations, executed with exacting detail, of fighting ships from those of the galleons of Frobisher and Ralegh,** fighting ships which included Drake's *The Golden Hinde* and the more recent four-deckers of Nelson and Hornblower. These were hung cheek by jowl with Ashanti javelins, "Dane guns," and the curved swords and matchlocks of the Afghan frontier.

Every senior officer who could inveigle his way into London for the event was there, as were some of the junior officers who had influential friends or who were marked for advancement. Almost, but not all, were accompanied by their ladies. I believe it could be safely said that no other quarter in the domain could boast the same aggregation of beauty which was present at the Army-Navy Club on that evening. The flowers alone created an air of sumptuousness, for many of the varieties were out of

* It is mere speculation, of course, but one cannot help but wonder if this Lord and Lady Tarleton might have met Sherlock later in a professional way, for Holmes mentioned to Dr. Watson that among the cases he had handled before he met the doctor was "the record of the Tarleton murders." The reference will be found in "The Musgrave Ritual," one of the stories in *The Memoirs of Sherlock Holmes*. MH/SMW

** Mycroft is not in error. Sir Walter preferred his surname to be spelled "Ralegh." MH/SMW

season. Indeed, the tropical flowers had been hothouse grown, especially for this evening. The profusion of orchids and roses, chrysanthemums, dahlias, and all the others were enough to steal away the breath from even the most jaded of the evening's guests.

A blare of trumpets announced the arrival of a party sufficiently well placed to merit the fanfare. There was some dodging of ceremonial swords and sabres as viscounts, admirals, dukes, and baronets rubbed shoulders with colonels, majors, generals, captains, and even an occasional lieutenant.

The guests were announced by a grizzled veteran as they made their way through the foyer and into the grand hall. Waiters circumspectly travelled amid the throng and I could see that their trays bearing champagne and other *apéritifs* were routinely emptied within fifty feet of their place of origin.

I entered and spent some few minutes circulating about the hall. I hoped to find Mr. Moriarty and the Southerners before all were hastened to the dining tables. My search was to no avail, however. They had not as yet arrived.

While the entire retinue of servants began patiently, yet prudently, to nurse the assemblage into their places at the magnificently set and ornamented tables, I took a stand behind a potted palm in the corner. It commanded a view of the entrance from the foyer so I might see the Americans as they entered.

I had just exchanged an empty goblet for a full one when I heard a voice hailing me: "Holmes! I say, Mycroft Holmes! Halloo!"

An elderly, white-haired man, bearing the insignia of a KCB propelled himself through the concourse. A strikingly beautiful young lady clung to his arm. She was having a little difficulty with her gown as she tried to keep up with him. The crowd was thick and the elderly man quite short in stature. But his bulldog manner gained him eventual headway or the obstacle was pushed aside, bodily. The aged knight was Sir Rodney Stevain Ploveson Fairndails, to to give his full name, a friend of my father.

"It's very good to see you, Sir Rodney," I said, as he liberated another glass of wine from a passing tray. He introduced his guest as he sipped.

"This is Miss Arabella Fitzwalter. M'dear, this is Mr. Mycroft Holmes, son of an old friend. Earned him a place in the Foreign Office, what, some five years ago, in'nit?"

"That's correct, Sir Rodney."

"Yes, of course. Work under that old ramrod, Jerrold Moriarty, what?"

I nodded. The noise of the multitude was building. Sir Rodney was nearly shouting as he continued the conversation.

"I was minded of you last evening, Holmes, when I received a wire from that old barley-brain, Moriarty."

I pricked up my ears. "A wire?"

"Yes, yes, of course. Damme but he's an odd duck. Wired me at Portsmouth last night. Something about a game of pocket billiards. Hah! Pocket billiards, would you believe. As though I'd allow that old biscuit-dome to drag me away from the charms of Miss Fitzwalter, here." He chuckled. "But then I made the mistake of telling Arabella about the wire and she thought the ball would be a good place to show off her new gown. Live and learn, eh, young man; live and learn."

He left off chuckling abruptly and fixed me with a gaze that has rendered junior officers mute with terror. "What does that mean, 'pocket billiards'? Has old Jerry gone dotty?"

"I've noticed nothing out of the ordinary, sir."

Sir Rodney relented. "Of course, pardon me for m'bad manners. It's just that Old Tar-belly has distressing timing. I wouldn't have come to this candle-waster but for Arabella. I was in the midst of the armaments supply for the ruddy fleet, checking on the ordnance and wallowing in cannon, rockets, and torpedoes last night. I have to finish up the report, you know. If Lord Wellesley hasn't looked at it by Wednesday next, he'll have my guts for garters." He turned to Miss Fitzwalter. "Begging your pardon, my dear." She giggled.

He took another sip of wine and drained his glass. Giving me a wave, he and Miss Fitzwalter made off toward a servant carrying another tray laden with full glasses, disappearing into the bright ribbands of the company.

It was very soon after this episode that the Americans arrived in the company of Jerrold Moriarty and two of his three sons. It may be indicative of my superior's level of imagination that all his sons were named James. How they sorted out the post-bag at home, I can only conjecture.

Of the two brothers in attendance this evening, Moriarty major was a professor at one of the less distinguished universities hereabout, while Moriarty minor was an army lieutenant who was present, I suspected, only because of his father's position. I did not know the lady he escorted, but his brother, the professor, seemed bent on social ostracism. He was escorting the French Creole woman whose presence in his company had caused quite a stir at Ascot earlier this year. Rumour had it that she was a quadroon.*

All the men in the Moriarty company, save the Lieutenant,** were dressed in tailcoats, as was I. But we were practically lost within all the scarlet, buff, blue and other hues of the regiments worn by the veterans. Taken with the tints and tinctures of the evening gowns worn by the women, the profusion of colour was almost too gorgeous to behold for any length of time. The knot of sombre black was a welcome relief.

The Americans stood in stiff discomfort, appraising their surroundings. Only the beautiful Rachel Leland was at ease in this milieu. I supposed that she would be unruffled in any similar circumstance. She wore an emerald-green gown, mantled in gossamer lace, a sable muff hanging from her arm. Her creamy *décolletage* was sure to gain her the enmity of every lady present, and the attention of every gentleman.

I caught Mr. Moriarty's eye and ploughed through the assembled multitude.

"Evening, Holmes," said Mr. Moriarty, with great affability. His thin hair was plastered down on his great forehead. "Wonderful evening, isn't it? You know the members of the Alabama delegation, and my sons?"

* This revelation bears out research made by a member of the Baker Street Irregulars, the late James Montgomery, in his monograph "Chip Off The Old Block?" as noted by the late William S. Baring-Gould in *The Annotated Sherlock Holmes* 2:304. MH/SMW

** The young Lieutenant James Moriarty, it can only be assumed, is the same James Moriarty who, as a colonel, wrote the "scurrilous letters" to the newspapers which forced Dr. Watson to write the true incidents of the Holmes-Moriarty struggle, as related in "The Final Problem" found in *The Memoirs of Sherlock Holmes*. MH/SMW

"Of course. How do you do? I'm terribly sorry that Colonel Leland was not able to attend."

"The doctor thought it would be advisable that my uncle remain undisturbed for the present," responded William Bankhead.

"I trust he will soon be well."

Bankhead made to respond, but his words were drowned in the booming voice of Sir Rodney, as he and Miss Fitzwalter burst through the crowd.

"Ho there, Moriarty, I say, *hello!*"

"Ah, Sir Rodney," Moriarty called back with his affected *bonhommie*. "What a delight to see you. I'm glad you received my message, and could attend at such short notice."

Once more, he made the introductions, concluding with ". . . and this is Sir Rodney Stevain . . ."

"Oh hang it all, Moriarty," Sir Rodney burst in. "They'll never remember it all, anyway." He turned to Miss Leland and smiled as he took up her hand to kiss.

"How'ja do, m'dear. Sir Rodney Fairndails, at your service." The little knight was at least a foot shorter than the lady and the scene would have been a trifle comic had not Miss Leland accepted his attention with complete serenity.

As this was happening, however, I noticed a look of petulance cross the sparkling, if somewhat vapid, brow of Miss Arabella Fitzwalter. After a moment's indecision, she dropped her own fan with a small startled cry. All the gentlemen in our group, excepting Sir Rodney and Captain Ravenswood, made an immediate dash for the fallen accessory. Carteret, having retrieved it, was rewarded with the glowing beneficence of Miss Fitzwalter's gracious smile. I managed to control my own amusement, but only with an effort.

Women in battle are not to be made light of in public. If ever Sherlock got back into my good graces, I'd tell him about the incident. Damn him for not coming!

Carteret now rejoined his companions, beaming from ear to ear, as Sir Rodney said to Mr. Moriarty, "Well now, Stinky, what's all this talk about a billiards match? I don't mind telling you that I was damned busy. Wasn't thinking about attending this *soirée* at all, you know, eh, what? Damned busy."

"I can well understand that, sir," said Moriarty smoothly. He turned to Ravenswood. "You know Sir Rodney is the fleet armoury officer, a position of grave responsibility."

"Grave enough not to drop my duties just to run up to London at every beckoning, I daresay," snapped the old man.

Mr. Moriarty went pale around the gills for an instant but gracefully recovered. "Yes, of course, Sir Rodney. But this will prove to be a game of high drama, one I know you would not want to miss." His eyes then darted toward me, but I took care to look absorbed in the study of the regimental colours of the Fifth Northumberland Fusiliers* hanging from the wall opposite. Captain Ravenswood suavely moved in to fill the gap.

"Pocket billiards is a game that I have found highly stimulating. I understand that there are one or two officers here tonight who possess a familiarity with the cue stick. I have even been led to believe that some of your compatriots have been known to wager upon the outcome of such a game."

Sir Rodney rose to the bait. "Yes, indeed they have. And they have been known to win. I know of a man present at this very ball in whom I would have the greatest confidence, eh, what?"

Ravenswood smiled wolfishly. "As a former officer in the service of my own country, I might be willing to accept such a challenge."

"Quite so, gentlemen," said Moriarty in an attempt to repair the breach. "Sometime soon, we may be able to have the Captain demonstrate his skill."

"What's wrong with tonight, eh? You invited us to a game of billiards. What about we have done with this colonial's boasting this night? I'm sure that Major Eggleston of the Guards will be happy to demonstrate his skill."

"Ah, yes," said Moriarty, hoping to regain control of the situation. "He is reputed to be excellent with a billiard cue, but this is hardly the time . . ."

---

* The Fifth Northumberland Fusiliers was the very same regiment to which Dr. Watson was attached following his course as a military surgeon, as he related in *A Study in Scarlet*. MH/SMW

"If he is as excellent as you say, Mr. Moriarty, I should be foolish to pass up the opportunity of meeting him. I might even learn a few tricks from him that I didn't know before," said Ravenswood, his hard, dark eyes blazing with unaccustomed amusement.

"Yes, but . . ."

"Then you accept the challenge, Captain Ravenswood?" asked Sir Rodney.

"It would be an insult to honour if I did not."

Sir Rodney smiled his bulldog smile. "Then it is done."

"And done," answered the portly Southerner, with a curt bow.

They shook hands and arrangements were made for after dinner. Sir Rodney left us, chirruping, to ferret out Major Eggleston. I then took charge of the matter of finding our places for the meal. This was not difficult for as yet less than half of the attendees were seated, much to the annoyance of the major-domo and his minions who had been struggling to accomplish this feat since first I entered.

As we made our way to the table, Mr. Moriarty stopped every so often to speak to this officer or that and a select civilian or two. The conversations lasted but a few moments each time, invariably concluding with a nod from the person met, followed by a glance at the ceiling, above which were the gaming rooms of the Army-Navy Club. I made no move to eavesdrop in these talks as the content was obvious. What was not so obvious was the reason behind Mr. Moriarty's sending telegrams to Sir Rodney as well as the gentlemen and officers with whom he stopped to chat. The pattern grew with each man he met. I recognised the individuals who were being sought out by Mr. Moriarty. Each of them was well placed in various departments within the ministries, yet none was in complete charge of any one department.

It then became clear to me. The telegrams had gone out to these subordinate department heads to meet in the gaming room; the pocket-billiards match was originally a ruse, or a code word. It was, at least until Sir Rodney brought the match into actuality. I chuckled. Mr. Moriarty had not counted on Sir Rodney's single-mindedness. He had only chosen that term as a code by which the Americans might meet with his friends and allies so as to lay out their plans.

Whatever was to be hatched at this affair had certainly not begun in the mind of my superior. The portly Captain Ravenswood had almost certainly suggested the strategem. What was really interesting was that the Americans had chosen Jerrold Moriarty to aid them. He was hardly the man to plan a *coup d'état,* but he certainly knew the right people to abet one.

Not having brought a partner, I took my place at the foot of one of the long tables. Little more than half of the guests had as yet been seated. I had Bankhead on my left and a retired lord of the Admiralty and his wife to my right. Making inconsequential small talk with my neighbors—his Lordship still thought that the steam engine was a passing fancy—I managed to appear the dutiful young diplomat. Yet the pose did not restrain me from paying close heed to the looks and gestures of Moriarty and Ravenswood. And to those of the enchanting Rachel Leland.

I was surprised at my reaction to Miss Leland this evening. She had not particularly impressed me during her visit to my office, although she had proved that she could rise to a situation on the night of the attack upon her father. Yet now I found myself gazing down the table to where she sat and allowing my gaze to linger. It was most disturbing.

Within a few minutes of our being seated, dinner was announced and a general commotion ensued as the remaining guests were seated. The meal itself, a compliment to a man of my tastes, proved uneventful, although there was a minor disturbance when a clumsy servant managed to pour wine into my custard. He murmured his apologies; I graciously brushed them aside. I looked up—and saw that I was being served by Sherlock!

He wore the proper livery, a large walrus moustache, slicked-down hair, and a bulbous nose. His apologetic demeanour was a masterpiece of underacting. But behind the *façade* were the steel-gray eyes of my brother, one of which fleetingly winked at me.

He called for a waiter to serve me another sweet, and then withdrew to continue pouring for the others at the table.

Thus did the meal come to a conclusion. The ladies separated from the gentlemen, trooping upstairs to repair their complexions and gowns from the ravages of dinner.

While a few of the gentlemen brandished after-dinner pipes, most of the assemblage awaited the cigars that were a speciality of the Army-Navy Club. The cigars were truly worth the wait, for they were made from a blend of finely-aged Djebel and Basibali tobaccos, skillfully cut with a brandy-cured Kentucky white Burley to retard the fast-burning Turkish tobaccos. I prided myself on being able to distinguish the difference between *yaka* and *ova* blends and was gratified to find that tonight's paradigm of the tobacconist's art was harvested in the Turkish uplands and therefore of the *yaka* variety.

The aroma of the rising smoke was filling the room before I caught my brother's eye. He dutifully responded to my silent summons. Standing by, he proffered me a cigar and then lit it with a vesta, bending low to do so.

"Meet me in the far corner under the Saxon shield five minutes after the port is served," he whispered. I imperceptibly nodded and blew a smoke ring in his face. He bowed stoically but I noticed with some satisfaction that his eyes watered. He blinked several times as he continued his ministrations to the others along the table.

The location he specified was to the rear of the dining hall and behind the Americans and Moriarty *père et fils*. It was no trouble to excuse myself and manœuvre to the corner as Sherlock finished his rounds with an almost empty decanter. He poured me a glass.

"What does all this mean?" I asked with some asperity.

"No details now," he answered. "The ladies will be returning soon."

"Now see here, Sherlock . . ."

"If you've been observant, you've seen as much as I," he said. "I hope to discover more while you observe the proprieties. By all means try to get into the gaming room after the ladies return."

With that he took his leave and I had no choice but to rejoin my party, still mystified by my brother's actions. And yet, his whole manner, melodramatic as it was, heightened my own sense of anticipation. Something was to take place this evening that could have earth-shaking consequences as I well knew.

I returned to the table as Sir Rodney and Major Herbert Eggleston presented themselves to Mr. Moriarty and Captain Ravenswood.

"Ah, hullo, Holmes," was Mr. Moriarty's unenthusiastic greeting.

"I thought to be of some service, sir."

"Thank you, but I don't believe you need trouble . . ."

"Wait a moment, Stinky," Sir Rodney interrupted. "What do you know about fourteen one-rack, Mycroft?"

"A game of pocket-billiards played with fourteen rather than the usual fifteen balls. The space for the single ball in the front of the rack is left vacant for the break. Points are scored by sinking the balls into the pockets, one point per ball. The game is usually played for three hundred points. An expert can run the table." I turned to Mr. Moriarty. "That is, should he hit every one of the three hundred balls in each of the twenty-one and a half rounds necessary to accomplish this feat, the game might take a minimum of three hours and thirty-three minutes. It could last more than twenty-one hours, under ordinary circumstances."

"But that's far too long!" Mr. Moriarty exclaimed.

"I might suggest a fifty-point game that would take less than one and one-half hours," I offered.

The parties accepted.

"I now suggest that we appoint an impartial marker to arbitrate the game," said Sir Rodney. "And because of his already proven expertise, I propose Mr. Mycroft Holmes."

Captain Ravenswood bristled and Moriarty began to stammer an objection.

"Now look here, Stinky, I refuse to take no for an answer. You and I both know that Holmes here is an honourable gentleman." He looked up to Captain Ravenswood's scowl. "I trust the Americans have no objection to him?" he said with a meaningful scowl.

I knew that the Captain would not risk the outcome of his larger plan on so niggling a point. But it took him a moment to shrug and say that it made no difference to him. I certainly did not relish the role; I would rather have remained an inconsequential bystander. It was apparent to me, however, that I had been excluded from the original plan by the American. Since there seemed no other way for me to learn what I could about the further plans that might be developed, I accepted.

"I hope that I might be invited to witness this event, too," came Rachel Leland's soft Southern drawl over the hubbub of the room.

"Of course, you may, m'dear," said the chivalrous Sir Rodney. "A lady is always welcome at these endeavours." He continued, turning to Captain Ravenswood. "So long as the Empire is equally represented."

The American nodded.

"Good!" Sir Rodney said happily. "I submit that Miss Arabella Fitzwalter be nominated." There were no objections and we proceeded to the upstairs gaming room. For those not familiar with the Army-Navy Club's interior, it might help to briefly describe the area to which we were adjourning.

It was a corner room, panelled in dark oak, about fifty feet square. Two large leaded-glass windows in the north and east walls opened into the room. A large fireplace, surrounded and surmounted by a carved Carrara marble mantlepiece, occupied most of the west wall, and the door in the southwest corner was screened from within so that the idle passersby might not intrude upon a game in play. A low platform was raised along the north and east walls, directly beneath the windows already mentioned. On the platform were built benches, upholstered with long, dark brown, leather-covered cushions and backs to accommodate a gallery in comfort.

The marker's place was simply a small, square platform set against the south wall, enclosed with a wrought-iron railing. Above it was a blackboard for scoring games. Along that same wall, in the southeast corner and beneath a petite oriel window, was a small writing table and chair. These areas commanded an unobstructed view of the table in play.

The billiard table was bolted into the floor in the very centre of the room. It was one of the very best examples of art and sport intermixed. The beautiful legs were of massive oak and carved with the heads of gargoyles and serpents amid foliage, done in very fine detail. The table was of a design so that either billiards or pocket billiards might be played on it, when small slats were taken out of the sides. The corner and sections of the side kerb, also removable, were made to reveal the leather-mesh pockets with their own kerbs. The rubber cushions and the playing field itself were covered with regulation blue felt, and two small smoothed-over putty "spots" were incorporated into the cloth. There were various baulk lines drawn on the cloth with pipeclay and these had to be brushed off before we could begin play. While the attendants were doing so, Eggleston and Ravenswood chose their respective cues from the rack hanging alongside the marker's stand.

The room was planned so that the fireplace was at the foot of the table, behind the players as they would break. The flickering firelight would therefore not become a serious distraction as the players shot. Four mineral-oil lamps were suspended above the field, their shields highly polished so that shadows would not interfere with the play.

The attendants had readied the table and set the triangular rack on it. As they placed the balls within, a servant entered to see to the liquid needs of the spectators. It was my brother. His gall stupified me and I prayed that none of the Americans would see through his disguise.

My attention was brought back to the rivals now lagging for break. The young major's ball returned the closest and he retired to watch the Captain's opening.

"Captain Ravenswood to break," I announced. One of the attendants stood beside me, ready to mark a score in either of the two columns labelled with the names of the contenders. Another sat at the writing table with pencil and paper to keep a check-score.

The Captain was given to flourishing his cue-stick, making constant back-and-forth motions with it as he drew a bead on his quarry, the cue ball. His shot was true, hitting slightly to the left of centre. The balls careened about the table, but none entered a pocket. Sir Rodney smiled.

"No score. Major Eggleston's shot," I called. The Major took careful aim at the fourteen-ball. He made a forcing shot, meant to get past the ten-ball which was a slight obstruction. There was too much screwback to the cue ball and so it was deflected by the ten-ball.

"No score. Captain Ravenswood's shot."

The Captain shot and hit the seven-ball and then the

twelve-ball into the side- and upper-left corner pockets. On the next shot, he missed the fourteen-ball.

"Two points for Captain Ravenswood. Major Eggleston to shoot." The Major's next shot was true and slightly to the left of the centre of the three-ball, the Major using what is called a "half-ball" stroke. Sir Rodney applauded vigorously. Eggleston missed his next attempt, a two-cushion bank shot at the eleven-ball.

And so the play continued. At the risk of incurring the charge of repetition and making an exciting game merely a detailed description of strokes and stances, I will summarise the remainder.

The two men battled back and forth around the table, constantly searching for the best shot. The Major was showing good form, but the American was like a dæmon as he sunk his shots with theatrical, though accurate, strokes. The Major was slow and methodical. He seldom tried for the difficult combination shots, whereas the Captain constantly attempted them.

The balls were racked at the start of the second game and racked another four times. At the conclusion of the sixth game, the score for the Captain was forty-one points, for the Major, forty-three. The seventh round would doubtless be decisive.

The Major made the break. Two balls were knocked into the upper-left corner. He then knocked another ball into the side pocket. He shot again and missed.

Captain Ravenswood dropped in a ball and missed his next shot. The score stood at forty-two for the Captain to forty-six for the Major.

Having a four-point lead, the Major became careless. He attempted a three-cushion bank shot to put the three-ball into the side pocket. He missed. Captain Ravenswood took advantage of the situation by striking two balls home. He shot again and missed.

Eggleston surveyed the table and sank the eleven-ball. It was now forty-four to forty-seven, Eggleston's favour. He next tried for the thirteen-ball, resting on the cushion between the lower-right corner and right side pockets. He banked it into the side pocket opposite. There was applause from the gallery. Overconfident, the Major attempted another bank shot and missed. The play passed to the Captain.

Ravenswood made his next shot, a combination. Both balls were dropped. He made three successive shots, before missing the five-ball.

"Captain Ravenswood, forty-nine points, Major Eggleston, forty-eight. Major Eggleston's shot."

There were but two balls left on the table: the eight- and the five-balls. The Major sent the five-ball the length of the table; it struck the upper cushion, returning to the lower part of the table, where it went into the right corner. The Major had tied his opponent.

With only the eight-ball remaining on the table, the Major regained his poise. He took careful aim. He slowly walked about the table, this way and that, looking for a way in which to make the next shot. His difficulty was that the ball rested between the cue ball and the cushion of the lower part of the table on the right side. It almost touched both of the objects it lay between. The Major had no shot at all. He might have tried for the opposite corner, but, after considering the odds, he refrained from that attempt. He might place the balls in too good a position. Instead, the Major called out a "safe" shot, meaning that he would not attempt to hit the ball into a pocket, forcing Captain Ravenswood to try it. He gave the cue ball a light tap. The blow brought the cue ball even closer to the eight-ball, so that they were almost touching, making the shot that much more difficult.

The Major retreated with a small smile as Ravenswood took in the situation. We had all become aware of the betting going on between the men in the gallery. Sir Rodney was acting the bookmaker to all these governmental figures and was chortling still from Major Eggleston's last score. For these men, the amounts were not too exacting, but the sums would have been beyond my means nonetheless. Bankhead and Carteret were tensely watching Ravenswood's every movement as he walked this way and that around the table.

The Captain took his time. He walked around the table slowly. His earlier bravura had passed and he was intent on the shot.

"Eight into the corner," he called out at last, indicating the lower left with his stick. "With two banks."

Eyebrows were raised around the room, not the least of which were those belonging to Sir Rodney. Everyone leaned forward in his place, as Ravenswood took his stance at the left of the table. He hit his cue into the downward side of the eight-ball. As he said, it banked twice, on the right cushion and onto the left, before sinking into the lower-left corner pocket.

There was a measurable silence before the room exploded into cheers and applause. The Major shook the American's hand as he had at the start. There was no need for me to announce the winner. Nor could I have been heard had I tried to do so.

Sherlock had taken pains to make himself unobtrusive while taking in as much of the game as possible amid his various duties as a waiter. The Americans had taken no notice of him, nor had Sir Rodney, who had known him as a youth, but who had not seen him for many years. I was still at a loss to explain his presence here at all. It had been a very neat trick to gain admittance. The few suppositions I had made were not able to answer all the circumstances. While bets were being collected and the winners were clapping Ravenswood's back, asking about his individual shots, Sherlock blithely walked over to the marker's stand.

"Don't worry," he said. "They'll be thinking that I'm asking you about further service."

"If no one has recognised you."

"Not to worry. No one is more invisible than a liveried servant." He made a slight motion with his head toward the gallery. "Sir Rodney certainly took a beating."

I looked at the old warhorse. His pained expression was sufficient corroboration of my brother's remark. "I'm sure that Moriarty means to make it up to him with the plans they'll be discussing later," I said.

"Then Moriarty told you?" Sherlock asked in surprise.

"No. I've only deduced that detail after looking over the guest list of witnesses here, Sir Rodney among them. There's a man here from each department whose good offices would be necessary for the success of the Americans' plans. I shouldn't be here at all, but Sir Rodney insisted."

"I see." Sherlock looked thoughtful. "They'll be asking you to leave on some pretext or other."

"You may count on it."

He looked up at me. "Then don't hesitate to leave when they ask."

"I may be able to have Sir Rodney keep me around."

"No, don't. The Americans are not very sympathetic to your continued presence. But don't worry; I'll be here."

"You think that they'll talk in front of servants?"

"They have no reason not to. It's all part of my plan."

I had no time to ask what his plan involved, for we saw Moriarty and Ravenswood conferring, Moriarty giving a brief glance in our direction.

"All right then, Sherlock. But for God's sake, be careful!"

I saw Moriarty and Ravenswood make a movement toward us. I gave Sherlock a nod and he withdrew.

"The servants would like to know if they should remain," I told the conspirators when they came within earshot. "Do you or any of the men wish to stay for a drink and a chat before returning to the dance?"

"Yes," said Moriarty. "I think that would be in order."

"In the meanwhile," said Ravenswood, with an uncomfortable smile, "I want to congratulate your calls. They were well done." I thanked him. "My friends and I shall be staying here to speak with Mr. Moriarty and I would be obliged to you if you would escort Miss Leland to the ballroom so that she may enjoy the remainder of the dancing."

So I was to be excluded from the meeting after all.

"I would be most honoured."

I thought I might also have to escort Miss Fitzwalter to the ballroom, but Sir Rodney refused to listen to any of Mr. Moriarty's importunities. He had lost his wagers, of course, and he said that he intended to enjoy the rest of the evening in the company of his beautiful partner. To say that this news was devastating to Mr. Moriarty would be an understatement. Sir Rodney would be of vast importance to the plans of the Americans. But they could do nothing else but watch as he left the gaming room with his companion. We followed them.

The dancing was in full sway as we entered the ballroom. The orchestra was in the midst of a waltz; the glittering couples made graceful patterns about the magnificent chamber. Their colours were made even more brilliant than before by the mirrored south wall and the majestic crystal chandeliers which magnified the opulence of the costumes into a glorious kaleidoscope.

Sir Rodney and Miss Fitzwalter had been caught up in the dance, but Miss Leland and I stood in a corner near the fireplace. A few moments passed before either of us spoke.

"I'm sorry you've been left to carry on alone with me for the rest of the evening," said Rachel Leland, looking at me with the same coquettishness she had demonstrated during the interview in my office.

"I wish that all my duties were so tiresome," I responded.

"Why, Mr. Holmes," she smiled, waving her fan coyly, "aren't you gallant."

I smiled. The waltz ended and was soon succeeded by a fiery mazurka. We remained in silence.

"May I bring you an ice?" I finally asked.

"I'd like that very much, Mr. Holmes. Thank you."

I left her seated in one of the red plush chairs in the corner and soon returned with a silver punch-cup filled with the softly frozen *sorbet*. After accepting the little silver spoon I handed her, she looked at it, exclaiming, "What beautiful tracery. I do wish we could get such fine silver back home."

"I am recalled that your patriot, Paul Revere, was a silversmith of no little merit," said I.

"Oh yes," she returned with a laugh. "So he was. But we don't talk much about him."

"Oh?"

"No; he was a Yankee."

We both laughed.

But the silence continued as she ate. The entire *sorbet* was gone before Miss Leland attempted another sally.

"Do you often attend such elegant parties?" she set the punch-cup on a little side-table and gestured at the graceful saltations of the dancers.

"No, hardly ever, in fact. I usually find them tedious. More often than not, I have business to complete in any case. Dispatches, reports . . ."

"It all sounds very important," she interjected, then dropped her eyes. "But very boring," she added frankly.

"Well, I shouldn't say that. My work in the Foreign Office is very important, sometimes crucial . . ."

"Would I be presumptuous if I asked you to dance with me, Mr. Holmes?"

I was about to make an excuse, but there was something in her manner that told me she would suffer no excuses.

"I would not think you forward, and I will be happy to dance with you."

I took her in my arms and we joined the resplendent company. The rich emblazonings became a blur. We lost ourselves in the swirling movements of the waltz as we danced upon the parquet floor.

"I simply cannot understand your hesitancy, Mr. Holmes," said Rachel Leland above the music. "You dance wonderfully."

"It's been a very long time," I replied into the air. "My father insisted that my brother and I learn. 'You never know when you'll have a use for it; besides, all gentlemen should know how to dance. It's expected of us,' he said. Well, right there and then, Sherlock and I determined never to become gentlemen. We were both of one accord."

She laughed and we whirled and flew with a grace and design which I was unaware I possessed. After some minutes, the music ended and we joined in the applause.

"I don't know how long I can keep up with you, Mr. Holmes," she gasped joyously, "but I simply must take a rest. Allow me to say that you are a marvel," she continued, as we left the floor. "Trying to make me believe that you're nothing but a wallflower. I'm sure that you've broken more hearts than you care to admit."

I blushed at her suggestion. "I have broken no hearts nor am I likely to."

"Dear me," was all she said for a while. When she spoke again she said, "Would you find me too demanding if I suggested that we catch our breath in the garden?" She pointed to the open French window. I agreed and she locked her arm within mine.

The heavy mist had lifted and the moon's radiance could

be perceived behind a thin layer of cloud. Every so often, the stratus would part to reveal one star or another. The air was invigorating and crisp after our cavortings and we luxuriated in its briskness.

The flowers were long vanished because of the early snow, but I imagined that I was wrapped in their fragrance. I explained it to myself as the bouquet of her perfume, but the feeling persisted.

There was a large garden beneath the portico upon which we stood, hands on its railing, watching the swiftly moving night sky and all the luminously outlined shapes taken by the clouds.

"I'm glad I brought my muff along," said she. "At least my hands are warm."

"If it's too cold we can . . ."

"Oh, no, I didn't mean . . . Oh, look!" She removed her hand from the muff and pointed a gloved finger skyward. "There! That's Dubhe. Let's see, where's Merak?" She searched the firmament for the other pointer star. "There it is. Now, six times their length—Polaris!"

I followed her finger to the North Star, for centuries the guide of mariners and all wayfaring men.

"I had an old Irish tutor," I said in the soft voice of remembrance. "He taught me the names of the stars in Gaelic. Some of which, I believe, were his own invention." I smiled diffidently. "I was always fascinated with the name he gave Merak. 'Cumhyll' he called it."

"Cumhyll," she repeated. "Does that have any special meaning?"

"Almost all names in Gaelic mean something. 'Cumhyll' means 'proud-walking' or 'life-leaper,' as he explained it." And as we looked at the star, occasionally blotted out by cloudy wisps, it twinkled and danced, giving veracity to my old tutor's explanation.

We watched in silence, a Strauss waltz welling up behind us. I saw her long, golden ringlets blaze with the ballroom's reflected radiance as her delicate veiling brushed the *boutonnière* in my lapel.

"I'm surprised that such a talented man isn't married," she said at last.

"I may be. How could you know otherwise?"

"Then where is your wife?" laughed Rachel Leland. "I cannot imagine that you would keep her away from this marvellous ball. Besides, one look at your necktie would tell any woman."

"My necktie?"

She laughed again. "It's always crooked." Her gloved hand brushed my chin as she reached under my collar to centre the tie. "I have been wanting to do that since I first met you."

She brought her hand down and we again turned to the garden below us. Her gloved hand stole into mine and once more, we regarded the stars.

"May I ask you to take me home, please, Mr. Holmes?" she said at last.

I was startled. "Miss Leland, your fiancé . . . ?"

"My fiancé," she said bitterly, "won't care in the least. In his eyes, I'm little more than a horse he's purchased, or a trophy he's won. Something to be admired, to be displayed; something to enhance his prestige. The fact that I breathe or think is immaterial to him. He frightens me, Mr. Holmes, he truly does."

She turned from me and took a few steps to the farther end of the veranda. In a voice little louder than a whisper, I heard her speak with an agonizing plaintiveness: "Dear God, release me from this life. I want to be free again, if only for a little while."

I was shocked and embarrassed to have been privy to so private a moment. I felt like an awkward youth, unable to do anything for this beautiful woman and frustrated at my helplessness.

Miss Leland pulled a handkerchief from the sable muff still draped on her arm and dabbed at her eyes.

"Will you escort me home?" she said, turning back to me.

"But surely Captain Ravenswood . . ."

"Never mind him, I say," Her eyes blazed. "Never mind any of them. They're all too busy to care about what I do. Please have no fear for me. I'll find an excuse for him later. A headache or something. Just please, please take me home!" The fire subsided and she was, once again, merely a beautiful woman. But a woman for whom I was beginning to feel compassion and, perhaps, even love.*

The carriage ride from the Army-Navy Club to the Langham is not a long one, but on that night so long ago, it lasted an eternity. I recall the shadows that crossed her face, the movements of her lips as she spoke. And it saddened me when I realised that the hotel drew near.

We were bowed into the lobby by the commissionaire and ascended the staircase. With each step, each breath I took, I felt a sense of impending loss, which I could not explain. If the carriage ride had seemed interminable, the walk to her door was unmercifully short.

As she put her key into the lock, she turned to bid me good night. I would have spoken, but she put her finger to my lips.

"Dear Mr. Holmes. You needn't say anything. Thank you for your kindness. I will remember this evening. I will remember the balcony and the garden. And I will remember my dear 'Cumhyll.' " Her eyes welled up with tears. "I will remember him for as long as I live." She blinked back her tears. "But now I must resume the rôle you helped me escape for a brief moment. My father may be needing me and so, dearest friend, good night." She opened the door and entered.

I watched her close the door, I was unable to move until she was quite entirely out of sight. The door shut and, with plodding feet and heavy heart, I lumbered back down the hall to the staircase.

My foot had only just found the first carpeted step when I heard Rachel Leland scream in terror.

---

* The following is a note clipped to this page of the manuscript (MH/SMW):

> I know how enthusiastic a reader of Watson's chronicles you are, Trent. Does this revelation come to you as a surprise? It certainly was one for me. Yet, in retrospect, I am quite sure that I was beginning to fall in love with Rachel Leland at this point. I have cudgelled my brain, even a half-century later, to understand how I could have taken such leave of my senses, forsaking the rigorous training which you, as a reader of my brother's cases, would come to associate with him and me. It is an embarrassment to chronicle this lapse, but it must be recorded with the other facts so that the reader might understand my actions in the events that followed this episode.

-M-

8

DEATH AND DEDUCTION

I found the door of the suite unlocked. This time, the sitting-room was a shambles, the chairs upended, the cushions of the couch thrown willy-nilly about the room. But I was too intent upon finding Rachel Leland to care much for the room's disarray.

I found her on her knees beside the Colonel's bed, her face lying on his hand, her body wracked with sobbing, the whole scene a tragic *pietà*. On the bed lay Mordecai Leland, his face still partially covered by the pillow used to smother him.

I rushed past Miss Leland and reached for the Colonel's pulse. The bluish pallor of his cyanotic hand told me that I would find none. The body was already in the early stages of rigor mortis.

Rachel looked up. "He's gone?"

"Yes, my dear."

She stared at me for a moment, then her eyes rolled up and she crumpled to the floor. Ever so gently, I lifted her up and carried her across the mayhem of the sitting-room to the bedroom she shared with Millicent Deane. The window was open and the room was cold and draughty, but I thought no more about it as I placed her on the bed. I looked about, wondering what had become of Millicent Deane. Could she be attempting to find the authorities? Or had she been abducted? The ladies' room had again been ransacked. It was not difficult to infer that the intruders had taken the only witness to the murder of Colonel Leland.

I left Rachel Leland on the bed without awakening her, closing the door to her room after me. Entering the sitting-room once more, I pawed through the secretary until I found a suitable sheet of stationery, pen, and ink.

"Come at once," I wrote. "Colonel Leland is dead." I

signed it, folded it and sealed the message in an envelope, addressing it to Captain Ravenswood. Scurrying down the stairs to the desk, I dispatched it by the commissionaire. I gave him a half-crown to deliver it within the quarter-hour to the Army-Navy Club and into Ravenswood's hands alone.

I returned to the suite and had barely closed the door when I heard a soft knocking upon it.

"Mycroft, open the door."

Sherlock was alone, wearing a long glen plaid macfarlane over his servant's livery, though the walrus moustache and putty nose had since disappeared. "I arrived in time to see you cast that commissionaire out into the night." He paused. "Now I see why." He quickly took in the room's disarray. "Well, your note gives us a little time."

"Time? Time for what? Why are you here?"

"I had to find you. This seemed a likely spot, since you quit the Admiralty Ball in the company of Miss Leland. As for time, or the lack of it, we must investigate while we have the chance." So saying, he whipped out a magnifying lens and proceeded to explore the damage.

"But why did you have to find me?"

"So that we might prevent the death of Colonel Leland, or at least capture his murderers," he answered, while on his knees peering at the carpet through his lens.

"You knew about it?"

"Not for certain. At least not until you hurried that commissionaire out into the cold." He rose, looking into the Colonel's bedroom.

"The pillow was used to smother him, I suppose."

"So it would seem."

"By the bye, where is Millicent Deane?"

"She was not here when I entered."

Sherlock looked puzzled. "She could have murdered Colonel Leland and then fled."

"Sherlock, what do you mean?" But it was no use. He was back on his knees, a tuneless humming escaping his lips, broken every now and then by clucks and snatches of words. He moved surely and swiftly, the gawky adolescent gone. I observed a man pursuing his chosen profession with relish. A bright "Aha!" broke the rhapsodic gibberish just once, but it resumed almost immediately. He finally stood up and surveyed the room, continuing his mutterings until he came to the threshold of Colonel Leland's room. We entered it together.

Removing the pillow, Sherlock gazed on the craggy face. "Well, whoever they were, they did their work well," he said grimly.

"I find it decidedly odd that the Colonel's bedroom is not disturbed, don't you?" I asked. He said nothing in return, but I saw the glimmer of understanding dawn within Sherlock's hooded eyes.

"Yes, yes," he said finally. "That would account for it." He slowly turned to face me. "This has been made to look as though it was another robbery, but it is not."

"Well, of course. That much is obvious. But what about the same men being here earlier?"

Sherlock shook his head and clucked disapprovingly. "My dear Mycroft, look here." He motioned me back to the front door. "Look at these smudges."

"Mud," I said.

He looked at me disparagingly.

"If only you'd stir yourself. You should have seen this when you first entered. Look at it!"

Labouriously, I descended and examined the mud at close range.

"Now look at this smaller mark near the door to Ravenswood's room. And this one."

I followed his finger, inspected the mud and finally rose. "Well?"

"The large smudge by the door is relatively fresh, whereas the other two smears are quite dry."

"Yes," said Sherlock, "and you'll notice that the mud is of the same type and consistency: black, with small, lighter-coloured pieces of grit."

"Rather like river mud, I should say."

"True, and it proves that the men who most likely perpetrated this crime are in league with someone who visited them earlier. Maybe Miss Deane, maybe Ravenswood. But what of Miss Leland?"

"She's fainted, poor child. I put her on the bed."

Sherlock nodded. "I was just exiting the gaming room when I saw you both walk to the staircase. I went to the chamberlain and explained that I was needed back at the hotel to prepare the Captain's bath and so took my leave."

Sherlock looked at the door to her bedroom.

"Was the door open or closed when you entered?"

"Closed. I had to open it when I carried her into the room."

"But I'll wager that you found the window open."

"Why yes, it was. It still is."

"Not very polite of you, Mycroft," said Sherlock, "leaving the lady exposed to the chill night air." The ghost of a smile played on his lips as he opened the door.

At that moment, we heard the sound of voices in the hallway, and the door was flung open to reveal Captain Ravenswood, pistol in hand, Bankhead and Carteret flanking him.

"What is the meaning of this?" His eyes darted around the room, his thumb cocked the hammer of his pistol. "What are you doing here?"

"Miss Leland asked that I escort her home from the ball," I answered. "We found the suite as you see it."

The duellist finally entered the room, his friends behind him. He shot a glance toward the Colonel's room and saw the lifeless body on the bed. His companion followed his gaze.

"Good Lord!" exclaimed Bankhead.

"I'll get the police," said Carteret, fitting action to his words. But before he could get fairly out the door, Captain Ravenswood barked out a sharp command for him to stop.

"You will stay here, Mister Carteret, and that's an order."

Both of the younger Americans were surprised at this direction.

"But Captain, sir . . ." began Carteret.

"I said that that's an order, sir. You will obey me." Ravenswood swung round to me. "Where is Miss Leland?"

I indicated the now open bedroom door. "She fainted and I carried her into her room."

He considered this for a moment. "Where is Miss Deane?"

"She was not here when I responded to Miss Leland's screams."

"What!" He ran into the bedroom. We all followed him

to the door. Rachel Leland was still unconscious, her cloak bundled about her, the large sable muff dragging the floor, as I had left her.

"Miss Deane must have been kidnapped!" cried Carteret. "Captain, I insist that I be allowed to notify the police."

"As Colonel Leland's nephew, I agree, sir," said Bankhead.

Ravenswood now swung on both of them as he exited the bedroom. "You will both be at ease." He strode to the door to block any possible exit with his bulk. "And I command you both to silence."

Sherlock and I exchanged veiled glances while Carteret opened his mouth and then closed it in frustrated obedience. Ravenswood now assumed a more reasonable tone to address us.

"Gentlemen, you will no doubt understand my reasons. The situation is the same as the previous attempt on our lives and the robbery attempt on Wednesday night. Our mission is of the utmost secrecy and it must not be jeopardised by any publicity. I must refuse the knowledge of this tragic circumstance to the police."

"I must inform my superiors," I said. "But Mr. Moriarty will have quite a task before him to keep this from the attention of Scotland Yard."

"I have every confidence in him," Ravenswood answered shortly. "I trust that he will be in touch tomorrow morning concerning arrangements for the body."

"Captain Ravenswood," said Sherlock, "I would be interested to know if there is anyone whom you suspect of committing these foul deeds."

Ravenswood walked to the sideboard and poured a brandy for himself before he spoke. "As baffling as these circumstances may be to you"—at this Sherlock gave him a bored look—"I'm sure that I know who is perpetrating these outrages." He turned from the sideboard and faced all of us. "You really needn't worry yourselves. Or the police." He looked at Sherlock and me significantly. "I have ways of dealing with this low life. Miss Deane shall be rescued, you have my word. I shall find this man and string him up."

This pronouncement had been delivered in a most stirring manner. I had no doubts but that he referred to

Captain Jericho and I half expected him to call down the fiery wrath of God upon Jericho's woolly head.

Sherlock, for one, remained unimpressed. A speech concerning the tariff proclaimed in Hyde Park would have roused him more.

"I presume that you speak of a certain adventurer, Captain Jericho, I believe he is called?" asked Sherlock impassively.

Ravenswood looked at him in surprise. "How do you come to know of that snake?"

Sherlock shrugged. "That is not important. I am certain that Miss Deane related to you the facts of the attack made upon her and my brother?"

"That is correct, sir. I was not able to express my . . . apologies that it should have happened here," said Captain Ravenswood, addressing himself to me. "I might say that I believe him to be responsible for both of these monstrous deeds."

"A thoroughly intriguing supposition, Captain Ravenswood," Sherlock said mildly. He had replaced his lens within the folds of his overcoat, and was now calmly lighting his briar-root pipe. "It is nonetheless thoroughly incorrect."

"You are very wrong, sir," said Ravenswood, his eyes narrowing.

"You may be assured that I know whereof I speak," replied Sherlock coldly amid the smoke of his pipe. "The Negro did not instigate this wreckage."

Ravenswood sneered, "And how can you be so positive of that, Mr. Cocksure?"

Sherlock followed the eddying smoke rising to the ceiling before he replied. "I call your attention to the state of the sitting-room."

The Americans' puzzled expressions surveyed the wanton destruction in the chamber.

"The room is a mess," cried Bankhead.

"What sort of game are you playing, Mr. Holmes?" demanded Carteret.

"I play no game, gentlemen," said Sherlock, unperturbed. "I ask only that you consider this point: this same suite of rooms was plundered in similar fashion a bare forty-eight hours ago, with no loss, I understand, but the deprivation of Colonel Leland's prize pistol. So I ask you, why would the same men burgle the same establishment when they had plenty of time to find what they sought during their first attempt?"

"Because their first search had proved fruitless," answered Ravenswood with a sneer.

"So you postulate, Captain, that they returned two nights later, murdered the Colonel, spent the rest of the evening in making this place a shambles and then abducted your fiancée's companion. Is that correct?"

"I suppose so," said the Captain.

Sherlock righted one of the velvet and mahogany armchairs and seated himself in it, resting his hands on the knob of his walkng stick.

"They spent the night in tearing up your rooms in very much the same way and in very much the same places as before?" my brother asked. "Not very likely, my dear Captain, not very likely." He removed his pipe from his mouth and replaced it in his pocket. "Now I should suggest that we are dealing with a different set of intruders altogether. They deliberately set out to murder Colonel Leland and created this disorder merely to conceal their true purpose."

Ravenswood walked over to the chair in which Sherlock sat and stood menacingly at his side.

"And what are your reasons for believing that anyone other than Jericho would wish to kill Colonel Leland?"

Sherlock leaned back in his chair. "They are the same reasons that tell me that Millicent Deane will be returned to you unharmed and within a very short time."

Before I could move, Ravenswood's pistol filled his hand, its muzzle pointed at my brother. "You seem very sure about that. You had best explain your reasons, sir."

"Of course," said my brother, straightening, "But first . . ." and with a swift motion, he brought the knob of his stick down upon the hand of the duellist. The pistol dropped onto his lap and Sherlock, without hesitation, picked it up, training it on its former owner.

"Not a move!" I called out to the others. "If you try anything, I shall be happy to allow my brother to fire at will."

"That will certainly make explanations to the authorities much simpler," said Sherlock, rising and beaming boyishly at the Americans. "I believe that we'd best depart, Mycroft."

"Oh, Captain," he called out from the door. "I shall be happy to return this to you," he said, indicating the pistol, "but I fear that you would act too precipitately with it. So perhaps it is best if I retain it for the while." He watched the American glower back at him in silent rage. "Of course if you promise to—but no. I can see that you have no wish to lie to me. Well, good night, gentlemen. I shall see that Miss Deane is found within forty-eight hours." So saying, he closed the door on the Americans and pocketed the pistol.

Throughout the brief ride in the chill morning mist, Sherlock wrapped the shoulder-cape of his overcoat closer and crowed about his success with Captain Ravenswood. It was not until the horse came to a halt that Sherlock decided to answer my silent questions. "If I may presume upon your hospitality for a cup of tea . . ." his voice trailed off.

Not until the steaming cup was in his hands did he begin his story.

"Now as to my actions today. It began with the notice that appeared in the agony column of this morning's *Daily Mail.*"

"You know I never read that twaddle if I can help it."

"Well, if you plan to be an investigator, even temporarily, you had best keep a sharp eye on it." He made a long arm and reached the newspaper from where I had left it on the couch. I sorted through it until I came upon the page in question. Squinting down the column of Babel, I came upon the only entry that could make even a little sense.

THE BIRDS FLY THE COPSE WHEN THE COCK CROWS THREE TWICE. T'WERE BEST DONE QUICKLY. 2 D & J

"I assume the initials to be those of the men to whom the message is intended?"

Sherlock nodded.

"It is certainly not very oblique," I continued. " 'The birds' refers to Ravenswood and his party. They 'fly the

ENTER THE LION 159

copse when the cock crows twice' must allude to the time when the Americans will leave their hotel suite, at six o'clock. 'T'were best done quickly' must mean the murder, since we both believe that the puerile endeavour to make the room appear to be burglarised to be an afterthought."

"Wait, Mycroft," Sherlock said quickly. "The mud-stains we found! The first ones must have been made by Ravenswood when he went to the Southwark pub, not by Millicent Deane. Therefore the latter, the fresh stains, were made by the men he hired there to murder Colonel Leland."

"That would fit in with what you were told about his visit last night."

"Of course. I just wish I had thought of it before. I might have been able to prevent the murder."

"Nonsense, Sherlock. You did not find the mud until tonight. You can't take such coincidental lapses upon yourself. Be glad that you did find them."

It was a long moment before Sherlock said, "I suppose you're right, Mycroft. But I am loath to admit a lost opportunity." Another moment passed before he continued.

"The moment I saw the notice, I decided not to accompany you to the Admiralty Ball. I sent a telegram and then disguised myself as a disreputable young groom,* eventually finding myself at home with the other ostlers in the mews beside the Langham.

"The drivers and farriers gather together throughout the day for a pipe and a pull at the flask. Within an hour, I had collected an astounding amount of extraneous gossip along with some rather enlightening discoveries, to wit: Captain Ravenswood's several journeys have been to Bankside . . ."

"Rachel Leland apprised me of his peregrinations to Southwark. You have narrowed the search to a specific section. Well done."

"He visited a pub called The Anchor, making his most

---

* Sherlock has a high regard for this disguise. He used it on at least one other occasion when, as "a drunken-looking groom, ill-kempt and side-whiskered' in Serpentine Mews, he learned what he could from the stablehands about the notorious inhabitant of Briony Lodge, Miss Irene Adler. The incident will be found in "A Scandal in Bohemia," a case contained in *The Adventures of Sherlock Holmes*. MH/SMW

recent visit late last night, but I'll wager that that was his destination on the day that Trevor lost him in the traffic."

"So now we have the name of the pub. You have done yeoman service."

"Ah, but Mycroft, I have learned even more."

"What else could you learn?"

"Well this will be a bit harder to follow up, but one of the farriers told me that two footpads from across the river were seen lurking about the Langham. They are so much a part of Bankside, that their appearance impressed itself in his mind."

I nodded. Sherlock had many times explained to me how the hoodlum gangs had made a vast division of London among themselves. The rigid boundaries were seldom trespassed with impunity.

"The game must be worth the candle for them to run the risk of being seen encroaching upon the territory of another group of ruffians."

"That's it exactly, Mycroft. But to continue: I had been in the mews for about an hour, when I espied the special messenger from the Foreign Office delivering what I discovered to be the invitations to this evening's grand event."

"They were left in the pigeonholes behind the desk, no doubt."

"Keen mind, brother, I've always admitted it," said Sherlock with a caustic little nod. "I recognized the size and shape, along with the crest in the corner.

"And it planted the germ of another scheme. Returning to my digs, I wrote a letter, in Ravenswood's name of course, to the chamberlain of the Army-Navy Club, identifying me as his American servant, the most recent member in a long line of family retainers.

"It seems that the Captain promised my father, his butler, to keep me by his side, so that I might serve him. Ravenswood apologised for this eccentricity, begging the club to understand that this was, in no wise, a reflection upon the staff of the Army-Navy Club."

"And the chamberlain swallowed that poppycock?"

"Certainly. Especially as the message was written on Langham stationery which I borrowed during my visit."

"That was taking something of a risk, Sherlock," I said disapprovingly.

"Perhaps, but it did gain me entrance."

"Yes. So now I suppose you've learned all sorts of interesting details about this plot."

"That was the idea," Sherlock replied brightly. "No one pays attention to a waiter. I was able to catch a few things in passing during the game. But after the game, after you were—ah—ejected, I was able to catch enough to corroborate Captain Jericho's information about their plan. And a frightening one it is. Jericho understated nothing." Sherlock's demeanor became serious.

"They plan to take over the Washington government so quickly that their sympathisers in Commons will force Parliament to accept the *coup d'état* as a *fait accompli*. There was talk about making the new United States a part of the Empire, but this is a matter that will take more definite form later. Their first consideration is to make certain that the overthrow proceeds smoothly."

I shook my head. "Those foolish men."

"No one there thought so. There are one or two immediate difficulties to be surmounted, what with the absence of Sir Rodney and Sir Edmund Darlington."

"They mentioned Sir Edmund?"

"Yes," said Sherlock. "I recall that Ravenswood was most particularly disappointed about his absence."

"Which means that Mr. Moriarty has worked well to inform Captain Ravenswood of the political situation. Sir Edmund is most influential within several ministry spheres. Should he be won over, the Americans will have a powerful advocate working for them within the government."

"So it would appear," said Sherlock, now beginning to chew his lower lip.

"So then they must have another planning session soon, so as to include him in the plotting."

"Can he be won over?"

"I'm sure of it. Sir Edmund would dearly love to add his name to the list of the monarch's first ministers. If he joins them, he would be able to consolidate enough feeling within the party to force the Queen to ask him to form a new government." We were silent a moment, thinking.

"Moriarty has chosen his men well," I said at last. "He has picked out every dissatisfied official of any consequence within the government. If they could not win over Sir

Rodney, they would find means to get around him, but his department is essential to their plans."

"That was the talk. Moriarty mentioned that it was an unfortunate circumstance altogether. But this was merely a preliminary meeting. I stayed long enough to find out quite a few things. There are some disadvantages to the waiter's disguise, but all in all, it worked out as I had planned."

"Before you go on to other matters, I would be grateful to learn more of this wild plot which the Americans are hatching with the aid of Mr. Moriarty."

"Very well." Sherlock removed his pipe and pouch and began to push tobacco into the bowl. "Colonel Leland, Captain Ravenswood, and the others are here on a secret mission to capture the good will of members of Her Majesty's Government, so that they will have aid and supplies enough to supplement their own when they recapture Washington City and bring about an end to the American government."

"So much we already learned from Jericho."

"They wish to return the nation as a Crown colony with various provisos, of course. The major points being that their committee be appointed the provisional government with powers of appointment under the Crown, the royal governor to be their own candidate. The state governments are to be retained, but only their verified candidates are to be allowed to hold office. They also want a parliament of their own choosing under a royal governor, or they may be content with parliamentary representation, at least for the first few years."

I smiled. "For someone who professes a complete lack of interest in politics, you did very well."

"There's more," said Sherlock. "And this caused a little debate. They want to re-establish the slave trade."

"Not much of a chance of that," I snorted. "That sounds as though it might be a negotiating point."

"I beg pardon? It seemed to make a difference tonight."

I chuckled. "My dear Sherlock, one ploy in diplomacy is to argue for a point that means little or nothing to you, so as to give it up for a matter of importance. I am quite sure that this committee knows that Her Majesty's Government will not allow slavery to exist in any part of the

Empire, certainly not in America, should it be recovered. This matter of slavery is simply a diversion."

"You may be right," said Sherlock dubiously, "but there is one important matter that will come to pass. Trent is correct. Ravenswood has the necklace. It is an important prelude to this entire enterprise that it be presented to Her Majesty. A gift to the nation, its acceptance would assure the Confederates of the Empire's material aid. A secret treaty will be written, to be concluded and ratified by Parliament after the *coup* has been successfully completed.

"I was not able to stay for all the haggling which took place during the meeting, but perhaps you're right about their terms being negotiable."

"Especially if the present government were to fall and one more favourable to the Americans were to come to power. Remember that the Judases mentioned by Captain Jericho are not confined to the New World. You think that they might try to force an election here?" he asked.

"Better than that. They'll be in a position to force Prime Minister Disraeli to resign in favour of a government more sympathetic to the annexation of the United States."

"You may be right," said Sherlock, "but I must admit that all these parliamentary machinations bore me."

"They may bore you, but they will be important to consider beforehand. When is the invasion planned? Did they discuss that?"

"Ah, Mycroft, this was inspired. Ravenswood was in his element when he announced this. It is sheer genius on the part of the Southerners. Learning this made all my play-acting worthwhile. One must compliment them for their . . ."

"When, Sherlock!"

"The Fourth of July. The greatest American Independence Day ever: the long-planned and long-awaited Centennial celebration." Sherlock sat wreathed in smoke, a wide smile on his face."

"The devil you say!" I exclaimed. "Well," I continued, "one must commend their sense of irony."

"Yes, a brilliant stroke, what? In shortly less than eight months, they plan to march into Washington City, Philadelphia, and other important Northern industrial centers of commerce, to upset the most important anniversary of the nation." He shook his head. "I would not have given them the flair for the dramatic with which they plan. Of course the major focus will be upon the capture of Washington. That General Grant is now the chief executive gives them even more enthusiasm and sense of purpose, I think. 'This time, Grant will be taken to Appomattox to negotiate *his* surrender,' said Ravenswood with a certain glee."

"Do you recall any discussion about him, when, say, a meeting could take place with Sir Edmund Darlington involved in the planning?"

"Not so much a planning conference, but I heard Moriarty tell Ravenswood that he would introduce Sir Edmund to him at the testing of some improbable flying craft. 'Based on the ideas of Leonardo da Vinci,' I heard Moriarty say. He spoke of it in wondrous terms as revolutionising warfare, or some other twaddle of the sort."

"The auto-gyro," I said, my heart sinking within me. "For a meeting that did not last very long, they certainly found time to mention a good many things."

"Yes, that's what they called it. An auto-gyro. What do you know about it?"

"I should say that your brief description sums it up."

"In that case, as an engine of destruction it sounds extremely uninteresting," said Sherlock, affecting a yawn.

"My dear brother, even with your complete lack of regard for warfare, even you must understand the practicalities involved. A group of men within such a craft could scrutinise enemy positions, could rain down projectiles on the enemy forces . . . why, the scope of such an invention defies limitation."

"That's all very nice," said Sherlock, "but could not this craft, like hot-air balloons, be shot down by cannon, or even by a single bullet that found a vulnerable target, its depending, as is likely, on the breeze for its movement?"

"Sherlock, you apparently do not understand the principles involved," I answered. "This craft will be completely self-propelled. Unlike a balloon, it will depend little on the velocity of the wind to direct it. I have not seen the plans, but I would suppose that it will be completely armoured."

"All except its moving parts," was Sherlock's skeptical reply. "But how come you to know so much of its history?"

"Only because of my superior's complete inability to keep a closed mouth in my presence. The upshot of this is that he has also informed the Southerners. I'll wager that he has even told them about the testing on Salisbury Plain."

Sherlock had grown introspective. "A heavier-than-air machine; a novel idea, I must admit. A bit impractical. I am only disturbed because it is being built as a warship."

"Why do you say that, Sherlock?"

"I am often disheartened by governments, even Her Majesty's, being so concerned with warfare. They show little interest in what may appear to be eccentric inventions unless they can be used as engines of destruction, or as a means to aid in such destruction, to somehow immobilise a real or imagined enemy." He shook his head. "More and more, I find that to be the whole end of government, Mycroft. And that is one reason why I can take so little interest in political manœuvering. Now tell me: how is this contraption powered?"

"By a steam-driven turbine."

"I see that they're mixing a little Hero of Alexandria with their Leonardo da Vinci," said Sherlock with a little smile. "It must be very unwieldy."

"Quite," I responded. "But use your imagination, Sherlock. Armed with bombs or grenades to be rained down from a great height, beyond the earthbound artillery of an opposing army, it becomes an utterly irresistible weapon. For all practical purposes, all targets on the ground become indefensible."

"Another threat to the world so as to maintain the *Pax Britannica,* eh?"said Sherlock, scornfully.

I looked hard at him. "Sometimes I question your loyalty to your Queen and country."

"You needn't," said Sherlock pulling again at his pipe. "Her Majesty has my greatest respect and loyalty, as much as the pride I have in the British stock whence we spring. But I put no trust in petty politicians," he scowled. "See that you never become one. I should be very sorry to think that the methods of grab and greed so indigenous to such vermin had become uppermost in your mind. It's as much a disease as the ambition to gain another people's territory, just a smaller, meaner strain." He brushed an ash from his waistcoat and said, "Now, should this auto-gyro prove successful, these men will use it to convince even more chair-warmers in Whitehall to help in this planned conquest of America."

"I don't believe that the craft will be perfected to the degree necessary for independent flight," I said curtly. Sherlock's attitude nettled me more and more. I wondered if his remarks were a veiled way of questioning my own integrity. He seemed eager to continue, so I swallowed any indignant response that we might go on with our planning.

"Have you any notion of how we might proceed to stop this business?"

"I have some few notions, as you call them. And a few hours of sleep will help to refine them," I said.

"Impossible," Sherlock replied shortly. "I refuse to allow you to drift off until I tell you of my deductions at the Langham."

"You told me about the mud already."

"But I made another discovery, Mycroft, one that you overlooked in your concern for Miss Leland."

I resented the tone of his remark, but I wanted to know what he had found, so, again I said nothing.

"Now, before I tell you about my findings, you agree that the death of Colonel Leland was the motive of to-night's attack, rather than another attempt at burglary?"

"Conceded," I said.

"The puerile endeavour to disguise the fact was an obvious afterthought."

"And your reasons?"

"One need only have seen the open window," said Sherlock, leaning forward in his chair, as though he were one of his own university dons. "Now why would that window be open, especially on such a bitterly cold night as this, except as a signal?"

"You therefore infer that someone opened the window to announce to someone outside, in Regent Street, that it was safe to enter the room."

"Precisely. And from the room's temperature, I would hypothesize that the window was raised either just before or very soon after the party departed the hotel for the Army-Navy Club."

"So then," I asked, "You believe that one of the Americans raised the window? The only person remaining ambulatory in the suite was Millicent Deane. Do you suppose that she is an accomplice to the murder and her own abduction?"

"Her absence may point to a connivance in the affair, as much as it may point to a forcible abduction. Don't forget," said Sherlock, "there may be more to the lady than meets the eye. But you overlook her companion, Rachel Leland. They did share the rooms."

"In that case," I said exasperatedly, "you may as well include the entire party, any one of whom could have opened the window."

"But the men would surely not tramp into the private chambers of the ladies. Their presence would be a trifle indelicate, to say the least. No, it is one of the women, I am sure. I believe that Miss Leland may be ruled out from the suspicion of murdering her own father. That would be too monstrous to presume."

I nodded, then said, "So you believe that it was Miss Deane who admitted the Colonel's attackers," I said. "Which leaves us with the original problem: Why is she gone?"

"Because it might prove an embarrassment to leave the only person who could describe the murderers," said Sherlock.

"I am sorry; I cannot find it within me to believe the worst of Millicent Deane, that her concern for Colonel Leland was mere playacting."

"I admit that it would be difficult to deceive you, Mycroft, but not impossible. She was here alone with Colonel Leland. She had every opportunity, and now she's gone."

"Suppose I concede your point about Miss Deane. How do you postulate her return?"

Sherlock rubbed his chin. "Well, it may be a bit thin, but, assuming her complicity, she may have left of her own will, as opposed to an outright kidnapping. Or, having accomplished the murder, she left with the men, who had ransacked the rooms again looking for the necklace."

"Or," I said, "she might have been abducted by those

same men to ensure payment for tonight's deed, the destruction of the rooms a mere ruse, as we have said."

"If that is so, those hired assassins are playing a dangerous game."

"I'd like to find Captain Jericho, to see what part he plays in this."

"What makes you think that Jericho is involved? I grant you that he has something of a motive, and I am even persuaded that he planned the Wednesday night search of the rooms. But I ask the same question I asked Ravenswood: Why would his men search in very much the same places they searched before? And what about the Colonel? He had just as much chance to be murdered on Wednesday night."

"But Jericho has an excellent motive to mix himself in this, especially if he is as preoccupied with the necklace as Trent believes," I countered.

"Yes, and Ravenswood might have implicated Jericho, if only to divert attention from himself," Sherlock replied. "Let's not forget that. I would be interested to know how Dr. Fordyce, the counterfeit physician, knew about the laudanum. There was no one in that room who might have told Jericho."

"Not unless one of the Americans is 'playing both sides of the street,' as they say in the States."

"An interesting supposition, Mycroft, and one that I might trace. Though I doubt much will come of it."

"Indeed you might," I said. "That notice in the paper could just as easily have been placed for Jericho, or even by Jericho."

My brother rose, put his hands behind his back and paced the room. I pressed my point.

"You must consider the man, Sherlock. He is an admitted criminal, outside the law of two continents. He threatened the lives of this delegation within our own hearing. He knows their habits; he's studied their movements. And he stands to gain a fortune for his efforts. He must be considered a prime suspect."

"Or a prime patriot," said Sherlock softly. "His whole background and appearance belie his being a common thief."

I smiled drily. "I would hardly call a jewelled necklace

worth a million and a quarter American dollars the prey of a common thief. It would surely be worth it to him to mouth a few hypocritical aphorisms to lull the suspicions of the proper English gentlemen who are aware of his background."

Sherlock sank back into his chair with a sigh. He went through the ritual of finding his pipe, emptying the dottle, filling it once more, packing the tobacco, and lighting it. I knew that his mind was working feverishly, but it was not until the blue-grey smoke of his acrid shag had enveloped him that he spoke again. "What you say about Captain Jericho is true, Mycroft, and there's no denying it. He's admitted to us that he's a man of, well, of opportunity, shall we say? His motivation is sufficient to hang him ten times over in any court in the realm."

"We must remember the principle of Occam's razor," I said matter-of-factly. " 'Always seek the simplest explanation.' "

"Meaning?"

"*Cui bono?* Who profits from the death of the Colonel? The prime beneficiary is Captain Samuel Ravenswood, headstrong, ambitious, unscrupulous. One would think that he would wish Leland to be at least a figurehead until the affair is consummated."

"Leland would have been a moderating force *after* the invasion, no doubt," Sherlock agreed. "But had he become too firmly entrenched after the plans had seen fruition, within either or both governments, Ravenswood could not have touched him without fear of reprisal."

I shook my head. "You have much to learn about politics," I said. "The back-benchers would tear him to pieces. Leland lacked the taste for the jugular, so ably demonstrated by his corpulent friend, Ravenswood. As it now stands, Ravenswood could have staged that attack in the street the night the Americans arrived, but no one can definitely point a finger at him with proof positive."

"To play *advocatus diaboli*," said Sherlock, "I can say that the next person to profit directly from the Colonel's death is our Negro acquaintance, if it were his only way to obtain this necklace."

"Accurately stated," I said. "Now, to return the favour,

I shall proceed as prosecuting attorney against another party by asking you a question."

"Your magnanimity knows no bounds," said Sherlock. "And if you don't stop raking in Mrs. Crosse's delicious pork pies, neither will your girth," he smiled.

"Remember the fate of flatterers in Dante's *Inferno,*" I said, arching my brow at him. "But let me repeat, I put to you a question: What is the worst possible thing for a thoughtful, intelligent, and ambitious person to be in this modern and enlightened age?"

He stared at me for an instant and then smiled bitterly. "Why, a woman, of course."

"Precisely. And why?"

"Because they have no direct exercise of will or power."

"You scintillate, Sherlock. Even the most powerful woman in the civilised world today—even our own gracious sovereign—must work her will by working her wiles upon men."

"I trust you are applying this theory to Miss Leland?"

"But of course. And for that reason I can exonerate her."

"So much for the prosecution," said Sherlock drily. "And how do you exclude the lady with such ease?"

"Because, my dear Sherlock, in order to work her wiles, Miss Leland must have some hold, some leverage upon a man, be it flirtation, infatuation . . ."

"Strangulation or flagellation," Sherlock interpolated.

"Or sensual gratification—or any one of a number of other ploys. And I can say that Miss Leland has no leverage with anyone in the delegation aside from perhaps, her father."

"Not even as the fiancée of Captain Ravenswood?"

"To bring the objective down to the subjective, not even as that. I am entrusted with a confidence, but I do not think that I violate that trust if I say to you that I am assured of Miss Leland's lack of leverage with Captain Ravenswood."

Sherlock's grunt was the only grudging agreement he would give me. He had again steepled his fingers and was now deep within a brown study.

"Yes," I said smugly, "There is not a doubt of it in my mind."

Sherlock looked up sharply. "Why exclude Rachel Leland? She has as much to gain as anyone else. Maybe she'd rather have a quarter of a million pounds than spend the rest of her life with Ravenswood. You told me about that interview in your office. She might very easily be trying to manipulate you. You wouldn't be the first to play the fool for a woman."

"My dear Sherlock!"

"Do you deny the possibility?"

"Well, of course!"

Sherlock's look of reproach was enough to check my denial.

"Mycroft," he said slowly, "you taught me the importance of reasoning, of putting my mind ahead of every emotion, to look at occurrences with dispassionate objectivity. You taught me that honour and reason are inseparable. Do not allow yourself any less rational or less disciplined behaviour, I implore you. Do not allow any infatuation to befuddle your brain. Cut through the cobwebs!"

My earlier annoyance once more welled up. He was, after all, my younger brother. How dare he attempt to rebuke me!

"My dear Sherlock," I began, only just barely able to control my anger. "Just what are you implying?"

He shrugged. "I just hope that your thoughts remain unclouded. And that you have the courage to proceed in an unbiased manner no matter what the outcome."

"You may be sure I will," I answered with biting scorn.

Without another word, he collected his hat and coat and departed. I watched him leave and felt anger—a foreign emotion so far as Sherlock was concerned—well up inside me again. It stayed with me as I prepared for bed until my ascendant need for sleep overcame the rage.

9

MR. MORIARTY
TIPS HIS HAND

I awoke the next morning before dawn in a cold sweat. Had I screamed or cried out? My bedclothes and sheets were sodden with perspiration. Had I been visited by some dream or nightmare? I could not recall what it was that had awakened me but I felt a sense of foreboding envelop me as closely as my clinging nightshirt.

It was this unknown dread that kept me abed, as surely as though I were a small child afraid of the dark. And for the same reason. That indefinable Unknown, not just in the darkness, but of the darkness, nonetheless terrified me. I felt very small and alone.

Was I running a fever? Had a mere disease taken such a grip of my senses? I wished it were so, but I knew it was not. My soul was shrivelling within me as my thoughts hastened back to the comforting presence of my mother's voice, reading to us from the family Bible:

. I am poured out like water, and all my bones are out of joint: my heart is like wax; it is melted in the midst of my bowels.

Hearing my mother's words recalled the anger I had felt toward Sherlock. I realised that it was an unwarranted emotion, for Sherlock had only wanted to help me. And I had sent him off still feeling this foolish wrath. In my guilt and despair, I thought of Mrs. Crosse and the consolation she found in her religion. Would to God that I had that comforting strength. Mrs. Crosse had weathered the death of her husband because she had an inner srength and security that I had forsaken in my youth. I had found the religion of my forebears to be empty and useless mummery. And the line from *Hamlet* came to me as though to underscore my feelings: "There are more things in heaven and earth, Horatio, than are dreamt of in your philosophy."

Are there? I asked myself. No. Reason, intellect, that is man's salvation. The only means one has to strive against what assails him.

But then a stray passage from the "Morte d'Arthur" of Tennyson's *Idylls of the King* struck me with a force I had never before experienced: "More things are wrought by prayer than this world dreams of."

No! Faith in a benevolent Diety was but a crutch for the credulous. Yet now I yearned for that Shoulder upon which to lean. I certainly found little solace in the remembrance of the shabby treatment I'd given my brother, the memory of Rachel Leland's hand in my own, my whole involvement in this drama to prevent the murder of hundreds of thousands, the slaughter of cities, and the destruction of what I found just and right. Again, I found myself longing for an Advocate to defend me from the forces that overwhelmed me.

Once more, my thoughts focused on Mrs. Crosse and her abiding trust and confidence in the powers of intercession she believed to reside in all those saints, whose reminders she almost daily presented to me. I drifted back to sleep, reflecting upon the possibility of an Almighty Providence. And, as though I was once again a little boy, I murmured a prayer, placing myself in the hands of God.

The sun was not yet full in my window as I again awakened. I felt the crusted residue of sleep in my eyes and upon my cheeks and was reminded of my despondent thoughts. I felt drained as I rose and weakly staggered across the room to don my dressing gown. By the clock on my bureau, I saw that it was just lacking five o'clock. I had a great thirst, I discovered, and I emptied the water pitcher beside my bed. I was thankful that my fear had subsided along with my self-reproach and recriminations.

Had that multitude of saints, whose likenesses took up a good part of one of my dresser drawers, interceded for me? I wondered. An empty feeling within me persisted, but I wondered if perhaps it was because of a lack of food, rather than a lack of faith. Both situations were correctible.

I walked back across the room to the wash-hand stand, poured water into the laver and rinsed my face in its refreshing coolness.* Reaching for the towel, I dried my face. I was not at all drowsy. The household was not yet up this early on a Saturday morning. I could go back to bed or I could put my mind to work and do something constructive. The desk beckoned me, so, lighting a lamp, I began to compose the notes that form the basis of this account. This proved to be the cathartic I needed to exorcise the dæmons within me by trapping them in writing.

It was sometime later, as I was glancing over these rather sketchy notes, that I heard a slight jiggling at the latch of my door. It was Mrs. Crosse, come to open the window shades in my sitting-room, as she did every morning.

"Why, Mr. Holmes!" she exclaimed. "I expected you to be asleep for another two hours, considering the late hours you kept last night."

"That's very kind of you, Mrs. Crosse, but old habits are hard to break."

"Would you be liking some breakfast, then?"

"The biggest in your larder, Mrs. Crosse, with a large pot of tea, if you please. I feel as empty as a cistern in a desert."

Her solicitous look vanished, at once replaced by a bright smile: Mycroft Holmes was hungry. All was right with the world.

I rose from my gargantuan meal feeling content and full. I walked to the window and raised the sash.

"It's such a beautiful day," said my landlady, noticing my present occupation, as she replaced the dishes and trays upon her waggon.

Indeed it is, I thought. A pale yet determined sun shone through the thick mist, not yet risen from the night before. Through intermittent patches, the sky could be discerned, a pale, autumnal blue.

---

* Wash-hand stands were prevalent during the age before indoor plumbing in every home. They resembled low sideboards, without the superstructure. In a long center drawer were kept toilet articles, and a small cabinet beneath held the "thunder-mug," or chamberpot. Atop the marble slab covering sat a ewer within a laver (basin), and a soap dish. Behind the counter, washcloths and towels hung from a wooden rack resembling a lyre. Even after the advent of indoor plumbing, wash-hand stands could be found aplenty, both in England and America, until after World War II. MH/SMW

"I'm surprised to see you so industrious this morning."

"No more than I, my dear Mrs. Crosse," I responded, still searching the awakening firmament. "No more than I."

A knock at the front door caught her attention, and she excused herself, leaving the remains of my repast on her waggon. She returned almost instantly, bearing a telegram.

"It's a telegram for you," she said apprehensively.

I was always struck by the fact that Mrs. Crosse invariably equated the arrival of telegrams with dolorous tidings. Perhaps because it was the manner in which she had been informed about her late husband's death. I had never asked.

Of course, it is well known that my brother would rather send a telegram than write, even where a handwritten note would be preferred, or correct.* I recall an occasion when I wrote a letter to him, asking if he would wish to attend the opening of a Gilbert and Sullivan comic operetta three days hence. I sent it by the first post, hoping to receive an answer by mid-afternoon, in the sixth or seventh post. Within the hour I received Sherlock's telegraphic answer consisting of the word "No." He spent a shilling or more where a penny would have sufficed. But I digress.

I slit open the envelope with the butter knife.

It was a message from Mr. Moriarty requesting that I appear at his residence this very forenoon. Reading between the lines, I determined that this interview would likely concern itself with the events of the evening just past. Mr. Moriarty would be seeking my advice. I wondered how he planned to make his way around the American, Ravenswood, who would be against my being included in these plans.

Mrs. Crosse's brogue broke in on my thoughts. "The commissionaire said that he was instructed to wait for a reply."

I hastily drafted my acceptance—compliance would be a better word—and sent it back through Mrs. Crosse's good offices to the commissionaire downstairs.

As I finished my morning ablutions and dressed, I real-

---

* This trait has lasted throughout Sherlock's life. In one of his later cases, "The Adventure of the Devil's Foot" (in the collection entitled *His Last Bow*), Watson makes the remark, "He has never been known to write where a telegram would serve." MH/SMW

ised that the matter was an urgent one to Mr. Moriarty.
The answer had been reply-paid.

Jerrold Moriarty, for all his mildly indiscreet ways within
the FO, had been notably silent about his life away from
government. I knew of his sons only because of their infrequent appearances in Whitehall. All three were named
James, as I have mentioned. But that was almost all I
knew about them, aside from office chatter. I had never
met Mrs. Moriarty, indeed I had no idea if she was still
living; my superior never mentioned her within my hearing. I had little respect for Mr. Moriarty's handling of his
department of the FO, as one has gathered by reading
these pages. I was not really sure of his intelligence, but
one thing I saw: The man was shrewd enough to surround
himself with talented and agile minds (I do not necessarily
refer to myself), and had ingratiated himself with influential patrons. His ambition was boundless, as I had been
aware for some time, but never as much as in these past
few days since the arrival of the Americans. The possibility
of such a man leading an area of a new government, more
highly placed than he was now, was an alarming thought.
But one met a great many of the same ilk in all spheres
and strata of government. That the political arena was yet
operable being staffed by such mediocrity was a source
of continual amazement to me.

The Moriarty home was located in Kensington, tradi-
tionally the stepping stone to Mayfair and the upper plane
of the elegant society among which my superior so ardently
yearned to be numbered. The building was a solid one,
comfortably large without being rambling. It was one of
many row-houses so prevalent along the broad avenues of
those neighbourhoods. It was fronted in brick and Portland
stone. An archway was built over the front door, composed
of irregular blocks of Portland stone, completely surrounding the entranceway. The same pleasing design was repeated around each of the windows of the three-storey
structure. The butler, scion of a family of manservants,
took my name and, with an economy of gesture, ushered
me into the large and spacious, though thoroughly clut-
tered, sitting-room. As I awaited the appearance of my
superior, I had time to take stock of my surroundings.

I was always appalled by the tasteless clutter of the typical English drawing room of this era. Sitting-rooms, drawing rooms, and parlours were filled to overflowing with potted palms, Oriental carpeting, the usual grotesquely carved, massive marble mantlepiece, and forests of lamps which somehow stood amid the ungainly, bulky, mahogany horrors of furniture.

The Moriarty household was no exception. In the not overly large room, I counted two couches, a settee, three overstuffed armchairs, a barrel-chair, three side-chairs, and three ottomans. In themselves, and in less profusion, each piece of furniture was acceptable, beautifully styled, well crafted and executed. The heavy mahogany and the wool frieze of the chairs and davenport were of the best quality. But they lent themselves to a more isolated manner of display. It was overwhelming when beaded valances materialised from out of the ether, atop the mantle, and over the entranceways. Potted palms sat in those places not already occupied by floor lamps, and a chandelier suspended from the centre of the ceiling reflected pinpoints of sun onto the gold-flecked floral wallpaper. The final touch was the fringed Persian carpet, spreading riotous swirls of colour the length and breadth of the room. For all the life of me, I felt that I had stepped into the middle of a jumble sale.

Had I been left alone much longer I would ultimately have had to be taken to Bedlam. Fortunately, the young Lieutenant Moriarty opened the sliding doors to admit himself into the clutter. He greeted me with the news that his father had been called to the Foreign Office "for some sort of emergency meeting" and would return directly. The information gave me pause, for I knew that the only emergency brewing must involve the American Southerners.

My anxious speculation was interrupted by the appearance of the oldest Moriarty brother, the university professor. He took my hand in greeting, but with a distracted sullenness, as opposed to the polite military graciousness displayed by his brother.

The two Moriartys were similar in appearance, having the same tall spare figure and thinning hair of their father, though the Lieutenant stood straight and firm, while the Professor was stooped and puckered. The younger Moriarty was dressed informally, doubtless a relief from his uniform, in a smoking jacket, while the Professor was frock-coated and dressed, one would suppose, as he would be for his classes. A distinguishing mark was his curious habit of oscillating his head while in conversation. It was a trifle disconcerting and must have been a source of terror to his students. We' all stood awkwardly until Lieutenant Moriarty offered me a drink.

"It is still a little early for me," I responded, "but I would be happy for some tea."

He pulled the bell rope and gave the butler the necessary instructions. The Professor had excused himself to wander about the room, apparently looking for something he had left there earlier.

"You must excuse my brother," said the young Lieutenant. "He is deep within some researches."

"I see."

"It is something about a mathematical measurement relative to the motion of asteroids.* I believe it will be a rather deep subject, if I haven't mixed metaphors too hopelessly," he smiled. "Do I state your case fairly, James?"

The Professor turned and flushed, firmly clutching his papers to his side. "Laugh if you will, James, but if you could see beyond the tip of your cannon, you would real-ise that my speculations apply to the field of ballistics. It will revolutionise your artillery. Dear me, yes, it will."

This whole speech was delivered with his swaying head moving menacingly back and forth. Had the man been speaking to me, I would have been petrified by his intimidating stance. Fortunately, his brother was used to him. Feigning disinterest, he yawned mightily.

"I'll believe that when you can prove it," he said.

"In that event, I had best return to my work. Excuse me, gentlemen," said the Professor curtly, and regally swept from the room, the picture of wounded dignity. The total effect was spoiled, however, by the appearance of the butler with the tea tray, who arrived in the doorway at precisely the same instant in which the Professor slid open the doors to make his exit. There was an awkward dance between the two men until the butler could manœuvre his

---

* The monograph was eventually published; Sherlock mentions it in *The Valley of Fear* as being entitled *The Dynamics of an Asteroid*. MH/SMW

tray around the unrelenting Moriarty. The Professor finally exited, in even higher dudgeon. The flustered, white-haired butler was left standing where he was until the Lieutenant was able to control his silent mirth.

"Set the tray on the library table, Dawes. We'll serve ourselves."

The butler followed his master's instructions and closed the connecting doors as he withdrew.

"James will be unapproachable for a week, I'll be bound," his brother said, good-naturedly. "I must really apologise for his bad manners."

"I can't help believing his words, though, Lieutenant. I should say that the future of the military lies in more scientific pursuits."

"Oh come, not you too," the young Lieutenant cried in mock despair. "And you a practical politician. You and my brother must be reading too much of that French fellow, Verne. Jimmy eats them up. Stories about submersible ships and rocket-trains to the moon. What blather!" He grimaced. "I must admit such ideas to be appealing to a certain sort of mind, but they are truly beyond the scope of the military."

"I should think that you, a military man, would see that weaponry becomes more sophisticated with each succeeding generation," I said.

"Oh yes, more sophisticated weapons, definitely. But there'll always be a place for the enlisted man, the infantry, and the cavalry," he said. "Nothing can do the job like charging a fortification with bayonets fixed!"

I kept my tongue in check without reminding this young man of the Light Brigade's disastrous charge at Balaclava during the Crimean War. One cannot argue with a wall. This Moriarty was bright, but he lacked the perception of his brother; he was very like his father in that way. He would go far in the service.

My thoughts were interrupted by the appearance of his father, who entered the connecting doors with the distracted air of a bewildered man. Seeing his son, he asked if we might be excused.

"Of course, Father," the Lieutenant answered. "I've enjoyed our discussion, Mr. Holmes," he said, turning and extending his hand once more. As I took it, he bowed respectfully.

After his son's departure, the father moved to the liquor cabinet and removed a decanter. He poured himself a tumbleful. As an afterthought he looked back to me and asked if I should care to partake. I indicated the teacup in my hands. He shrugged.

"Frankly, Holmes," said he, taking a chair and placing it opposite me, "this thing has me in a quandary."

"What thing is that, sir?"

"This American thing, you know," he said, looking into his glass. "The fact is, that Ravenswood fellow doesn't like you, you know. He insisted that you be kept out of this matter, that you are in no way involved. It seems you rubbed him the wrong way right from the first."

"Not intentionally, I assure you, sir."

"No, no, of course not. I know you better than that. But the deed is done and that's all." He took a drink and looked up from the glass. "You know that I've always found your thoughts—ah—very instructive. I should be grateful for your—perspective—in this matter." He shrugged again, as if to indicate his difficulty. "But I cannot include you in this matter officially without gaining the enmity of Ravenswood and his fellows. My hands are tied."

"I understand your dilemma, sir."

"What I plan to do is this: Without letting him on to the fact, we can work together—unofficially. If you take my meaning. Especially after he and his cohorts have returned to America."

"I am under your orders, sir."

"I knew you'd understand," he smiled painfully. He had another swallow of his whisky and became introspective. "You know, Holmes, after this matter is resolved, I shall hold much responsibility in the government. I don't mind telling you that your advice has been most constructive on occasion. It has saved me from . . ." He paused and considered his next words, then changed his mind before continuing ". . . from using other tactics in the past. Your information is always succinct, and you are usually correct in your observations.

"You can't know what has been taking place or the plans

that some individuals within Her Majesty's Government have been making. We cannot help but succeed. As I said" —he now puffed at a cigar—"I will be a force to contend with in the FO and in a new government." He now stared at me. "If you work with me now, as you have in the past, I'll be sure that you will always have a place near me. You may be sure of it."

I was not altogether surprised at this speech. As I have mentioned already in these pages, Mr. Moriarty was a man who was intelligent enough to realise his own limitations and to keep talent around him. I did not allow any emotion to show as I asked, "You seem to have had some information that disturbs you, beyond Captain Ravenswood's views concerning me. If I can unofficially advise you now . . . ?"

"Yes, yes." He straightened in his chair and his eyes gleamed from within his deep sockets as he told me of some of the details of the conspiracy plotted during the last twenty-four hours.

"This began even before I sent the Americans down to see you on Tuesday. Or, should I say, when Cyril Harvey sent that note with them and told them to say 'The lion looks in all directions.' Cyril and I have been friendly for some twenty years. He was instrumental in gaining my position for me in the FO. Somehow, he became enmeshed in these plans of the Southerners, who needed to involve someone within the foreign service who would be sympathetic to their plans. And Harvey was chosen specifically after being 'sounded out,' to use Captain Ravenswood's colourful phrase.

"When they first arrived, I sent them to you because I know that you are familiar with some of the codes. Ames told me that they had a note from Harvey, but I wanted you to assess these men. Harvey had already sent me a circumspect cable, preparing me for this delegation in veiled terms, which hinted at the true nature of their mission." He shifted in his chair, relighting his cigar which had gone out.

"I don't mind telling you again, Holmes, that I have come to rely on your assessment of situations, so I told Ames to send this delegation on to you. And you handled the affair in precisely the manner I had expected of you. I apologise for deceiving you, but it was imperative that

I hear your estimation of them before I made my decision to join them or to send them packing."

This news startled me. My first reaction was that Moriarty was saving face for relegating what was an important delegation to a relatively minor official. But all he said had the ring of truth and probability. My respect for his own arts of politic discretion rose considerably. At the same time, I considered trying to dissuade him from his course. But as he continued, I realised that my convictions could not turn him; he would reject my objections out of hand now. He was in a position to dismiss me from the service altogether, and I would not be privy to the information with which he was now entrusting me.

"The plan to capture Washington City is simplicity itself," he continued. "We shall repeat the successful invasion Ross made in 1814. General Sir Valentine Theodosius will sail into Chesapeake Bay, march across Bladensburg and enter Washington, just as before."*

I was startled. These were war plans being spun out before me. But were they Moriarty's plans alone? Like as not he was repeating Ravenswood.

"But sir, won't the Americans be watching our ships? If they are unscheduled and land without warrants, the United States government might sense some kind of unfriendly action. Troops might then be assembled if our regiments attempt to disembark. If this is to be an unexpected attack, surely we will have to lull the suspicions of the Americans,

---

* Jerrold Moriarty is referring to the Battle of Bladensburg and the subsequent burning of Washington City, as it was then known, on August 24, 1814. General Robert Ross and a force of 4,500 troops were escorted by a British fleet to Chesapeake Bay, defeating a small force of American regulars at Bladensburg under the personal command of President James Madison. When Madison perceived the outcome of the battle, he returned to the Executive Mansion. He and his wife, Dolley, escaped with little else but a brace of dueling pistols, a portrait of George Washington, and the original of the Declaration of Independence. Ross proceeded to set fire to certain public buildings in Washington, the Executive Mansion and the Capital among them. A rain put out the fire, saving the walls. The building's architect, James Hoban, restored the interior, the walls being whitewashed to remove the marks of the burning. The mansion was popularly called the "White House" afterward, but not until President Theodore Roosevelt had stationery printed with that name, in 1901, did it become the official name. MH/SMW

or their capital will be defended before we can even enter Chesapeake Bay."

"Well thought out, Holmes," Mr. Moriarty smiled. "That is where the new Confederate forces will come into play." He leaned back and blew a smoke ring into the air. "The Southern forces will be ready to engage Federal troops in Georgetown, drawing away military forces from our attack in sufficient numbers so that the resistance in Bladensburg will prove to be negligible. The two fronts will then become a pincers that will crush the resistance forces, while preventing the escape of the Washington politicians." His fingers gave a corresponding squeeze to his cigar, graphically illustrating the plan.

I kept calm while I framed all I heard into an orderly sequence. I was determined to tell the Prime Minister, to tell Trent—anyone who was in a position to help. I was diametrically opposed to this undertaking. Nothing of lasting value could be gained and there was much to be lost for the Crown, for the Empire—for England.

Resistance would appear, not only on the continent— France would be among the first, if not Germany, to declare war—but the whole world would explode upon Great Britain. The foreign press would have a field day, delighting to describe the treachery of "Perfidious Albion." Such an unprecedented catastrophe as would then be fomented would destroy the many blessings brought to the world through the English-speaking peoples. I inwardly shuddered at the thought of the rampant anarchy that would engulf the world.

The circumstances brought to mind the effects of the French Revolution and our own Civil War. The monarchy would be toppled, the flower of British youth would be withered, as had been the young men of France in this and the last century. We would be racked by endless warfare within and without, and eventually sink into the oblivion we would so richly deserve.

I saw now that the seeds of petty despotism sown by Moriarty within the Foreign Office would blossom forth with the fruits of war and death. And all this because of the ambition of Moriarty and men like him, seeking to impose their influence on others, becoming the tool of power and the source of grief to millions. I was determined to stop them. As I listened to the catalogue of the war's aftermath as Moriarty described it, I found my resolve strengthened. Trent would have this information and together we would save the beauty and grandeur that was England.

I continued to draw out Moriarty's plans and asked leading questions, mentally jotting down the designs of war. I discovered that the rebel forces would commandeer trains in Virginia and North Carolina, the goods waggons would be filled with troops and brought into the city undetected the day before. There would be an attempt made on the life of President Grant, and he would be advised not to leave the city, as he was planning, to open the Centennial celebration in Philadelphia.

"But that will make little difference," Moriarty continued, "for attacks will commence upon a dozen major industrial cities in the North in much the same way, Philadelphia among them. So, should President Grant be determined to attend the opening ceremonies, he will be captured nonetheless."

"But what of the other states? We will surely have to conquer each one of them before the fighting is done. That might take years, expending troops needed in other parts of the Empire. The colonial system will be weakened and revolts encouraged throughout the Empire."

Moriarty chuckled. "Well done, Holmes. That was a question which had originally troubled me. But I have been convinced by Captain Ravenswood that such a lightning-fast attack upon the capital city will demoralise the country before anyone can plan a counterattack. We will make prisoners of the entire American government and ship them away before the 'dis-United' States can make any kind of stand against us." He laughed again. "Do you remember the remark made by our minister when we signed away the colonies at Paris? He sneeringly asked the American representatives if he should make out one treaty or thirteen, one for each of the states.

"We have little to fear. Just ten years ago the country was torn apart, so divided against itself as to fight, one section against another. The same division still exists and more schisms have begun to grow. Each portion of that country is eternally jealous of the other, continually at the others' throats, not only within their own legislatures, but within the Congress also. And without the central authority at Washington, politicians in all the divers states will be quaking in their boots, begging their legislatures to make separate treaties of peace with us at any price. You'll see, Holmes. One by one, in quick succession, each state will humbly ask for Her Majesty's protection in exchange for its loyalty." Moriarty bared his teeth in a scornful grin, intently believing all that he said. "You will see that the American politicians will sign away their loyalty to the 'Grand Republic' so as to join the largest nation, the strongest power on the face of the earth. The Empire will stretch from sea to sea, encircling the earth as one mighty nation, headed by Victoria, the first Empress of the World!"

"That is a grand ambition, sir," I said. "But there will be state militias and citizens who will not bend to us . . ."

"Humph. As there are in India. And what have they done to us?" was Moriarty's response. "Besides, they will be unready and will become the more unwilling to fight the strength of Great Britain, a power they cannot hope to overcome." He leaned forward, conspiratorially. "We may even have mercenary reinforcements from Mexico and South America to press into service should we need them. The United States is hated in the Latin countries and especially in Mexico, where the Washington government is still looked upon as a landgrabber." He sat back with a contented smile. "You do well to question our potential weaknesses. I knew that you would be a help to me. That is why I have chosen you to assist me. And, as soon as that fool Ravenswood sails back to his country, you'll continue to be my advisor."

He chuckled to himself once more. "Can you imagine Dizzy's face when I march into his office and present him with a map of the entire North American continent, telling him that once more the British Sovereign rules the entire area? We may even annex Mexico."

"I suppose Prime Minister Disraeli will have little time to savour such triumphs."

He paused in his laughter. "You show yourself indeed wise in the ways of government, Holmes." His eyes became hooded, cobra-like, though his smile persisted. "He will be sent packing, Holmes, very soon after the news reaches us that the conquest has succeeded."

I was apprehensive about those hooded eyes. Moriarty suspected me now because I was too astute. What has been said of megalomania was true, I saw at close hand: The disease moves slowly, causing each of its victims to forever suspect his advisors. I had best prove less clever, I thought, and so give him an opportunity to demonstrate his superiority.

"Then Mr. Gladstone will receive the news and act with you to consolidate the gains made by the Crown."

This had precisely the pacifying effect for which I had hoped. Gladstone had retired from politics the year before. My remark would be typical of a minor official who spoke before thinking. Moriarty relaxed and cocked his head to one side.

"That is what one would expect, if one were unwise to political trends. If the Jew falls, then Gladstone returns from Hawarden to pick up the pieces." Moriarty grinned mockingly. "I see that you still lack the subtlety of deceit, Holmes. But Gladstone is as bad as the Jew."

I was relieved to see that Moriarty's suspicions had been lulled. My response was one of incredulity: "But why should Mr. Disraeli be forced to resign? He caused the annexation of the Fiji Islands and he's made known his plans to annex the Transvaal next year."

"But look at what he did *this* year," Moriarty shot back. "The farm labour law, the factory worker law. He's now let it be known that he plans to clean up the rabble in the slums and build new homes for them." He shook his head slowly, his disgust evident. "The man's a romantic. Those novels of his"—Moriarty grimaced—"full of sentimental nonsense. He's a mollycoddle. He annexes the Fiji Islands, which have no army, and takes the Transvaal, which might just as well have none. Would that Hebrew milksop try to annex France or Germany?" he glowered. "Or the United States?"

I admitted that the prospect was doubtful. He dropped the ash from his cigar and his disposition lightened.

"Gladstone, as I said, is just as bad. Another reformer, another do-gooder. Patting the Bengalis on their greasy heads and calling them his brothers, trying to reclaim the whores of Whitechapel . . . no, Holmes. Both of them are redundant to our plans. That is why Disraeli will topple and Gladstone be discarded." He looked me full in the face. "You may have determined that those men in the billiards room were not brought together by accident."

"I had not considered them, sir," I lied. "I was too busy during the game."

"Well," he smirked, "if you had noticed them, you would have seen that they represent a great many departments of the government." He regarded his cigar a moment. "One man was not present, Sir Edmund Darlington."

So my worst fears were realised. Sherlock was right. Sir Edmund would take charge of the Liberal party, calling in his debts from among the party leaders to pass over Gladstone and support him to run for Gladstone's former seat in Parliament.

"Sir Edmund was the first person to whom I mentioned these plans," Moriarty said. "Failing to appear at the Admiralty Ball, Sir Edmund was to meet the Americans this morning in my office. But Gladstone returned today and demanded a meeting of the party leaders. Therefore, Sir Edmund was forced to send his regrets." Resentment built within Moriarty as he said, "He didn't even make his excuses until I sent word to him enquiring as to procedure this morning."

So the new "government" was not as united as I was being led to believe. This would be valuable to know in the future. I tucked the information away as Mr. Moriarty continued.

"Now Sir Edmund will not be able to see the Americans until the test of that air-device on Monday. And there he will not be able to discuss plans in detail." He was lost in his bitterness. Then, remembering that I was there, he continued with a false heartiness. "But, not to worry. After we complete our planning, he will bring pressure against those who owe him favours. He'll then be nominated to Gladstone's former seat in Parliament, be named the new leader of the party. Gladstone will then be sent to the banks of Lethe and the Tories to the depths of Hell, their leader, Disraeli, first and foremost among them."

"I suppose that, with the death of Colonel Leland, it will

be proper now to work with Captain Ravenswood as the ranking member of the delegation."

Moriarty's face took on a quizzical look. "What are you babbling about?" he asked.

"It occurred last night in the American's suite at the Langham Hotel. The Colonel was apparently the victim of a gang of thieves." No need to tell Mr. Moriarty about my deductions as to his real murderer. He would find out soon enough.

"Thieves, you say, eh?" He grew alert. "Was anything of—value—missing?" So he knew about the necklace too. Ravenswood had told him of its value—and its use. Sherlock had been correct on all counts.

"When I returned Miss Leland to her suite, she discovered her father's body. In addition, Miss Deane, her companion, is missing, under mysterious circumstances."

He thought on my words for a moment. "That's too bad," he said at last, but his mind was still on the necklace.

"The room was a shambles and Miss Leland was terribly distraught. I'm amazed that you have not been informed of it by the Captain."

His eyes once more filled with suspicion. "I am surprised also, Holmes. You've proven yourself to be observant once more. I shall find out what I can from Ravenswood later. So the police believe it to be a robbery attempt, eh?"

"I left before the police were informed. Captain Ravenswood, in fact, refused to allow either of his two compatriots to put the police in touch with the matter while I was present. He mentioned that the Foreign Office would have to find a way to keep the matter quiet and to satisfy Scotland Yard. I'm surprised that he mentioned nothing about it to you."

"It surprises me, too, Holmes." Moriarty would be having some words with Ravenswood now, before their plans proceeded much further. Perhaps after he became disenchanted with the Southern captain, I could persuade him of the futility of the plans to capture America. Until then, I was happy to see that the suspicion now settling on his brow was directed toward the sullen American. I could have little to do with them after last night; therefore I had need to plot a Napoleonic strategy now. I had to sow feelings of discord among the members of the alliance and then step back to let them fight among themselves: *divide et vince*. I could only hope to exploit any feelings of mistrust that might spring up between the British and Southerners for future conferences with Mr. Moriarty.

The appearance of the butler ended further discussion, as he announced the presence of Captain Ravenswood. Moriarty would have had him wait until I was able to exit, but his plans were frustrated when Ravenswood pushed himself past the startled servant.

"I knew I'd find this lily-liver here," he raged. "I told you that this man was to have nothing more to do with this plan!"

The butler was dismissed and Moriarty rose in wounded dignity.

"How dare you burst into my home, sir! You must : . ."

"Not another word, Moriarty," Ravenswood snapped, his imperial bristling electrically. His voice was low and deadly when he added, "If you say anything else, I'll have you ruined, do you understand. I'll create the biggest scandal that this country's ever seen, and you'll be right in the middle of it."

Moriarty's face took on a ghastly pallour. "Now see here, Ravenswood," he began in a more reasonable tone.

"No. *You* see here. This man will be gotten rid of and immediately, do you hear? He's forced his attentions upon my fiancée, and he is now meddling in the death of my late commander, Colonel Leland. Now then," he growled, "make your choice, Moriarty. Are you with us or are you out? Is it Holmes or me?"

Mr. Moriarty was uncertain as he looked at the both of us. But it took a very few moments before he spoke—the choice was inevitable.

"I don't know what goes on between you and the Captain here, Holmes, but there has been too much time and effort invested in these plans to throw them up for some insignificant junior clerk. I hereby suspend you from any further duties in the service until I determine what may be at the bottom of these accusations." He melodramatically pointed at the door. "You will be informed of your future in Her Majesty's service. As for now, you may take your leave."

Ravenswood opened the door and stood to one side. I

passed through it, only to have the American take hold of my arm as he did in my office at the conclusion of our first interview.

"And if I find you disturbing Miss Leland again," he said in a low snarl, "I will have the great pleasure of killing you." He then gave me a push clear of the aperture and slammed the connecting doors shut behind me. The butler solicitously handed me my hat and stick, though I fear I paid him little heed for my thoughts were racing madly now. I found myself on Moriarty's front step, furiously trying to determine my course of action. Should I go to the PM? Yes, but I might also try around at Grosvenor Square. No doubt I could interest American Ambassador Schenck in this matter and that would take it out of Moriarty's hands altogether.

I gave second thoughts to this plan of action, recalling that I was under orders from Moriarty to say nothing to the Americans about the affair. If I did, I could find myself without a position.

My position. I was suspended in any case; what harm could be done my position now? Mr. Moriarty could do little else to me; I was as good as booted out of the government. No doubt Ravenswood would try to have that accomplished. He was already attempting to implicate me in the murder of Colonel Leland. But I dared not go to the American Ambassador or to Calvin Trent; the Southerners would surely have the embassy under surveillance.

I summoned a hansom, bidding the driver to take me along the Embankment. I wanted to think this business through and the short ride under the trees might help me.

Should I try to see the Foreign Secretary, hoping to make him believe this outrageous plan? No, he was away, salmon fishing in Scotland. I laughed to myself bitterly. He will surely be sent further away than Scotland when the Southerners' plans near fruition. Some minor emergency, just important enough to keep him away from London for a few days would suffice.

And there would no doubt be some urgent itineraries set for the General Staff within the next few weeks, all coming during the end of June and the beginning of July next year. Their deputies would be happy to keep their offices in good order during the generals' absence. And while they were away, ships, regiments, and commanders would be mobilised, no one knowing that war had not yet been declared, and they would remain in ignorance until the telegraphs carried back the news of victory in Washington, Philadelphia, and a half-dozen other cities.

So why would anyone give this outlandish plan any credence? I could scarcely believe it myself. And if I found it incredible, how much more so would the Foreign Secretary, the Home Secretary, or any other government minister in Whitehall? I might just as well attempt to make the Prime Minister believe it.

The Prime Minister? Well, why not? I would first defy whatever lookouts might be watching the embassy, get to Ambassador Schenck, and bring his message to Mr. Disraeli which would ensure me an entrance past his officious secretary, Alexander Stafford-Clark. The PM was the only person who could bring this to an end now, short of my storming Windsor Castle. But no, I thought bitterly, the Queen is at Balmoral. No, the only person who could act quickly and decisively was Benjamin Disraeli.

I rapped up to the driver. The trap in the roof was opened.

"The American Embassy in Grosvenor Square. And please to hurry."

10

THE "RASPBERRY MITRE"

"The Ambassador is extremely ill at this time, sir." These words were my greeting in Grosvenor Square. I recalled his unkempt appearance on Thursday. I could do nothing but leave word for Trent, then proceed to the Prime Minister's residence, and hope for the best.

"Number Ten, Downing Street, driver."

My Foreign Office credentials allowed me past the policeman outside the door, as well as the stony-visaged butler within. I was ushered into an antechamber to cool my heels while awaiting Mr. Disraeli's secretary. Within a few minutes, that personage entered.

Alexander Stafford-Clark was a man with whom I had had no previous meetings. Mr. Disraeli had assumed office a little more than a year before and my good offices had not, as yet, been called upon by him for any purposes of statecraft. Mr. Stafford-Clark was a dapper young man, with longish hair, always immaculate and impeccably attired. This afternoon he wore an elegant tan cutaway, brown- and tan-striped trousers, and a heavy gold Albert chain was hung across his dark waistcoat. His manner and voice were an obvious emulation of his master's.

"Ah, Mr. Holmes. Terribly sorry to keep you, but the meeting with the Servian Minister is imminent and we've been busy. Those people delight in being inconvenient. It is only because of his visit that Mr. Disraeli has remained in the city today."

"I cannot tell you how grateful I am to find . . ."

"I have to be sure they are all properly greeted, in French, by Stephens. And you know how Stephens detests speaking that language, even for the sake of diplomacy. But then, there it is. Now, how can I help you? Can you divulge a few of the details about this—ah—emergency?"

"I could, Mr. Stafford-Clark, but I prefer to tell the PM directly."

He sat down, a thoughtful look disarranging his finely chiseled features. "Please believe that I understand your haste, Mr. Holmes, but also please understand that I must know the nature of this errand if I am to disrupt the PM's meeting. I should want to be sure that it was for a good reason. I have my position, you understand, as well as the importance of this impending visit, to consider."

"I understand," I said, nodding, "that this meeting with the Servian representative is of great moment, but I can say, without exaggeration, that my news is even more imperative. But I understand your situation."

I had best speak with the tongues of angels to get myself past this officious little man.

"I have information that there is a mutiny in most, if not every area of the several ministries. It is a mutiny that will consolidate the efforts of a band of Americans, in England now, to bring about the overthrow of the government of the United States and the downfall of Prime Minister Disraeli and the Tory government."

Stafford-Clark looked at his hands gravely, saying nothing.

"I can supply the names of most, if not all, of the officials involved, and give you an unfortunately incomplete timetable of events."

Stafford-Clark continued to say nothing.

"I have this information directly from my own superior officer within the Foreign Office, Mr. Jerrold Moriarty, who is, unhappily at the center of this mælstrom."

Stafford-Clark finally looked up. "You say that you are privy to these plans and can identify those who are involved. How did you become involved?"

"Mr. Moriarty believes me to be sympathetic to these plans." My words were now coming out in a rush. "Mr. Stafford-Clark, I must impress upon you the urgency of this matter. The plan is to disrupt the July Independence Day celebrations in America by sailing Her Majesty's ships of the line into Chesapeake Bay and debarking troops to invade the city of Washington on the very day of their centennial celebration."

"And how can they do this without the knowledge and consent of the Lords of the Admiralty? You know that ships and troops must be deployed only with their consent and the approval of the PM?"

"I don't know how they plan to do it, sir, I only know that they will forge authorisations, if they have to. They may have one or more of the Lords of the Admiralty within their conspiracy for all I know, and they could send the proper documents on to the commanders involved. There are one or two generals already implicated, whom I saw in a meeting with the Americans and Mr. Moriarty."

"You say you were privy to the information?"

"But not the complete details." I was getting desperate now. This officious secretary would not allow me in, I knew. But I went on, hoping that there might be one relevant detail that would move him.

"The plans are only now being formulated. Within a week, two at most, they will be crystallised. These men will then be ready to strike with the ships and the troops on the deadline as mentioned.

The secretary looked at me gravely. "Mr. Holmes, do you believe that a few shiploads of men, even British troops, can demolish the entire government of the United States?" He smiled benignly. "I am second to none in the admiration I have for the British soldier, but do you really believe that so few . . ."

"There are insurrectionists throughout the southern half of the United States. They are training and are already mobilised. All they lack is the command to group and attack. That will be given to them in time to invade Washington through Georgetown, allowing the main bulk of our soldiers to harass the forces from the northern sector of the city. It will be a secret attack and they hope to catch the Grant administration off guard, if not completely asleep. For all I know, they may attack at night and raise the Union Jack over the Capitol dome that morning, the morning of the one hundredth anniversary of the American Revolution."

"That sounds like the very melodramatic touch that the affair needed," smiled Stafford-Clark. "All in all, it has the ring of a very suspenseful novel." He looked at me. "How long has it been since you've been on holiday from your work, Mr. Holmes?"

I rose. "If you do not let me in to see the Prime Minister," I roared, "you will be a party to destroying the entire civilised world."

"Now, please, Mr. Holmes. Calm down," Stafford-Clark said, also rising. "You'll not prove your point by bellowing."

"I must get in to see Mr. Disraeli, and you'll not impede me any longer." And with that, I made a rush to the door of the inner office. With a speed I had not reckoned upon, Stafford-Clark pushed his chair aside and stood in front of that door. His response to my action stopped me.

"Now understand me, Holmes," he said severely. "I know that you must be tired and distraught. But I warn you. If you attempt to see Mr. Disraeli, I shall stand my ground here and call for the entire staff to come in here and eject you. Calm yourself!"

I was breathing deeply, and I was ready to pick up the young man and throw him to the other side of the room. But I realised that such an action on my part would evoke exactly the consequences threatened by the PM's secretary.

"Very well, sir. I have no other recourse." He relaxed a little at his stand. "But I warn you. If this plan is put through, you'll find yourself seeking a new position, if you do not find yourself in the deepest dungeon of the Tower for your mistake today."

I turned and left the office, slamming the door loudly. I brushed the servant away as he attempted to escort me to the street door, opening it myself and slamming it with equal force. The constable looked back to me, but decided not to interfere, apparently thinking me a disappointed office-seeker or something of the like.

I stood in front of Number Ten, collecting my thoughts. I took a couple of steps, turned and looked back at the residence. An athletic man might scale the front. I thought of Sherlock. Ah, if only he were here, I mused bitterly, he might climb the pergola or the wall or a drainpipe. He could sneak past that damnable Stafford-Clark a shade better than I. I looked at my expanding girth and saw that such an attempt was beyond me. Scaling anything but a short flight of stairs would have been an impossible folly. I dismissed these farcical thoughts and hailed a passing hansom, directing the driver to take me home to St. Chad's Street, home, and Mrs. Crosse's luncheon.

The cab moved spasmodically through the usual Saturday afternoon congestion in the Strand. The shadows were lengthening as my chances to halt the senseless carnage dwindled. I was the epitome of irresolution. After my abortive interview with Stafford-Clark—even before—my mind was unable to focus on the events piling atop each other. Intermingling incidents of a personal nature intruded upon my professional mind. My fine talks to Sherlock about logic and reason seemed to be so much fluff now. I had to end this conspiracy before it swallowed up the nation, but my rebuff from Stafford-Clark and the rebuke from Moriarty had been so unexpected.

And behind it all remained the thoughts of Rachel Leland as she appeared the night before at the ball, a beckoning wraith, quite beyond my powers of holding. I sought to dispel this thought from my mind, but irrevocably, it returned, taking pre-eminence over the cataclysmic events spawned over the week past.

I arrived at Number 42 thoroughly disgusted with myself, that I could not shake the memory of the evening past nor avert the tragedy I foresaw. I had a thought to reject Mrs. Crosse's kindly urging that I take lunch, but I was hungry, and such relaxation would be a welcome, calming influence. I splashed water into the laver and rinsed off my face and hands while Mrs. Crosse set out the substantial meal on her waggon: shepherd's pie, scotch eggs, venison *pâté*, bread, butter, and jam. I was spreading the *pâté* when I saw Mrs. Crosse's latest attempt at religious coercion tucked under the napkin. It was an essay by Father Newman, entitled "A Letter to His Grace, the Duke of Norfolk, on the Occasion of Mr. Gladstone's Recent Expostulations."

"Rather a long title for so small a pamphlet," said I with a wry smile.

"Father Newman felt that he had to defend the Pope against that terrible black Protestant from Scotland," she returned with good humour, as she fluffed up the pillows on the divan. "Imagine Mr. Gladstone mixing into our religion, and he a turncoat Scotsman," she said with faintly concealed disdain.

Dear Mrs. Crosse, I thought, smiling amidst my other worries.

"Ah yes," said I with a little sigh, "and John Henry Newman a turncoat Anglican. Yes, it is a shame that we cannot keep the issues clear."

"Humph," said the young woman with righteous indignation. "Father Newman just saw the light and abandoned his former ways."

"A *kindly* light, I should say."

Mrs. Crosse took her leave in a cloud of incense, while I took a bite of bread and *pâté* and perused the tract. It was well written, as were all of Newman's literary endeavours. It was, as the title took pains to say, a reply to Mr. Gladstone's essay, an effort to refute the recently defined dogma of papal infallibility for his former C. of E. constituents. I pondered the situation with a brief chuckle. It was well that the former Prime Minister was out of office, for the Catholic pulpits had rung with denunciations of his intrusion. It would have gone badly for him in the press if he were still leading the government.

My thoughts turned to the career of William Ewart Gladstone. An able man, he was not only a politician of consummate skill, but a well-respected scholar. Many years before, he had written his own translation of Homer from the Greek.

In the House of Commons, he had been a member of the Conservative party, now in the minority, until fairly recently. But his reforming spirit did not sit well with the leaders of the Tories. Finally, he saw that he had no alternative but to cross the aisle. Thus, the "Grand Old Man" joined the Liberal camp. Just last year, he had called for a vote of confidence and failed. Mr. Disraeli, as the leader of the Tories, swept into the premiership and a disgusted Gladstone had resigned his seat in Parliament, announcing his retirement. The press now occasionally reported on his efforts to rehabilitate Hawarden, the restored castle that was his country home in Wales.

Then it struck me. Perhaps I could persuade Gladstone to intercede for me with Mr. Disraeli. It seemed rather silly at the time, and no less now, as I write these words, fifty-nine years later. But I just might be able to convince him. All I had to do now was to locate him. But where was he? Mr. Moriarty mentioned a meeting of the leaders of the Whigs that Darlington had seen to be more important than to meet with the Southerners. Gladstone doubtless attended. It was held somewhere in Whitehall. But where would a man, a fine scholar and deeply religious, betake himself while spending some time in London? Would he perhaps spend some time in meditation? Perhaps—especially after conferring with sordid minds beleaguered in petty politics. I thought of St Paul's. No, too big and too public. All Hallows? No, too far out of the way, as was St. George the Martyr which I also rejected, although its drab interior might appeal to him. St. Martin's-in-the-Fields? Small and private, it would appeal to him. The church was near enough Whitehall. That might be the one. Without another thought for lunch, I dashed out to the street and hailed a cab.

Upon my arrival, I ran ino the little church near Ludgate. He was not there. Considering their vast numbers, I knew it would be impossible to search through every church in London. But where else could he be? I gave the matter more thought.

A religious man could avail himself of prayer and meditation best in his own home. A man who was a scholar might wish to continue his researches and study. He might want to dispel the paltry meddlings of the petty politicians of today with the great thoughts of philosophers from the past. And if that man be a student of Greek literature, he might best appreciate those thoughts in their original language. And where else would a student of Greek literature go in London to study such manuscripts, but a place wherein he would find them in profusion? Therefore, it would not be beyond the realm of probability to find William Gladstone in the manuscript room of the British Museum. Well, I had nothing to lose by trying to find him there.

Arriving at the museum, I made for the manuscript collection. There are several small rooms for serious students surrounding the major collection, and my only delay was to find in which of these rooms Mr. Gladstone had secreted himself. I found him, his white head in faded contrast to the ivory of the mouldering piles of ancient writings stacked on the table before him. A pair of spectacles was perched on his nose, as the well-known, craggy face perused the antique manuscript spread out before him. His pince-nez was attached to a cord that lay across one of his hoary side-whiskers before descending to the button on his lapel where it was fixed. His coarse, ruddy features were screwed up in a look of perplexity as he tapped his pencil against the paper on the desk containing his constructions of the *reliquiae* before him. He had been often pilloried by the Tories as a vulgar, ill-bred "man of the people," to use Mr. Disraeli's phrase. He was, in fact, the very picture of a respectably prosperous shopkeeper.

"Mr. Gladstone?"

The leonine head raised and the large expressive eyes peered over the rim of his glasses. "You have the advantage of me, young man."

"My name is Mycroft Holmes, of the Foreign Office," I said, by way of introduction. He looked at me for a moment, then returned to his labours.

"I am retired from public service, young man," he said, with a quiet, weary impatience into the aged parchments. "Or hasn't the word yet reached down into the calcified depths of the Foreign Office whence you come?"

"Have you also retired from your country's need?" I answered, in a voice weary enough to match his own. He did not stir. "Besides," I continued, remembering the momentous phrase used in my office in what seemed to be a long age before, " 'the lion looks in all directions.' "

He tensed, made a mark on his paper, and without looking up, responded, " 'Yet protects the cubs within its den.' " This was the countersign!

"You are either very indiscreet, Mr. Holmes," said he, finally setting down his pencil, "or you are upon a rather important mission. If the former and if I were still first minister, I would sack you on the spot. If it is the latter, you must be in dire straits."

"As it stands now, sir, I am in peril in either way."

"I see." He indicated the wooden chair across the table from him, the only other furnishing in the bare cubicle. "I suppose I had best hear you out."

"But here, sir? The matter is grave."

"Of course it is, else you'd not have used that phrase. But who will bother us here?" He smiled crookedly as he surveyed the walls, then frowned, saying, "unless there are more of you people coming from the Home Office?"

"The Foreign Office, sir, and the answer is no."

"Little difference between the two these days, what with that land-grabbing romanticist at the helm." He turned back to his manuscripts. "You know, Mr. Holmes, I've been grateful for this chance away from public life. I have been splitting logs, as did the late Mr. Lincoln, and I heartily recommend the occupation for the members of this regime. I'd swear that those tree stumps have as much imagination as my honourable opponents." He chuckled drily. "Now, what have you to say for yourself?"

I quickly outlined the intended conspiracy. Mr. Gladstone did not interrupt my recitation of events, but he waved aside my explanations of political implications. He knew them better than I.

"I told that man some while ago to get rid of that foppish dandy, Stafford-Clark. Was he aware of the implications contained within the code, or do you think, as I do, that he's merely a simpleton?"

"To be fair, sir, I must say that I did not use the phrase in front of him. I felt that, if I could get to Mr. Disraeli, I would tell him."

"Of course, evidence of your good sense—'because he is an hireling and careth not for the sheep.' You'll find that in John, 10:13. Very well, then, what do you expect me to do?"

"I would like a letter of introduction from you, sir. A note I can take with me to Downing Street."

"To get past the invidious Mr. Stafford-Clark. A sensible thing, I must say. But one that may be easier for my friend here"—he pointed to a bust of Aristotle standing just inside the door—"than for me. I carry little weight in the thoughts of the present occupant of Number Ten."

"More weight than I carry, sir."

"Mr. Holmes," he said seriously, "I have retired from public service. And I would just as soon take a sheet of blotting paper to the Embankment and try to dry up the Thames with it, as to ask Disraeli for a favour."

"Mr. Gladstone," I answered, "this is not politics. It is patriotism."

His craggy brow arched imperiously. "I will not be lectured on patriotism by you, Mr. Mycroft Holmes. I have served Queen and country for several decades, sir. And I was shouting down the back-benchers in Commons before ever you were born. As for now, I intend to have some time for myself and my family!"

I saw my last hope ebbing away in his rhetoric. But he relaxed and continued in a milder intonation, "Besides, my boy, I am not at all sure that I believe you."

"I am not lying, or inventing a story, sir, you must . . ."

That mighty hand again waved me into silence. "I don't doubt that *you* believe it. But there are too many gaps in your tale. Nothing about the War Office, or how this cabal intends to thwart the Chancellor of the Exchequer to find the monies necessary for the undertaking."

"Representatives from both ministries were in the billiards room last night."

He sat back in the hard wooden chair. "I see," was his only comment before he fell silent for many minutes. He sat motionless, his chin propped in his hands, his elbows resting on the arms of the chair. I thought, after some time had passed, that he might have fallen asleep. But then he raised his eyes to mine.

"No," he rumbled.

"Sir?"

"My answer is no."

I would have spoken, but he raised his hand. "Don't misunderstand me, Holmes. It took great courage for you to seek me out. And your sincerity is quite evident. But I've been forty years in the Commons, and close within the machinery of government. I can assure you that it is not the well-greased machine sometimes portrayed by our ministers.

"The plot you outline depends on a smoothly co-ordinated, well-timed operation, implemented by like-thinking men who are in agreement on each possible element making up the whole. As you have outlined it, the intrigue makes no contingency for the bellyache of the commissary officer, nor the shrewish wife of the armaments sub-minister. It is the pettifoggery of mundane matters which will defeat your conspirators, Mr. Holmes.

"You may be aware that whilst I held the premiership, it was said that I cared little for implanting the British flag on foreign lands, that I cared little for empire. That is true." He paused. "But that I do not care for *the* Empire, for England, that is a gross and unjust lie. I wish to see and do the best possible work for England. So also, I can say, does Mr. Disraeli. Oh, we have our own methods, each of us, but our ends are identical: that the Empire—England—shall always lead, never follow the parade of nations." Once more, he put his head in his hands.

"I have told you that I don't doubt your sincerity. I understand your wish to overthrow what you believe to be incipient threat to the realm, wisely perceiving that it leads only to anarchy and death, and heaven knows what other evils brought on by the overthrow of established order.

"But I am assured of one thing: it is the plan of the Almighty that sets the foreign and domestic policies of nations. Whoever assumes the title of the Queen's First Minister is merely carrying out that plan. Yes, even Benjamin Disraeli.

"We are all God's servants, Mr. Holmes. And I tell you now that if it is God's will that we regain the entire North American continent, I for one, shall not attempt to thwart Providence, lest I find myself fighting God Himself!"

With a great weariness, I picked up my hat and stick. Then I turned to him. "And supposing, Mr. Gladstone, that this be not God's will but the will of a consorted band of men seeking to force His hand for their own motives and gain? What will you do when the nations begin their march upon us, to cast down all that has been built up by generations of scholars and statesmen?" I looked hard into his eyes. "What will you do then, sir?"

I turned away, my feet like lead as I left him among his papers.

Outside, the biting cold and darkening sky chilled and dismayed me only a little less than the memory of Mr. Gladstone's rhetoric. I walked along Great Russell Street, until I came to Montague Street. Deciding against visiting my brother's rooms, I caught a hansom to take me home.

The cab was about a block away from my home, stopped

for cross-traffic in the Euston Road. I looked out and saw a familiar and friendly-looking pub sign. I had often noted its incongruous name, "The Raspberry Mitre," but had never visited its precincts. On a sudden impulse, I handed the driver my fare and alighted in the street. It was not my usual custom to partake of spirits this early in the afternoon, but my present circumstance and depression prompted the action. Thinking to myself that a drink would settle my stomach and calm me, I hoped for a chance to sort through the scrambled events of last night and this afternoon, to put them in some kind of order. Then I would plot another strategy to see Disraeli.

There were no other patrons within the pub when I entered.* I ordered a whisky and soda. The liquid burned my throat as I poured it down. The glass now empty, I asked for another. I went to a booth and continued to sip. I had a fleeting thought that I might become intoxicated, imbibing as I was with only a bite of bread and *pâté* for lunch. But Mrs. Crosse's breakfast had been substantial, I rationalised; all would be well.

I was mistaken in my reasoning.

The incident last night with Rachel Leland, my vengeful feelings toward Sherlock, not to mention the murder and my morning's frustrations with Moriarty, Stafford-Clark, and Gladstone, all crowded together. Was I beginning to fall in love with Rachel Leland? In an adolescent way, I found myself thinking about her manner, her looks. No, certainly not love. Or was it? Was it merely an infatuation? I could not say. I only know that I found myself, again and again, on the veranda overlooking the garden, with her hand in mine. Was this what my brother meant by my "less disciplined behaviour" last night? And if this love was not scorned by the woman, it was surely endangered by Ravenswood. I recalled his threat and felt a great wave of anger wash over me.

---

* London's now notorious "pub hours," which prohibit the opening of establishments before the hour of 11:00 A.M., close them in the middle of the day, from about 2:00, and then allow reopening from about 5:00 to 11:00 P.M., did not come in until a few years past the turn of the century. Before that, the rule was that the pub could remain open from dawn until midnight, even on Sunday. MH/SMW

How many glasses were on the table? The two had become four, the four had become eight. I blinked and looked again. I was not sure but that the eight had now become sixteen. And again I thought of Rachel Leland.

I was trifling with the affections of an affianced woman. That it was not a trifling matter to me, but the innocent flowering of love, meant little. My mood changed as I became angrier with myself. I was the interloper and I should be treated as such. "I should offer myself to Ravenswood, the great duellist. I will allow him to challenge me and draw first blood," I muttered to no one in particular, "It's the only decent thing left for me." The family honour would not be shamed: I was a Holmes and I would, by God, conduct myself in the best traditions of the family!

Having convinced myself of the chivalry of that sentiment, I took another drink.

The memory of the remainder of the evening is unclear. I vaguely recall that there was a disturbance in another part of the pub and I set upon myself the task of quelling it.

"I know a great many things you probably don't know yourself," I ringingly declared to the barmaid. Pointing to the argument I said, "I can solve their problems for them logically. Deductive reasoning, you know." I then asked her if she was aware that the man she had met that afternoon was in the habit of using moustache wax.

A constable was summoned and I recall a short walk through the wintry air to what must have been my abode, for Mrs. Crosse's face suddenly loomed before me, a portrait of fear and consternation. I remembered nothing else until the next morning, for suddenly a great, palpable darkness descended and everything went black.

11

MISS LELAND LEAVES
WITHOUT ME

The room was still black when I awoke. The pulsing in my head beat with Wagnerian vengeance; my mouth was as dry as though Brünnehilde and vast legions of the *Walküre* had galloped through it. All in all, as I sorted out my extraordinary performance of the evening past, it was, with but one exception, the most embarrassing memory of my entire life. I was thankful that I was unable to recollect more.

With palsied limbs, I struggled to my feet. I saw in the dim forelight of dawn that I still wore my shirt (*sans* collar), braces, trousers, and stockings. It had probably been all that Mrs. Crosse could do to remove the rest of my garments and put me to bed. My efforts brought on another sensation. I quickly opened the cabinet of the wash-hand stand and removed the chamber pot. On my hands and knees, I vowed never to drink to excess again, for I now knew how it must feel to be the victim of an apoplectic stroke. As I felt at that time, a cerebral hæmorrhage could be no less than the pounding in my head.

Gaining some control of myself, I rose to my feet, occasionally reaching out and taking hold of whatever solid pieces of furniture made themselves available. I was tremendously thirsty. I roundly cursed my landlady for leaving but a tumblerful of water, which I gulped down quickly. By doing so, I made myself dizzy once more and I carefully walked back to my bed. It was evident that Mrs. Crosse had more sense about these things than I.

Lying there, I stared at the mottled ceiling, and immersed myself in thoughts of my terminated career. Professionally ruined, I saw that not only had I been dismissed, but I had ensured my fate by insulting the PM's secretary and by slighting the most able and proficient statesman of the age. I'd have no luck with Mr. Gladstone if there was a change of government and I sought to reclaim my position in the FO. In other words, I had not only dug my own grave, I had nailed shut the coffin lid and shovelled dirt on top.

All this was because my efforts to stop the ambition of a single knot of men had proven feeble and disjointed. The independent history of the United States would come to an end because of me, while stupid, vainglorious men swept over me, the one person who dared oppose them. I was to be consigned to the sewer of defeat, to moulder there amidst the other ruined lives of weak and vacillating men.

If I was a fool professionally, I was, romantically, a buffoon. Poor naïve Mycroft Holmes, who sought to pluck a star from the heavens, could not upset the plans of an arranged union.

Nor was that the end of my misery. I had earned the contempt of my brother, convinced in my own smugness that he was the fool, not I. It was plain to me now to whom the cap and bells truly belonged.

I will not weary the reader with a litany of the misery to which I subjected myself in the early hours of that Sunday morning. But I suffered the wretchedness of a man who is forced to admit defeat and disgrace.

Even after I heard the sounds of the household come to life and the dawn was full upon my windows, I continued to stare at the ceiling. The door to the street below opened and closed. That would be Mrs. Crosse leaving for early Mass. When she returned, more than an hour later, I was still abed. I was not cheered, as on other mornings, by the happy clatter of pots and pans announcing the breakfast being prepared in the kitchen. I had broken out in a sweat and kicked the blankets from me. I was ashamed of the unpleasant task through which I had put Mrs. Crosse. I was ashamed also because I lacked the strength to don my robe and face her within her own domain. I would have apologised for last night's inconvenience and told her that her food was wasted on me this morning.

Then there was the sound of softly treading footsteps on the carpeted steps leading to my room and a faint, almost indiscernible knocking at my door. It opened to the solicitous face of my young landlady, her black curls under a mob-cap, a long apron around her neck and tied at the waist.

"Mr. Holmes?" she called softly. "Are you awake?"

"I am, Mrs. Crosse," I rasped. "And more's the pity."

She entered my flat, a restrained bundle of energetic good will, slowly yet anxiously making her way through the sitting-room to my bedstead. I hurriedly attempted to draw the covers around me, but she arrived before I could grasp the sheet. I had endeavoured to pick it up three times before she shooed me back and raised the blankets to my chin herself. Noticing the chamber-pot, she shook her head.

"Mr. Crosse once did the same thing that you've done. And I told him that he could forget all about me if ever he drank that much again." She picked up the foul-smelling pot, holding it at arm's distance, and made a face, saying, "I'll have this emptied and return directly."

When she did return, she had a glass tumbler in her hand and a water pitcher. She held up the tumbler, full of a liquid of indescribable colour. "This is a sovereign cure for gentlemen who indulge the drink when they don't know how to handle it," she said, by way of introducing me to this universal specific, which was, she told me, a vile concoction consisting of orange juice, a raw, whole egg, cayenne, garlic, Worcestershire sauce "and plenty of salt and pepper." Had she not stood over me watching, I should have thrown the mess across the room at first taste. But she handed it to me and crossed her arms defiantly, as though daring me to refuse.

"Come now, Mr. Holmes, you won't taste a thing," she said, her bullying posture belying the sweetness in her voice.

I put the tumbler to my lips, swallowed, and paid the penalty for trust. Good Lord, but that witches' brew was nauseating! As I downed the contents, Mrs. Crosse smiled, relaxed her stance and looked encouraging. I could not have felt worse. The concoction blazed a trail of molten lava through my throat and stomach. I coughed and dropped the glass.

"You lied!" I said through rigid lips. "You made that brew from dead toads. My *lungs* are on fire!"

"Oh, pish-tosh," said she, with a toss of her dark curls. "My husband called that a Bombay Bomb. Why, he could polish one off with not so much as a by-your-leave." She rinsed out the glass and poured more water for me.

"Now you just rest, Mr. Holmes," said she. "Drink this slowly. I will be back later."

She was out the door before I could tell her to leave the pitcher. But, within a few minutes, my limbs ceased their St. Vitus rituals, and the putrid taste in my mouth was cleansed away. After a short rest, I began to feel better. I became convinced that Mrs. Crosse had inherited the "healing touch" reputed in mediæval times to reside in the monarch.

I must have stayed abed for another hour before my mind rebelled in stagnation. I betook myself to wash, shave, and dress. I still had need of some intellectual stimulation to free myself from the chains I had forged. I then remembered the manuscript that I had begun the previous morning and removed it from its place in my drawer. "The very thing," I said aloud.

I read over the words I had written and saw that I had not gotten very far with it, so I began to write once more. I detailed William Bankhead's dramatic interruption of the meal at Goldini's; our cramped ride by landau and my remark about aglets; our meeting with Dr. Agar, and Ravenswood's cigar. And, as obliquely as possible, my first meeting with Rachel Leland. When I came to the end of this episode, I looked over the many pages of foolscap. This was taking too long, I thought. So I set down the major incidents as they had happened, while they remained fresh in my mind, devoid of conversation or parenthetical comment. I hoped to gain a clearer perspective of all the elements comprising the whole of this adventure, and perhaps find a key to unlock some of the mysteries that remained. Then perhaps I could dispel the murky shadows that were now cast upon my somewhat clouded career.

I examined motivations as I noted them, weighed the facts, and transcribed my observations alongside them. I had done a good deal of this when Mrs. Crosse knocked again. She wanted to inspect her patient to see how he had progressed, I thought, as I bid her enter.

Her sternly determined face told me that nothing could have been further from the truth.

"You have a visitor," she said coldly, "by the name of Miss Rachel Leland. Shall I say that you are at home?"

I nodded vacantly, not daring to believe her words.

"Then I'll tell the young lady that you will be seeing her directly," she said curtly. I was sorry that my landlady did not seem to approve of Miss Leland. She would not presume to tell me of her feelings in so many words, of course, but she closed the door with a sonorous bang.

Hastily brushing my hair, replacing my carpet slippers with proper shoes, and donning an informal house-jacket, I descended the steps. The door to the downstairs parlour was open and Rachel Leland, clad in a warm woollen cloak of the colour of thick chocolate, was pacing the floor. She was deeply upset, I saw, and did not intend to stay long, for she still carried her fur muff, and her satiny blonde hair was yet enclosed within the folds of her hood. She moved with quick, nervous steps.

I was overcome by the sight of her, unable to speak a word. Miss Leland came to the end of the parlour, turned, and took a step before looking up and seeing me. I must say that the sight of her face, wreathed as it was with her golden curls and framed in her sable hood, would have melted the stoniest male heart. With a small cry, she ran across the room, and would have come into my arms, had I so wished. As it was, she stopped in front of me and looked into my eyes. Her own were filled with a deep anguish.

"Mr. Holmes, Mr. Holmes, I need your help! He's insane!" And so saying, she exploded into tears and then buried her face in my shoulder.

I was nonplussed by this turn of events, tentatively placing my arms about her shoulders, over the deep brown cloak she wore. As I did, her hood fell off her head and her hair brushed my chin. All I could say was, "Please calm yourself, Miss Leland, of course I'll help you," as soothingly as I was able. "But of whom do you speak? Who is insane?"

"Captain Ravenswood. He's challenged Tyler to a duel," she said. "He'll kill him, Mr. Holmes, he'll kill him."

"Ravenswood? He could never fight a duel in the city without being arrested before things were properly begun." More than that, I thought, he could not risk the adverse feelings such an action would generate among his would-be allies. "But please, Miss Leland," I gently asked her, "how did this begin? Please tell me what happened."

She drew a handkerchief from her muff with which she dried her tears. I recognised it as my own.

"After you and your brother left us Friday night, Tyler wasn't so sure that Samuel was doing the right thing by not letting us call in the police to investigate father's murder. He kept on about how we should go to Scotland Yard and see that it was done properly."

Her face became hard and her eyes blazed with blue fire as she continued. "But the Captain would have none of it. Tyler became more adamant about the police, but Samuel resisted his arguments, until finally he ordered Tyler to refrain from any more mention of the matter, and to respect the commands of his superior officer. 'There will be no police nor will there be any insubordination,' he said.

"At that, Tyler became furious and he told the Captain that he could go to the Devil, if my father meant that little to him, but that he would not stand by while murder was done. So saying, he opened the door to our suite and would have been out, had not the Captain fairly leaped across the room, pulling Tyler back by the scruff of his neck. Then he slammed the door shut. He turned on Tyler and threw him against the wall, just as though he were a puppet. Then he hurled him to the floor. Tyler got up and Captain Ravenswood slapped him across the face and challenged him to a duel."

She looked up at me with the face of a Madonna, so much beauty and so much sorrow to be seen in her eyes. "Tyler and the Captain never got on together. When Tyler and I were younger, we used to play together. I believe Samuel has resented our friendship."

"Then Tyler went into the army and the Captain was in the same regiment. The Captain would sometimes rag him and belittle him in front of the troops. After the war, Tyler and he would get into violent arguments—'discussions,' said my father, 'that had no purpose but to show up the other.' Well, Tyler became interested in the group of men who began the talk about the South becoming powerful again. The arguments between him and Captain Ravenswood stopped when Tyler told him of the group of men. They seemed to have finally found some common ground. And now this."

I wondered how much Rachel Leland knew about this plan. "Tell me, Miss Leland, what is planned for the South?"

She looked startled and then avoided my eyes as she said, "Why, Mr. Holmes, I don't know very much at all. Just some talk about making the South as powerful as it was before."

I might be in love with her, but I could tell that she was not being completely honest. I broke away from her arms and took her to the settee.

"When and where is this duel to be fought?"

"Tyler hasn't said. As the challenged, he has the choice of time and weapons. But he was so stunned that he didn't say a word. He just went to the room he shares with Billy Bankhead and locked the door."

"But I thought all this had been resolved when I left you last night. Tyler and Billy were both shocked that the Captain would not inform Scotland Yard about your father's death."

"It began again when the undertakers came to take my father away, before they left for Mr. Moriarty's office this morning. I've been doing my best to keep everyone calm."

"What with your father's murder and the disappearance of your friend, I can well imagine that all this must be causing you a great strain," I said kindly. "But if they all went to Mr. Moriarty's office this morning, then things must have cooled down, don't you think?"

She shook her head vigourously. "Mr. Holmes, don't you understand? Tyler and Samuel have pledged themselves to this cause, above all things."

"Then, if they are still working together, I fail to understand the urgency."

Rachel Leland flushed. "Don't you understand?" she said again. "They are together now because of their oath, because of their honour. When Tyler makes his decision, he and Samuel will be forced by a code of honour to see it through to the first blood.

"But if the Captain wants to be spiteful, he can say that honour is not satisfied and demand that the duel be to the death." She began again to weep. "And Captain Ravenswood thinks he has the advantage. It would be just like him to want to fight to the death."

"But how can I stop Captain Ravenswood?" I asked her. "He would not hesitate to challenge me also."

"I know," she said. "I might be able to talk to him, to turn him from this dreadful charade. But Tyler may force him to make good his challenge. I want you to try to dissuade him from that course and to accept my fiancé's apology and retraction of the challenge. Honour would then be satisfied." She began to cry again. "But only you can talk some sense into Tyler." Once more she rested her head on my shoulder. Again I gently pushed her away. She looked up at me.

"Is this to save your fiancé or to save Tyler?" I asked.

She looked at me in disbelief. "Why, to spare them both," said she.

"I'm sorry," said I. "I hoped that would be your answer."

"Why?"

The words came with difficulty. "I wanted to be sure that you weren't using me. I'm sorry to have entertained these suspicions." I thought of my brother. "I had to be sure in my own mind."

"Mr. Holmes," she said gently, "Mycroft, have you so soon forgotten what I told you Friday night?"

"No, Miss Leland, not a word." I looked away from her. "But I have no wish to compromise you. There are proprieties to be considered, you understand. You are going to be married soon."

"To a man I do not love; to a man I grow to despise and hate with each passing day," she said passionately, her eyes beseeching me to say something to soften her pain. I saw her anguish, but I could do nothing. My own sense of honour forbade me to interfere with her betrothal. She saw my despair.

"I am sorry."

"So you abandon me to my fate."

"I must. My honour demands it."

She stared at me and her lips set in a straight line. "Damn your customs and proprieties," she said as she rose from the settee. A wild look now took possession of her eyes. "Damn your honour. Why are you afraid? To protect me? To protect yourself?"

" would not have you held up to reproach," I said softly.

"You would condemn me to a life of emptiness for the sake of some artificial ideal?" Then she laughed scornfully. "Or is it because it would cause gossip about you in your ous Foreign Office?"

Her implication caught me off guard. "What do you mean?"

"Would the Prime Minister look down his nose at you because you dared take the woman you love? Is your career worth more to you than I?"

" dear, such a thought is monstrous! It never occurred . . ."

"And I thought you were brave," she sneered. "I wanted you to prevent a duel. I thought you would defy anything for me, for what you know is true. You are nothing more than a snivelling coward." She laughed again, wickedly. "You call yourself a diplomat! Would you try to save the world, little man, while your own crumbles about you?"

by her attack and my silence infuriated her.

"I thought you were a leader, that you were above petty rules, but I now see that you wouldn't have the strength to lead. weakling!"

to the depths by her spoken contempt, but I found m gue.

spoke to me of honour. What I say may sound pretentious, but my honour is the very touchstone of my life. I cannot throw over nearly three decades of my life for a whim. Such a lack of discipline leads to chaos and anarchy.

"All my life I have cultivated my integrity. My proudest boast is that my word is my bond. Can't you understand that? Can't you see . . . ?"

"All I see is a spineless slavey who seeks to curry favour with his superiors," she said coldly. "No, I cannot understand that you can refuse the one thing, the best thing, I can ever give to any man."

She opened the parlour door.

"You are the most contemptible man I've ever known,"

she said, making her way to the front door. "I'm sure you will learn to live with your cowardice. But I can't and I won't. I will return to a man, a man, do you hear? One who is not afraid to take that which he desires. I am too proud to be content with less. Goodbye."

She pushed her way past me and swept regally out the door and into the carriage awaiting her return. Through the sash, I saw her beautiful head, the hood now fallen away, her proud chin thrust forward. The carriage drove off, leaving me, stricken, in the front hall.

For long moments I stood there, staring into the street. I was rooted to the spot. Finally, the measured tread of my landlady activated me. I shut the door as she descended the stairs behind me.

"Is there anything I can do for you, Mr. Holmes?" said Mrs. Crosse.

"No, thank you, Mrs. Crosse," I replied, in a green and hollow voice. I turned to go, but she took my hand in her own.

"Dear Mr. Holmes," said she, with warmth and loyalty, "If that lady doesn't know what a prize she's throwing away, then Devil take her."

I looked into her kindly eyes. She pressed my hand in a gesture of sympathetic good will that was touching. I shrugged and smiled brokenly. Then, slowly and silently, I left her on the stairs and walked back to my room.

The chimes of St. Pancras Church finished striking the hour of four. If not for their quarterly tolling, I should have lost all conception of time. As daylight waned, I sat within my darkening room, staring fixedly at the wall opposite. I had been thus since Rachel Leland's vociferous departure. All motivation had been drained from me. Her contempt had plunged me back into that fit of depression I had so keenly felt in the early hours of that bleak day. Within less than forty-eight hours I had found a treasure, only to watch it sink beneath a quagmire and vanish.

My solitary vigil was interrupted by Mrs. Crosse's insistent knocking.

"A man to see you, sir," she said, darkly. "He told me that he was come from the Prime Minister."

"From the . . . Prime Minister!" I cried. "Are you sure that you heard him correctly?"

"Oh, quite, Mr. Holmes." Her eyes were wild with apprehension. "I hope you are not in some kind of trouble."

"Humm? No, Mrs. Crosse; not any longer!" I exclaimed jubilantly.

I dashed past the startled young woman and almost leapt down the entire flight of stairs in my anxiety to greet the messenger.

"Mr. Holmes?" he enquired rather dubiously.

"Yes, most definitely so."

"The Prime Minister would be grateful if you would be able to see him . . ."

"When?" I interrupted, ignoring the proper etiquette.

"At once, if you do not find it inconvenient. I have been asked to escort you. A coach awaits without."

It took me a very brief time to make myself presentable, donning the clothing proper for the occasion in a trice. Then I was whisked away by a handsome coach and four to Number Ten, Downing Street.

12

IN DEFENCE
OF THE EMPIRE

When we arrived in Downing Street, there was another short wait before Alexander Stafford-Clark made his appearance. Upon this occasion he was the perfect picture of courtesy and deference.

"The Prime Minister is expecting you, Mr. Holmes. If you will follow me, please?"

We went through the door that I had threatened to shatter the day before. We passed through one office and then another. The secretary opened a door and announced my arrival. He stood back, allowing me to enter.

Behind a large oaken desk, in a study whose walls seemed composed of nothing but very full bookshelves, sat Benjamin Disraeli, First Minister to Her Britannic Majesty. I had seen him before, of course; he was as familiar in the vicinity of Parliament as Big Ben. The tall, thin gentleman slowly rose to his feet and offered me a languid hand in welcome.

"Mr. Holmes, how do you do. Please take a seat."

"Thank you, sir."

"It was good of you to come on such short notice."

"Had I been roused from sleep, I should have come as quickly, sir. The matter is that important."

"My secretary did not at first agree with you, I understand."

"I am happy to see that he changed his mind and told you."

The Prime Minister raised his finely arched brow in surprise. "It was not Stafford-Clark who arranged for this conference, Mr. Holmes, I assure you."

"Then who else . . . ?"

"I did," rumbled a deep voice behind me. I whirled to

see William Gladstone rise from his seat and come forward with his hand extended.

"Mr. Gladstone thought you would be taken unawares," smiled Disraeli. "I recall that he took great delight in mocking my sense of the dramatic on the floor of Commons. I shall remember this incident for your return, Mr. Gladstone."

"As though I would come back with you at the helm, Mr. Disraeli," Gladstone retorted. "And you, Holmes, don't look so startled," he said gruffly. "Our conversation yesterday afternoon persuaded me to think that your so-called conspiracy might not be such a fanciful idea at that. You turned out to be quite right to challenge me.

"And don't thank me either," he continued, as I began to express my gratitude. "All I have done is gain you entry. Now you must convince this parliamentary paragon of your tale. And myself as well."

"Mr. Gladstone speaks truly, Mr. Holmes." said Disraeli. "I agreed to see you as a favour to my old opponent here. I am not convinced by what he told me, which he admitted was incomplete. I am afraid you will still have to plead your case as though this were the Queen's bench and I were Mr. Justice Hume." He paused. "In all fairness, I should tell you that you had best be eloquent, for your credibility is not of the highest. Stafford-Clark mentioned that you almost came to blows yesterday."

"That is true, sir,"

"Don't try to frighten the young man, Dizzy," said Gladstone. "That piercing stare and Semitic nose of yours might shake some green back-bencher in Commons, but I think you should know something about our Mr. Holmes before you try to intimidate him."

The Prime Minister resumed his seat behind the desk, while Gladstone and I sat in the red-velvet and mahogany chairs facing him.

"Well, then," Gladstone began, pulling some sheets of foolscap from his pocket, "I've made some hurried yet discreet enquiries as to the character of Mr. Mycroft Holmes." He donned his pince-nez, searching through the papers. "Ah—no that's Plato. Ah, here it is. Mycroft Holmes has been in the Foreign Office for a little more than five years." He peered over the rim of his glasses at

Disraeli. "D'ya remember that embassy we sent to Herzegovina early this year during that Balkan crisis? Well, if this young man had not been with Davies, we could have had a fine mess of things there, and the commission would have had nothing to show for its efforts. Davies himself put it into the dispatches, which makes me change my opinion of Davies a little." He read from the paper: " 'Mr. Holmes has been with us for some five years, joining the government directly from university, upon the recommendation of Sir Rodney Fairndails. But for his efforts and prodigious capacity for detail, the Herzegovinian ambassadors would have blinded our labours in that country. He is to be commended for his timely insistence that they honour their pledge of 1570, a year before the battle of Lepanto, of which none other of Her Majesty's ministers had the slightest knowledge.' Deucedly good work, young man.* ·

"Now then, I could go on, quoting Alec Caldecott of the Home Office and David Randall of the Exchequer and others, but on this they all agree: Mycroft Holmes is devoted to his work and has a knack for pulling true and verifiable details seemingly out of thin air. More than once Holmes has had facts at his fingertips which others could not have gleaned from the archives in five years of constant searching."

Gladstone folded his papers and replaced them in his pocket. "So much for Mr. Holmes' credibility," he said in conclusion.

"I withdraw the remark, Mr. Holmes." Disraeli smiled with easy grace. "And Mr. Gladstone, I had no idea that you had become so interested. Or that you would find yourself so highly applauded by your peers, Mr. Holmes."

"I merely wanted to see him receive a fair hearing."

"And rightly so, William. Now, Mr. Holmes, please relate the pertinent facts as you have learned them."

---

* There is no other historical mention of this secret "pledge," but a case may be made for it as a partial explanation for the refusal of Queen Elizabeth I to join the Spanish and Papal armies called to a "crusade" by Pope St. Pius V against the Ottoman Empire, of which Herzegovina was then a part. The "Balkan Crisis" of 1875 occurred when Herzegovina seceded from the Empire, which had become, at that time, the dissolute, corrupt "Sick Man of Europe." MH/SMW

"Go on, Holmes," Gladstone urged me. "From the beginning, just as you told them to me."

Carefully, I recounted the circumstances as they had occurred, beginning with the Americans' use of the code phrase. I proceeded to tell of the attack on Colonel Leland and Captain Ravenswood, and of my own involvement. I told of how I had been rushed from dinner twice, when Colonel Leland was shot and when Sherlock deduced an attack on the Americans, only to be knocked unconscious myself. I was heartened when Gladstone slammed his fist against the arm of his chair, saying "Good for them," when I told how Sherlock and Trevor had amazed Jericho with their dramatic appearance and turned the tables on him. I spoke of the men invited to the billiards room during the Admiralty Ball, and concluded with the murder of Colonel Leland and my conversations with Moriarty and Stafford-Clark. Disraeli allowed himself a wry smile when I told of how his secretary prepared to prevent my onslaught.

"So Stafford-Clark was ready to leap into the breach for my safety," mused the PM. "I am happy you didn't pick him up and toss him aside; I doubt he'd have been able to withstand you."

Gladstone snorted, "That pipsqueak couldn't withstand a steady breeze in Regent's Park."

I was about to detail how I found Mr. Gladstone when the former prime minister lifted his hand.

"Mr. Disraeli knows we met," he said. "Now then, Benjamin; do we believe him?" Disraeli followed the smoke of his cigar as it wafted its way to the ceiling. "I see that he has converted you, William," he said finally. There was no answer from Gladstone. The Premier rose and walked across the room to a large globe sitting within a richly carved oaken frame. His back to us, he spun the globe. Gladstone continued to face the desk, sitting with an air of calm. Yet his eyes were charged with a sense of expectancy. Was he awaiting some ringing address from this man who had opposed him these many years in Commons? Or were they both awaiting some analysis from me?

There was only the sound of the spinning globe, and of Disraeli's long, artistic fingers skidding along the enamelled surface. Without turning from it, he quietly asked, "Do you believe him, William?"

"What possible difference could that make upon the face of the earth?" Gladstone asked with a low-pitched testiness. "You are the Prime Minister now." The PM turned to face him.

"The tale is fanciful and sensational. You are a novelist, Benjamin. Such fancy folderol alone should appeal to you." Mr. Disraeli smiled where he stood, as the "Grand Old Man" continued to regale him. "You and I both know what truth, and how much there is of it, is contained in what we have heard. I am not yet that far removed from the leadership of Commons that I do not recognise whereof young Mr. Holmes speaks.

"His assessment of Jerrold Moriarty is accurate. That man curries favour as other men seek love. Such a scheme would certainly enjoy his support, as well as some others whom I could name in the vicinity of Whitehall.

"Besides," Gladstone continued, "Moriarty is a stupid man."

"You are right, William," said Disraeli. "Moriarty is easily led. Why you ever allowed him to remain on in the FO is quite beyond me." He sat behind the desk again, staring at his folded hands. "That man is not a Machiavelli to weave a web of empire from the separate strands of dissent and discord found in the government agencies, the property of would-be leaders. Moriarty is merely one of those strands himself."

"He didn't say that Moriarty was leading the bloody conspiracy," Gladstone growled. "Moriarty has only brought the separate elements together. Do you not listen to what is said any longer?"

The Prime Minister raised his head, a fixed smile on his lips as he contemplated his old foe. "I listen. Oh yes, William; I listen well. And I remember. I remember, for instance, the sight of you waving a copy of the Budget; waving it in the face of the Commons in '52. I remember how you kept pounding away at, how did you put it? at 'this document of destruction.'"

"And your government fell," Gladstone replied cozily.

Disraeli's smile vanished. "Only because you whipped the Commons into a frenzy; because you replaced the pool of logic with a torrent of emotion, and *that*, my dear adversary, is precisely why I shall not be harried or bullied into accepting this young man's story so quickly. I have no intention of taking some rash action before I can be fully acquainted—*fully* acquainted, I say—with all the facts."

Gladstone lifted his hand, but only to rub his forehead as he muttered, "Father forgive him, for he knows not what he does."

"That's Luke, 23:34, only slightly paraphrased," came Disraeli's swift reply. Gladstone dropped his hand, utter amazement on his face. The PM smiled slowly, "You see, the old Jew has done his lessons. But I beg you not forget the remainder of the passage: 'And they parted his raiment and cast lots.' You may be sure that I shall not allow the Empire to be parted, nor be gambled over by rogues and sharpers."

"If you are determined to rake over the ashes of history, Benjamin, why not try to find something a bit more germane to our discussion," said Gladstone with an utterly false smile. "The *Alabama* settlement has more relevance to this matter than some twenty-three-year-old Budget."

"Indeed it has." Disraeli quickly snapped up the subject. "And how did the *Times* describe you in that instance, William? 'Pusillanimous' was, if memory serves, one of the kinder epithets used in the article."

Gladstone flushed. "If we are to be dependent upon notices and editorials in the public press to guide the policies of the ministers of this nation, it could surely be no worse than what leadership you are providing now! You know as well as I that the *Alabama* arbitration staved off a serious crisis. And even though we lost the case, arbitration by the Geneva tribunal was an excellent precedent to set, and one that will be turned to our advantage someday."

"Exactly, my dear boy," said Disraeli, "that's exactly the point. I'm happy that you see it now."

"See what? What do you mean, Benjamin?"

"I mean," said the Prime Minister gravely, "that action hastily conceived and hurriedly executed will not be condoned by this government as it is unfitted to the governing of this nation." He smiled and raised his hands. "Arbitration, that's all I want."

"I agree," said Gladstone, without a pause. "Now may we return to the matter at hand?"

"But of course, William," said Disraeli, now the soul of amiability once more. "I am sorry to have neglected you for so long, Mr. Holmes," he continued, turning to me once more. "But this is the result you must expect when you bring two recalcitrant old bucks together: The first thing each does is to search for the other's weak points."

"As well as digging at old wounds," Gladstone quietly grumbled. "You see the reception given the bearer of ill-tidings, Holmes? Thank God this isn't ancient Rome with Mr. Disraeli as Cæsar. You and I would no doubt be presently covered in pitch and illuminating the imperial gardens."

"Now William," said Disraeli, affecting an impatient wheedle, "you yourself said that you had not the information necessary to form a valid judgement in this matter. I should appreciate it if you would refrain from hectoring me as I try to gather such information for my own judgement."

"Now, Benjamin," said Gladstone, adopting the same tone, "I have only submitted that no one but you can have your plot and eat it too. If this young man had brought you knowledge confirming your own suspicions, you cannot in good conscience condemn him to Pentonville Prison."

"But William, he has brought me no such corroboration."

"Then I further submit to Your Worship," said Gladstone, as though he were proceeding in court, "that you may not challenge the testimony presented to you by this young man for no other reason but that you lack the certain knowledge to which he has become privy." He cleared his throat. "Now may we return to the matter at hand?"

"Yes," said Disraeli, with furrowed brow, his hands folded on his desk top once more. "Mr. Holmes, in all candor, I must say that I find your tale far-fetched. And, while it appeals to me as a novellist, I must confess that as Prime Minister, I am unconvinced. Such a massive scheme is unreasonable and illogical, not to say that it is fatuous and absurd."

"Yes, sir," I said. "And I am the first to admit as much."

"Ah, that speaks well for the lad, Benjamin. His quiet assurance is impressive, is it not? Why, if some hysterical maniac from Speakers' Corner dashed in here, pounding my desk and ranting at the top of his lungs for me to do something . . ."

"Someone like yourself, eh, Mr. Gladstone?" said Disraeli, smiling.

Gladstone narrowed his eyes. "If I myself came in the door with this tale, I should escort myself to the door and have myself ejected. And with a kick for good measure."

"I agree that Mr. Holmes is no rabble-rouser . . ."

"I don't know if Mr. Stafford-Clark will agree with that," I said.

"A touch, my dear Mr. Holmes," said the PM appreciatively. "That says even more for him, William. Lunatics have little or no humour." The Premier cocked an eye toward Gladstone, "that I have noticed, anyway." Even Gladstone chuckled.

"All right then, I've threatened, bullied, denounced, and insulted you in the House. I shall let you have that one, Prime Minister," Gladstone said with a smile. "But there is one man to whom I shall not give the time of day until we get to the bottom of this infernal cabal."

"You must mean the ubiquitous Sir Edmund Darlington," said the PM.

"You're damned right," Gladstone retorted. "He has the key to this Rosetta Stone of intrigue, I'll wager." He sighed. "I hate to admit that he's a member of my own party, for he reminds me of Cassius."

" 'Such men are dangerous,' " Disraeli quoted.

"Aye, that they are. And Sir Edmund has been making himself a veritable good Samaritan of late. He garners political favours in the same manner that other men net butterflies." Gladstone slapped the arm of his chair again, and winked at me. "He has a good net, but he'll have no issue to catch this time, I warrant you."

"Until now," I said. "The winning of America may be a very good issue to change his credits into political currency."

"Yes," said Disraeli. "In a way, Sir Edmund will be able to despatch us both to the outer darkness where there will be a weeping and gnashing of teeth."

"*You* may wish to weep and gnash teeth, but I shall not, by jingo!" Gladstone thundered.

"Nor do I," said Disraeli smoothly, "but I may spare

myself the threat of a vote of confidence in the Commons by taking up the invasion and championing the conquest of America myself. A nation the size of America, possessing her wealth and potential, is a tempting prize for the Empire . . ." His voice trailed off.

"Ah, don't talk daft, man," said Gladstone. "That could only bring about the greatest military momentum since that little Corsican upstart began his endless chain of conquests."

"I don't know, William," the Prime Minister mused, "America has no allies, none at all, with the possible exception of France."

"Ah, but France hasn't an army to spare. And do not forget that, although President Grant has not begun to search for allies, there are any number of countries on the continent who would offer their services. They would be happy for the chance to use that as an excuse to fight against us. And let us not forget Russia. The entire world would then declare war upon the United Kingdom and none else would stand in defence of the Empire. And when it was over, we would find our country devastated and our population decimated."

The old man stood. "And if ever you allowed that to come to pass," he declared, his finger pointing to Heaven, "then by all the powers above, I would fight you in the Commons, bending every effort to destroy you, and not be satisfied until you and every last one of your creatures were expelled from Parliament."

Disraeli turned in his chair and faced me. "I do believe that Mr. Gladstone is making a speech," he drawled.

Gladstone looked up at his hand and realised that he was making an expostulation worthy of the floor of the Commons in the small study. He joined in with the quiet laughter of the PM.

My interview over, I left Number Ten much heartened. With a firm resolve to seek out my brother and find the necessary proof to win the Prime Minister's intervention, I left the two statesmen and returned home.

I left the coach and dashed up the stairs with the unbecoming haste that so characterised me in those days. I wished to remove the formal attire I had changed into for my meeting, put on my comfortable greatcoat and scour the city for the shred of evidence that mattered to the PM.

I unlocked the door to my rooms and turned to light the gas.

"Don't bother, Mr. Holmes," came a familiar voice out of the shadows. "Please extinguish the match." I did so.

"Well, Captain Jericho," I said, facing the wall. "Did you use the front door this time, or the outside window, as have so many others of late?"

"We haven't much time, sir," said the Negro, as though I had not spoken, "I must bring you alive, and I would be unhappy if you gave me any reason to fail the promise I gave my friends."

"Which friends?" I snapped. "Those who shot Colonel Leland on Tuesday night, those who ransacked his rooms on Wednesday night, or those who murdered him Friday night?"

"We haven't much time," he said again.

"And if I choose not to accompany you?"

"You'd cause me to resort to a most unpleasant sort of persuasion."

I considered my alternatives and found them wanting.

"Very well, Jericho. You take this round. Where are we going?"

"That must remain my secret for the present time." His voice came from just behind me. "You'll pardon me if I remove your hat?"

He did so.

"Now, would you get into this coat? One arm at a time, please." He wrapped a long, greasy mackintosh around me. It smelled like a horseblanket. He then placed an overly large bowler on my head.

"Are you taking me to a masquerade or to a rendezvous?" I asked with weary scorn.

"You simply must be patient, Mr. Holmes," Jericho answered, his inflection as steady as ever. But I sensed a feeling of urgency in his voice. He was anxious to be off.

"Tonight is the consummation of all your plans, is it not?"

He was silent.

"Only I stand in your way now, eh?"

"In a manner of speaking, Mr. Holmes." His voice

moved to the door. "Let us be off now. And I would ask you to not disturb your gracious landlady or any of the rest of the household, if you take my meaning. I have a loaded revolver in my hand."

"Much like the first time we met in these rooms," I quietly replied. I would have no opportunity to send word to Sherlock, I thought with my heart sinking, without placing my life in jeopardy. I could only see this part of the adventure through for myself and hope for the best. Perhaps a later chance for escape would present itself. The only good would be that I would learn more of the plans that Jericho was hatching before I fled.

We were down the stairs and out the door with silent celerity. A closed coach awaited us. One of Jericho's henchmen opened the door and my unwished-for escort and I mounted the vehicle. The door was closed and the shutters made secure.

"I don't want you to anticipate our destination before we arrive," said Jericho, in explanation for the mysterious manner in which we were being conveyed. "I wouldn't want you to bother yourself to mark the way."

His teeth gleamed in the darkness as he smiled sardonically. And with just a trifle too much menace, I thought.

13

KIDNAPPED!

The horses' gait settled into a brisk trot after leaving the usual congestion in the area surrounding King's Cross and St. Pancras Stations. Travelling along the Pentonville Road, there would be little traffic at this hour on a Sunday night.

Jericho had not spoken since the time we entered the brougham, and so I had an easy time concentrating on our direction (east) and the course followed by our driver. Upon reaching the intersection of Pentonville with three other avenues, namely the City Road, Goswell Road, and St. John Street, we proceeded along the City Road. I inferred this by the angle of the turn taken by the horses. I prided myself upon gleaning a fairly accurate knowledge of London's streets during the years of my residence. This information was to stand me in good stead that night.

After passing Finsbury Square, the driver seemed to take several gratuitous turns, judging by the short span of time between each one. My sense of direction did not fail me, though. I reasoned that, no matter the convolutions of our itinerary, our general course, and Jericho's intent, was to reach the river. The American spoke not a word from the time we had entered. He sat opposite me, the pistol still in his dusky hand.

"You carry a different pistol tonight," I mentioned casually. "Your previous weapon was a much smaller gun. A Derringer, was it not?"

He said nothing, but I was determined to draw him out.

"Let me see—this revolver is manufactured by Colt, I believe. You take very good care of it, I must say. It almost shines in the dark." The sound of the horses' hooves on the pavement was my only answer. "It must be very special to you to keep it in such perfect condition."

"The fortunes of war," Jericho said finally. Hoping that his answer was oblique, I thought.

"Perhaps 'spoils of war' would better describe it," I said grimly. "Spoils of the American Civil War, to make an even more precise reference."

There was no answer, but Jericho's teeth appeared again in his broad smile. We travelled on.

In the silence following our brief exchange, I calculated that our time spent in travel had been about fifty minutes. The air was becoming colder. We could not be in the Embankment Road, I thought, it was too far west of our route. We were still east of St. Paul's, I knew, although we were now travelling in a westerly direction. I closed my eyes. We must be along the Wapping Wall, I decided, taking a course along Wapping High Street to St. Katherine's Way. Would we cross the river, I asked myself? Or would we stop in the deserted waiting room of a railway station; a vacant warehouse on this side of the river might be our destination. And then what? a bullet? a garrote? a blow to the head . . . ?

I willed myself to be quit of these morbid reflections. I must concentrate upon our itinerary, I told myself. If we crossed the river, over what bridge would we travel? The two nearest would be the Tower Bridge and Southwark Bridge. But which one?

"It's getting cold," I said, grateful that I had been left my gloves.

"It will get warmer," my companion answered. His meaning was clear enough.

"Quite," I responded.

The carriage was now turning to the left. The hollow sound of the horses' hooves told me that we had indeed come to a bridge. But which one?

I strained to feel a small swelling in the road. Was that it, or was it merely a loose stone in the roadway? A few minutes later, a pronounced jostle of the coach wheels confirmed that we were on Tower Bridge, heading south. The first tumefaction had indicated the bridge articulation, followed by the junction where the ends of the draw-bridge road overlapped. Only Tower Bridge would have these features for it is a draw-bridge.*

---

* This is certainly a puzzling statement. Tower Bridge was completed in 1894, some 19 years after this adventure took place. Mycroft must surely mean that he took Southwark Bridge, a short dis-

We left the bridge and turned right. We were entering the slums of Bankside.

I swiftly recalled that Captain Ravenswood had earlier visited Bankside, according to Sherlock. Were Jericho and Ravenswood in league?

"We will soon arrive at our destination," said Jericho, looking at his pistol, "and I regret that I must blindfold you."

"What!"

"I'm afraid I must, Mr. Holmes. I can't risk the chance that you could know where you are. I have friends to protect."

"And if I resist your idea?"

"I shall be forced to deliver you to my friends as damaged goods."

"I see that I have little choice in the matter," said I, as the coach wheels screeched to a halt against the kerb.

"I am obliged to you, Mr. Holmes," said Jericho as he bandaged my eyes. "Please allow me to lead you out of the carriage."

I was pushed out of the coach and left alone while Jericho spoke to his driver in a voice low enough to prevent me from overhearing. He then brushed past me and opened a door near to us. A dozen raucous voices chorused past me from a distance and the foul reek of vomit, stale tobacco smoke, and cheap gin assailed my nostrils.

"You are sure that no one inside this pub will think it odd that a black man is leading a blindfolded white man through the establishment?"

"Not at all," came Jericho's cheerful response. "We're going in the back door."

It was, in fact, a very small back door, I discovered as we squeezed through it. I caught a snatch of a conversation: ". . . so she pawned her gloves. Then Rainy, coy lady what she is, sent 'er right around to fetch 'em back."

---

tance to the south of where Tower Bridge would stand. That he goes into such detail of deduction would be grounds to doubt the veracity of his account. One can only believe that this lapse is intended for the ease of the reader who might not have readily understood Mycroft's reasons for knowing that he was being taken across Southwark Bridge, a much more refined problem, no doubt. MH/SMW

Cacophonous laughter greeted this apparent witticism. We might be entering the back door, but we were still very close to the pub's main room. That made little matter, for I was led up a flight of stairs, past a spacious room at the landing, and immediately guided up another flight into another room. The voices drifted up from the public room below until Jericho shut the heavy oaken door.

"I trust that you've suffered no great inconvenience, Mr. Holmes?" said Jericho, removing my blindfold.

I said nothing, but blinked several times, although the only light was the dim glow coming from a mineral-oil lamp hung from the ceiling. We were the only tenants of the room, a small loft above the pub downstairs. I made a mental note of my surroundings. To this very day, I can accurately recall it in every detail: the rickety wooden chairs, ten of them around a large rectangular table of roughly fashioned oak in the centre of the room, the lamp suspended above it.

Looking about me, I had no doubts but that the pub, approximately three hundred years old, was on the bank of the river. I could just make out some distant lights across the Thames from the large oriel window at the north end of the room.

The room's dimensions were not necessarily small, but it had a feeling of closeness, derived from the low roof and the heavily timbered ceiling and walls, for the timbers ran along the ceiling and were continued down along the walls to the floor. The wood was thick with accumulations of smoke, dust, and cobwebs, imparting to the beams the whiskers of age. The entire chamber had a nautical look withal: I felt as if I were in a cabin aboard an old three-masted man o' war.

Captain Jericho sat down and pulled out a chair next to him.

"No need to stand on ceremony here, Mr. Holmes. Be seated."

I did so and again looked to the window. The abundance of heavy grime on the leaded glass made it impossible to see anything else but the lights along the riverside.

All at once, the door opened to admit a short man, who quickly shut the door behind him. He wore a bowler, a comforter wound around his neck, and the collar of a long, ragged coat turned up. He had a yellow complexion under a two-day growth of beard. Several sticking-plasters adorned as much of his face as I could see, as though he had cut himself shaving. This, perhaps, accounted for the whiskers. He sat at the opposite end of the long table and said not a word.

Within a short time, another man entered, a stooped Lascar sailor, dark-skinned, with long hair poking out from under a dark blue stocking cap and gathered behind with a cord. He wore a thick-knit fisherman's sweater with a high-rolled neck under a navy-blue pea-coat. As he walked under the soft glare of the hanging mineral lamp, I saw his black, bushy eyebrows, the surly look on his thin lips and the long and livid scar which ran from under his left eye to the corner of his mouth. He said nothing to us, but walked over to the first man and spoke to him in a low voice which I was unable to hear distinctly. A reek of garlic had entered with the Lascar and became overpowering as the man returned to our side of the table. It was all I could do to keep from choking as he leaned across the table, his garlic stench like a shield and buckler to him. My eyes watered as he said:

"Hullo, Mycroft."

It was Sherlock!

The door opened before I could reply, and the publican entered.

"Four pints of bitter," said Jericho.

The publican nodded and left us. I allowed him to shut the door before I exclaimed, "Sherlock! what is all this?"

Smiling, my brother nodded to Jericho. I looked at the Negro and repeated my query.

"You'll have to wait and see, Mr. Holmes. It won't be long now."

"But why all the mystery?"

"Our friend here," said Sherlock, glancing at Jericho, "thought it was a necessary precaution to protect his friends. It also appealed to my sense of the dramatic."

"I have only recently been in the presence of the two greatest actors of the age," I said. "By comparison, this is sheer mummery. But Sherlock . . . ?"

"Yes?"

"Who is the man at the end of the table?"

"You don't recognise our old friend, Sergeant Lestrade?"

"Lestrade!"

"Yes, but don't talk to him now. He told me that he was portraying a policeman and he has to concentrate to stay in character," Sherlock smiled.

"Very funny, I'm sure, Mr. Holmes," the Sergeant called out from the far end of the table. "I just hope that your bully-boys arrive soon, for your own sake. The law is very severe with those who give false information to the authorities and detain them from more important work."

Sherlock smiled. "You'll find this work important enough, my dear Lestrade, you have my word on it."

The publican chose this time to reappear with the swill that passed for dark in this establishment. I grimaced as I drank it.

"Don't worry, Mycroft. The ale is more for appearance than anything else," said Sherlock.

"I am certainly happy to hear that. But why was I brought here at all?"

"We had to bring you here like this," said Jericho, "because we wanted you in on the capture."

"What capture, would you care to tell me?"

"Do you remember the attack described by William Bankhead?" began Sherlock. "The one that occurred on the night they arrived? He said that two men were involved. One wore a plaid greatcoat and there was some mention of a duke. After Leland's murder last night, I became convinced that the two incidents must be related. I therefore found Jericho here, and Trent and Trevor also. I pressed them all into service and the results will be made manifest tonight, with any luck."

"In all honesty, Mr. Holmes," said Jericho, "your brother did not have to use much persuasion. As soon as I heard of Colonel Leland's murder I knew you would suspect me. It happened despite the precautions I had taken, so I wanted to help to clear myself. That's why I'm here."

"But Calvin Trent also?" I said, turning back to Sherlock. "You say that he allied himself with you. And with Captain Jericho?"

Sherlock smiled. "I convinced him to call a truce. I pointed out to him that it would be worth more to his career to prevent another civil war from breaking out in his country than to run Jericho to earth. He'll be arriving later." He took out his watch. "In fact, it is just time for our appointment, gentlemen. Shall we go to the public room?"

The publican must have been part of the plans conceived by Sherlock and Jericho: he had carefully kept a rear table vacant among the throng in his saloon-bar. We all found seats and I gasped as I located a virtually unrecognisable Victor Trevor. The young Beau Brummell was incongruously attired in a shabby suit, a dirty, checked cravat wrapped about his neck. With his tousled hair and a face begrimed by lampblack, he was giving a convincing portrayal of a local dockhand.

"Trevor is to bring the men we want to us. Keep watching him."

I sipped my dark and kept watching Trevor. Eddying around the gigantic young man was a current of humanity which seemed to include every kind of low life inhabiting Bankside. Trevor himself was engaged in a spirited conversation with another fellow, who was attempting to placate the young colossus. At one point, Trevor pounded his fist on the bar, upsetting the drink of another man standing next to him. His neighbor began to complain, but after taking note of Trevor's size and menacing attitude, he quickly subsided and called for another pint.

"I was not aware that Trevor was so good an actor," I said to Sherlock.

"He's had a pint or two to fortify himself," was the amused answer.

"A pint or two?" exclaimed Jericho, "It looks like he's put away so much dark that he'll soon be looking like my cousin Ethan. But here's our other quarry arrived," Jericho added, cutting through our laughter.

Indeed, another man had made his way to the bar and Trevor called to the barman to bring another pint for him. Sherlock smiled into his glass.

"Just one more character, and our little drama will be under way."

A minute or so later, Sherlock's hopes were realised as another familiar figure came into our den of thieves, entering the narrow side door behind our table, the same one through which I had been earlier led. Calvin Trent caught sight of us and Jericho found him a chair by the simple expedient of pulling one out from under its besotted occupant at a nearby table. The drunk crashed to the floor and lay, undisturbed in his alcoholic stupor.

"It came," said Trent, taking the now-vacant seat. "I've got it here in my pocket."

He started to reach for something in his coat, but Sherlock halted him, laying a hunting crop across his arm. The crop had been fished from within Sherlock's pea-jacket and was familiar to me. Sherlock had found the leaded crop some years ago and he loved to brandish it about the house as though he were a field marshall and the crop was his baton.

"Well, gentlemen, now that we are all here, shall we repair to our former quarters?" said Jericho nodding to the stairs.

We rose and, hidden amid the crush of tosspots around us, made our way past the middle room and up into the loft. We all took seats around one end of the table, Trent coming in last and sitting at the head.

"I gave your friend the high-sign," said Trent to Sherlock. "He'll be up in ten minutes."

Sherlock acknowledged this information with a nod, then turned to me, saying, "You may recall that, after the Admiralty Ball, you decided that I should further investigate the death of Colonel Leland. I discarded your theory of Jericho's responsibility for the first and third attacks, which left me with the problem of the second attack."

"Your brother knows about that already," said Jericho, a little ruefully. "It *was* my doing and . . ."

"I confirmed it this evening when I saw your pistol," I interrupted.

"That's right," the black man admitted. "But, in my defence, I can say that my men were under orders to search for the necklace. They were to incapacitate but not injure anyone they might find in the hotel suite who threatened to interfere in that search. Hence the chloroform."

"And the pistol butt?" I asked meaningfully.

"It might have been worse, Mr. Holmes," was Jericho's veiled reply.

"And did you find the necklace?" Trent asked quietly.

"I leave that for the Secret Service to discover," Jericho said, with his usual sardonic grin.

"To return to my original theme," said Sherlock, with a little emphasis, "it was left to me to follow up the inadvertent clue given us by William Bankhead on Tuesday night."

"What clue was that, Sherlock?" I said. "He seemed to know very little, actually."

"Ah, but he did repeat something mentioned by the attackers. 'Get the duke,' he thought they said. Well, he could just as easily have heard 'Get him, Duke.'

"Proceeding on this supposition, I returned to the Langham mews and asked the ostler who originally told me of the Bankside felons to accompany Jericho and me to Bankside to see if they might be found." Sherlock was warming to his description of the chase. "Considering that I was then in the same disguise in which you now behold me, this was something of a problem."

"But we finally persuaded him that it would be in his best interests," added Jericho.

Sherlock looked again at his watch. "We have little time now. I can only ask you to sit back and follow our lead. Mr. Trent?" The thin little American turned to him. "Please give your walking stick to my brother. I'm sure you are otherwise armed, and he might have need for it before the evening is ended."

Sherlock then turned to Lestrade. "Did you procure the extra constables for the swift removal of our guests after we have done with them?"

"I've been told to take my orders from Mr. Trent, sir, not you," was Lestrade's haughty reply. "But the men have been posted," he added grudgingly. "I have been a plainclothes policeman for some while now, young Mr. Holmes, and I will do my job well."

"Of course, Lestrade, of course," said Sherlock soothingly. Then he gave me a wink as he said, "We're only here to augment your usual blend of cunning and audacity."*

---

* This would seem to be a favorite taunt of Lestrade by Holmes. He is recorded as saying the same thing to him in "The Adventure of the Empty House," the first case collected in *The Return Of Sherlock Holmes.* It might also be noted that Lestrade's remark

"I almost forgot," said Trent. "You'd best see this telegram first, Mr. Holmes." He reached into his coat-pocket, finally able to get to the message, and handed it to Sherlock, who read it and then gave it to me.

"This may come as a bit of a shock," he said, not unkindly. I read it.

> TRENT:
>
> IN RESPONSE TO YOUR ENQUIRY, THE FOLLOWING FOUND IN REGISTRY, ST MICHAEL'S CHURCH, IN PLAQUEMINES PARISH, LOUISIANA:
>
> CAPT. SAML. RAVENSWOOD AND MISS RACHEL LELAND MARRIED 28 APRIL 1875.
>
> HOPE THIS ANSWERS YOUR QUESTION.
>
> D.F. BENJAMIN

"Your brother wondered about them," said Trent. "He and I thought it might be best to find out some more about them. There are many things that Ravenswood has to answer for, aside from the murder charge mentioned by Ambassador Schenck. Miss Leland seems to know about a good many of them." He paused. "And a wife cannot be made to testify against her husband."

My brother placed his hand on my shoulder. "Rachel Leland is one of the guiding lights of this intrigue, Mycroft. Do you remember our discussion? The worst thing for an intelligent person to be is a woman, because she cannot wield power in her own right but must rely upon the willingness of a man. In Ravenswood she found a ruthless tool, driven, as she is, by the lust for power and ambition." He paused. "She was using you also, Mycroft, and for the same ends."

It was a while before I could say anything. I remembered her visit earlier that day and the one she paid me at my office. Her apparent hatred for Ravenswood, her proffered love—she must have recognised my own mental ability and she sought to divert me. Divide and conquer. It all fit together now; it all made sense.

---

about being on the force "some while now" is no idle boast. By the time of *A Study in Scarlet*, in 1881, he had been in the Criminal Investigation Department (the CID) and its predecessor, the Detective Department, for some twenty years. MH/SMW

When I was once again in command of my faculties, I saw that everyone, with the exception of Lestrade, was looking at me. I took a deep breath of the fetid air and turned to Sherlock.

"You are right. It is the only rational conclusion. Leland had to be eliminated; his moderation would have gained him the acclaim of his people at home and the trust of the government here. Using such prestige, he would have halted Ravenswood's drive for power, and Rachel would become mere window dressing. He and whoever else there is in America planning this overthrow would soon find that Ravenswood was an unnecessary luxury. So, because the Captain is too much the hothead to have organised the attempts on Leland, he did little but carry out the orders—most likely put as suggestions—of his wife, Rachel Leland. It could only have been she. There is no doubt in my mind that he did the actual hiring of the thugs, but that his wife was the instigator of the plan itself."

There was no time to say any more. Footsteps were heard on the stairway. The door opened and Trevor entered behind the two men we had seen standing with him at the bar.

"Here they are, gen'nlemen," said Trevor thickly to his new-found companions. "I told you they'd be up here awaitin' us."

He ushered them forward. "They got maybe a dozen or so mates downstairs," Trevor announced to us. "But these are the two who deserve the bank notes. The big 'un's name is Jim and the chap in the plaid overcoat's Duke."

The man identified as Duke nervously peered about the chamber, probably seeking an escape route. There was none. There was no other entrance to our exit from the room other than the heavy oaken door, now being surreptitiously bolted by Trevor.

"Are these the men?" said Trent in a surprisingly harsh growl. The ploy was obviously to have the American act as leader of the proceedings. The two felons had dealt with Ravenswood, ergo, an American accent would allay any fears the two might have. No one but Trent could play the role; Jericho was disqualified by his colour. I was astounded by the degree to which Trent, usually the mildest

of men, had changed his demeanour as the theatrical un-
folded. I sat back expecting to enjoy the interrogation and
Trent's performance.

Trent's question had been addressed to Sherlock, who,
as the Lascar sailor, was playing his part to the hilt.

"Yuh," he answered in a brutish snarl. "They is the men
I foun'. I tol' thum they botch the first job, but they still
want the hunner' pounds."

"Don't you listen to 'im, mate,"—said Duke, in a loud
Cockney bawl. "We did just like the guv'nor told us."

"'At's right," agreed Jim. "Duke would'a had the old
man on the street, but he missed 'is aim. I only had time to
give 'is Worship a clout alongside 'is head, the way it was
planned, when a couple of toffs was on us."

"So because you murdered the old man in his hotel
room," said Jericho in his newly affected West Indian lilt,
"you say that the money is due you. Is that right?" he said,
looking to Trent, his palms raised enquiringly. Then he
laughed. "I do not see how they could have walked past
the manager's desk without being thrown out on their ears,
the way that they are dressed now."

"'Ere now, mate," said Duke nervously, "we din'nt go
in the front door as big as you please. There's a maze o' fire
stairs in the back of the Langham, what lead hup the back
and across the buildings behind. We went hup ten minutes
after the window was opened, just as was planned."

"'At's just 'ow it were done," Jim added defensively.

"Yus," said Duke again. "An' I'm not sayin' 'at we
wouldn't'a finished the old man right then and there, but
the blighter was snuffed b'fore we got there. Someone beat
us to 'im and smovvered 'im wi' a pillow."

"Pillow," grunted the Lascar Sherlock. "Woman's weapon."

Sherlock flashed me a quick look and saw that my face
was stone. With those three words, he told me that Rachel
Leland had murdered her own father.

"We're tellin' you this because your frien's done right
by us, so we're playin' it square wiv you."

"Not all that square," I said grimly, "You took a woman
with you."

"Only 'cause she sawr us. We dinn't know if she done

the killin' or not, so we took 'er wiv us," whined the little Cockney.

"That wasn't part of the bargain," said Trent, picking up the cue. "You will not see a farthing of the money owed you until the woman is safely returned." He sat down with an air of finality.

"You see what you did," said Duke to Jim, "I tol' you she was in on it."

"Well, 'ow did I know? I just wanted to be safe," his friend returned. Then, in a more respectful voice to us, "I just wanted to make sure we'd be gettin' the hundred quid what was promised."

"So now we're straight," said Duke with a strained smile. "We wasn't gonna 'arm 'er." He giggled unconvincingly. "Jim 'ere was just havin' a lit'le bit o' fun." The cold stares he met while he looked about the table choked his laughter back into his throat.

"Where is she now?" growled Trent.

"She's wiv a mate downstairs, I mean outside," Jim quickly answered. "We was gonna bring 'er hup hafter we got our pay."

"Bring her up here," roared Trent. "Now!"

"Right now, Yer Worship," said Jim, with a hasty tug at his fiery-red forelock. Trent motioned to Trevor, who went out the door with the burly, red-haired Cockney.

We said nothing while Duke stood waiting, awkwardly turning his hat round in his hands. Within a minute or two, there was a clatter of feet upon the steps and Trevor opened the door, followed by Jim and a strapping dock worker. Between them, they had the heavily cloaked and hooded Millicent Deane in tow. Miss Deane was still blind-folded and gagged—fortunately, I thought, or else she might have alerted the miscreants to our true identities. Trevor moved back to the door and bolted it.

"We kep' 'er in good condition," said Jim with a patently false heartiness. "Nary a scratch on 'er."

"Very well then," said Trent, slowly. "I believe that you've earned your compensation."

He made as if to reach out his purse from an inner coat-pocket. "Yes indeed, you have earned it," he went on, and so saying, drew out a service revolver. "And the first of you who makes a move will take a slug along with him."

As the astounded hoodlums raised their hands, I hurried to release Miss Deane from her bonds. "You can go to the window and call in your police, Lestrade," said Sherlock, taking his hunting crop from inside his coat. The sergeant nodded and opened the window facing the street.

"Mr. Holmes?" asked the surprised Millicent Deane, after I had unbound her eyes.

"Yes, my dear. And my brother and a few friends."

Miss Deane would have said something more, but Jim chose that moment to make a desperate bid for freedom. He threw himself at me and I fell onto the table and into Trent and Jericho. Trent's pistol fired and the shot went into the ceiling. The massive dock hand then threw Trevor aside, unbolted the door and the room exploded in violence. The door was thrown open and the man would have bolted out of it but for Trevor. Reacting quickly, Sherlock's brawny friend grabbed hold of him and threw the man into the runty Duke.

In an instant, the room was filled with airborne chairs, half-filled pints, shouting, and the occasional body. Lestrade was still in the window-seat, blowing his whistle forlornly while the fighting erupted about him. With an abrupt oath, he replaced it in his pocket and joined in the melee.

Duke slipped out of Trent's clutches and was able to make his way out the door, with Sherlock in hot pursuit. I deflected a fist with Trent's walking stick and took Miss Deane into a corner of the room, away from the thick of the fighting. Jim now broke away from Jericho and Trent, dashing out of the room and down the stairs, the two Americans right behind him.

After making sure that Trevor and Lestrade had the dock worker firmly secured, I left the lady with them, to see what fate had befallen our fellows.

Coming down the stairs, I looked into the middle room, to see if any combatants had taken refuge therein. Two sailors were sitting in the window alcove, unperturbedly finishing their meal, oblivious to the noise rising from the public room below. Apparently this was a common occurrence to them.

As I descended the stairway, the noise of battle became

all the more distinct. As the main room came in sight, I found that "the dozen or so mates" Trevor mentioned earlier had acted to assist their friends by provoking the most singular barroom brawl that I could ever have imagined. Fists and ale flew in all directions. The sound of splintering tables and chairs crescendoed as I reached the bottom third of the staircase, trying to make out the forms of my companions in the uproar.

I finally found Sherlock in the back of the tangle. My brother had somehow taken charge of Jim and, as I looked, brought down the leaded hunting crop on the red head of his antagonist. The man went down as I watched. A stranger aimed a punch at my brother, but Sherlock neatly deflected the blow and sent the man flying into the nearest press of combatants, battling under a picture of the Queen. One of the bruisers grabbed it from the wall and brought it down over the head of the intruder.

Trent and Jericho were trying to corner the slippery Duke amidst the wild fighting. But he kept eluding them, as his pursuers were obliged to defend themselves every few feet. The little Cockney, his long comforter flowing out behind him like a cape, was edging ever nearer to the narrow back door. Although Sherlock was close by, he was engaged with an old sot who clung to him, too drunk to fight.

Taking the initiative, I leapt the remaining stairs and picked up an overturned spittoon. I had the space to move and was at the door before Duke. He saw me and would have ducked back into the throng, had I not swung out with the cuspidor, catching him neatly on the side of the head. He went down with a crash.

As he sank, Sherlock propelled his bewhiskered companion onto another man and found a place by my side.

"Is everything all right?" he yelled above the tumult.

"Yes," I shouted back, making a swipe with the walking stick at a man who was cocking his fist and aiming it at Sherlock. My brother swung around and shoved him back into the din as a winded Trent arrived beside us, Jericho close behind him.

"Take care of these men for Lestrade and the regulars," barked Sherlock to Trent. "And take Miss Deane to my brother's house. Mrs. Crosse will look after her, at least until the police wish to question her. I think we have to be somewhere else."

"What?" I cried.

"I understand, sir," Trent called back. "We can take care of ourselves." He indicated Jericho.

The black man smiled. "Nothing like a good fight to make fast friends," he roared over the pandemonium.

A pitcher crashed on the wall behind us, reminding us of the donnybrook that had engulfed the pub and was now spilling out the front door.

"Here," I cried out, handing Trent his stick. "Thanks for the use."

"I saw that you put it to good purpose," he smiled. "Good luck!"

We slipped out the side door, into the dank and narrow side street.

Walking around to the front of the pub, we saw that the fighting had filled the street in front. The brawlers were thick along the brick-paved street, swallowing up the uniformed police brought by Lestrade's whistle. A few of the combatants had even climbed onto the small Bankside pier opposite the pub.

"So," I muttered, looking at the pub sign, "he did bring me to The Anchor."

"Jericho assured me that he'd be able to deceive you," said Sherlock.

"Only as to the exact destination, dear brother. He made the fatal error of taking Tower Bridge across.* After that, it seemed possible that I might end up here."

Sherlock shook his head resignedly. "Foolish man," he said.

I turned and stalked back down the side-street. Sherlock turned and ran after me.

"Mycroft," he cried out, "where are you going?"

"To find Rachel Leland," I declared over my shoulder.

"I thought you might. I'm coming with you."

I stopped. He looked at me and smiled, albeit grimly. I returned his smile and clapped him on the shoulder. "Right," I said, and together we set off for the Langham.

Neither the lateness of the hour nor the condition of our

---

* Read "Southwark Bridge." MH/SMW

costume was conducive to attracting the few cabs there were. We crossed Southwark Bridge on foot before we found a hansom that would stop for us. In the cab, I lit a cigar and discarded my comic-opera bowler, the latter to Sherlock's dismay. We gave no further thought to my greasy waterproof or to Sherlock's Lascar disguise until we entered the lobby of the posh Langham Hotel. The desk-clerk made a move to stop us.

"I beg your pardon," he said indignantly, beginning to round the desk. But we had no time for him.

"It's all right," I said jerking my thumb back at Sherlock, cigar clamped firmly between my teeth, "he's with me." We left the man in silent consternation.

Taking the steps two at a time, I recalled the evening in which I had been so winded by the task. But tonight, my rage had given me new strength. We knocked on the door of the Americans' suite. There was no answer. We knocked all the louder. Still no response. Just then, a page came past.

"Begging your pardon, Mr. Holmes," he said, "I can save you the trouble of knocking. The Americans left over an hour ago."

"You know us?" asked Sherlock incredulously.

"You are in Captain Jericho's employ, are you not, my boy?" I asked.

"Yes, sir."

"Do you know the location of The Anchor pub in Cheapside?"

"Yes, sir. I was just on my way. He told me to meet him there, as soon as I was able."

"Did the Americans leave word as to their new address?"

"No sir, but I saw that they left with a swell who'd come 'round in a carriage to pick 'em up."

"Good lad," I said, handing him a shilling. "Go quickly to your master and tell him that we were here. Ask him to meet me in my rooms tonight in company with Mr. Trent. He'll understand."

"Yes, sir. Thank you, sir." And the boy was down the stairs like a shot.

"Interesting idea, using hotel personnel and little boys,"

mused Sherlock.* "That little lad had his ears to the keyhole all the time, I'll wager."

"Obviously," I agreed. "That was how the sham doctor discovered the prescription without being told about it. Millicent Deane didn't find that odd, but I did."

"Yes, but he mentioned 'a swell' just now. That will be Moriarty," he said.

"To be sure," I replied. "But he would not be so foolish as to take them to his home. He would not be that audacious."

"Then the Americans are flown for sure."

"But not for long. They will be at the test site tomorrow to meet with Sir Edmund Darlington. We can nab them there." I set my jaw resolutely. "Right now, I have a settlement to make with the Right Honourable Jerrold Moriarty."

"Let's be off."

"No, Sherlock. I'm going there alone. Find Lestrade and ask him to send some detectives to Kensington. I'll meet you at my flat after Moriarty has been taken."

He nodded. "You won't mind if Victor Trevor comes along, I trust?"

"By all means bring him, Sherlock. He may prove his usefulness again. In any case . . ."

". . . he's a good audience for us," smiled Sherlock. I laughed with him. My bitter feelings from Friday night were dispelled.

A solitary light was on in the front window of the Moriarty home in Kensington. I knocked at the door and it was opened by Jerrold Moriarty himself. I forced my way past him, into the vestibule of his home.

"I say, Holmes! What is the meaning of this intrusion?"

"It's all over, Moriarty. For you, Ravenswood, and for Rachel Leland, too."

"Rachel Leland? What—what are you raving about?"

"I know all about the plan of conquest; I know even

---

* Could this be the inspiration for Sherlock's use of the street urchins he employed as "the Baker Street Division of the detective police force" which he called "the Baker Street irregulars" in *A Study in Scarlet* and in *The Sign of the Four?* MH/SMW

more than you-told me. I may even know more about the entire plot than you've been told."

His face went white and a great fear shone in his deep-set eyes. Still, he kept up his nescient pose. "Come into my study," he said at last, his voice quavering.

I followed him into his sanctum, a room off the vestibule, just opposite the sitting-room wherein he had been so triumphant just a few hours before.

"Now, then," he said, sitting behind his desk in strained indignation. "What am I to make of your speech, sir? Just why are you here?"

"Your conniving is over. The Southerners will be rounded up when they appear at the test site in Salisbury and will no doubt be deported to their own country to stand trial for treason."

"I ordered you to stay out of this. I suspended you from your duties to the Crown."

"That was your last order, Moriarty, and I have no doubt but that you have performed your final duties to the Crown. I've been with the Prime Minister, and by this time he will have all the proof he will need to order your arrest for conspiracy to commit treason against Her Majesty's Government."

That sense of dignity, which I had seen only once before, now enveloped him closely. "I believe that you have been misinformed, Holmes. My actions were in support of the Crown. There is no evidence against me, save the word of an embittered junior clerk, recently relieved of his duties. Whatever you have to say will be easily refuted."

"I would not be too secure in that knowledge, sir. I am not the only one who has been keeping your movements under surveillance. And their words will be heeded, even if I am discredited."

Even though his face was in the shadow cast by the shade of the student lamp on his desk, I could see it go ashen as the full import of my words struck him.

"Now, you will please tell me where you have hidden the Americans."

He appeared not to hear for a moment, then he said, "Who is it you want?"

"The Americans! Ravenswood, his wife—Rachel Leland

—and the others. I know that you would not bring them here. I also know that Rachel Leland murdered her father. Now, where are they?"

He smiled, but I could see the hatred in his eyes. "Do you think that I shall betray The Cause now? Now, even before it is properly under way? The Americans are safe and they shall remain so." His lip curled into a sneer. "We have better minds behind this plan than you, with all your cleverness, could have imagined."

"More devious minds, that I'll grant you," I answered. "But if you want the law to be easier with you, you had best tell me where you have secreted them. Is it with Perkins of the Home Office? Neville of the War Office . . ."

He held up a warning finger and absently wagged it back and forth. "That would incriminate them," he said, his smile becoming more ghastly as his eyes became vacant and glassy. "We are too cunning for you, Holmes. We have taken better care of them than your puny mind could ever fathom." Abruptly, the vacant look disappeared, and he turned his gaze full upon me. "You were always so showy with those great displays of memory and analysis. I trusted you with my plans, with my future. I trusted you with the great plan we had of creating the most magnificent empire ever known upon the face of the earth."

"And I trusted you, sir," I said quietly. "I trusted you to tell me what you knew of these plans for chaos and war. And what you knew convinced me of the enormity of the suffering you were ready to have unleashed upon the earth. Empire? Yes. But what you were spawning was to be an empire built on war and persecution. Many good people who want only to live in comfort and security would die. And for what? Not for something as sacred as their home or their honour, no! All they would do is pave your way of greed and ambition with their lives." My anger waxed hot as the words poured out of me.

"Your ambition is to command lives, not serve them. You want people to live in fear of you, not to respect you. You propose a tyranny to crush the people underfoot, taking not only their lives, but their sons' and daughters' as well, condemning all to ignominious deaths. Colonel Leland was only the first; there would soon be others, as you and your cohorts chased through the shadows to find all those who dared oppose you.

"I used to pity you, Moriarty. I pitied you because you strove beyond your grasp and then had not the faintest idea of what to do with the information you obtained. So how long do you think you would have remained a power? Five years? Ten? Twenty? You would have remained for as long as it took for some other one of your underlings to insinuate himself close to those who commanded you.

"Prince Albert had you and all those like you in mind when he guided the Queen's hand in our American policy fourteen years ago. Had he lived and remained a potent force for good, you should never have attained the position you have today." I looked at him with undisguised loathing. "And he is dead while you and your friends live to plot and plan, no better than beasts becoming drunk on human blood."

"Yes," he smiled again, toying with the cord of his dressing gown. "I live. And my sons shall live after me. Neither you nor Gladstone nor Disraeli will halt the destiny of this family. We shall yet attain greatness."

"No," I said, turning my head slowly from side to side. "If they follow your example, they will achieve little but hatred and fear and infamy. It is only fortunate for them that they have chosen different paths from yours and will not plague mankind with petty schemes, to control and bend destiny to their whims."

The sound of a cab on the cobbled street drifted in through the window of the study. The vehicle stopped in front of the house.

"Do you hear that, Moriarty? That will be the men from Scotland Yard, sent to take you into arrest. We shall find the Americans too. And they will share the fate reaching out to all of you."

I turned, so as to open the door for the police. I heard a movement behind me and I looked back at Moriarty. He was still smiling. His skin was drawn tight across his brow and his cavernous face took on the aspect of a death's-head. Even after all these years, I can see the madness and frenzy that had taken charge of his expression, etching his features with ghastly precision. I was in the hall when I heard the single shot.

I raced back to the study and found him sprawled on the floor. The pistol was still clutched in his hand as Jerrold Moriarty lay in an ever-spreading pool of blood. He was, even yet, grinning hideously, his eyes open in death as they beheld me for the last time.

Choking down my revulsion, I fled the room of death. Once more I entered the hall, when, out of the corner of my eye, I caught a movement. The Professor, Jerrold Moriarty's eldest son, glided down the steps.

Taking no notice of me, he entered the room. I was anchored where I stood, the police knocking at the door all the while. The Professor turned and, before I moved to admit the authorities, we exchanged one silent look. But that look told me that, in the eyes of his son, I was branded with the mark of Cain. I would be forever looked upon as the murderer of his father.

14

TAKING THE AIR
IN SALISBURY

Upon my return to St. Chad's Street, I had little time to reflect upon the death of Jerrold Moriarty. Trevor, Jericho, Trent, and my brother were all in animated conversation, once more reliving the events just past. They were yet attired in parts of the various disguises they had worn earlier. And despite the lateness of the hour, they were, every man, still keen and alert.

I enquired after Miss Deane.

"Your landlady is in charge, right now, Mycroft," Sherlock said. "But on the way here, Miss Deane told me what happened to her. She went to the hotel lobby soon after her companions left for the Army-Navy Club. She wanted a copy of the *Evening Standard,* it seems, and did not know how to get hold of the buttons.* When she returned, our friends Duke and Jim had the place in an uproar. They panicked and took her along with them."

"Her story jibes with what those men told us at the pub," said Trent. "I don't believe we'll be holding her. She seems to know little else about the real errand her friends were on."

I silently acknowledged this information and called down for Mrs. Crosse, who was still about, bringing some late-night refreshment up to us. I spoke with her briefly in the hall and returned to the rooms with her tray.

I then told my guests about the harrowing episode in Kensington: Jerrold Moriarty's suicide and the silent judgement of his son. Sherlock shook his head when I concluded. "There may be trouble from that quarter. I have always distrusted silent, brooding scholars. They are as

_____
* Sherlock is referring to the page mentioned earlier. The appellation *buttons* refers to the uniforms worn by pages. MH/SMW

much to be feared as doctors, if they turn to the ways of crime."*

There was a knock on the door, as Mrs. Crosse returned.

"Did you do as I asked, Mrs. Crosse?" I asked.

"Yes, sir," she replied. "There was nothing out of the ordinary."

I thanked her and she took her leave.

"What was that all about?" enquired Sherlock.

"There is no time to tell you," said I. "We must press on to the more important matter right now: the taking of the Southerners."

I outlined my plans, while the others contributed to them. All, that is but Captain Jericho. The tall Negro stopped me as I turned to plan his role with him.

"I'm sorry, Mr. Holmes," he said, "but I believe you can finish this business without me." A faint smile played on his large lips. "After all, everything I wanted to do has been accomplished. I've even contributed my share to help bring this conspiracy to an end."

"And more, if you ask me," was Victor Trevor's enthusiastic outburst.

"Hear, hear," said Sherlock quietly.

"As for now, I must plead the press of other business too long neglected," he said, picking up the low-crowned, broad-brimmed white hat he had worn as part of his West Indian disguise. "I must take my leave now, gentlemen, but I would be remiss if I did not express my gratitude for your help." He looked at each of us as he continued.

"Perhaps my country will never know of what we did. But I assure you that, should you ever be in need, or if there is anything you desire, it will be the pleasure of Joshua Horn to procure whatsoever you lack.

"Gentlemen," he said with a low bow, "good evening."

With those words, the Negro departed, virtually vanishing through the door to my room.

"Joshua Horn, eh?" mused Sherlock. "His will make an interesting item to file in my commonplace book.**

* These same thoughts are echoed in "The Speckled Band," when Sherlock discusses Dr. Grimesby Roylott with his friend, Watson: "When a doctor goes wrong, he is the first of criminals." Sherlock apparently learned his lesson early on. MH/SMW

** This comment makes the Irregular student wonder if Captain

"A most extraordinary man," Calvin Trent. "I know little more about him than when last we spoke in these rooms. But I can tell you this: He proved himself a true patriot in that saloon tonight. I could have been dispatched several times, yet he remained to assist us until the conspirators were turned over to your Sergeant Lestrade, and returned in our company to this flat. He's a good man in a fight and a good and loyal comrade to his friends. I could wish no better said of myself."

"If we are to do without him now," said I, "we had best continue making plans for the capture of the others on the morrow."

We then made our arrangements. Calvin Trent had some scruples about leaving to relate our exploits of the evening, but I insisted that he must. Mr. Disraeli would need these facts if we were to make the arrests we needed on the morrow.

"I don't know, Mr. Holmes." Trent scratched his head. "I doubt that he will be kindly disposed to being awakened at this hour, despite his pledge to you."

"If your government hung in the balance," said Sherlock, with a quietly sardonic smile, "I doubt your President Grant would begrudge you a few hours of sleep." With that, Trent surrendered himself to the inevitable. He picked up his hat, saying, "Sooner begun is sooner ended. A good evening to you all, gentlemen. I'll meet you tomorrow at Waterloo Station."

He was soon followed out the door by Victor Trevor and my brother. I went to bed and, considering all the activity and excitement of which I had been a part, I slept very soundly.

My household was awakened very early the next morning. A special messenger from the PM delivered the special credentials necessary to board the trains to Salisbury Plain to witness the official testing of the auto-gyro.

"It must be a very special occasion to get a body up this early," Mrs. Crosse told me with a yawn.

Jericho will be indexed under *C* for "Captain" or *J* for "Joshua Horn." Sherlock's methods of indexing have been the cause for merriment among several commentators who delight in pointing out that in *The Adventure of the Sussex Vampire* Holmes notes the listing of "Victor Lynch the forger" under the letter 'V'. MH/SMW

"Indeed it is. What we see today could affect the future of the entire world."

My landlady's eyebrows shot up in surprise and dismay, "Well then, I'll be sure to offer my Mass this morning for your intentions, Mr. Holmes," was her earnest reply.

"Thank you, Mrs. Crosse," I said, touched by her concern. "And how is Miss Deane?"

"Ah," she said, "I put her in the spare bedroom, you know, and I don't believe that she'll waken much before noon. The poor child was all in when your brother brought her around last night." I didn't doubt that for a minute.

I arrived at Waterloo Station some fifteen minutes before the train was scheduled to leave. The train, a special express chartered by the government, was due to leave Waterloo at 6.55 that morning, to arrive in Salisbury at 8.25

The normal railway personnel had been augmented by men provided by the government, who interviewed each passenger before boarding to certify his pass. The most influential and important members of Parliament were to attend the test, as well as other members of the Queen's service, so every precaution was being taken. Considering the number of people in attendance, it was a wonder that word had not somehow leaked out to the British or the foreign press.

Sherlock, Trevor, Trent, and I found a compartment to ourselves and while we awaited the last few passengers, I explained the meaning of the test we would witness that morning.

"You see, the inventor has proposed that a heavier-than-air machine can rise under its own power, using some basic principles discovered in ancient times, as well as by more recent thinkers. Using the principle of the gyro, he has stated that his machine will not only rise, but will be able to hover in one spot, as the hummingbird is able to do. I need not tell you about the military applications of such an engine, as well as the civilian uses that may develop from such a craft."

"I understand the scientific applications of such an engine," said Trent, looking out the window. "But one wonders just what kind of Aladdin's lamp this flying machine portends for the future. I hope that man was not meant to fly, for he would soon find an evil application for such a miracle. Mankind is like that."

"What about ballooning?" Trevor put in. "It's a marvelous sport . . ."

"But ballooning," said Sherlock, "is not directional flight, which is what William H. Phillips hopes to accomplish this morning."

"Yes," I agreed, cocking an eye at Sherlock, as I recalled our discussion of Friday morning along these same lines. "Phillips tried this once before, in 1842 to be exact, again in the Salisbury Plain. In that experiment, the auto-gyro rose too rapidly and broke its moorings. It was fortunate that there was no one aboard, for the craft was never seen again."

"But how does a piece of metal rise from the ground?" asked a perplexed Victor Trevor.

"Calling it 'a piece of metal' is stating the matter rather too simply." Trevor leaned forward in his seat.

"The craft is a very complex piece of machinery," I said. "It is steam driven, I know. The model in 1842 was attached to a flexible pipe and was supposed to have attained an altitude of one hundred feet before it broke loose."

"But how does the thing get off the ground?" asked Trevor impatiently.

"Well, as I recall, the dynamic lift was achieved by two contrarotating aerofoils made of aluminium, the lightest metal known to man. These were located in the trailing edges, through which slits had been made. The jets of highly pressurised steam were therein located and, by action of the steam pushing against the ground, the auto-gyro left terra-firma."

"Oh," was Trevor's subdued reply as he settled back into his seat.

The train was, by this time, fully loaded and ready to leave the station. The signals were given and within seconds, we achieved speed and were rocketing out of the terminus. The buildings of the city shortly gave way to the bucolic scenery of the countryside. The ride to Salisbury from London took an hour and a half. We had all brought various books and newspapers to while away the time.

About midway through the journey, Sherlock took out his watch. "I should say that we will be arriving in Salisbury in some forty minutes," he said, still gazing at his hunter.

"Forty-two minutes, actually, Sherlock," I corrected.

"I was merely aproximating for the benefit of our friends," he replied with a laboured sigh.

"But how can you be so sure?" asked Trent, with no little amazement.

Sherlock and I exchanged glances. "May I?"

"By all means, Mycroft."

"Well then, my dear Trent, it is evident, is it not? The train at present is travelling at a rate of fifty-eight miles an hour, gauging from the time it takes to pass between the telegraph posts on this line. If we allow the train a mile and a half in which to attain speed at the beginning of our journey, and the same distance in which to decrease speed at its conclusion, why, then, the calculation is a simple one." I sat back in modest pride at my explanation.

"Very good, brother," said Sherlock with a sly wink to Trent. "Now, I knew the same by looking at my watch when the train left Waterloo, and knowing that it is scheduled to arrive exactly one and a half hours later in Salisbury. But I'm glad that I now know the reason why."*

I sheepishly joined in the laughter.

Forty-one minutes after this episode, the special express pulled into Salisbury Station. As we disembarked, we were met by a fleet of vehicles which transported us the five miles or so across the flat, grassy countryside to the actual testing site. They had situated it in the centre of the plain, an area dominated by a large observation balloon of the Montgolfier type. North of the balloon stood the pavillion from which the PM, the cabinet, and members of Parliament would be observing the test and the auto-gyro itself. It was as yet cloaked by a large canvas tarpaulin. The morning breeze had blown one or two loops free of their pegs, allowing several tantalising glimpses of the mechanical air-ship, its metal-riveted body resting on steel limbs,

---

* As we know from Dr. Watson's accounts, Sherlock became proficient in gauging distance and speed while on board trains. One example will be found in the case entitled "Silver Blaze," found in *The Memoirs of Sherlock Holmes.* MH/SMW

which terminated in wheels made of hard rubber tyres, two in front, one behind.

The balloon, covered by a stout rope netting and anchored about two hundred yards north of the contraption, was no doubt to be used as an aerial observation post, providing that the auto-gyro left the ground. The great shape of the balloon lent an air of frivolity to its otherwise utilitarian purpose. Even the brown and green of Salisbury Plain itself appeared somber in comparison. The mood was not cheered by the mist, which could be seen rising in tendrils of cloud, obscuring the wintry sun.

A number of soldiers moved briskly through the cold and damp, bent on various tasks. There was very little movement in the roped-off area surrounding the two vehicles and my eye was next drawn to a small group of men who stood conferring at the edge of the test site. As we drew near, I saw that one of the men was Sergeant Lestrade who, upon seeing us, excused himself and walked over to us.

"Hello, Mr. Holmes," he said, a broad smile on his face. My brother received a somewhat stiffer welcome, but the presence of Trevor and Trent rekindled the detective's warmth.

"Good to see you, Sergeant," said Trevor, "I must say your appearance is much improved without all that sticking-plaster and candle wax."

"Now, now, Mr. Trevor," said Lestrade. "No more of that. Your association with your friend Sherlock Holmes here should not ingrain a sense of impertinence within you for the law."

"Not at all, my dear Lestrade," returned my brother, good naturedly. "Why, what with your efforts at The Anchor last night, and the successful capture of the Americans today, I should say that you'd be in line for a promotion soon. I see you already have been put in command of the Scotland Yard detail here. Yes," he continued with affability. "Yes, 'Inspector' Lestrade. The title suits you. And I see you've also been given a decoration."

Sherlock allowed himself a smile as the detective gingerly touched the swelling beneath his left eye. "A small price to pay," he said proudly. "And, Mr. Holmes"——his voice became low as he leaned over to my brother in a confidential way—"when I do get that promotion, you can be sure that I won't forget to tell my superiors that you were of great assistance to me in this matter."

"Why, thank you, Lestrade," said my brother gravely. "I am sure that you will do the right thing." Lestrade pulled away. "Sooner or later," my brother added, *sotto voce*. I believe I was the only one who heard those final words, and I was hard put to keep my face in a proper expression of gravity.

"My men are keeping a sharp eye on the carriages as they arrive. We'll allow the Americans to get out and strut around for a while before we clap on the irons."

"An excellent plan, Inspector, er, Sergeant," said Trent, drawing him away. "If I may go over the details with you . . ." And he walked away from us with Lestrade to the group awaiting Lestrade's return.

Sherlock, Trevor, and I strolled over to the balloon, Trevor animatedly explaining the various details of the balloon: the purpose of the ballast bags, the construction of the gondola, and so forth. I dare say that, though Sherlock listened with polite attentiveness, he could have explained it to Trevor in as much detail. My brother has a penchant for obscure, out-of-the-way information.

An army colonel materialised from out of the mist and walked to my side. "Mr. Mycroft Holmes?" he asked.

"Yes?"

"All is in readiness, and the Prime Minister would be obliged if you would see him before the test."

I turned to follow him, and found Sherlock at my side.

"Do you mind if I come along, Mycroft?"

"Not at all, Sherlock, but I can't speak for the PM."

"I'll take my chances," my brother smiled back.

"Colonel, my brother will be accompanying us."

We were led to a large open-fronted tent, not unlike a lean-to, which had been prepared for the Prime Minister's party. Among the some two-dozen dignitaries therein assembled I was surprised to see the features of William Gladstone much in evidence. He was in conversation with Disraeli as we approached, but they broke it off when they caught sight of us.

"Ah," said Disraeli, after greeting me. "You would be Sherlock Holmes."

My brother was impressed. "Why yes, sir, you are very quick at identification."

"Nothing to it, young man. There's a marked family resemblance," said Disraeli, with a twinkle in his eye. "I also had a detailed description of you from Mr. Calvin Trent. He had glowing things to tell us about you both."

"Indeed," said Gladstone, "the Holmes family seems to contain nothing but remarkable young men."

"And it appears as though the Empire owes you a very great debt," Disraeli added. "A debt that may be lightened somewhat when the next birthday honours list is made known."

My brother and I turned to each other. Sherlock looked to be slightly amused. I most definitely was not.

"I thank you," said Sherlock with a polite bow, "but aren't such honours perhaps a little premature? The Americans are not as yet in custody. Something could go amiss."

"It is possible, Mr. Holmes, said Disraeli, with an amused air, "but I like to prepare for successful conclusions."

"Such as that given to Sir Edmund Darlington," said Gladstone with a chuckle, turning to me. "Mr. Holmes, it went like clockwork! I allowed myself the pleasure of bearding him in his den last evening. Of course I took some Scotland Yarders along with me, but it was delightful! The man was so astounded that I knew anything at all about the conspiracy that he didn't even bother to lie about it. 'How'd you find out?' was all he could say. I tell you, I've not had so much pleasure since I translated Homer." He laughed. "By this time, Sir Edmund is enjoying the comforts of a holding cell in Pentonville awaiting his arraignment. And I have no doubt but that his American friends will be keeping him company before too long." Gladstone chuckled again, gleefully.

"About the honours you propose," I said, in an awkward attempt to return to our earlier topic, "I don't believe that we would really want our names on the birthday list."

"What?" Gladstone and Disraeli chorused in surprise.

"Please don't misunderstand," said Sherlock, quickly jumping in. "It's not that we wouldn't appreciate knighthoods . . ."

I picked up at my brother's pause.

". . . That is entirely true, sir. But we both believe that such an honour would be a handicap to us at this stage of our lives."

"A handicap?" came the hollow echo of the shaken Prime Minister.

"Yes, sir," I said. "You see, I am but a minor cog in the wheels of Her Majesty's Government. I therefore have some amount of security and all I really desire is a small rise in salary. Such a rise would allow me to take some rather nice rooms in St. James, on Pall Mall. Nothing fancy, you understand," I added quickly. "It would merely be somewhat closer to the Foreign Office."

Gladstone was attempting to smother another chuckle as the PM regained his composure.

"A modest man," said Mr. Disraeli. "Commendable, Mr. Holmes, quite commendable, I'm sure. But I must say, I'm not in the habit of hearing men in my government refuse their rightfully won honours."

"Ah, Benjamin," said Gladstone with a snort. "That's because you so rarely attract the right kind of man. Now, I understand Mr. Holmes perfectly. But I am curious why young Mr. Sherlock Holmes would reject a knighthood?"

"Yes, Mr. Gladstone, well," said Sherlock, "you see, I am but a student, hoping in time to become a consulting detective . . ."

"Ah," said the PM, "that too is commendable. I am sure that we can arrange something with Scotland Yard . . ."

"That is not quite what I meant. You see, I wish to be an independent consultant, putting to use the talents for logic and inference that my brother and I have so far developed, working within my own methods."

"Well, all right," said Disraeli, "but I do not understand how the granting of a knighthood will hinder you in this profession."

"Well, you understand, sir, that if my face and movements became widely reported, as would certainly occur if I were honoured with a title, then it would prove much more difficult for me to infiltrate the haunts of criminal classes with impunity. And even law-abiding folk, who would not mind working with *Mister* Sherlock Holmes, may be put off by serving *Sir* Sherlock Holmes."

The Prime Minister said nothing for an instant, considering what my brother had told him. Then he looked again at Sherlock and extended his hand, saying, "It is most gratifying to see that wisdom is not yet extinct in England." Sherlock took his hand and inclined his head graciously.

"This is all very well," said Mr. Gladstone. "But see here, Prime Minister, we should do something—ah, but wait. You say that you are a student, sir?"

My brother nodded.

"Then, as your brother has mentioned his own lack of sufficient, ah, financial wherewithal, may I assume that you too are somewhat lacking in funds? I assure you, I mean you no embarrassment," he added quickly.

Sherlock shrugged. "Well, Mr. Gladstone, I certainly do not live in Mayfair."

"Well then," beamed Gladstone, "there you are, gentlemen. Benjamin," he said, addressing the Premier, "a simple note to the Chancellor of the Exchequer could provide a pension . . ."

Disraeli favoured Sherlock with a shrewd look. "Despite Mr. Gladstone's love for simple solutions and despite the government's undeniable gratitude, I fear I must limit the spending here." He paused. "But I think a *modest* sum might be obtained from our discretionary accounts. Say of one hundred pounds annually."

"Say three hundred pounds, Mr. Disraeli," said Gladstone firmly.

"Say one hundred seventy-five, Mr. Gladstone!"

The former Prime Minister considered this for a moment and then nodded his assent.

"Good," said Disraeli. "So there will be a rise in the salary of Mr. Mycroft Holmes by one hundred seventy-five pounds and an equal amount for his brother, so long as he shall remain at university taking classes," he concluded briskly.* Gladstone would have opened his mouth to protest the condition, but thought better of it and merely shrugged, saying, "Now you know why Mr. Disraeli is the Queen's First Minister and why I fell trees and study Greek."

"Lest you leave believing that I conduct all the govern-

---

* This was certainly an excellent deal for Sherlock. He was still taking classes when he met Dr. Watson in 1881, and seems to have continued for at least a year thereafter. MH/SMW

ment's transactions in so speedy a manner," said Disraeli, "let me assure you that I will welcome both of you in the future. The door of Number Ten, Downing Street will always be open to you."

"No matter who may be tenanting the premises," Gladstone added with a wink to his colleague.

With another round of handshaking and well-wishing, we concluded the interview.

Although the air remained chill, the sun had finally broken through the overcast. As we returned to the test-site, the tarpaulin was being removed from the auto-gyro. The large propeller on top of the craft, as well as the smaller propeller forward, gleamed brightly in the sunlight. Beside it, the tall, stationary boiler was being stoked and billows of smoke issued from the smokestack as the tenders shovelled in the coal. All the while this was being done, another group of men were making final arrangements on the balloon and the crew was going over the plans for ascension.

Sergeant Lestrade and Calvin Trent, with Trevor in tow, hurriedly cut through the crowd when they caught sight of us.

"I was afraid we would be making the pinch without you two," said the American. He turned and we followed his gaze to a group of people standing near the rope which had been put up to keep the press of people away from the various craft and the boiler. I saw that the Southerners had arrived, silk hatted, with Rachel Leland cloaked and hooded in chocolate brown. That she once more carried her sable muff confirmed something to my mind. They were speaking to some of the men they had met at the Admiralty Ball.

"They arrived about two minutes after you left," said Lestrade, "walking up, as cool as you please. The blonde lady even smiled at me, she did," he added indignantly.

"I see that the pigeons have found some mates," said Trent.

"And mates they are indeed," I said grimly. "Sergeant, those seven men standing with the Americans are to be placed under arrest also. Some of them are connected with the government, but do not allow that to deter you. Mind that you take them all."

"No trouble about that, sir. They are as good as in the Old Bailey," said Lestrade with happy anticipation. "Will you be accompanying us?"

"No," said Sherlock before I could speak. "My brother and I will go over together first. They will be less suspicious. You and your men will follow us when I signal you." He turned to me.

"That's right, Sergeant. I'm sure that Mr. Trent, here, has informed you of our plan for capture."

"Very well, sir," said Sergeant Lestrade, "but do let us get this over quickly."

The Americans were about fifty yards from where we stood and, as casually as we could manage, Sherlock and I headed toward them. At each step, my uneasiness increased. I fought down my feelings and prepared myself to become the instrument of Rachel Leland's—Rachel Ravenswood's—capture.

Sherlock must have sensed my mood, for as we walked, he quietly said, "Mycroft—remember that this woman is evil. She murdered her father; she'll murder anyone who stands to thwart her ambition. You know there is nothing she would stop at to achieve her bid for power."

"That knowledge doesn't make it any the easier for me."

"Brace up. Smile," he said, as we came closer to them. "Wider. They'll see us in a moment."

My lips pulled themselves into the smile my brother wanted.

"I'm leaving you here. Going behind them, just in case."

Clapping me on the back, he disappeared into the sea of silk hats and bowlers. I intermittently saw his head bobbing through the crowd as he pushed toward the Southerners.

As I approached, Rachel turned, looking bored with the wait. She caught sight of me and smiled. Ravenswood, whose back was toward us, was left behind as she moved away from him. He was deep in conversation with two of the men I'd ordered apprehended. She cautiously looked back, her movements finally concealed from him by the crowd.

I stopped and waited for her.

"Oh Mycroft," she said holding her hands out to me. I took them. My palms were cold within the gloves I wore.

She looked up at me. "I want to apologise for the terrible things I said yesterday. It was dreadful of me and I want you to know that I agree with you. You were right and I know that now."

Yesterday, these words would have meant a great deal to me, even after learning of her marriage. Now, as I saw Sherlock waving his tourist's ear-flapped travelling cap to Trent and Lestrade, my heart became stone.

"I thank you for the apology, but I think it would be best if we rejoined your friends."

She looked confused. "Mycroft—what are you saying? I told you I was sorry . . ."

"And I accepted your apology, Miss Leland. Or do I better address myself to Mrs. Ravenswood?"

Her face blanched as she stammered, "I—I don't know what you're saying, Mycroft. I . . ."

"You've played the innocent long enough, my dear. Now it is time that we go back to your friends and husband. You're all to be taken back to London together, where I believe Ambassador Schenck will have some questions for you about an attempt to overthrow the government of the United States."

I took her firmly by the arm and led her back to the conspirators. All the while, my heart was being drawn and quartered within me. She offered no resistance, but her face had become hard and her eyes had narrowed. I now saw the true visage of Rachel Leland.

We were almost upon the men when Ravenswood looked around and saw me with Rachel. His face went wild with rage as he barked, "Rachel! Get away from that man!" Before she could say anything, he pulled us apart. Trent and Lestrade were still some distance off and Sherlock was blocked by the crowd.

"You," he said glaring at me with unbridled frenzy. "I thought you were suspended."

"Not I, but you soon will be when you are returned to the United States. I'm only sorry that I won't be there to see how high the gallows will be."

"Samuel, he knows," said Rachel, gasping. "He knows everything."

Ravenswood turned back to me. "You bastard," he cried, and with all his force, he brought his gloved fist across my face, sending me to my knees, my head reeling. He took a step and would have kicked me, had I not had the presence of mind to anticipate his movement and so cracked my walking stick across his shins. As he went down with a howl, I supported myself with my stick and got to my feet.

"I would refrain from any more resistance," I wheezed. "Scotland Yard . . ." Before I could finish, a large, six-chambered pistol appeared in his hand as he lay on the ground. The bystanders gasped and melted away from us. The duellist took aim. I was too dazed to move. I am a dead man, I thought.

Then a leaded hunting crop came down upon the American's wrist. The pistol flew from his hand as, once more, he yelped with pain. Sherlock put his foot on the gun and looked at the companions of the fallen Captain.

"I hope none other of you men thinks to stop us," said he. "The police are training their arms on you at this moment." No one made any movement; the spectators stood frozen, watching the tableau. No one, that is, save Rachel Ravenswood. And not even I saw her reach into her muff and bring out the gleaming little pistol which she turned on me. Impulsively, Trent came forward, but she held him off with the pistol.

"You had best leave," she said with cold deliberation. "I am not afraid to use this, and I will be forced to kill Mr. Holmes here, if you do not withdraw." The men retreated and Ravenswood was able to raise himself and retrieve his weapon.

"What'll we do now, Rachel?" he asked.

"You still remember how to navigate a balloon, I trust. You sent up enough of them during the war for aerial observation."

"You don't suppose that you'll get away. That balloon could be dangerous," said Sherlock.

"Save your advice for those who need it, little brother," snapped Rachel. "And I would not advise you to do anything rash, or else your large, older brother will sing with the tongues of angels by day's end."

As if by magic, a corridor was made for us as we passed through the crowd to the roped-off area. Ravenswood's pistol waved off the balloon's attendants and Rachel kept me under cover with her weapon as he clambered in. The balloon swayed in the breeze as Ravenswood made space for Rachel and me in the gondola. Sherlock, Trent, and the police ran to the balloon, stopping a few yards away from it.

"You know," I said in as casual a voice as I could find. "They only have to shoot the balloon for you to be caught like rats in a trap."

"You really can't believe us to be that stupid, dear Mycroft," said she, with a cruel laugh. "The balloon is filled with hydrogen. If those police are so feeble minded as to shoot it, the explosion would kill half the people on this plain. As close as Mr. Disraeli is sitting, he might have that pompous little curl on his forehead singed off, or it might burn off that ridiculous little goatee. Neither will they attempt to shoot us in the g dola. If they miss their aim, their bullets may strike you. No, Mycroft. The balloon is the safest way for us."

Just then, Bankhead and Carteret, with the other conspirators who had been following behind, undecided what to do, made an attempt to join us. Rachel's pistol halted them.

"I'm very sorry, gentlemen," the sweetness of her Southern accent a mocking cruelty, "there is no more room."

Their voices rose in protest.

"Shut up, all of you," she said shortly. "The balloon won't take any more passengers." Then the sugary tone came back. "I'm just afraid that you'll all have to stay here." Seeing that Ravenswood had made everything secure, she now said to her former comrades, "Would one of you please cut the lines?"

No one moved.

"Tyler," she ordered. "Cut that line or have your head blown off."

Never taking his eyes from her, Tyler moved as if in a dream. His eyes spoke volumes to her, and each silent word was wrung from his depths. Even so, the young man extracted a pocketknife and sawed at the tethers. The last strand finally severed, we floated free of the gathered officials.

But we had not risen very high, when Carteret seized a rifle from one of the startled soldiers. He took quick aim and would surely have burst the balloon had not William Bankhead come to his senses and knocked the rifle barrel away. The shot rang out, but the bullet went wild.

In the gondola, all the while, a couple of lines that had been overlooked by Ravenswood proceeded to cross, opening the gas valve. We were thus prevented from attaining further altitude. The gondola lurched drunkenly as the Captain tried to secure the errant ropes.

We were but some forty feet above the crowd and pandemonium had broken out. I glimpsed Sherlock and Calvin Trent running to the auto-gyro through the crowd. The steam had reached a sufficient degree to provide power to the air-craft, and, within a few moments, a churning noise filled the air, as one of the attendants gave a tug to the forward propeller and it began to spin. At the same time, the large horizontal propeller projecting from the hull over the short metal wings began to turn slowly.

I remembered that Phillips, the inventor, had attained a height of one hundred feet during his first attempt, and the flexible umbilical that attached it to the boiler's steam was doubtless longer than that.

Ravenswood, hanging from the balloon's rigging, became apprehensive.

"Rachel, if they get that thing aloft . . ."

"Don't worry, Samuel, just get those lines untangled. Besides," she smiled evilly, "even if they do get that junk-pile into the air, they'll still have a hard time getting Mr. Holmes off without killing him."

The propellers were spinning faster now and we all watched the bright, gleaming metal-riveted craft in almost rapt attention. The jets of steam from the runners were sending up billows of dust and dirt from beneath the air-ship. With a great shudder, the auto-gyro rose.

The stokers were back at the furnace, shovelling in the coal to keep up the steam pressure. And the metallic bird continued its slow vertical ascent.

Ravenswood had secured the lines now, closing the gas valve. He dropped a bag of ballast and, once more, we began to rise.

But so also did the auto-gyro. We were about seventy feet above the ground now and the auto-gyro had risen some forty feet. Even Rachel was becoming apprehensive now, as the great machine steadily rose. But when it was about half as high as we were, the air-ship gave off a loud explosion and a large cloud of steam roared out of its depths. The crew on the ground made a mad dash away from the roped-off area, as they sensed the impending disaster.

Another noise—a grinding—emanated from the autogyro, and another burst of steam. The ship hung suspended for a moment, then fell back to earth, its umbilical snapped, landing with a loud crash, a cloud of dust suddenly concealing it from view. The dust settled and we saw that the air-ship had become a pile of wreckage, the large propeller still spinning slowly, one of the four blades snapped in the middle and dangling crazily from its rotor. Rachel read my thoughts.

"Poor Sherlock Holmes," she said. "He died in the service of his country." She laughed with a savage delight as I swung around to face her, my eyes blazing with anger.

"It would seem that your inventor's dream has died aborning. Your rescuers will have to find some other way to save you," she laughed.

Ravenswood had put his pistol away and was now adjusting the ballast bags. "Let's dump him over the side," he snarled. "We don't need the extra weight."

"No, Samuel."

"Why not? We're about two hundred feet up now. Let's kill him and be done with it."

"I said no, Samuel; there's no need to argue. We've done things my way so far and . . ."

"Yes," Ravenswood interrupted her. "We've done things your way and where has it gotten us? Into a balloon, criminals escaping from what should be a friendly government. No, blast it all, Rachel! Get rid of him!"

The winds had blown the balloon away from the test area, and we were sailing over the Salisbury Plain at a swift rate on the easterly wind. Stonehenge, which was about ten miles from the test site, could just be made out in the distance. At the rate in which the prevailing winds were blowing, we might reach Dover by midday.

"I say throw him out!" cried Ravenswood. His high silk hat was blown off his head just as he said this again. I watched its meandering descent, wondering if I might be following it soon.

"No, Samuel," said Rachel calmly.

"Rachel." Ravenswood began to take a step to her, but a gust of wind upset the gondola and everyone grabbed for an anchorage, while the basket swung like a pendulum, back and forth, until it regained its stability. Before Ravenswood or I could move, Rachel had the pistol in her hand once more. But Ravenswood's rage had not abated, and once more he let loose a stream of invective. When he had done, he was still of a mind to cast me from the gondola.

"Don't be foolish, Samuel. We still need him."

"The hell we do!"

"I tell you, Samuel, don't be a fool."

"Fool? You call me a fool? You filthy strumpet! I've had enough of your insults. You've tricked and deceived me . . ." He took a step toward her.

"I warn you, Samuel. That's far enough . . ."

Rachel was very pale and very tense as she told him: "Samuel, you had better stop your nonsense and pay attention to the balloon . . ."

His lip curled, "So you and your fancy-man will land safely?"

Her nose and forehead were red; the lines of her cheeks were stark and white against the crimson.

"One more word from you in that vein and, husband or no, I swear I'll shoot you. I'll kill you, so help me!" There was no anger in her voice, but I recoiled from the tone she used, for there was no feeling, no emotion; only a bitter chill that underscored each word she spoke.

Ravenswood was startled by her coldness, but he knew no restraint. "Shoot me? You haven't shot a gun since you were running about in your slaves' hand-me-downs." He laughed nastily. "You were no better than white trash when I took you in."

"Don't push me, Samuel . . ."

"Push *you*? You pushed *me!* You've always pushed me, in every way: the council, the plans, even in my business, madam. It's been your ambition that's driven us to where we are now. Hell, you even tried to have me kill your own father!"

"Yes," she said softly. "I did. Because I thought you were a man, because I thought you wanted to be someone who wanted to control your own destiny . . ."

"That's a laugh; since I met you, *you* controlled my destiny. Well, no longer."

With that, he lunged for her. She fired the gun in her hand. The first shot stopped him for a moment, but he pressed on. She fired again, coolly and deliberately, as he staggered forward. This time, the bullet struck him in the shoulder and the impact spun him around like a rag doll. He grabbed for a rope where there was none. The momentum carried him over the side and he fell backward, out and into the void. He missed taking me with him by bare inches.

Now the pistol was levelled at me. Her hand was firm and steady.

"Well, Mycroft, we are now rid of him," she said calmly. "He really was a fool to oppose me." She looked past the balloon, to the darting wisps of cloud. "Now we are literally as free as the wind."

Her eyes settled on me now, directly across the gondola from her.

"Samuel was always too hotheaded for his own good. You will be much better for me than he was."

"My dear Miss Leland, what are you proposing?"

She smiled sweetly. "We're here together, Mycroft. We might as well stay together." I must have looked at her incredulously; what she was suggesting was insane.

"Mrs. Ravenswood, you have murdered your husband just now, your father less than three days ago, and may have caused the death of my brother. Do you really think that I shall want you, never knowing when I may join the list of those affected by your fatal charm?"

"Don't you see, Mycroft? It was fated to be thus. Father could never have had the power, not the real power, we need to break away from the Union. He told me that he wanted to live in harmony with the Yankees, separate and distinct. He never really wanted a full-scale war. He wanted that surprise attack to take place, to immobilise and demoralise the North, to force it to concede our independence and that was all. Then he would go back to 'Ilium' having no more to do with what was set in motion. That was what The Cause meant to him.

"Samuel's ruthlessness attracted me at first, but he was too unstable. I'm afraid I misrepresented myself when I first came to your office last week. I wanted him before he wanted me. I goaded him into joining the committee after Tyler told us about the movement to free the South once more. He had the necklace, you see. He would have sold it, or broken it up piece by piece. But I knew that we could ensure our independence with it. That's why we came to England."

"He may have had it," I said, as the ancient circle of Stonehenge passed beneath us, "but I know that you've had it ever since you left America."

She laughed, "But how could you . . . All right, where is it?"

The woman seemed to be reverting to some childish memory of hide-and-seek. If I wanted to stay alive, I thought, I must keep her mind occupied.

"I had my suspicions when those ruffians were unable to find the necklace on Wednesday night last, when I visited your father and Millicent Deane."

"Ah, poor Millicent," said Rachel Leland. "It's so sad about her. She thought my father was the most dashing man she had ever known. I think she had some kind of infatuation for him, the way she used to look at him back home." She seemed lost in some memory of the past, yet her hand never wavered; the pistol never moved. "Alas, poor Millicent is now the victim of chloroform or a bullet."

"You will be happy to know that Millicent Deane is alive and in the custody of my landlady. And the authorities will soon be happy to question her about what she knows of this plan."

Rachel laughed. "They won't be happy for very long. Millicent knows absolutely nothing about The Cause, or the committee, or anything. She is merely an acquaintance I brought with me as a chaperone."

I was becoming more and more concerned about the distance we were travelling. Just after Captain Ravenswood had fallen, and we had passed Stonehenge, I thought that I had seen a horseman spring out of a clearing. I wondered if he was following us. I had not seen him for the past few minutes, however. I had little time to think about solitary horsemen. I had to keep Rachel Leland's mind busy on what I was saying rather than on what I might be thinking as I worked out a strategy to distract her.

"But you were telling me about how you know the location of the necklace," said the young lady.

"Ah, yes," I said. "Well, when Jericho came to my rooms last night, I realised that he still did not have possession of the gems. Therefore they must still be hidden. I also realised that they must be on the person of someone of your delegation. The size of the necklace automatically ruled out any of the men, and I knew then that either you or Miss Deane must have it on your person. I positively ruled out Miss Deane last night. I asked my landlady to search her clothing after she went to sleep. She found nothing. Therefore, by the process of elimination, you must, at this time be carrying over two hundred fifty thousand pounds on your person."

The breeze blew her curls and the sun glinted off golden hair as she laughed again and asked, "You surely wouldn't search through my clothing now, would you, Mycroft?"

"Certainly not," I said. "I know where you have the necklace without having to do anything of the sort."

"Do you now?" she asked mockingly. "So you're going to be one up on Joshua. Yes,"—she smiled shrewdly—"I know that he sent those men to ransack our rooms. As soon as he discovered that Samuel had possession of them, he had an itch for those diamonds. So tell me now: where are they?"

"In the one article of clothing you have never been without at any time that I've seen you. I thought it odd that you had it at the Admiralty Ball, but that was before I realised what you were concealing. The lost diamond necklace of the Confederacy is in your sable muff."

Still holding the gun on me, she reached into the same pocket from which she had drawn her gleaming pistol, in the lining of the muff. When she dropped her accessory, a large multijewelled necklace caught the sunlight in every facet of every diamond in her hand. The sight of it was awesome as she turned it this way and that; the necklace fairly blazed in her hand. I needed no jeweller's glass to tell me that every gem was a diamond and every diamond was flawless. As the sun cascaded forth from it, I had no doubts that Calvin Trent's estimation of its value was correct. The diamonds, their golden settings affixed with consummate art to the several golden ropes in the shape of an inverted pyramid, probably weighed no more than thirty ounces. Yet such a tiny artifact of crystallised coal and metal was worth some quarter of a million in pounds sterling.

This glittering bauble, the merest bagatelle of which would keep me comfortable for the rest of my days, now lay dripping from her fingers. I was captivated by the shimmering rainbow-prisms of light until they were once again hidden away in the secret pouch in the lining of the sable muff.

"You see, Mycroft? We can come down here, make our way across the countryside and take the boat-train to France before ever our pursuers know where we've gone. We can roam the continent, Asia—anywhere we wish—for we have the most negotiable items on earth." She looked at me now in the same way as she had gazed into my eyes on the veranda at the Admiralty Ball. Her voice was soft and tender, as she told me, "I admire you, Mycroft. I saw at once that you were no fool. I saw that Ravenswood was never a threat to you, for his mind was nothing compared to your own, he was . . . Do you know what Daddy said the night before he died? He told me that I was a pretty little girl and that if I married Samuel, I would be happy forever because we would be able to keep 'Ilium' in the manner it used to be before the war. He never knew that we had been secretly married in a little church in Louisiana. But that was before I realised that there was no softening the sharp edges. I thought I could do it, but as you saw, there is just no reasoning with him.

"I recognised that Samuel could lead those other doddering old fools, talking about John C. Calhoun and states' rights and all. They lacked the drive to blend all the separate elements together into a unit. Samuel could do it, but he needed me to guide him. We came so far together, then . . ."

Her voice trailed off eerily. She was trying to sway my emotions as she had done at the Admiralty Ball. She would not succeed again.

"So you and Ravenswood hired the men who attacked you the first night, who almost killed your father."

"Yes, it would have been better that way," she said softly, never moving her pistol the slightest degree.

"And Carteret and Bankhead had no idea of what you were planning. They were really trying to capture those men that night."

She sneered. "They were trying to be heroes. I hoped to keep them far enough away by looking into the window of a dress shop, so that Samuel could keep walking with Daddy."

"So then, afterward, you did it yourself. You murdered your father."

She looked surprised. "I told you," she said impatiently. "He was getting in the way."

We were long past Stonehenge now, still travelling east. Was that the same rider I had seen before in the distance? From our height I could not tell. I only wanted to give this balloon some direction. Otherwise, we stood a good chance of being carried out to sea.

A hamlet loomed up about a mile from where we were, directly on our course. Rachel saw it too. This bit of civilisation seemed to bring her back to our present condition.

"Well now, Mycroft. Shall we escape together, make our way to the continent, and live like royalty?"

"I fear that your admiration would soon cease, Miss Leland. I am sure that I should sooner or later suffer the same fate as your father and Captain Ravenswood. Neither could I find myself content to live as your paramour, satisfied with the crumbs that you would care to drop me . . ."

"Crumbs?" she exclaimed. She smiled, the breeze catching her loosened curls in a brilliant golden halo. "Never that, Mycroft. We would be equal, we would be sharing . . ."

". . . the necklace which belongs to neither of us? No, Rachel. You would soon come to hate that kind of existence, as I should come to hate being pursued from one country to the next, with no place to call home." My voice was hard as I said, "You can't share the important and valuable things that I find in life, because they have no part in you. Things like . . ."

"Honour?" she smiled and in that second, her smile changed from the essence of purity to a contemptuous obscenity. "You're a bigger fool than Samuel. You have the ability to rule nations, and you cast it all aside."

"That is not quite true, Miss Leland. I am not throwing away power," I said coldly. "I am only casting you aside."

"Shut up!" Her anger flared to incandescence. "I *should* have thrown you out." Her lips became a straight line. "You will do me one favour before you die. You'll bring this balloon down first, and then I'll derive a great amount of pleasure from seeing you shot. Now—bring us down!"

"Are you sure you can trust me, Miss Leland? Besides, you cannot shoot me. You need me as a hostage."

"Don't fool yourself about your own importance, Mr. Holmes," she sneered. "I can get along much easier by myself with a great deal more freedom than if I had to watch you out of the corner of my eyes every minute."

"Why don't you shoot me now and be done with it?"

"I want you to take this balloon down, sir. No more talk. Get us down—and pronto!"

I had no choice. She gave a sidelong glance earthward and directed me to bring down the balloon in a clearing in the midst of the trees to the north of the hamlet. I had watched Ravenswood preparing the balloon before flight, and how he handled the lines and gas-valve during the emergency we encountered as we took flight. The only way we could descend would be by releasing the gas in the balloon. I pulled slowly at the rope that controlled the spring-lever on the gas-valve, and the gas began to seep out. We descended.

The breezes we encountered at the higher level were turning to blustery gusts as we dropped. I didn't know if we could land in exactly the space pointed out by Rachel, but at least we were headed in that direction. The gondola continued to be buffeted by the winds, but Rachel never took her eyes from me. She steadied herself with one hand, but she never lowered the pistol.

We were now some five hundred yards away from the clearing. "Release more gas," Rachel commanded. I pulled the rope again and the valve opened wider. A little too wide, in fact, for we began to plummet. I frantically closed the valve and thus ended the swiftness of our descent. Rachel Leland still had her pistol trained on me, the muff safe about her left arm.

The trees now loomed up and I opened the valve a little so that we could set the balloon down in the clearing. We

were now little more than fifty feet above them and the
wind had died down completely. I sighed with relief as
the gondola entered the clearing, the branches yawning
open for our entry.

Holding on to part of the rigging, I leaned over the side
to check our position. That was a mistake. I lost my foot-
ing and reached for one of the other ropes. That too, was
a mistake. I grabbed hold of the rope that was the gas-valve
control. The valve opened completely and the balloon
lurched, throwing me back into the gondola. Rachel
screamed as her gun went flying and the ballon dropped
to the grassy knoll below us.

We were too close to the trees and, although we missed
the topmost branches, the rigging became caught in the
jutting branch of an ancient oak, some thirty feet above
the ground. We were thrown against each other, Rachel
instinctively throwing her arms about me. The bag and
rigging became firmly braced against the tree and the gondola was upended. With Rachel's muff close against her, we
were separated as we fell some twenty feet, to the grassy
slope below.

When I came to myself, I was lying in the grass. A familiar
figure, dressed in tweed, smelling of horse, knelt over me,
care etching his dusky features.

"Captain Jericho," I said feebly, trying to rise. "We
meet under the most preposterous circumstances."

"Forget the manners," said he, gently pushing me back
onto the grass. He smiled. "No need to stand on ceremony
for me, remember."

I returned his smile, recalling the time in the pub when
he had said the same thing, under slightly different circumstances.

"How do you feel? Any broken bones?"

"The wind's been knocked out of me, but I seem to be
in one piece. Rachel Leland?"

"She's still unconscious, but she'll live. In fact, you're
both lucky to be alive. You don't know the first thing about
ballooning." He smiled.

"So I discovered." The cobwebs were clearing. "But how
is it that you found us? You were leaving, I thought." Then

I remembered the horseman. "It was you who was following us!"

He sat on the grass and shrugged. "Guilty as charged. I hid out overnight in a barn nearby, taking advantage of some farmer's unintentional hospitality."

"But why?"

"Well, I thought that Sergeant Lestrade would be by before the test began, and I had some business to conduct with him."

I thought there was some other meaning to his words, but at the time, I wasn't quite able to focus my thoughts. He continued.

"I was on the road awaiting him, when I saw the balloon take off without the auto-gyro, then it started coming toward me. I thought that was odd, but it wasn't until I saw you and Miss Rachel and Ravenswood were in the gondola that I knew something was wrong.

"After a bit, I heard two shots and saw Ravenswood fall out of the basket of that soapbubble. There was too long a space between the shots, so I knew that it wasn't you who pulled the trigger: The shots were deliberate, with the intention of killing. That's when I knew that the ringleader of all this madness was Miss Rachel. You might hope to stun him, but you'd never deliberately kill Ravenswood." He smiled. "You had too many questions for him to answer." He looked past me to where Rachel Leland lay unconscious.

"When I was a slave, I knew Miss Rachel as a most willful little girl. I found it hard to believe that the demure, retiring young woman I heard was accompanying her father was the same person. As a child, she was always putting little boys up to do things for her, and it dawned on me that she was doing the same to Captain Ravenswood." He looked back to me. "Well, I just thought I had best follow you, to see if I could be of any assistance when you came down." He smiled again and said, "I had no idea that you'd need this kind of assistance, though."

"Did you have any trouble with the equivocal Miss Leland?"

Jericho smiled. "She was unconscious when I arrived. I have just made quite sure that she was secure in her new surroundings. She'll not be getting away any too quickly and that's a fact."

He stood up. "And now that I find you in one piece, I'll be taking my leave."

My mind began to work. There was something wrong about all this.

"Jericho—a moment, please."

He stopped and looked down as I rose to a sitting position.

"Jericho—how long have we been here?"

"Some fifteen minutes. That's why I want to be off. Your brother and half a regiment of troops will be here any minute. Trent will most likely be with them"—his smile broadened—"and I don't want to find out if our truce is still on or not." He walked to his horse on the edge of the clearing.

"Jericho!" I called out. "Wait!"

He wheeled his horse around to face me.

"Thank you, Jeri . . . Mr. Horn. Thank you for all you've done."

He gave me a stately nod from his saddle. "Don't mention it, Mr. Holmes. Just one friend doing a favour for another. If ever I get knocked down in a ditch, I'll expect to see you trot up in a hansom cab to minister to me." Then he said something I didn't understand. "Actually, I should be thanking you." But he gave his usual paradoxical smile and galloped off, through the trees and out of sight.

I struggled to my feet and stumbled weakly to the tree from which the gondola still hung. The balloon, now an empty silken bag, was flapping against the branches. I could not have asked for a better signal for Sherlock and our friends to find us. If Sherlock still lived, I thought sadly.

I looked over to where Rachel lay, comfortably but nonetheless securely bound with ropes from the balloon. She was yet unconscious and her muff still hung from her arm. I would have removed its precious contents then but decided that it would be best to recover the necklace in the presence of witnesses.

I returned to where Captain Jericho found me and stretched out once more. The sky was a deep blue with only vagrant clouds scurrying past. For the last of November, having spent the past week in snow and rain, this was an anomaly of which I thought I should take advantage.

Within ten minutes, a great noise of men, carriages and horses became heard and Trevor, Trent, Lestrade—and to my great joy, Sherlock—appeared on the scene, along with some fifty others: soldiers, police, and civilan politicos who came storming into the clearing in some of the broughams and landaus that had taken us to the test site from Salisbury Station.

"Isn't that just like my brother," said Sherlock as he jumped from a carriage and strolled over to me. "Half the country looking for him and he's having a fine time, lazing in the sun." The mockery of his tongue could not conceal the concern in his eyes, however. I assured him that I was sound, that Miss Leland was captured and that all was safely concluded. Trent and Trevor were glad to find me as well. Even Lestrade was able to commend my actions.

"You've made the capture and no mistake," said the wiry little sergeant, with a ferretlike grin.

I had struggled to my feet and now led them to where Rachel lay, near the shredded remnants of the gondola hanging from the oak. "Just like Absalom," said Lestrade.

The sight of it made me remember the crash of the auto-gyro. "Sherlock," I turned to him. "What about the auto-gyro? I was sure . . ."

Sherlock winced and rubbed his shoulder.

"When the contraption exploded, it threw us clear of the wreckage." Sherlock smiled ruefully. "I fell on Lestrade."

The next day, we were back in my rooms in St. Chad's Street. Having been fortified by one of Mrs. Crosse's hearty dinners, I broke out a bottle of excellent brandy and everyone was given a generous dollop.

Sherlock was in one of his introspective moods, smoking the long cherrywood pipe that he had made for himself a few years before. It was now an infrequent companion, usually smoked when my brother was in a querulous frame of mind. Trevor was listening intently to Trent as he informed us of how the two younger revolutionaries had broken down and confessed to all they knew. It wasn't very much, but, when taken together with my testimony and the evidence that Trent had been collecting, it was evident that there would be a great cleaning of house in Whitehall and the pseudo-military council in Alabama would be answering to charges of treason.

I poured another round of brandy as I made things clear to my friends. Millicent Deane, it came out, was nothing to the plot, as Rachel Leland had told me—simply part of the disguised "continental tour" plans that Rachel had devised. She returned to the States no worse for her adventure but certainly the wiser for it. And as for Rachel Ravenswood, she was to be charged with conspiracy to commit treason in the United States while answering to the charge of her husband's and her father's murders, here in England. She would not be seen again.

In answer to a question from Victor Trevor, I clarified Jericho's motives for having his men attack us at the Langham.

"Jericho's men were undoubtedly told to take the Colonel's pistol if they could not locate the diamond necklace, as a threatening gesture. If my memory serves me well, I recall a similar circumstance occurring in the Bible, between David and Saul. First Samuel, I would suppose."*

Sherlock said little throughout the evening. Looking back, I remember the look of annoyance he wore. Something was lacking. The problem was solved, but some fact of it was left unclear to him.

It was left to Trevor to give voice to the question that everyone was pondering. "So tell us, Mr. Holmes, what happened to the necklace?"

"Yes," said Calvin Trent. "We searched Ravenswood's body, one of the matrons went through all of the clothing worn by Rachel Le . . . Ravenswood, and the other Southerners profess no knowledge of the necklace, other than that they were told it was being carried by Ravenswood. How do you explain it, Mr. Holmes?"

I gave a noncommittal gesture. "For all I know, it might have been buried with Leland. Or it might not have existed at all. Captain Ravenswood might never have had it to

---

* Mycroft's memory served him well indeed. The reference will be found in the first book of Samuel. Sherlock, it will be recalled, also referred to the first book of Samuel in "The Crooked Man," a case found in *The Memoirs of Sherlock Holmes*. MH/SMW

begin with." I thought I knew with whom it now resided, but I was loath to disclose that information. I had made no mention of Jericho's finding us after the descent of the balloon. For all I cared, Joshua Horn could keep anything he wished from this venture and welcome. No one else had any better explanation, and the matter was dropped.

"Something I'd like to know Mr. Holmes," said Calvin Trent, addressing my brother, "is how you were so sure that the men you followed at the behest of the ostler were really the same who attacked Colonel Leland and Captain Ravenswood on the night they arrived in London."

Sherlock assumed a bored expression as he took his pipe from his mouth. "The ostler identified them," was his laconic reply, after which he replaced the long cherrywood.

"But Holmes," said Trevor, now taking up the cudgel. "They could have been innocent bystanders, or the ostler could have been mistaken."

"Or he might have been lying, just to get away from a crazy Jamaican and a taciturn Lascar," said Trent with a wry grin.

"It is as I told you earlier, Trevor. I acted under the supposition that Bankhead misunderstood one of the assailants, when he thought he heard him say, 'Get the duke.' As it turned out, he said, 'Get him, Duke!' I had only to call out his name after we followed him for a few short blocks. I said, 'That one is Duke,' and the short man turned around, startled at hearing his name spoken by a stranger. I made his acquaintance by describing his actions that Friday night, and his instructions from Ravenswood. I did this so well, in fact, that he was convinced that Captain Jericho and I were sent from the Southerner with the second half of their payment. Following that encounter, it was easy to persuade him and his friend Jim to meet with us at The Anchor."

"I have to admit," said Trevor with a laugh, "I could have never mistaken him from the description you provided."

"Certainly," said Sherlock with a touch of petulance. "The whole thing was a rudimentary application of inference and observation."

We learned part of the reason for my brother's ill-humour when he said, "Of course, to read the account of the matter in the newspapers, one would be forced to believe that the regulars had planned the entire capture. Just look at this," he said, handing me that day's *Daily News*. "It is representative of the rest."

A headline announced the capture of the Southerners and the thwarted conspiracy.

The section indicated by Sherlock read as follows:

> . . . The sensational capture of the Americans and the rescue of Mr. Mycroft Holmes of the Foreign Office from the Montgolfier aerial balloon was accomplished through the industry of the newly promoted Inspector G. Lestrade of the Detective Department of Scotland Yard. Inspector Lestrade had earlier been responsible for the apprehension in Bankside late Sunday night of two suspects having a connexion with the conspirators. It would appear, from remarks made by the Inspector, that these men had laid open the conspiracy which threatened the safety of the Crown, as well as jeopardising the friendly relations between the United Kingdom and the United States of America.
>
> The Prime Minister has made no statement concerning the matter aside from his remarks noted earlier. Mr. William E. Gladstone, in London on holiday, has called upon Mr. Disraeli to initiate a thorough investigation of all governmental departments and agencies. He further urged Parliament to enact appropriate legislation providing for periodic scrutiny into the divers ministries . . .

"I can understand it of Lestrade, taking all the credit," said Sherlock, "but I should have supposed that Gladstone or Disraeli might have said some little word concerning the roles that we played in this little drama."

"I would suppose that they are merely taking us at our word," I replied, lighting one of my favourite Havana cigars. "We refused knighthoods; we told them that we did not wish the publicity. Actually, I believe we did rather well by them."

"That's only because your name appeared in the newspaper account," said Sherlock peevishly. "Which is inaccurate and incomplete," he added, "just as this case is."

He gave me an arch look. "I'd almost swear that you were keeping something from us."

"Now, Sherlock, you were there when I gave my testimony to the police. They don't question my story. Besides" —I blew a smoke ring into the air, resuming an avuncular manner—"you know that I was unconscious until just before you found me."

"That doesn't explain the knots I found in the rope used to bind Rachel Ravenswood. I have some knowledge of knots, and those were a special type called harness hitches. You surely didn't tie them; you know nothing about horsemanship."

I raised an eyebrow at him.

"Well, no practical knowledge, anyway," he amended. "But I could almost swear that someone else tied those knots."

"Well, perhaps someone else did come on the scene and left before I knew it. I was unconscious part of the time, you know."

"Yes, you mentioned that," he answered drily, while Victor Trevor and Calvin Trent laughed amid the remnants of our feast.

There was a knock at the door.

"That will be Mrs. Crosse to clear the dishes," I said, bidding her enter.

"This package just came for you, sir," said Mrs. Crosse. "It was hand delivered by a special messenger. I hope it bodes no ill . . ."

"No, no, Mrs. Crosse, I'm sure it doesn't," I said. "Just put it on the sideboard, thank you."

"Of course, sir. It's just so queer to have one special delivery following so closely after another," she said. "Are you gentlemen finished dining?"

I said that we were indeed finished.

"Well, I'll be right back with my waggon to . . ." She broke off, seeing Sherlock's unfinished plate. "And you two are brothers," she clucked disapprovingly.

I turned to my companions after Mrs. Crosse had shut the door. "I'm asking her to run my new household when I move into Pall Mall, you know," I said, picking up the package.

"You're sure to become even more gluttonous than you

are now," Sherlock muttered, more to Trent than to me. Trent smiled and turned to Trevor.

"Any time you want to ask her to leave your new establishment"—he gave Trevor a wink—"ask her to come to Baltimore. I wouldn't mind having meals like this on a regular basis."

I smiled, picking up a pair of shears to cut the twine and brown paper from around the package. I opened the box while Trevor regaled the others with a humourous anecdote concerning the lack of a proper cuisine displayed at a university luncheon for a retiring don.

I lifted the lid and pulled out the cotton-wool batting. Within was a small, silvery pistol. I recognised it as the one used by Rachel Leland, cast out of the balloon when we landed and supposed lost by the police.

A small card that was packed with it lay on the bottom of the box. "Compliments of a Friend," it read. I replaced it with the pistol and closed the box.

Sherlock came over and picked up the string, examining it closely. He removed a small lens and inspected the knot. He looked up at me, his brow arching once more.

He said not a word, but replaced the lens into his pocket. He then picked up the twine and wrapping paper and tossed them into my fireplace. We watched them blaze up, the laughter of our guests behind us as Trevor finished his story.

"Did you find anything of interest, Sherlock?" I asked.

"No," he said quietly. "Nothing at all."

ACKNOWLEDGMENTS

The people and publications listed herein played an important part in the creation and development of this book. They are entitled to share in whatever good impressions you might have of this work, while any negative criticism should be directed at, and belongs solely to, the authors.

In listing those who helped, pride of place belongs to Miss Nancy Senter. Because of her good offices, the authors have a more thorough—and exact—knowledge of the boroughs and precincts of London. In addition, from her Sherlockian scholarship to the use of her self-correcting typewriter, she provided us with help, inspiration, and exactly the right phrase when needed.

Terry Hodel believed in this project before anyone else. Her quiet voice asked many logical questions that made the authors strive to create real and believable characters and situations. For whatever success we achieved, Terry deserves the credit.

Mary Aldin saw the manuscript in its early stages and was able to give it some depth and direction when it seemed to be floundering.

Throughout the writing of this novel, the authors sought the advice and the freely given comments of the friends and relatives listed below.

Robert Bisio must take album credit for his crucial Civil War information. Ed Kolpin, founder of The Tinder Box chain of pipe shops, contributed an exact knowledge of tobacco. The authors sought out John Farrell, head of The Tigers of San Pedro, a California scion of the BSI, for vignettes of British life, which were further supplemented by Edwina Iredale of the library of the British consulate in Los Angeles and by Robin Sanders Clark who, in his youth, was a close friend of Sir Arthur Conan Doyle and his family. Anthony Howlett, guiding light of The Sherlock Holmes Society of London, spoke with Mr. Wright and

Miss Senter at Flanagan's Restaurant (in Baker Street) one evening, corroborating, expanding—and refuting—some of the author's theories. If there is any man today who puts one in mind of Mycroft Holmes, it is Tony. DeForeest B. Wright, historian and genealogist, set his son straight on the usage of Victorian habiliments, especially of wash-hand stands. Miss Helen Wright, librarian, and the resources of the Santa Fe Springs City Library, kept her brother literate during some of his less lucid moments.

During convalescence from hip surgery, Daws Butler forsook Yogi Bear, Huckleberry Hound, and his other vocal creations, yet found time to read through this manuscript and discuss character development and plot with the authors. Ira Fistell, founder of two Holmes societies in Wisconsin (The Notorious Canary Trainers and The Bagatelle Card Club), and at present a radio personality in Los Angeles on KABC-Radio, took time to read through the manuscript, making suggestions and corrections throughout. Thanks are also due to Miss Alix Feldman for her thorough research on aerial ballooning.

The authors wish to thank the good offices of their agent, Julian Portman, for finding a home for this history. And we must also acknowledge the considerate help of our editor, Sandra Choron, who took her introduction into Holmesian studies with great good humor and took on a fair share of work in assisting the author's native shrewdness while refining their thoughts, language, spelling, and grammar. Her one fault is telephoning the authors at 7:30 in the morning to ask about grey studies. But we have forgiven her.

In recognizing literary sources, it is, first and foremost, necessary to give credit to Sir Arthur Conan Doyle, the good friend of Dr. John H. Watson, who gave the world so many diverting tales, that make for good reading at all times and in all climes. His genius lives through his compelling and entertaining stories.

We are also grateful to the authors of the publications listed below, part of the ever-expanding body of Sherlockian literature.

Baring-Gould, William S., ed. *The Annotated Sherlock*

Holmes. New York: Clarkson N. Potter, 1967. The single most significant compilation of the Holmes Canon.

Hardwick, Michael and Mollie. *The Sherlock Holmes Companion.* London: John Murray, 1970. Contains many quotations selected for immediate use and referral.

Harrison, Michael. *The London of Sherlock Holmes.* New York: Drake Publishers, Inc., 1972.

In the Footsteps of Sherlock Holmes. New York: Drake Publishers, Inc., 1973.

The World of Sherlock Holmes. New York: E.P. Dutton, 1975. These three volumes are all chock full of the color and character of Victorian England.

Tracy, Jack, ed. *The Encyclopædia Sherlockiana.* New York: Doubleday Publishing Co., 1977. A useful, if erratic, source.

The Baker Street Journal, founded by Edgar W. Smith in 1946, has devoted many pages to articles about Mycroft Holmes, some of which were mentioned in the Introduction. Through the editorship of Dr. Julian Wolff, Commissionaire of the Baker Street Irregulars, it has remained the single most outstanding quarterly by which students of the Baker Street studies have kept green the memory of the Master. Now, as it begins a new phase under the tripartite editorship of John Linsenmeyer, Chris Steinbrunner, and the Hon. Albert Rosenblatt, it is evident that the sun never sets on Sherlockian studies.

Non-Sherlockian sources must also be listed:

The Great Democracies (volume four of Sir Winston Churchill's monumental *A History of the English-Speaking Peoples*), New York: Dodd, Mead, 1974.

David Thomson's *England in the Nineteenth Century,* London: Penguin Books, 1977 (volume eight of *The Pelican History of England*), also provided useful details.

The Widow of Windsor, by Tyler Whittle, New York: Warner, 1977, gives a well-rounded look at politics at the time during which the action of this story takes place.

Gore Vidal's *1876,* New York: Ballantine, 1977, has several sharply-focused comments and observations about people and institutions during that time.

Henry Morton Robinson's *The Cardinal*, New York: Simon and Schuster, 1950, a novel about Roman Catholic people and politics, contained an example of the Gaelic language which suggested an episode to the authors. Thanks are due Mr. Robinson.

Strange, Unsolved Mysteries, by Emile C. Schumacher, New York: Popular Library, 1966, provided the introductory details concerning the Lost Necklace of the Confederacy.

MICHAEL P. HODEL AND SEAN M. WRIGHT

Great detective novels "in the American
MICHAEL COLLINS MYSTERIES
private-eye tradition of Chandler, Hammet and MacDonald."
—NEW YORK TIMES BOOK REVIEW